Hello, lovely people –

Little did I know that an evening spent feeding orphaned baby lambs would lead to the inspiration for my latest novel, ...ness for Beginners.

...e Farm, the setting for my story, is based on the fabulous ...l Antiks farm – a place which helps children and young ... with learning difficulties, mental health issues and ... They do great work and have very generously allowed ...pend time there in the name of research. There's more ...is wonderful place in the back of the book if you'd like ...out about their work. They are simply amazing.

...ank you for picking up my book. I hope that you enjoy ...tory is, obviously, pure fiction, but the heart behind it is ... real.

...ppy reading!

...e Carole :) xx

...f you want to keep up with what's happening – new books, ... of chit-chat and some fab giveaways – I spend far too ...h time on social media, especially Facebook and Twitter, so ...can always find me there. I have a newsletter which you ...gn up to at www.carolematthews.com. I don't share your ...rmation and you can unsubscribe at any time. I'm also ...stagram, but never seem able to find my messages there!

🅵 www.facebook.com/carolematthewsbooks
🐦 @carolematthews
📷 Matthews.Carole
  www.carolematthews.com

Also by Carole Matthews

THE CHOCOLATE LOVERS NOVELS

Carole Matthews

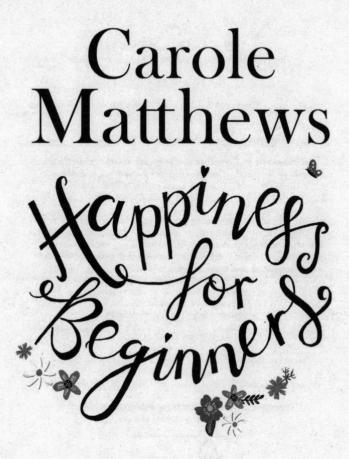

Happiness for Beginners

sphere

SPHERE

First published in Great Britain in 2019 by Sphere
This paperback edition published by Sphere in 2019

1 3 5 7 9 10 8 6 4 2

A CIP catalogue record for this book
is available from the British Library.

ISBN 978-0-7515-7212-4

Typeset in Sabon LT Std by Palimpsest Book Production Ltd,
Falkirk, Stirlingshire
Printed and bound in Great Britain by Clays Ltd, Elcograf S.p.A.

Papers used by Sphere are from well-managed forests
and other responsible sources.

Sphere
An imprint of
Little, Brown Book Group
Carmelite House
50 Victoria Embankment
London EC4Y 0DZ

An Hachette UK Company
www.hachette.co.uk

www.littlebrown.co.uk

Carole Matthews is the *Sunday Times* bestselling author of over thirty novels, including the top ten bestsellers *Let's Meet on Platform 8*, *A Whiff of Scandal*, *For Better, For Worse*, *A Minor Indiscretion*, *With or Without You*, *The Cake Shop in the Garden*, *Paper Hearts and Summer Kisses*, *A Cottage by the Sea*, *The Chocolate Lovers' Club*, *The Chocolate Lovers' Christmas*, *The Chocolate Lovers' Wedding*, *Million Love Songs* and *Christmas Cakes & Mistletoe Nights*. Carole has been awarded the RNA Outstanding Achievement Award. Her novels dazzle and delight readers all over the world and she is published in more than thirty countries.

For all the latest news from Carole, visit www.carolematthews.com and sign up to her newsletter. You can also follow Carole on Twitter (@carolematthews) and Instagram (matthews.carole) or join the thousands of readers who have become Carole's friend on Facebook (carolematthewsbooks).

To Sylvia Simpkin – a crazy crafting lady
who will be much missed.
Your crafting legacy will live on,
bringing so much pleasure to many people.
30th July 1959 - 26th March 2018.

Chapter One

Anthony the Anti-Social Sheep lowers his head and growls. I hold up a hand, trying to establish myself as the head of the pack – which, if I'm honest, I'm not even sure is a sheep thing. It certainly doesn't cut the mustard with Anthony. He squares his not-inconsiderable shoulders and makes eye contact. I can, however, tell a sheep with an evil glint in its eye and Anthony, as so often, has one now.

When he's in this kind of mood there's really no reckoning with him and I know that I have no option but to make a dash for the gate. Anthony, in turn, knows that I'm too far away to make it. Three times this week he's charged and up-ended unsuspecting ramblers who've strayed into his field. I've lost count of the muddy walkers that I've patted down while apologising profusely as they try to re-set their spectacles and gather their backpacks. It took the last one two hastily brewed cups of tea and a sizeable wedge of lemon drizzle cake before they were right again. One of these days someone will sue me for a sheep-based assault.

'Good boy, Anthony,' I coo, as I back slowly away. 'You're not really the devil incarnate. You're just misunderstood.'

Unappeased, he starts his run towards me and, as the other

infinitely more placid sheep lift their heads to watch, I turn on my heels, sprinting as fast as my wellies will allow. 'Play nicely, Anthony!'

He is unheeding.

The five-barred gate is coming tantalisingly closer, but I can hear Anthony's hooves thundering behind me. He's one hell of a size for a sheep, with a big, square head and the posture of a seasoned pugilist. Technically, he's a ram, but on this farm we try not to complicate matters. He was recently parted from the elements that specifically made him a ram in the hope that it would make him more docile. Sadly, it didn't work.

I don't know what's made him so bad-tempered and disgruntled with life. I love him as much as a human can love a sheep without it being illegal. He has the prime choice of fields. He's first in line for food. If only he could learn to love me back or at least not want to knock me over every time I enter his territory then I'm sure we would both be happier. The dogs are, quite wisely, terrified of him and he certainly has a more menacing growl than either of them. Anthony has long eschewed baa-ing as a form of communication.

As I run, Little Dog is barking encouragement at the gate. He's been on the wrong side of Anthony many times before now and has learned not to venture into his field. Little Dog knows how much a prod with his battering-ram nose in your nether regions hurts. Big Dog, possibly brighter than either of us, is staying well clear and is, quite sensibly, cowering behind the wheels of the tractor.

'No, Anthony,' I shout as fiercely as I can over my shoulder. 'NO!'

But it's too late. His massive head makes contact with my bottom and he tosses me as hard as he can. As I'm catapulted forwards, I can feel clear air between me and the ground. Lots of it.

2

I land, face forward, with an inelegant 'ouff' in the muddiest part of the field, the bit where we open the gate, the bit that's trodden to sludge by the hooves of many more amenable sheep. Even though I'm short and sturdily built, I'm no match for Anthony.

His work for the day done, a contented Anthony trots off to find someone else to terrorise. I swear that sheep is smiling. Little Dog, braver now that the surly Anthony has gone, squeezes under the gate and comes to lick my face.

'You're not much use as a guard dog, are you?' I admonish as I push myself up on my elbows.

He looks at me with his one eye and his expression seems to say that he wholeheartedly agrees. Like everything and everyone here, Little Dog came to us damaged. I think that he must have been kicked in the face or something equally dreadful in the past, because as well as losing an eye, he has suffered nerve damage which means that his lips are permanently pulled back so he looks as if he's always smiling. Thankfully, he doesn't seem any the worse for it now and his weird grin makes him look like the cutest thing there ever was. Which is just as well as he's a pretty hopeless guard dog. Unless licking a burglar to death would count.

Little Dog is probably some kind of Jack Russell/random terrier combo. He's got stubby legs and a white coat with brown patches that's the texture of a paintbrush.

Then there's Big Dog. He's my second contender for the prize of Most Useless Guard Dog. He's blessed with only three legs, breath that would floor a dinosaur and a fear of anyone wearing a red jumper. He's a huge beast with a tail that can clear a coffee table in one wag. He might be Alsatian-based somewhere in there, possibly crossed with a mountain dog or wolf – yet he is the scarediest dog ever.

I haul myself up, grateful that no bones are broken, and

hobble to the gate. I'll probably have a corking bruise or two in the morning, but I'll live to fight another day.

As I don't want Anthony making a break for it today and terrorising any random strangers, I make sure that I secure the bolt very carefully behind me. 'You're going nowhere today, Big Man,' I tell him, sternly. 'I want you to take time out to think about your behaviour.'

He gives me a scornful look and goes to annoy his fellow field companions. He's not well-liked, my dear Anthony, and that makes me love him more. We acquired him because he was considered too much of a handful for anyone else. It seems to have set a pattern.

I brush the dirt from my hands, my jeans, my shirt. I should introduce myself to you. How rude of me not to have done it before. I'm Molly Baker. I'm thirty-eight – no idea how that's even possible. I'm single, but I'm not a mad cat lady. I'm a mad all-kinds-of-animals lady. Welcome to my life at Hope Farm.

Chapter Two

I'd have a shower, but there's really no point. I usually end the day filthy, so I might as well start out that way too. The animals won't mind and the people joining me on the farm today couldn't care less what I look like. It can wait until later.

Besides — a small but not inconsiderable point — there's no hot water on tap. That's due to the fact that I live on-site at the farm in a small, but perfectly formed caravan — this place was never blessed with a sprawling farmhouse — and my only bathing facility is an open-air bucket shower at the back of one of the barns. Al fresco bathing is fine in the summer months and, sometimes, I hook the bucket shower up to the hosepipe for the horse wash and go with ice-cold water. Bracing, yet enjoyable in its own way. But in the depths of December the appeal of staying dirty can be quite over-whelming. Most of the time, I quite like the process of boiling myself a kettle of water to do my ablutions, or maybe I'm just used to it. It's time-consuming though and I don't have the luxury of being able to set it up right now — there's so much else to do.

My home is modest, but I do my best to make it cosy. It

was originally my aunt Hettie's home and is as old as the hills. To cheer it up, I recently gave the outside a coat of paint and strung up a bit of pretty bunting to disguise the fact that it's living on borrowed time. I've made it homely on the inside and I'm constantly doing running repairs to keep it going. Mind you, as I spend most of my time out on the farm, it's purely a place to sleep and I don't need much in the way of creature comforts. My assistant Bev bought me some nice cushions, embroidered with cutesy farm animals, which the dogs probably love more than I do. One of our casual volunteers crochets, and has hooked me a matching blanket – again possibly more appreciated by the canine inhabitants. Although I do like to snuggle under it if I can wrest if from them. I changed Hettie's orange 1960s curtains for pale blue gingham numbers which do look pretty. What else do I need? Bev tells me that mismatched crockery is all the rage, which is just as well as mine has achieved that status quite by accident – usually an over-waggy tail. In the summer, I swelter and in the winter it's like living in a freezer, but it's a small price to pay for the freedom of the land.

Today, the spring weather is excelling itself and it feels as if we've finally cast off the harsh mantle of winter. A hearty dump of late snow in February seemed particularly cruel when the early snowdrops were out in full force. That's all forgotten now, as spring is most definitely in the air and the day is balmy with a gentle breeze, when so often up here in our exposed position it can be howling a gale. The sky is the palest of blues dotted with clouds tinged with grey, hinting that we might be in for a spot of seasonal rain later.

I stretch my back, which is already tight due to my lumpy mattress. The one extravagance I do occasionally miss here is a long, hot bath, particularly when I've got a lot of aches and pains, but then everything else makes up for that. At Hope Farm

I live in a most idyllic slice of Buckinghamshire countryside, with no nosy neighbours – in fact, no near neighbours at all. This place is situated in a spot of splendid isolation – just as I like it. I look around and know that every morning I wake up here I am truly blessed.

Little Dog falls into step at my heels – his favourite place in the world. Warily, Big Dog decides that it's safe to come out of his hiding place and joins us.

'Come on then, you two. Before we open our doors for business, let's see how everyone else is.'

We head first to pick up our two pygmy goats, letting them out of their overnight pen. Dumb and Dumber spend the day out in the paddock with the horses who don't mind them as company. The alpacas tolerate them occasionally too – when they're in the mood. They are goats of very small brain, but they're undeniably cute and set up a plaintive bleat whenever they see us.

'Morning, lovelies,' I say as I let them out into the yard. 'Are you hungry?'

Goats are always hungry.

The dogs give them a good sniff in greeting. After they've been fed and fussed over, the goats wait patiently to be taken up to the paddock, already familiar with the routine.

I should tell you that Hope Farm isn't what you might call a 'traditional' farm. Oh, no. We don't grow crops, we don't have cows, we don't *lowers voice to whisper* *kill* any of our animals for food. Instead, our residents live a life of pampered luxury. They've all had tough starts in one way and another and I think they deserve a little TLC and understanding. Much like the young people who come to spend their time here, too. You see, I run the farm as an alternative way of educating kids who have special needs or behavioural issues. How I came to be doing that is quite a convoluted tale. We should sit down with a cup

7

of tea and I'll give you chapter and verse. Now, I've just got to crack on.

Our next resident is our 'pet' lamb, Fifty, who is at the opposite end of the spectrum to Anthony. Where Anthony is more often in an evil humour, Fifty is one of life's most affable sheep. He's convinced that he's a human or a dog or a pig – anything but a lamb – and, as such, he's pretty much given the free rein of our farmyard. If you drew a cartoon sheep, you'd draw Fifty. He has a handsome brown face, ears that are quite possibly big enough for him to take flight and a doleful expression in his big brown eyes. He has eyelashes to die for.

He's best friends with our monster-sized pig, Teacup, and usually snuggles up at night beside him in Teacup's pen. Now and then, when I'm feeling particularly soft, Fifty beds down in my caravan. When he hears us, he comes up for his early morning cuddle.

'Hello, Fifty. What's good today?' He leans into my hand for his favourite itch behind the ear.

Fifty was an orphaned lamb who came to us with a fifty-fifty chance of survival. He was weak, underfed and literally on his last legs. He preferred to nestle in my lap rather than feeding, so I spent hours with my finger in his mouth teaching him how to suck. Eventually, he thrived with warm milk on tap and me with many sleepless nights beside him in the hay under a heat lamp. His legs were bent and buckled beneath him, so I massaged them with lavender oil every day to cajole his wasted muscles into life and bandaged his spindly limbs until he was strong enough to support his own weight. He still walks with an ungainly limp now but it never stops him from bossing the dogs around.

Teacup wakes up and hauls himself to see us, always open to the offer of food. Teacup's only issue was to grow into a piggy the size of a Sherman tank when his owner foolishly bought one he was told would fit into a teacup. Hence the name. Living in the tiny garden of a semi-detached house in Hemel Hempstead soon wasn't a viable option, so someone told someone who knew someone who knew us and that's how we inherited him.

'Morning, boy. Did you have a good night?' I scratch his cheeks and the pig gives me a cheery grunt in reply.

I feed and water them all, holding the dogs away with my foot so they don't nick their brekky. We have two domestic white geese who come wandering into the yard, obviously worried that they're missing some breakfast action. We keep Snowy and Blossom for their eggs which are popular and Bev likes to put jaunty neckerchiefs on them which they usually surrender to after a few protest pecks.

Next to Teacup we have two more pigs – Salt and Pepper. They're New Zealand Kunekunes and are short, fat and hairy. Pepper, the lady pig, is very vocal and bossy. Poor old Salt mostly stands in the corner of his pen being the epitome of a long-suffering and hen-pecked husband. If you go to fuss them, Pepper barges him out of the way so that he doesn't get a look-in – poor thing – so we try to sneak him treats when she's not looking. They get their breakfast too.

Further along is a run with a dozen or more rabbits of all shapes and sizes who are used to being cuddled to within an inch of their life and seem none the worse for it. Many of the kids who come here aren't used to animals at all, so they're great for introducing them to the work of the farm and in learning to how to look after another creature. The alpacas will give you a nip or a swift kick if you do something they don't like, but the bunnies are altogether more agreeable. They're all content to sit quietly soothing a troubled teen in return for a carrot.

'Do you want to stay with Teacup?' I ask Fifty. 'Or will you come with us?'

Chapter Three

It's not yet eight o'clock, but the sun is climbing high and it looks set to be a warm day. Big Dog wanders ahead as we meander up to the field, sniffing anything he comes to with an intensity that's admirable. Little Dog stays contentedly by my side, my constant companion.

As always, when I'm striding out across the farm, I feel my soul settle. This is my home, the place where I belong. It's only here that I can be myself and am truly happy. I should tell you some more about it as we go. Hope Farm was left to me by my aunt Hettie, my godmother and my mother's older sister. I spent most of my childhood at this place and she was more of a mum to me than my real mother ever was. I don't remember even calling my mother 'Mum'. It was always Joan. And poor Joan was an alcoholic and never really had the time or the ability to look after a child. Her mothering skills could best be described as erratic. By the time I was born my father had long gone, so he was never in my life.

Hettie was the one who was always there for me. Joan saw me as an unwelcome interruption to her social life and made it abundantly clear. So Hettie would sweep me away from our awful, loveless home and take me to the farm where I'd tell all my troubles to the animals and find my comfort in caring for them all. Hettie was always patient, nurturing and showed me what to do. I looked after her small flock of sheep, her menagerie of pets and her rag-tag brood of chickens, learning what feed they needed, how to collect the eggs from the hens and what to do when they weren't well.

When, eventually, my mother cared more about the bottle than anything else in her life, Hettie took me on permanently before Social Services did. Just after I started secondary school, she installed me in her run-down caravan on the farm, making me take the only bed while she slept on the sofa-cum-bed in the living area. I didn't know that the best word to describe my aunt then was 'recluse'. I just thought she was shy. The truth of it was that for years she'd pretty much shut herself off in this green and pleasant part of Buckinghamshire, shunning neighbours, family and friends – pretty much everyone apart from me. I never thought to question why. It was more of a case of 'why wouldn't you?' After all, I was 'shy' too.

We never had visits from friends or neighbours and I never thought it strange. If Hettie didn't miss contact with the outside world, then neither did I. Going to school was torture. Every day, I used to sit at my desk and count the hours until home time. I wanted nothing more than for the lessons to be over so that I could run straight back to the farm. The other girls might hang around in the village or have play-dates for tea at each other's houses, but not me. I was a loner, the odd one out, the one who didn't get invited and I didn't mind at all. Hettie taught me a lot about animals, but nothing about social skills. The idea of being up here surrounded by all this beauty with creatures that didn't judge you or expect anything of you was more appealing to me as well.

When Hettie died I took over the running of the farm and

the mantle of family weirdo. Not that I see any of our relatives now. When my mother and then Hettie passed away, I lost any tenuous contact I had with the remaining cousins and whatever. The few phone calls I did get from them after Hettie's funeral I never quite managed to return and, eventually, they stopped. What did I have to talk to them about, anyway? They had normal office jobs, families, holidays in Majorca. I had my animals and, beyond that, no discernible life. Trust me, there's only so much mileage in talking about alpaca poo.

We cross the stream on our well-trodden path, both dogs running ahead of me now I check and feed the animals three times a day: once early in the morning before everyone else arrives, then again late afternoon and usually I do another round again at sunset, just to make sure that everyone's all right.

My aunt was young and strong when I joined her here. I was eleven, self-sufficient out of necessity and a willing helper. I helped her to feed the animals before I went to school and when I came home, I'd throw off my uniform and race back out into the fields again, usually finding her up to her elbows in muck somewhere. At the weekends, I rarely left the farm. It won't surprise you to know that I never spent my Saturday afternoons shopping for eyeshadow or at the cinema in giggly groups. I could count the number of friends on one hand. Well, one finger actually.

Hettie never said so but, as the years went on, I think the land was becoming too much for her. Although she was as strong as an ox for her age, there are twenty-five acres here which is not a lot in farming circles, but is more than enough to manage for two and is almost impossible to cope with single-handedly. Until I arrived, Hettie would never have anyone here to help her – she wouldn't have considered having strangers on her land – but somehow she kept it going. When I joined her, we divided up the tasks between the two of us. As I was younger, I took on the heavier labour and, in my teens, became a dab-hand at tractor driving while she tended the animals, always preferring to be with her beloved beasts. Yet, as Hettie aged, I gradually shouldered the bulk of the work and happily so. My aunt never owned the land, but rented it from the neighbouring farmer and when she'd gone the arrangement continued seamlessly.

I did once have a job in the real world. Hettie insisted. When I left school I trained as a teacher as I had no idea what else to do and Hettie wanted me to continue with my education. I'd have happily stayed on at the farm, but one of us needed to bring in some money. Hettie had largely funded us both out of money left to her from her parents and I knew that was becoming increasingly sparse.

Teaching was the obvious thing, I suppose. I liked the idea of helping children. At school, I'd had no one to turn to when times were tough at home and I thought I'd like to make a difference to kids who might be suffering in similar ways. So, very reluctantly, I left the farm every day and went off to the local college and completed a City and Guilds course in teaching, fitting my studies in around looking after the animals. After that, I landed a job at a local secondary school. It wasn't as I'd imagined and, to be honest, I felt as much out of my depth there as I had done as a pupil. I don't easily fit in.

I had no idea how noisy schools had become since I'd been at one and I'd disliked it then. My experience of it as a teacher was little better. The class sizes were enormous and somehow turned children who started out with real potential into surly, badly behaved monsters. I felt ill-equipped to deal with it all. I couldn't connect emotionally with the children when they needed it and I couldn't make a difference as I'd wanted to because I was bogged down with the curriculum and exam targets. The workload was never-ending and the bureaucracy of the state school system was too constraining. I found it all so stressful. I began to wonder if there was another way to educate those, like me, who were square pegs in round holes, the ones who had difficult home lives, as I had, the ones who didn't conform to the 'norm'.

Then, one day, I'd just finished a lesson where I barely had control over a small but foul-tempered, foul-mouthed rabble who were riding roughshod over any desire the other pupils might have had to learn and was so disheartened and disillusioned that, instead of walking to the staffroom for a group moan and a restorative cup of tea, I just kept walking, down the corridors, out of the door, beyond the bounds of the playground and never went back. Some might call it a breakdown. Some might call it coming to my senses. Whichever way, I wasn't required to work my resignation.

So that was it. I simply retreated to the world of the farm and found that, like Hettie, I was so much happier surrounded by animals rather than people. But I worried about those children. The thought of the ones who were lost or angry with no one to turn to kept me awake at night. I wasn't cut out to deal with kids en masse – I'd learned that quickly enough – but I did want to help. Surely there had to be a better way?

I found it. Eventually. And quite by accident. It seems ironic that Hope Farm is now the home to an alternative school for some of the most challenging youngsters in our society. With me, the most reluctant of teachers, as the founder, principal and chief dogsbody. Who'd have thought? Yet I love my job and find it so rewarding. This square peg forged herself a square hole.

But I'll have to tell you all about that later as I need to press on with my tasks and high-tail it back to the yard before today's students arrive.

Chapter Four

Up here in the big field we have two enormous Shire horses, Sweeney and Carter, both ex-police mounts. Sweeney suffers from anxiety. One riot too many, maybe. Carter has Seasonal Affective Disorder and is a nightmare in the winter months. Talk about grumpy. If he could stay huddled up in his stall and never venture outdoors, he would. Thankfully, he's a different boy altogether during the summer and loves to be out in the paddock. They're both fine, handsome lads and, other than being a huge expense, give us little trouble.

I fill two buckets from the shed and feed them both their breakfast. When they've finished, I give them each a sneaky carrot I have in my pocket as an extra treat. Bev, my assistant, comes to the farm pretty much every day and she rides them regularly to keep them exercised. I miss sharing the task as we used to, but I never seem to have the time to ride any more. There's always something more pressing demanding my attention. I can't think when I was last on a horse. I still have no idea what possessed me to take on these hulking great beasts, but someone asked me to and so I did.

I make a note that the top plank of their fence is broken –

again – and will add it to the never-ending list of jobs that need doing. All these boys have to do is lean their weight on it and the wood snaps like a matchstick.

'You're very naughty,' I tell them. 'You're always breaking your fence.' But I stroke their noses so that they know I'm not really cross.

At the other end of the scale we have two miniature Shetland ponies, who look as cute as you can imagine. Ringo, however, suffers from permanent sweet itch as he's allergic to his own hair. I tell you, I spend half of my life hacking at Ringo's fringe with my kitchen scissors – much as I do with my own hair. I try to keep his mane brutally short so that it doesn't touch his face and am constantly rubbing him with antihistamine cream which seems to help as well. He's a dear little soul, though, and bears his horsey eczema stoically. His companion is Buzz Lightyear who fancies himself an escape artist. Despite being short in the leg, he's always trying to jump his fence to get out to infinity and beyond. He very rarely manages it and, when he does, we always catch him before he gets too far as he's easily distracted by butterflies, flowers and streams.

'I bring breakfast and your friends,' I tell them and dish out the feed buckets I brought from the shed.

While Ringo and Buzz are eating, I put the goats in the ponies' paddock. They have a complaining bleat – I've never known goats with separation anxiety before – so I fuss them for a bit longer. They'll be fine when they settle and the goats and ponies do love each other's company.

Once everyone in the top fields are fed, I whistle for the dogs and they come hurtling towards me. We stride out back down the hill and I can already see from the cars parked in the yard that Bev and Alan have arrived. They are my stalwarts and I couldn't manage without them.

Bev and Alan are the main people who help me to run this

place and, generally, keep me on track. I make a mental note to tell Alan about the broken fence. He can go up there later and knock a few nails in – something he does on a weekly basis, if not more often. The rest of the time he systematically works his way through all the jobs written on the chalkboard in the barn.

'Morning, lovely!' Bev shouts as she closes the gate. 'Nice day for it!'

'Glorious,' I agree.

Bev Adams is in her mid-fifties, an ex-body builder who is still in great shape. She has muscles that pop up everywhere and is as fit as a fiddle. I think I'm quite strong after years of physical work, but I've never seen anyone chuck hay bales round like she can. If you saw her, you'd think she was quite hard – her face always bears a 'don't mess with me' expression – but she's a total softie. Her skin is tanned and quite lined from working outside – don't *ever* tell her I said that. God, she'd kill me. Her hair is long and home-bleached, but spends most of its time scraped back in a ponytail. And, as she's as busy as I am, it's not often that she gets time to bleach it so she usually has an inch of grey roots peeping through. She too favours my minimal style of hairdressing. My hair is short, brown and, as I mentioned, I cut it myself with the kitchen scissors. I like to think I've achieved a funky, choppy cut. A professional hair stylist might think otherwise. But when I'm showering outside under a bucket, the last thing I want to do is fiddle with my hair. I'm seriously low-maintenance all the way. I'd rather groom a horse for an hour than titivate myself.

'I bet you've been up and at it since the crack of sparrows,' Bev observes.

'Pretty much.'

'I'm knackered.' She yawns. 'I was on the lash last night at the Queen's Head. Open mic night. Poets and shit. It was wicked. Everyone was there. You should have come along.'

18

Bev knows that I'd rather stick pins in my own eyes than spend an evening in a pub, but she never gives up trying.

After Hettie died, I lost my way a bit, let myself go. Turning to drink was always a worry given my mother's history. I didn't know if a tendency to that kind of addiction would be in my genes. You never know, do you – and I certainly didn't want to risk it. Even now I rarely touch the hard stuff and, when I do, I'm usually cajoled into it by Bev. I enjoy a sip or two but, to my eternal relief, I can always take it or leave it.

I was lonely up here without Hettie. Goodness only knows, I like the isolated life, but everyone needs someone and I had no one. If I'm honest with you, I could have just joyfully let myself fade away. Who would have noticed anyway? I simply couldn't face going into the town, a trip to the supermarket began to terrify me and, like my aunt before me, I was only comfortable when I was around the animals. It's probably having to look after them that kept me going.

When I was younger Bev had always been kind to me when my mum was at her worst. The only true friend I had at school was her daughter, Stella. Bev was a young mum, having had Stella at just sixteen, so she felt more like a friend than a grown-up. As their house was between mine and our secondary school, I used to walk with Stella every day, picking her up on the way.

Bev knew what my home life was like – all the neighbours did as they'd hear mum shouting incoherently when she was drunk or weaving down the street clinging to lamp-posts for support. Bev would check every morning that I'd had breakfast and that there was something in my schoolbag for lunch. Usually, there wasn't so Bev would give me a bowl of cereal or some toast and there'd be a sandwich already wrapped alongside Stella's for my lunch break. As I said, she'd always been kind. In fact, her urge to feed me has never really waned.

When we left school, Stella went on to do wonderful things. University first and then some fabulous job in America – a lawyer or something. She comes home once in a while and Bev has been out to see her, but she doesn't like the flight. I'm with her on that. It would be my idea of hell too.

To fill the gap Bev became carer to a young girl, Trina, who had Asperger's Syndrome. Her parents both had high-flying professional jobs so could afford personal care for her. I didn't know what Asperger's Syndrome was, but I knew it took up a lot of Bev's time and I saw less of her.

But when Bev heard about Hettie passing away, she came straight up to see me. She came along to the funeral too. There were only a few of us there. Me, Bev and . . . no, I think that was it. Unless, you count the celebrant. We went to the local pub afterwards and had a cheese sandwich and a glass of decent white wine. There was no fanfare, no farewell tune, no letting off of helium balloons into the ether. It was quiet, dignified and involved as few humans as possible. It was how Hettie would have wanted it. I threw her ashes into the air at the farm and let the wind carry them over the land.

Afterwards, Bev insisted on setting up a routine of regular visits to the farm. In truth, I welcomed and dreaded Bev 'dropping by' in equal measure. The effort of talking to people had become enormous. Yet, despite my unenthusiastic response, she brought me food, home-baked pies and Tupperware containers brimming with wholesome soup on a thrice-weekly basis. When I was at my most pathetic, Bev's husband, Steve, rigged up a freezer for me in the barn and she filled it with food that would provide me with a staple diet. For a long time, I lived entirely on Bev's dinners that I only needed to microwave. She'll never know how grateful I am to her for that.

Sometimes, she brought the little girl she looked after with her. Which I think was for her own sake as much as mine. Bev was endlessly patient and kind with her charge, but I could see that it was demanding work. At the time, Trina didn't speak much at all yet I still found it difficult coping with them both in the cramped space of the caravan. The sense of claustrophobia could feel overwhelming, but I knew that Bev enjoyed bringing Trina up to the farm and it seemed as if it was the least I could do for her. She'd always been there for me. Despite her own commitments, Bev carried on visiting me, regardless. She was a constant and dogged companion, carrying on a stream of chatter even when Trina and I stared blankly at each other, willing her to stop.

Even in my self-absorbed and insular state, I could see that Trina's behaviour could be challenging. She was quite a handful, restless and frustrated, always difficult to entertain. Bev was wonderful and seemed to have the knack of dealing with her. Not everyone could do it. I think it's because Bev is one of life's nice people, a natural carer.

'I could kill for a bacon buttie,' Bev complains, bringing me from my reverie. 'But I suppose I'll have to make do with a biscuit.'

Like the animals, Bev's thoughts never stray far from her food. And, despite her love of our four-legged friends – or *mostly* four-legged in our case – I've never managed to convince her of the joys of being a vegetarian.

'One of the parents brought us some Tunnock's Teacakes,' I tell her.

'Food of the Gods!' Bev looks beside herself with glee. We all love it when we get unexpected treats. 'What have we got on today?'

'I haven't written up the list of tasks on the board yet,' I confess. 'That'll be my next job.'

'Slacker,' Bev teases. 'You've normally got that done by six o'clock. Have we got a full house?'

'Just four students, I think.' Our students all have different

Chapter Five

'Where's Alan?' I ask Bev.

'Disappeared into the barn the minute we got here,' she says. No change there.

Whereas Bev is an open book, Alan Taylor is one of life's mysteries. Hettie would have called him a 'conundrum'. Alan's probably in his sixties and is a minimal communicator. I'm only glad that he managed to land at our door. In one of his more voluble moments, I managed to wheedle out of him that he's a retired engineer of some sort – he might have said defence industry, but I don't like to ask him again. Apparently, early retirement – even with a generous pay-off and pension – wasn't all it was cracked up to be and he was looking for a few hours of volunteer work to fill his day. Some kind soul pointed him in our direction, so one day he just rocked up, got stuck in and never left. He says very little, can fix everything and won't take any payment from me. That's it. I can tell you nothing else about his work or personal background. He has his Enhanced DBS check that enables him to work with children, so that's all I need to know.

I sometimes think he might fancy Bev but it's quite hard to

tell. Occasionally, I sense that his expression softens when he looks at her. I might be imagining it, though. The only time he shows any real emotion is if I splash out and tell Bev to get some chocolate Hobnobs with the weekly shop – then his eyes truly light up.

His appearance is a bit of an enigma too. Alan has a surfeit of grey hair that sticks out in all directions and a long, straggly beard that ZZ Top might envy. Like me, he is a stranger to grooming products. He favours baggy trousers, a ripped check shirt and ancient Hunter wellies.

'Did you see what he's wearing today?' Bev widens her eyes – which are more than a little bloodshot after last night's enthusiastic pub session.

The only excitement we get from Alan – and our lives in general – is that he wears a different band T-shirt every day under his unbuttoned shirt. Some surprising ones too. Yesterday, for instance, was a Pulp day. We vie for the first glimpse which can send us into a frenzy. Every evening Bev and I take bets on who he'll turn up in, usually wagering cake or biscuits for the winner. We are normally way off. Though, in fairness, neither of us would have guessed Alan was a Bucks Fizz fan.

'No. Did you catch it? Were we anywhere close?'

'Remind me?' Bev says. 'What did you have?'

'Kings of Leon.'

'I went for Kaiser Chiefs.'

'And?'

'Florence and the Machine.' We both sigh our defeat. Didn't see him as a Florence fan either. He is a man of deep mystery.

'Not a hope,' I complain. 'He's always one step ahead of us. It's as if he knows.'

'Tomorrow's another day,' Bev says, consoling. 'We will crack the band T-shirt code. Fancy joining me for a quick tea and a teacake in commiseration at our abject failure?'

'Why not?'

So, dogs in tow, we head towards our communal tea room for a welcome break and a breakfast of biscuits for me.

Chapter Six

When I was slowly surfacing from my trough – I don't like to call it depression, but it may have been – someone asked me to take on a Shetland pony that had been neglected. I had no idea how to say no, so Tiny joined us.

He arrived malnourished and unkempt. Bev and I would walk out into the fields together with Trina to take care of him. It was then that we found that Trina loved the animals and, in turn, they seemed to calm her. Tiny was a particular favourite and she'd stand stroking the little pony and brushing his mane for as long as he'd let her. I've since discovered that some horses have a knack of knowing how to treat kids who need that bit of extra attention and Tiny was one of them. He was always kind and gentle, despite never having been treated that way himself. He was with us for a long time and had a good life here. We missed him terribly when he went to that big, open paddock in the sky.

Over that first summer, the improvement in Trina was incredible. She still never spoke directly to either Bev or me, but she began to coo away contentedly to the animals. When we acquired poor, battered Little Dog as not much more than a puppy, he joined her inner circle of three. She'd grin back at his weird perma-smile and, when she thought we weren't looking, we'd hear her chatting away to him, Little Dog cocking his ears as if listening intently.

That was ten years ago and, since then, Trina has blossomed into a lovely, and remarkably chatty, young woman. She's now at a local college doing an art foundation course. She still needs extra tuition and extended time for exams – and some days she has a complete meltdown out of nowhere – but her achievements are nothing to be sneezed at. She paints big, bold, beautiful landscapes with vivid, expressive colours. In her spare time, she rides ponies and helps out at nearby stables. Sometimes, she still comes up here to see us and it's always a joy to be with her.

When the local press found out about Trina's visits here and how they'd helped her, they sent a journalist who looked about twelve to interview us all. Then a photographer came and took some pictures of our very photogenic animals which we still have hanging in the tea room. When the piece appeared in the paper, I got phone calls from other parents – mostly stressed people at the end of their tether – asking if they could bring their children here. With Bev's help, we had a few informal open days – where I would do my best to hide in a barn. The children would arrive, pet the animals, maybe try riding a pony, collect eggs from the hens or some other simple, supervised tasks around the farm. Without exception, they loved it. So their relieved parents told other people and the word spread.

So, after much deliberation and angst, I decided to make it a formal arrangement and set up a permanent school here. Soon I had about ten people coming on a weekly basis. I generally have children over the age of ten up to about sixteen, with either behavioural difficulties or mental health issues. Some of them are brought here by harried parents who just need a few hours respite. Some come here because no one can think what else to do with them. We take students from the school down the road that caters for children with special education needs when they just need time out of the classroom to let off steam – mucking out a stable is an excellent way to burn off excess, destructive energy. Now we have about fifty kids in total on our books and just try to help them to overcome their fears and build self-confidence.

It's hard to say what we do exactly, but what we most definitely *don't* do is try to force square pegs into round holes. The students here are encouraged to develop at their own pace. We build self-confidence, self-esteem and responsibility. We teach them to learn by doing rather than by lessons. They look after the animals, they look after each other and they work on the farm. To the outside observer, it may seem haphazard – dare I say chaotic. No day is the same. But somehow, with a bit of luck and a following wind, it works. You know me well enough by now to realise that I like to stay as off-grid as possible but, of course, we have to jump through hoops with all the paperwork required for a place like this. Bev cajoled me into setting up a charity and I'm glad that I did as it certainly made this strange and unique little establishment feel more rooted. With Bev's guidance we've grown, developed and, not wishing to blow my own trumpet, helped so many kids to reach their full potential – especially the ones who would have foundered in the usual school set-up. I didn't exactly enjoy my teacher training or my work in state schools, but it was a means to an end and has certainly stood me in good stead for what I do now.

So that's kind of how we started and it's still what we do now. We just help people.

Chapter Seven

While we're having our first cuppa of the day, the students start to arrive. Some are brought by parents, others arrive in taxis – most of whom now know how to find us tucked away in our little satnav-teaser spot.

We've got some of our easier students today. First to arrive are two lovely young men, Jack and Seb. They're both fourteen and are on the autism spectrum. They've been coming here for roughly a year or so now, during which time they've become firm friends. If all of our kids were like this, then our job would be easy-peasy, lemon-squeezy. Set them a task – whether it's collecting eggs or mucking out a stable – and, generally, they'll carry it out without faltering.

Jack's favourite task is making tea for everyone and so his first job is always to put the kettle on. His routine is more precise than any Japanese tea-house, I'm sure. We like to meet up with the students here in our tea room each morning before we start the day with them, so that we can have time to chat through any issues. We also have our breaks here and our lunch. It's where everyone congregates for tea and sympathy. We call it the tea room, but that makes it sounds an awful lot more glamorous than it is. Essentially, it's a knackered old outbuilding with windows that are draughtier than I'd like. It could do with a lick of paint too, but we brighten it up with bunting made by the students and photos of their achievements. There's a wall of photos of our animals too, and granny blankets scattered everywhere thanks to our tame crochet fan – no one should be without a blanky in their lives.

There's a small kitchen at the back with a newish oven that was donated to us. Bev whips up our lunches here. She likes to bake too so there are often cakes to be had. But mostly it's just sitting around. Often that's the easiest way to get kids to open up. Then again, there are times when they just need to be quiet with their own thoughts and the modern world doesn't allow for much of that. If it was up to me, I'd confiscate everyone's phones the minute they came through the gate. Mobile phones are the devil's work, I'm convinced.

Jack makes a beeline for his favourite kettle and Bev and I oblige by having another brew while he and Seb tell us what they've been up to since they were last here a couple of days ago.

Jack lives at home with his parents – which not all of our students do – and has a couple of hens in the garden there, so we always get the lowdown on what his girls have been up to. His favourite job here is to collect the eggs from our scraggy brood and to write it up in the ledger.

Seb lives with foster parents and it seems as if his entire evenings are spent on his PlayStation, which sometimes worries me. I'd like to see him have some other interests, but we do everything in tiny bites here and that's something I can work on in the future.

'Who'd like to write up the list of tasks for the day?' I ask.

'I will.' Seb volunteers first. I reel off the jobs we have to do and slowly Seb writes them in his meticulous handwriting on the whiteboard in red marker pen, his favourite colour.

'The hens will be waiting for us.' There's a note of anxiety in Jack's voice as he dries the last of the mugs. 'They won't like that.'

'You go,' Bev says to me. 'I'll wait here for the other students to arrive and then I'll take them up to the field.'

'Come on then, Jack. Don't forget your bucket.' We head out together and Jack collects his pail from the barn en route. We walk up to the chicken coop which is set behind the tea room, close enough that I can see it from my caravan window. We have about twenty chickens now. It varies as we have a very active and determined fox in the vicinity. No matter what I do, he somehow finds his way in to their high-security unit. The chicken coops and run have recently been relocated so if I hear any kerfuffle in the dead of night, I'm up, out of my bed and there like a shot. No one messes with my girls.

'I think I saw Phantom,' Jack says as he swings the bucket next to him. 'Hiding behind the hay bales.'

'Really?' We have a cat with half a face, probably due to a past traffic accident, who lives in our barn. He wasn't brought here like the others; Phantom just moved in by himself about six months ago. Perhaps he just felt it would be a safe haven for him. I haven't ever been able to get close enough to him to fully ascertain that he is a 'he'. Phantom walks with a goose-step, lives mostly on the mice he catches, has fits occasionally and rarely comes out to see us. Every now and then, I try to cajole him to come and talk to me so that I can check he's all right, but he's a very reluctant patient. 'Did he look OK?'

'He has half a face,' Jack reminds me. 'He looks awful.'

'I meant did he seem to be healthy?'

'I don't know,' Jack says and I realise that will perplex him for the rest of the day.

Needless to say, Little Dog and Big Dog come along to help with the chickens too.

'How many eggs do you think there'll be today, Molly?' Jack asks, slightly anxious at the unknown.

'A dozen,' I guess. 'What do you think?'

Jack ponders for a while as we walk through the yard in the sunshine. 'Ten,' he says eventually. 'Is that less than a dozen?'

'Two less.'

He nods, happy with that information.

'I'm going to leave you to collect the eggs by yourself, while I go and check on the alpacas. Are you OK with that today?'

He nods again that he is.

'Don't forget to put the net over the door before you go in.' In fairness, Jack very rarely slips up, but we've had so many chickens bolt for freedom when one or more of our students have left the door to the coop open that it's worth repeating myself. Though we now have so many security measures that our chicken run is more like an escape room.

'I'll be back in five minutes, Jack. Just shout out if you need me.'

I see him check his watch.

'I might be ten minutes,' I correct. 'I'm only in the next paddock. Don't worry if I'm a little bit longer.'

'I won't worry,' he says with a worried frown and I wait and watch him until he's safely inside the chicken run with his favourite girls.

Chapter Eight

The dogs and I reach the alpacas. 'Hello, lovelies,' I shout out as I dig a handful of pellets out of their feed bucket. 'Here's your breakfast.'

They trot over, always eager to see me if there's food on offer. I hold out a hand and they jostle each other out of the way to have a nibble on the food and, where possible, my fingers.

'Don't nip,' I admonish. 'Play nicely.'

Alpacas will get away with blue murder if you let them. We have three here, and they are all total divas. I'd never intended to keep alpacas. I inherited them from a couple whose work was taking them abroad for a few years and, having got them as rather high-maintenance ornaments for their fields, had no further use for them. I got a phone call out of the blue – they knew someone who knew someone else who knew me through someone in the village, something like that. They thought I'd be *ideal* to take them on. Or a mug.

I suspect that they'd previously tried many other places but with no luck. Both with students and with animals, we are so often the last resort.

I said yes. Of course I did. What else was I to do?

The three of them stay together in one field and share the same stable. Rarely are they pleased about that. Tina Turner likes to be the boss. She's brown all over and has by far the most lavish chocolate-coloured pom-pom hair tipped with black, which she loves to flick about. Rod Stewart is white, with skinny legs and knobbly knees. Mostly, he sits there humming happily to himself on one note – the sound that alpacas make when they're content – and gazing blissfully into middle distance. Johnny Rotten is our most troubled alpaca – our post-punk bad boy. He'll nip your elbow if you're foolish enough to turn your back on him. As his name suggests, his hair is more Mohican than pom-pom and where his body is generally a tan colour, his top-knot is borderline orange. He's also pretty vacant.

Alpacas are herd animals and really, we should have more of them. They're supposed to thrive much better when they're surrounded by company. No one has told Johnny Rotten this. He, more than the other two, hates his fellow field-dwellers and will also hiss at you as soon as look at you. Our fluffy friends may look cute and have endearingly smiley faces but they are a skittish and temperamental bunch who need careful handling. Upset them and they'll give you a sharp back-heel with a hoof given half the chance. Technically, they don't spit, but they hiss if they're pissed off and it's pretty much the same thing. Tina is also prone to hold a grudge.

The upside is that their droppings – of which there are many – are a useful sideline. Bags of Alpaca Gold sell to keen gardeners for a small fortune. It's a hundred per cent organic and all the rage among the local allotment glitterati. We don't advertise it widely, but we're open every day to the public to sell our surplus eggs and alpaca manure. I don't like doing it, as anyone can come through the gate and my social skills when it comes to dealing with the general public I'm sure leave a lot to be desired. But we need the money and that's all there is to it. However, it is a great learning opportunity for the kids, so I try to focus on the positive aspects of it. If they're able to, the young people serve the sporadic customers, count out the eggs into our recycled boxes, haul the bags of Alpaca Gold to 4x4s and are responsible for giving change, then writing up the transaction into our Egg and Poo Ledger. Learning by stealth.

'How are we doing today, Tina?' Our diva waggles her head at me. I don't usually stroke the alpacas as they're not that fond of being touched. Much like myself. When you don't have much human contact, you kind of forget what it's like and tend to shy away from it. When I go to the supermarket now – if I've failed in my quest to make Bev do it instead – I'm aware that people don't respect your personal space any more. Half of the women still seem to be in their pyjamas and they're forever pushing past or bumping into you. Perhaps that's why I have an affinity with the alpacas. They're pretty aloof too.

We give the kids jobs to do every day like feeding the animals or grooming them, maybe some small maintenance jobs like mucking out or, if they're safe to handle tools, mending a fence. Each according to their abilities. Some of our students stay for as little as a week, a couple have been here since we began.

Bev helps me out permanently now and frankly, I don't think I could cope without her. A few years ago, her husband left her for a younger model and, to help her get over the pain, she threw herself into the farm in the same way that I have. She spent a lot of time kicking buckets around the farmyard or crying into the shoulder of a Shetland pony until she was over him. For me, she's invaluable. While I hide away here, Bev's the public face of the farm. She's the one who goes to meetings with the council, as required. She's the one who deals with our inspections. I'm the coward who lurks in the background messing about with chicken feed and pony tack, exuding anxiety. She's my rock, my friend, the closest thing I have to family and I love her to bits.

Chapter Nine

When I've dealt with the alpacas and the three of them are reasonably happy, I go back to see how Jack's getting on with the chickens.

He's busy changing the water in their drinkers and I smile when I see the meticulous care that he's lavishing onto this small task.

'How are you doing?'

Jack stands up, careful not to spill a precious drop of water. 'Ten eggs,' he says proudly. 'I thought so. One of them has laid a giant egg.' He comes to the bucket and shows me.

'Wow. That is a whopper.' We examine the egg together. It's an egg that looks as if it's on steroids. 'I bet that made her eyes pop out of her head.'

Jack looks at the hen in question. 'I don't think it did.'

'You remember what we discussed about people not meaning exactly what they say? Sometimes they try to be a bit funny?'

'Ah,' Jack says. 'That was you being funny.'

'Kind of,' I agree.

'What's funny about a chicken's eyes popping out?'

'Not much,' I have to concede.

'People are strange,' Jack concludes.

They are, indeed. That's why I stick mainly to animals.

All our hens are ex-battery and tend to have shorter lifespans than your regular chicken. So, unfortunately, it means that our students also get fairly regular lessons on what death means. I try to make the time that our all poultry visitors have here as happy as possible. They usually arrive looking truly terrible, in an 'oven-ready' state with no feathers or with floppy combs. They're often weak too as they've had no exercise at all, but it's good to see them strengthen and thrive with a bit of tender, loving care.

A big brown one struts over to see us. She's called Bouncer and is the doorlady of the hen house. No one gets past Bouncer if she doesn't want them in there. Then there's our survivor, Gloria Gaynor, who's been attacked three times by the fox and yet is still here to tell the tale. We've got a blind chicken, Mrs Magoo, and Peg is our one-legged chicken. We've got featherless chickens, anxious chickens and even one or two with all their limbs, feathers and faculties. I love chickens. I'm sure there are a lot of the world's ills that could be cured by cuddling a chicken.

Our only cockerel has become known as Dick the Cock – thanks for that, Bev – and it's a good job we haven't got any neighbours as he makes an almighty racket cock-a-doodle-doing throughout the day. But he's a very fine specimen and likes everyone to know it.

'Do you want to take the eggs and wash them so they're ready to sell?' I ask Jack.

'Yes.'

'How many eggs did we have yesterday?'

Jack thinks. 'Twelve.' He thinks again. 'A dozen.'

'Good. So how many eggs altogether?'

'Twenty-two.'

'Egg-cellent,' I quip.

He frowns at me. 'That's a joke too, isn't it?'

'Yeah. But a bad one.' Jack picks up the egg bucket and I link my arm through his. 'I'll walk you back to the yard.'

'That was an easy sum, Molly,' he mutters at me. 'A child could have done that.'

Chapter Ten

I should tell you about the rest of the gang. Time's pressing on and we have a lot to get through this morning before our communal get-together at lunchtime. If I miss that I have Bev to answer to. Sometimes, I get caught up in other things but Bev's right, it's another useful time to chat to the kids about their day and their concerns or worries if I've missed them when they arrive. So I try hard not to skip it no matter how busy I am.

Leaving Jack in Alan's care in the barn, I wander up to the big field at the top of the hill. Bev's up here with Lottie and Erin, two more of our regular students. Lottie and Erin are eleven and twelve, respectively, but are both going on thirty-five. There's nothing that you can tell them that they don't already know. They're in their usual uniform of neon leggings with matching neon nail polish. Lottie has been with us for about a year now, but Erin is fairly new. They've both come to us with challenging behaviour that often excludes them from mainstream schooling and their home lives are complicated and chaotic. If you could see them now, petting the goats and giggling with each other, you would never think it. When they want to, they can look angelic, but looks can be deceiving. When they kick off, they go big time and both swear like troopers. I've not been bitten by either of my dogs, but these two have both taken lumps out of me in the past. When Bev is fed up with them she calls them The Biters. Still, you know the saying about two equal and opposite forces cancelling each other out? I think that's what's going on here. Lottie and Erin have met their match in each other and when they're together, their challenging behaviour has been largely negated. It doesn't stop them trying it on with other people though.

'How's it going, ladies?' I ask them.

'OK,' Erin examines her nail polish and shrugs.

Lottie just does an echoing shrug.

'We're all good,' Bev says. 'When we're done up here, we'll come back to the yard and do some weeding in the herb garden.'

It's a little optimistic to call it a garden yet, but we've made a start on it. We have a couple of old feed troughs that have been planted up with herbs – thyme, rosemary, mint – and some salad leaves. Bev does most of the cooking and we try to use our own herbs when we can. I have plans to turn that part of the farm into a vegetable garden. If I'm honest, I've had those plans for some time now, but I never have the time or the money to see them into fruition. There's always something that needs repairing and the cash gets diverted. Wouldn't it be great, though, to see if we could grow all our own veg and add another strand of learning for the kids? One day.

Lottie and Erin don't really like doing much in the way of hard work, so we find them lighter jobs to do. They'll fiddle about with the herbs when pushed or will groom the ponies and do a stint collecting eggs. If we left them to their own devices they'd be happier sitting doing each other's hair all day or playing games on their phones. To give them a more structured day, the kids also have a couple of hours tutoring during the afternoon when they're here – which, of course, they resent bitterly and never fail to show it. We have an informal classroom set up inside one of the outbuildings by the tea room and have a raft of supply teachers who come in to conduct their lessons and I don't envy them their job. I've been there, done that, bought the T-shirt and so try to give them all the support that I can. We do all we can to keep regulars as that helps the kids too – many of them don't cope well with change – but that's easier said than done.

After I've chatted to the girls, I call the dogs to heel and they're already eager to move on. We walk along the path back towards the yard. My earlier Tunnock's Teacake breakfast didn't quite hit the spot and my tummy grumbles with hunger, so I leave the dogs mooching about in the yard for a minute and swerve into the caravan. Quickly, I grab a bowl of muesli to keep me going until lunchtime, making a mental note to add it to the next shopping list as I'm running low. I'm always running low on everything. Funds particularly. I only charge a modest sum for kids to come here and it really isn't enough. Bev's always nagging me to put the prices up, but I'm reluctant. A handful of students get council funding, but most of the parents have to pay for it themselves and, call me a fool, but I really don't want to cane it. The parents generally need respite, not more pressure – especially financial. I know all about that. As a result, I do struggle to meet overheads and the price of things seems to rise at an alarming rate – feed, utilities, vet bills, all of that.

We're quiet today, but some days we have a stream of vehicles coming and going. Several of our students come in taxis paid for by the local authority; one student we occasionally have comes in a minibus with armed security as he's had a troubled past involving knife crime; some are brought by frazzled parents in ageing Ford Fiestas with dented panels and they're the ones that my heart goes out to. As I finish my cereal, I hear the crunch of tyres on gravel and look out of the window to see if Bev is back in the yard and can open the gate. She's nowhere in sight, so I lob the bowl into the sink to be dealt with later and dash out to open it. A great big posh Bentley sweeps past me.

Wow. That's pretty impressive. Our kids might come in all forms of transport but I can safely say that I've never seen anything anywhere near as flashy as this in my farmyard.

Chapter Eleven

The shiny red car is incongruous against all the dirt and slightly rusty farm equipment. I stand and gape at it for a moment before mobilising myself to go and find out who it is.

As I approach, a well-groomed and devastatingly handsome man gets out. He's just as immaculate as his swanky car and has film-star looks the like of which we've never quite seen before at Hope Farm. Not when I've been awake, anyway.

Our unexpected visitor is tall, quite muscular. The jeans and dark jacket he's wearing suit his frame. His hair is fair, wavy and swept back. His skin is tanned but smooth rather than weathered and I speak as someone who is used to wind-burned cheeks. As he comes to greet me, I wish that I wasn't sporting an extra layer of mud this morning courtesy of Anthony and, as you have probably gathered by now, I'm not generally that worried about how I look. I even wonder if I've remembered to comb my hair this week.

In the passenger seat is the figure of a slight teenage boy, arms folded, jaw rigid. Even from this distance, I can tell that he's oozing hostility. He's staring fixedly out of the window in the direction of the sheep, but I know that he's not seeing them.

The man holds out his hand and, after I've given my palms a quick wipe on my jeans, he grips my fingers firmly as he says, 'Shelby Dacre.'

I recognise the name, but I'm not sure why. 'Molly Baker.'

'Sorry to turn up unannounced,' he adds in a voice that's strong, confident. A voice that sounds like it's used to public speaking, every syllable clearly enunciated.

'It's not a problem,' I assure him. Despite his dashing good looks, I can tell when he's closer that he looks tired, worn out. His eyes say that he's weary of the world. 'What can I do for you?'

He glances back at the boy in the passenger seat nervously. 'A friend told me about you. She said that you do good work here.'

'I like to think so.'

He lowers his voice. 'I've been having trouble with my son. They said you'd be able to help. I didn't know what I had to do. Whether we need to be referred or . . . ' His voice tails away.

'To be honest, most people just turn up,' I tell him. 'We take it from there. What kind of problems is your son facing?'

'He's been excluded from school for anti-social behaviour,' he confides. 'Pretty serious stuff.'

'Such as?'

'Lucas has been caught setting fires at the school. This time to rubbish in the grounds behind the sports block.' Mr Dacre shakes his head, bewildered. 'It's not the first occasion. Lucas has a bit of history.'

Ah, an arsonist in the making. That's new for me. We haven't had one of those before and we've had most things. We've had kids who have been invited to leave their schools because of bullying, knife crimes, assaulting teachers, indiscriminate use of weed and many more things.

'He was lucky to escape with only a police caution,' Mr Dacre

45

continues. 'I thought we'd be looking at much worse. Thankfully, the school didn't press charges. They just kicked him out. Now I've not a clue what to do. He just stays in his room all day and night. I can't reach him.' He lowers his voice further and his distress is evident when he says, 'I'm at the end of my tether. Please help.'

He looks like a man who likes to be in control, so I can understand why this must be a challenge for him. 'I can't promise a miracle fix, much as I'd like to, but we'll do our best.'

Mr Dacre is slightly embarrassed when he says, 'I've actually no idea what it is that you do here.'

I can't help but laugh at his candour. 'We're kind of the last chance saloon,' I supply. 'We help children and adults who have behavioural or mental health issues – sometimes both. I try to run a place that strives to support young people who are struggling by giving them a positive space to learn and grow.' He nods at that, so I carry on. 'They learn by helping on the farm – looking after the animals and each other. Because none of our students have the same needs or requirements, we tailor each experience to suit individual needs. We also have some structured education for our students. There's a supply teacher who comes in every day to cover some basics, but a lot of it is about confidence-building, providing structure and responsibility.'

'Christ, he needs some of that.'

I don't mention that so often with our students it can be the parents who are part of the problem. 'It's hard to say what exactly your son would be doing if he came here but, generally, the students spend their days involved in different tasks. They might feed the chickens, muck out a stable, groom the horses or feed the lambs.' And we'll be getting plenty of those soon as it's lambing season. 'They tackle whatever needs to be done. We try to make the days as varied for them as possible. It helps to get them working as a team and it's quite relaxed. We don't force anyone to do anything, but they're encouraged to be fully engaged. Does your son like animals?'

He gives me a reluctant smile. 'Not that you'd notice.'

'Then we might have an issue.' I smile back because what else is there to do? 'As you're here, would you and your son like to have a look around? That would be a good starting point.'

'I'll see if I can coax him out of the car. It's fair to say that he's not exactly thrilled to be here.'

'We're used to dealing with that too,' I assure him. 'Shall I come and say hello?'

'Maybe that would help. There are some vestiges of good manners lurking deep within him.'

So we head back to his car and, as we do, Bev appears in the yard, broom in hand, sweeping frantically at nothing in particular. She appears to be wearing red lipstick. A lot of it. As we near the car, she heads us off at the pass.

'Hi there,' she says and sounds rather more husky than she normally does.

'Hello,' Mr Dacre replies.

'I'm Bev.' For some reason, she's all of a dither and is giggling girlishly and, believe me, Bev isn't a natural giggler. She generally embraces the more brusque personality type.

Mr Dacre takes her hand and, for a moment, I actually think that she might faint. She goes all swoony and silly.

Behind his back, I mouth, *What's wrong with you?*

She winks at me and I've no idea why. Or is she winking at him? Does she fancy this man? It appears so and I've never known Bev say anything particularly good about the male of the species. When her husband left her for a younger, more East European model it left her heart badly scarred.

When Mr Dacre lets go of her hand, she strikes up a weird pin-up style pose with her broom. The woman's gone mad. She told me yesterday that she'd accidentally rubbed toothpaste into her arms rather than her HRT gel. Perhaps that's what's wrong. The minty fresh approach to menopause isn't suiting her.

I give her a wide berth and follow Mr Dacre to the shiny car. I hope he doesn't notice that Little Dog is weeing up against his back tyre. My dog views this as being friendly. I think if you have such a fancy car, you might view it as otherwise. We reach the passenger door and Mr Dacre's son gives us a sideways glance from beneath his fringe and I can tell that his heart sinks. The poor boy looks as if he'd rather be anywhere else in the world.

Shelby Dacre opens the passenger door for me. I stick out my hand and put on my perkiest voice. 'Hi Lucas, I'm Molly. Want to come and have a look around? See what we do here?'

'It's a farm,' he says, exuding boredom. 'I should be able to work that out for myself.'

'You're here now, though,' I say. 'Might as well have a look.'

By my side, Mr Dacre is all of a twitch. 'Give it a go, Lucas. You said you would.'

Lucas glares at his father. Then he sighs deeply, ignores my hand and gets out of the car. His slight frame is entirely clad in black – T-shirt, skinny jeans and boots. His arms are like threads of white cotton. His face, equally pale, is framed by an unruly mop of dark hair. He looks as if he combs it even less than I comb mine. His eyes might be brown, but it's hard to tell as his hair mostly covers them. I'd guess that he spends a lot of time indoors on his computer rather than running round in the sunshine.

'It seems as if I have no choice,' he mutters.

'Come and see what's on offer,' I say brightly. 'You might find that you're surprised.'

'I doubt it.' Yet he plods off into the farmyard, hands stuffed into his pockets, scuffing up clouds of dust as he goes.

I consider that excellent progress.

Chapter Twelve

In truth, I don't really want to take on anyone else at the moment. Each student is quite demanding and needs a lot of time, especially newcomers. They usually take a lot of settling in and Lucas certainly looks as if he won't be the exception that proves the rule. On the other hand, we are desperately short of cash and it's always a balancing act. If Lucas comes here full-time, and I suspect that's what Mr Dacre would like, then it would be more than welcome income. My bill for animal feed alone would make your eyes water. The phrase 'eat like a horse' is firmly based in truth.

'Bev, I'm just going to show Mr Dacre and Lucas around the farm.'

'Could I have a moment of your time please, Molly?' She snatches at my arm and holds me back.

'I'll catch you up in a second,' I say to them. 'Do feel free to have a look in some of the pens in the barn over there.' I point them towards our piggies and our geese, helpfully, usher them there.

As soon as they're out of earshot, my strangely acting operative hisses, 'Do you know who that is?'

'Shelby Dacre and his son, Lucas Dacre?' I venture.

'God, you're hopeless,' she tuts. I wonder if he's a local councillor or the mayor. Bev knows these things. Whoever he is, local dignitary or not, he's got her in a right tizzy. When I continue to look at her blankly, she supplies, 'It's Farmer Gordon Flinton, nitwit.' There's a slightly drooly expression on her face.

'Who?'

Bev rolls her eyes. 'Oh, for pity's sake, Molly. *Gordon Flinton.* THE Gordon Flinton.'

I fear I still look vacant.

'*Flinton's Farm,*' she persists as if saying it over and over will make me understand. 'The soap opera. The one that everyone has watched three times a week for the last twenty years. Everyone apart from you, obvs.'

'Ah.' Still none the wiser really. I have heard of it. I think. But, as Bev said, I've never actually watched it. Mainly because I don't possess a television. I can't even remember the last time I did have a telly. Not since I've lived on the farm, that's for sure. Hettie never had time for anything like that. Which is why all of these things pass me by. I only know what goes on in the *Big Brother* house or that there even *is* a *Big Brother* house because Bev insists on telling me.

'He's a bloody massive heart-throb! Surely even you can see that?'

'Yes,' I agree. He definitely is heart-throb material. 'I'd go along with that.'

'He induces mass hysteria in women of a certain age.' Bev puts a hand to her forehead. 'God, my head's all hot and my flipping legs have gone to jelly. He'd have it *all* night.'

'I'm sure he'd be pleased to know.'

'I'd beg you to get me a date, but sadly he favours the scrawny actress kind of woman.' She sighs at Shelby Dacre's back. 'The

50

man might look fifty shades of fabulous but he clearly hasn't got any taste.'

'I'm not sure I'd have any influence over his love life, having met him only ten minutes ago.'

'A girl can dream,' Bev sighs somewhat dreamily and leans on her broom in a lovesick manner. 'His wife died a year or so ago.'

'In real-life or on the soap?'

'Keep up, Mols. In real life. Cancer or something. Awful. He's gone a bit off the rails since then if you believe the TV mags. His current squeeze doesn't look much older than his kid.'

Hmm. That makes me think. Perhaps there's a very simple explanation why his son is lost and angry and trying to burn his school down.

'I'd better catch up with them,' I say. 'I'm not after his body, but I could probably do with some of his money. I think we can help Lucas. I hope he'll agree to coming here.'

'We weren't going to take anyone else on.'

'You should have realised by now that I can't say no.'

Bev brightens. 'Excellent. That means Farmer Gordon will be a regular visitor?'

I shrug. 'I guess so.'

Bev puts her hands together in prayer. 'There is a God.'

'I don't know exactly what you were pretending to do with that broom, but you'd better get back to it. If we don't impress Mr Dacre, then he might take Lucas elsewhere.' Though I wonder where that actually might be. I don't like to show off too much, but we're kind of unique in our approach here.

I leave Bev and hurry after Mr Dacre and Lucas. They're both looking into Teacup's pen when I catch up with them. Little Dog has taken up residence next to Lucas's leg and is fluttering the lashes of his remaining eye in a puppyish manner. His weird, nervy smile is out in full force. Not even the coldest of hearts could ignore that and, of course, Lucas bends to fuss him. Little Dog is ninja at getting cuddles. There might even be a hint of a smile on Lucas's lips, but I wouldn't stake my life on it.

'This is Teacup,' I supply. 'We inherited him because he grew too big. Most of our animals come here for similar reasons. Either their owners can't cope with them or they outgrow their space or usefulness.' Close to, Shelby Dacre smells very clean and fragrant, especially if you bear in mind that we're standing next to a pig. Still, I mustn't be distracted by a bit of posh aftershave. 'The students who come here are allocated jobs to do throughout the day. It's busy, Lucas, but can be enjoyable. Everyone does a couple of hours of structured tuition each day too, so that you can keep up with your studies.'

'Oh, joy,' he mutters.

'Lucas,' Mr Dacre says, sharply.

'We collected the hen's eggs this morning, but haven't changed their bedding yet. Plus the eggs need to be washed and boxed up for sale. Would you like to help out with that? You can meet a couple of the other young people.'

Lucas looks as if he's about to tell me to get stuffed, but then he lets out a weary sigh and says in a voice loaded with sarcasm, 'I'd be delighted.'

'I'm sorry, but I need to leave.' Shelby Dacre says, glancing anxiously at his watch, and I can tell that he's itching to get away. Which is a shame as it would do Lucas good if his father could remain and help him to integrate. 'I do apologise but work calls. You know how it is.'

Lucas's expression darkens and I suspect that he feels he has far too much experience of his dad putting work before him. To me it seems as if Mr Dacre's just eager to hand the problem of his 'difficult' son onto someone else. I'd prefer that person was me.

'Lucas can still stay with us. There's no need for him to rush off too.' I glance at Lucas. 'If you want to.'

'Can you manage without me?' Shelby asks.

He's addressing me, but Lucas spits out. 'I'm perfectly used to managing without you, Father.'

'We'll be fine,' I chip in. 'You can have a good look round, Lucas, and see what you think of us. Can you collect Lucas at five o'clock?'

'I'll send a car.' Mr Dacre addresses his son through gritted teeth. 'Try, Lucas. Please. For my sake and for your own.'

'I'll love every minute,' Lucas deadpans.

Shelby Dacre looks as if he's about to speak, but clearly bites it down. We both watch him as he walks back to his car. He looks as if he has the weight of the world on his shoulders. And Lucas smirks as he goes.

Chapter Thirteen

'Tosser,' Lucas says under his breath as his father drives away. I close the gate behind him.

'Everyone thinks that about their parents, you know.'

'In this case I'm right.' But his face is as sad as it is bitter.

'We have some great chickens,' I say to try to distract him. Lucas looks doubtful. 'Want to come and meet our girls?'

'If you insist.'

It's a gentle introduction to farm duties and one that most people enjoy, so I take him over to the chicken run. 'Grab a basket, just in case there's a stray egg or two that we missed earlier.' He does as he's told without protest – but without much enthusiasm either – and we go towards the enclosure together.

'We've got a few blind hens, so if you move too quickly they panic and run into things,' I explain to Lucas as we duck beneath the escape netting. 'Some have only got one leg, so they can over-balance.'

'You've got all of the fun things here,' he says.

'We cater for as many needs as we can.' I show him how to open the coops and look in the straw for eggs. There are one or two in each coop and Lucas collects the eggs with surprising care. 'We collect the eggs twice in a morning and once again later in the afternoon. Jack did it this morning. It's his favourite job. You could help him to do it later, if you want to.'

'Seriously?'

'It keeps the eggs clean and less likely to become damaged. In hot weather you don't want them in the nest for too long. We sell the eggs from the tea room to help our income.'

He doesn't look thrilled by that either.

Next I show Lucas how to refresh the bedding straw and, again, he applies himself without complaint. Perhaps we're both being on our best behaviour. When everything's fresh and clean, we head out and I take Lucas to the outhouse so that we can wash the eggs. The rest of the farm might be a little bit untidy and, well, farm-like, but this is the place that we keep spic and span so that our eggs are fit to sell. Jack hasn't yet prepared the ones from earlier, so Lucas and I stand side by side at the double sink and, together, gently scrub the shells to get all the straw, dirt and unspeakable off them. It's quite a relaxing, therapeutic job.

'I've only been here an hour and this is making me want to be vegetarian,' Lucas says.

'I am. I couldn't ever contemplate touching chicken, lamb or pork. It would be like eating one of my best friends.'

'I'm just looking at all the shit.' He wrinkles his nose as he washes an egg that's been particularly well christened and I laugh.

'There's a lot of that here,' I tell him. 'If you decided to stay, you'd better get used to it.'

'I'm not entirely sure that I'm going to have any say in the matter.' And a dark scowl descends on his boyishly handsome face.

We do the rest in what I'd like to call companiable silence, but I can still feel the waves of tension coming from Lucas. I show him how we put the eggs into recycled cartons. Customers get twenty pence back if they return their boxes.

'Aren't you going to try and psychoanalyse me?' he eventually asks. 'Everyone else does.'

'I hadn't planned on it. But I was thinking that we might need a cup of tea and a biscuit before we head up to the big field so that you can see the horses. Are you any good at brewing up?'

'Dunno.'

'Let's find out then. It's an essential skill if you're going to fit in here.'

He bristles at that. 'Who says that I want to fit in?'

I smile softly. 'Even rebels like a good cuppa. Come on.'

We fall into step across the yard and Little Dog trots along too. He knows that the biscuit tin will be opening and he's ever hopeful for some crumbs.

Chapter Fourteen

'He just wants to dump me on you,' Lucas says as he slams the mugs about on the table. 'You know that, right? Then he can pretend that he cares.'

'You think?' I only asked him an innocuous question and he launched straight into this. He's obviously been holding onto his anger for some time.

'I *know*,' he says, firmly. He stands fidgeting while the kettle boils and then he crashes about some more. Crashing complete, Lucas hands me a mug of tea and I take a grateful sip. Even though it's edging closer to lunchtime, I help myself to a chocolate digestive biscuit. I offer the packet to Lucas and, after examining it carefully, he takes one too.

'Come and sit with me for a minute before I find you something else to do.'

'I'd rather stand.' He leans against the wall, sullenly and scowls at his biscuit as if it's the enemy.

'Your dad seems to be very concerned about you,' I venture.

'He's an actor. Appearing to be something he's not is what he does best.'

'Bev told me that he's in a soap opera.'

Lucas's eyes widen. 'You didn't recognise him?'

'No. I haven't got a telly,' I say by way of explanation.

Lucas laughs out loud. 'That's hilarious. I wondered why you weren't throwing yourself at him like other women do.' I think of the usually unimpressed Bev going to pieces and feel that Lucas may have a point. 'You must be the only person on the planet who doesn't know who Shelby Dacre is. He's a National Treasure. Like The Queen.' Scathing. 'Apparently.'

'Is it any good? Do you watch it?'

'It's complete crap and I don't.' Lucas throws himself into the sofa next to me and pulls a crumpled packet of cigarettes from his pocket.

'No smoking,' I say.

He looks horrified. 'Not anywhere?'

'Hay and smouldering cigarette ends aren't a good mix.'

He sighs again, but puts them back in his pocket without further argument. I'm not even going to ask if his dad knows he smokes.

'So you spend a lot of time by yourself?'

'He's at the studio every day during the week. The show goes out on three nights. Omnibus on Sunday,' he mocks. 'Every weekend he's opening something or another. He'll do anything. He has no idea how to say no.'

'What do you do when you're alone?'

Lucas folds his arms and scowls. 'I thought you weren't going to pick through my brain.'

'I'm not. I'm just trying to find out a bit about you. We normally know more about our students before they arrive, but if you don't feel like talking we can walk up to the horses. They've knocked a bit of the fence down and I want to see if it's been fixed.' I'm sure Alan will be hard at work by now. I saw he'd arrived this morning, but that's rare. Alan just slides quietly in most days. He does have a battered old car, but he often walks here from his cottage in the village. Sometimes he even risks coming through Anthony's field if he's feeling brave. 'Fancy it?'

'I don't suppose you've got any computer games?'

'No.'

He puffs out a breath filled with misery. 'Horses it is.'

'I'll pick up an extra hammer on the way. You might feel like helping Alan.'

'What if I don't?'

'You can sit and watch him. We don't *make* you do anything here. If you want to waste your time, then you can.'

He frowns at that. If the kids push against you and you don't push back, it often throws them.

I turn to the sink to hide my smile and rinse the cups under the tap, promising to wash them properly later. Then we head out into the warmth of the spring day and grab a hammer from the barn before we walk up towards the field. The geese come and have a cursory check that they're not missing out on anything. I whistle for the dogs and, magically, they appear from behind one of the sheds where they've probably been hunting down a poor unsuspecting mouse. Little Dog and Big Dog come to heel. Kind of. They run ahead usually, sniffing everything there is to sniff. As we cross the yard, Lucas keeps pace with me, but he says nothing and neither do I.

Chapter Fifteen

The sun is overhead now, warm and bright. Without a breeze to cool the air, I can feel the rays hot on my skin. I'd better not keep Lucas out for too long as he looks like a vampire. Any sun on that lily-white skin and he might well go up in flames. I have some sunscreen in the caravan that he can use tomorrow. If he comes back.

I flick a finger at my van as we pass it. 'That's where I live.'

Lucas looks horrified. 'Seriously?'

I nod. 'Home sweet home.'

'Holy fuck, you are dedicated.'

'All my money goes on the animals.'

'That's why you take in brats like me?'

I laugh. 'We've yet to see if you're a brat or not.'

'I am,' he says. 'I promise you. Everyone says so. I like being that way, then no one gets close to me.'

'We're not all the same. Some people like being surrounded by others. Some thrive by themselves.'

'You like being by yourself?'

'I generally prefer animals to people.'

'I don't know whether I do or not. We've never been able to

have animals at home. Not even a guinea pig. Mum was desperate for a dog, but it was a no go.' The first time he's mentioned his mother. 'My father's allergic to everything. Even feather cushions.'

'Yet he plays a farmer in a soap?'

'I told you, he's a fucking fake.'

I can't help but chuckle at that. 'How on earth does he manage? Surely he has to go near the animals while he's filming.'

'His drug of choice is antihistamine. He mainlines it.'

'Oh, dear. I don't suppose we'll be seeing much of him here then.'

'No. But not for that reason. He has a girlfriend who's too young for him. She keeps him busy when he's not at award ceremonies or on *The One Show*.' Behind the bitterness in his voice there's pain too.

As we leave the yard, Fifty comes out of the shade of the pens to join us. It looks as if he's been hanging out with Teacup or the rabbits. He hobbles along next to us with his strange gait. 'This is our pet lamb,' I say to Lucas.

'A pet lamb? Why does that not surprise me?'

Fifty bleats at him and Lucas gives the lamb a sideways glance, determined to be unmoved by his obvious charm.

'He doesn't mind if you fuss him,' I say.

Exuding reluctance, he bends to ruffle Fifty's ears who bleats in joy and rubs against Lucas's leg. 'Friendly.'

'Most of us don't bite,' I tease. Then I correct myself: 'Actually, quite a lot of things do bite.' Students as much as animals. 'You just need to know how to handle them.'

The alpacas are all lying down in their stall, humming tune-lessly together and studiously ignoring us. The ponies are up in the far corner of their field, so we'll leave them until another time. Besides, I want to see if I can get Lucas doing something. So we make our way straight to Sweeney and Carter.

'Here are our big boys,' I say as we approach the field that contains – most of the time – our Shire horses. 'They're lovely but they keep breaking the fence.'

Alan, as I anticipated, is getting ready to fix it. He's come up here on the quad bike with the small trailer attached and it's loaded with planks. Fifty bleats until I pick him up and put him in the trailer. He settles down in the corner for a snooze. I guess he'll be having a ride home.

'Morning, Alan.'

Alan nods. 'Aye.'

As Bev said, today he's wearing Florence and the Machine.

'This is Lucas. He's giving us a try out. Thought you might like a hand.'

Alan looks him up and down but says nothing.

I hand Lucas the hammer. 'Here you go. You're on.'

He regards the hammer with disdain. 'I have *absolutely* no idea what to do with this.'

'Good. Alan will show you.'

Alan, obligingly, says, 'This is a hammer. This is nails. We use a hammer to knock nails in planks. We fix the fence. Horses knock it over again.'

'There you go,' I say. 'Simples.'

Lucas gives me the face that says, *Seriously?*

Alan might be sparing and somewhat obvious in his instructions, but he has infinite patience with our students. While working with him you might not engage in witty banter or find out about his history, his life, his hobbies or anything else for that matter. He is not the go-to man if you want amusing anecdotes. It took me about two years to find out that he liked chocolate Hobnobs. But spend time with Alan and you will usually come away able to tinker with a tractor or build a bird box or repair a window frame. Skills that should never be underestimated.

'Before you start, come and say hello to the culprits, our Shire horses. Sweeney has anxiety issues and Carter has SAD and is generally miserable from September to April.'

'I can see why they push the fence over.'

They're both over seventeen hands high and built like tanks. 'You can stroke their noses. They might be big, but they're gentle giants.' I show him how and, hesitantly, he follows.

'Ever ridden?'

He shakes his head. 'Never been this close to a horse before.'

'Bev exercises them and could do with some help if you fancy that. She gives riding lessons too.'

'Not sure if it's my thing.'

I pat Sweeney. 'I love to ride, but I rarely have the time these days.' Which reminds me. 'I've got a lot to do and I need to spend time with the other kids who are in today. Can I leave you with Alan?'

'Sure.' He hugs his skinny white arms and looks like a little kid next to the bulk of Alan. I can see that, despite his posturing, he's nervous.

'We'll catch up at lunchtime. Veg chilli on the menu.'

'Be still my beating heart,' Lucas deadpans which makes me laugh.

Already, I feel myself connecting with Lucas. That's a good sign. Some of the students are really hard to bond with – particularly those on the autistic spectrum – and though I have a lot to learn about him, I think this troubled boy might give me lots to work with beneath that brittle shell.

Chapter Sixteen

At the end of the day a chauffeured car turns up for Lucas. One of those huge, four-wheeled drive things. Perfect for farm duties. Less useful when only shopping at Sainsbury's. It has blacked-out windows and a driver in mirrored shades who sits stock-still, behind the wheel. Everyone else has gone and Lucas is the last of the students here.

'Travelling in style,' I say as we walk together to the car, Little Dog and Fifty in tow.

'It's only because my father's too busy to come himself and he thinks this makes up for it.'

I let that pass without comment even though I agree it would have been nice if Shelby Dacre had come to collect his son after his first day. No matter how old they are, they're still your babies and it's clear that Lucas needs some love and attention right now. But I guess if you're some hot-shot television star then you can't just halt filming to fit round your family commitments. I say it as if I have any knowledge of that world. 'Have you enjoyed today?'

'I'd rather have been playing computer games.' There's a flush of pink across his cheeks and his forearms. He spent a lot of time out in the big field mending the fence with Alan and in the afternoon, rather than put him in with the day's lesson, I found him some wellies and we mucked out the pigs together. If I'm not very much mistaken he might even have enjoyed that. Well, 'enjoyed' might be stretching it, but he didn't complain too much. Actually, he complained a lot, but not in a heartfelt way. I suspect he complained simply because that's what he's used to doing.

'We'll see you tomorrow?' I venture.

Lucas shrugs. 'I don't think I have any choice.'

'We can work on that,' I tell him. 'It's been nice having you here. Alan said you did well with him. Mending fences might be your forte.'

'The Alan bit was OK,' he admits, grudgingly. 'Though I did get a blister.' He shows me the afflicted finger and I pull a suitably sympathetic face.

'Take care, Lucas,' I say and I feel genuinely sad that we might not see him again. I think we could do a lot for him here. 'I hope you give us another go.'

He risks giving Fifty a tentative pat, then bends to fuss Little Dog and the dog's weird smile widens. Lucas makes a little noise that might be a laugh – not really sure though. Then he climbs into the passenger seat and the driver with dark sunglasses turns full circle in the yard and drives him away.

Bev appears at my elbow. 'Is he coming back?'

'I don't know, Bev. Usually, I can tell, but I can't call this one.'

My friend links her arm through mine. 'Let's have a cuppa and I'll fill you in on Shelby Dacre.'

'Are you sure that I want to know?'

'Forewarned is forearmed.'

Chapter Seventeen

'Have you got something to eat for your tea?' Bev asks as we climb into my van. 'You must be getting low on shopping.'

'I've got eggs.' We're never short of those. 'I'll knock together an omelette later.'

'You're looking too thin,' Bev admonishes. 'You need some flesh on those bones.'

For the record, I'm not thin at all.

'Why don't you come with me to the pub on Sunday for a roasty dinner?' she cajoles. 'I'm going with a couple of friends. You'd like them.'

'I might,' I say. 'Thanks for the offer.'

'You *might*.' Bev tuts. 'What you mean is that you won't. All you want to do is stay here with the chickens and Tina Turner.'

'Yeah,' I admit. Tina needs me. All the animals do. Their need is greater than my desire for a nut roast.

'Don't lose touch with the world completely, Mols. Your aunt did and, if it wasn't for you, she wouldn't have had anyone. Come and meet the girls. You need *some* friends.'

'I've got you,' I remind her. 'And Alan.'

'Between us we cannot supply all a woman needs.'

'I have *no* needs,' I remind Bev. 'Stop worrying about me.'

Bev takes in her surroundings and grimaces. 'You don't have a bathroom for a start,' Bev notes as she casts her beady eye round my van for signs that I'm not looking after myself properly – as she always does. 'That's not normal. *Everyone* needs a bathroom.'

I laugh. 'I'm sure my bucket shower could be considered romantic in certain circumstances.'

She shakes her head at me. 'Only by people who've never been in a hot tub.'

Though I scoff, it's true to say that my home could be better supplied with amenities. But it has what I require – mostly. There's a combined living and kitchen area that's reasonably well equipped. I'm not the world's best or most regular cook. There's an oven, but to be honest, my hairdryer probably puts out more hot air. It doesn't matter though as I use it on high days and holidays. Actually, I don't think I even use it then. I could use the one in the tea room kitchen, but that's Bev's domain and, besides, it's got far too many things that beep and buzz for my requirements. Someone, more than likely Bev, gave me a cast-off slow cooker so I give than an airing once in a while and can rustle up a hearty stew in the winter if need be.

There's a separate bedroom with a small bed that might, if we were being generous, be classed as a neat double. You can't walk round it so making it up requires some gymnastics, but I like to think that it keeps me fit. It has a pretty patchwork quilt on it that Hettie made before her eyesight got too bad to do fiddly work – a family heirloom, I suppose. I can't hoard a lot of stuff because there's nowhere to store it, so I travel light.

'It would be nice to see you living somewhere proper before winter sets in again,' Bev says.

'I'm fine here,' I tell her. 'I've survived every winter, so far.

I'll just put an extra blanket on the bed.' And snuggle a dog. 'I don't feel the cold.'

'You wouldn't admit it if you did,' Bev says.

Probably not. I know she frets about me, but I'm used to it. I don't think I could live in a proper house now. All those rooms! I'd just rattle around.

I put the kettle on and Bev gets out the cups while I find some milk. When the tea's brewed we sit curled up on the bench seat in the window.

'The money from Shelby Dacre will come in handy,' she continues. 'You should charge him twice as much as everyone else. He can afford it.'

'I can't do that! It wouldn't be right.'

She tuts at my obvious morals. 'Still, it will be useful.'

I can pay Alan, for one thing. '*If* Lucas comes back.'

'I could not believe my eyes when Farmer Gordon rocked up here this morning. I had to pinch myself. He's flipping *lush*.'

He is. Even I can appreciate that.

'I think he looks better in real life than he does on the telly. He's a right old playboy on screen. Especially for a farmer.' She pulls a wistful face at me. 'None of the farmers we know look like that. More's the pity.'

I'll second that. The guy we rent the farm from, George Brown, is a crusty old devil with a red nose that has the texture of a cauliflower. He's a nice enough bloke but luckily we don't see much of him. We're good tenants, don't cause a fuss and always pay up on time. He keeps out of our way. We keep out of his. What more could a landlord want? The rent review is due soon and I'm dreading it though he's always been quite fair in the past. Even a few hundred quid makes a massive difference here.

'He's dating a young bit of stuff off the telly too.'

We're back on Gordon Wotsit. 'You said.' And so did Lucas, so this is something I need to know more about.

'Scarlett Vincent. She's gorgeous, but in a very obvious way.'

I take it from Bev's tone that's a Bad Thing. 'How young?'

'Ridiculously so. He's clearly got too much testosterone knocking around his veins. What he needs is a more mature woman.'

'Like you?'

Bev grins wickedly. 'Now that you come to mention it, *exactly* like me.'

'You're not going to start coming to work in low-cut tops and leopard-skin-print mini-skirts.'

'Perish the thought,' she says. 'It might frighten the alpacas. Sensitive souls. Though I might go through my wardrobe when I get home. One can be *too* scruffy.'

'Even when mucking out horses.'

Bev taps into her phone. 'She's twenty-eight.'

'Who?'

'Scarlett Vincent,' she says in an exasperated manner. 'Keep up.' She turns her phone to me so that I can see her picture.

'Pretty.'

'Yeah. I suppose. She's not as young as she looks though.'

'She's hardly ancient.'

'He's forty-two. Dirty old dog. He should know better.'

'Perhaps he's immature.'

'God, I really fancy him,' Bev sighs longingly. 'I'm going to go home and watch *Flinton's Farm* with renewed interest tonight. You should watch it too.'

'I don't have a telly.'

'You can get it on your phone,' she points out. 'Even you're that modern.' She downs her tea. 'Gotta shoot. Thanks for the brew. I'll see you in the morning.'

'Thanks, Bev. What would I do without you?'

'Starve? Moulder away?'

'Probably.'

At the door, she turns back. 'Nearly forgot! What are you betting on for Alan's band T-shirt tomorrow? We both drew a blank with Florence and the Machine.'

'Er . . . ' I rifle my brain cells for band names we haven't already covered many, many times. 'I'll take Oasis.'

Bev sucks in a breath. 'Good call. Though he might go left field after Florence.' She strokes her chin as she ruminates. 'I'm going to go Mumford & Sons.'

'Nice,' I say.

'I bet he rocks up with Kylie on his chest just to spite us. You know what he's like.' She kisses my cheek. 'Love you. Make sure you lock up carefully.'

She says that every night and I know that she worries about me living up here alone.

'You know where I am.'

'I know where you are.'

Then she leaves and I finish my tea before I go out to do the last egg collection of the day.

they look as if they've been drawn for a children's story book.

By nine o'clock I'm ready to face the world, which is just as well as the students are starting to arrive. We've got a different lot here today and just four of them, so I'll be able to give everyone plenty of attention. In theory. If we have too many students and we become outnumbered, that's the day that something will kick off. Sometimes, in addition to our usual students, we have a surprise extra when one of the local schools will send a pupil here at short notice – someone they're having difficulty with who might need a day or two out of the classroom to cool down or to give the teacher some respite.

Jody is the first to arrive. She's twelve and has struggled to fit into the confines of traditional education. Her mum is home-schooling her and she comes here once a week to mix with other kids. You have to give Jody one simple task at a time which she undertakes with a methodical perfection until it's complete. Try to distract her from it or engage her in something else and she goes completely to pieces. We just have to be careful to give her things that are within her limits, as otherwise she'd stay here until midnight to get it done. I learned that the hard way.

We have an eleven-year-old boy called Asha three days a week. He's currently out of school as he hacked into their computer and they took it quite badly. He's diagnosed as having ADHD, but he spends his days here permanently attached to Alan. They can both spend hours in silent concentration stripping down an old tractor together and if there's ever anything wrong with your mobile phone or laptop, Asha is the one to fix it.

Tamara is thirteen and, if you saw her, you'd wonder why she was spending time with us at all, but she has lots of mental health issues and can self-harm when stressed. She likes to take many, many photographs on her phone to share on her Snapchat account. I've never been photographed so much in my life, but I try to bear it with good humour as I know how much she enjoys it. Thus far, I've avoided involving myself with social media. We don't have a Twitter feed or a Facebook page or Instagram. I know – positively archaic. Bev tells me off all the time. She says it would be a great way to advertise the farm and our work, but I just can't face it. The whole social media thing seems like such an invasion of privacy. I do, however, realise that I'm in the minority in that thinking. Bev says I should put myself out there, but the idea fills me with dread. Still, Tamara is with us two days a week and maybe it's something that I could develop with her.

Then there's Hugo, who's also thirteen. Our dear Hugo has OCD that manifests itself in many different ways. Not least of which is the desire to be spotlessly clean, which on a farm is a bit of a challenge. We try to give him tasks that don't involve him getting dirty, otherwise he'll scrub his hands until they're raw, but we're making slow progress and he's now able to clean the eggs. Even though they end up so spotless that you'd never think they'd been near a hen's bottom. Hugo does two days too, but we'd like to get him funding for more time. I've had a lot of conversations with the council about that. Tricky ones.

Both Tamara and Hugh live at home with their parents and we offer them much-needed breaks. Asha and Jody have a supply teacher coming in and as they're capable of some structured learning, they'll do an hour of maths and an hour of English after lunch. When they get here, we settle them all in with a drink. The older ones are very much used to caring for the youngsters and that's part of the learning curve that we encourage.

When Bev arrives she is, indeed, wearing a low-cut animal print top and some kind of wet-look leggings that appear to be in danger of cutting off her circulation.

'Obvious,' I say to her.

'No idea what you mean,' she bats back.

Then Alan turns up in a Blur T-shirt. 'Aye,' he says and does a slight, barely discernible double-take at Bev's outfit. Then he disappears into the barn. We both watch him go.

'That is a hair's breadth away from Oasis,' I point out to Bev.

She rolls her eyes at me. 'Close but no cigar,' is her verdict.

'He actually seemed very taken with *your* choice of clothing today.'

'My heart belongs to one man,' Bev says.

Then, talk of the devil, Shelby Dacre's big posh car rolls in and something like relief washes over me when I see Lucas in the back seat. If humanly possible, he looks even more sullen than he did yesterday.

Bev fluffs her hair and, I kid you not, rearranges her boobs.

'Is that a push-up bra?'

'Sod off, Mols,' she hisses and we both step forward to greet them.

Chapter Nineteen

Mr Dacre steps out of the driver's seat and, goodness me, he's looking very suave and handsome today. He's wearing a cream jacket with a light blue denim shirt underneath it and navy trousers. All of it is crisp and spotless. I'm in a flowery charity shop pinafore that's seen better days and wellies – not even festival style wellies, proper industrial farm-style ones. He takes off his sunglasses as he comes towards me. I glance over at Bev and she looks as if she's about to faint. The impact he had on her yesterday hasn't lessened on second viewing.

Lucas gets out of the car too. He pushes his hair back from his face when he sees us so that we can enjoy the full extent of his moody manner. There's a little bit of pink across his nose where he caught the sun yesterday. I give him my happiest smile and he stares at me stony-faced.

But before I say or do anything else, I realise that today they're not alone. From the passenger seat a vision in white emerges. Surely this is the woman that Bev was talking about to me. Scarlett Vincent? She looks like the photo Bev showed me on her phone. Though that didn't convey quite how beautiful she is. This woman is tall – almost as tall as Shelby Dacre – and she's slender with flawless olive skin and glossy black hair that hangs in a heavy sheath down to her waist. The long-sleeved white maxi dress she's wearing is slashed down to her navel and up to her thigh. Huge gold sunglasses hide her eyes and co-ordinate with her gold sandals. The look is topped with a floppy, wide-brimmed hat and a multitude of gold bangles which jingle-jangle as she moves. She couldn't look more fabulous if she tried – or more out of place.

Bev glowers at her. Alan's eyes nearly pop out of his head – I think he'd only come out of the barn to ogle the posh car. I pick up Little Dog and hang onto him in case he's tempted to wee on her.

I'm nudged sharply in the ribs by Bev. 'That's the one I was telling you about,' she hisses under her breath.

'She's very pretty,' I whisper back.

Bev curls her lip. 'If you like that kind of obvious beauty.'

'It may only be skin deep,' I offer in an attempt to stay loyal to Bev.

By then Shelby is in front of us and runs a hand through his unruly mop of hair. In the sunshine there seem to be a million different flecks of colour in it. A kind of gulp catches in my throat. Lucas hangs back sulking nearly as much as Anthony the Anti-Social Sheep.

'Hello, Lucas. It's good to see you back.' He stands there, arms folded, all angles and hostility, clearly seething.

I hold out my hand and Shelby shakes it. I'm aware that his hands are soft like velvet, whereas mine are calloused and rough. I don't think his Farmer Gordon character must actually get involved in much physical stuff. He must be more of a striding-about gentleman farmer.

'Good morning, Milly.'

'Molly,' I correct. 'An easy mistake.'

'Ah. Apologies. Lucas has deigned to come again.' There's so much tension in his voice that I wonder how he can speak at all.

'He did very well yesterday,' I tell him. 'He was a great help to Alan.'

Scarlett joins Shelby Dacre and leans up against him on the other side of Lucas, slipping her hands around his waist possessively.

'This is Scarlett Vincent,' Shelby says.

'Nice to meet you.' I don't hold out my hand to her as I really don't want her manicured fingers within touching distance of my sandpaper palms. Besides, she doesn't look as if she's keen to let go of her man. 'Would you like me to show you around?'

We both look down at her tiny, strappy sandals.

'I don't think so,' she purrs.

'We can't stay,' Shelby says, apologetically. 'We're on our way to an event. A magazine lunch.'

That goes some way towards explaining Scarlett's outfit, at least. Shelby gives a quick glance at his watch and, behind him, Lucas tuts like a mardy toddler. Shelby ignores him.

'We've got some delights lined up for you today, Lucas.'

'More grovelling about in animal shit until I realise the error of my ways?'

'Yeah,' I say. 'You'll love it.' Despite his best efforts to remain moody, there might be the glimmer of a smile lurking. Though maybe I'm being too optimistic.

'Why don't you go and put the kettle on. You know the ropes. There are some of the younger students in there,' I instruct. 'It will be nice for you to meet them.' He looks very doubtful about that. 'And there's a fresh packet of biscuits. I'll be with you in sec.'

Lucas slopes off and Shelby watches him go. 'See you later, kid,' he shouts after Lucas but the boy completely ignores him.

He turns to me. 'You're good with him.'

'He's a nice lad.'

'That's not something that many people say about him.'

'That's a shame,' I say. 'He's lovely.' That may be over-egging the pudding, but I can see a lost, angry boy, not a troublemaker. Sometimes it's easier for people to wear the badge that they're given than struggle to prove otherwise.

'I'm filming again after the lunch,' Shelby says. 'Late finish. So I'll send a car again.'

'I'm really sorry that I didn't know who you were. I can only apologise. I don't have a television. I'm afraid your show has passed me by.'

He laughs at that. 'Too busy on a real-life farm.'

'Something like that.'

'I love it, though,' Bev pipes up, looking a little pink in the cheeks. 'I watch every night.'

He gives her a pleased little nod and I'm glad that she's made up for my shortcomings in the hero-worship stakes. 'Thank you.'

'I hope you get your fight with your son-in-law and wotsit sorted out,' she blurts. 'Families, eh?'

I've no idea what she's talking about.

'My fate is entirely in the hands of the script-writers,' he demurs. 'I am merely a pawn.'

Scarlett Vincent doesn't attempt to hide the fact that she's bored out of her head and I see her tug surreptitiously at Shelby's hand.

'We should be going,' he says, slightly embarrassed.

'If Lucas is going to be a regular visitor, then I need you to sign some paperwork. Insurance, health and safety. All the boring things.' Plus money. I need to make sure that we get his payments set up. Sounds mercenary, I know, but it's essential. I haven't looked at my bank balance in the last few days, simply because I haven't dared. My finances are scraping the very bottom of the barrel.

'I can't do it now, but could you call my PA to sort out a time?' He fishes inside his wallet and hands me a business card. He suddenly sounds a lot more irritable than he did yesterday. Perhaps Lucas is right, he might be a bit of a twat who can only do fake niceness for a short while. We've seen it all here.

'That's fine.'

He sets off, Miss Perfect in tow. They climb into the posh car and, looking exactly like movie stars, they swing out of the yard.

'See what I mean,' Bev says. 'Unsuitable.'

'Yeah.' I can't help but agree.

Bev's sigh is full of yearning as she watches him drive away down our lane. 'I still would.'

'I probably would too,' I admit and we both have a good schoolgirl snigger.

Chapter Twenty

Lucas and I have a cup of tea together, but he doesn't say much. I try to introduce him to the other students who are here, but he's not terribly interested. They, in turn, look at him as if he's the coolest thing they've ever seen. It was exactly the same yesterday. He sits in the corner, disdainful, staring at his phone while I allocate tasks for the day.

I send Tamara and Jody off with Bev to do the morning egg collection. Asha and Hugo have already gone with Alan back to the barn, but I decide to keep Lucas close to me today. Before I take Shelby Dacre's money, I should make sure that this will work out.

'As it's a nice warm day, I could do with washing the Shetland ponies.' I actually need to check the milk sack and nipples of one of the new ewes we acquired. I think she might be pregnant, but I don't want to get too excited. I also need to get Teacup to wee into a bowl so that I can take a urine sample to the vet, which is going to be fun. But both of these things may well be a step too far for Lucas. He might faint if I suggested helping with either of them. Perhaps I'll leave those tasks until everyone's gone. 'They've both been rolling in the mud and look a right state. Up for that?'

Lucas shrugs his indifference but follows me out of the tea room and falls into step with me as we go through the yard and up to the small field – which is actually quite big, but not as big as the big field. Little Dog and Big Dog come along to help.

I know that the girls would have liked to have joined in with washing the ponies too as they love anything to do with Ringo and Buzz, but I'm kind of indulging Lucas for the time being. Jody and Tamara can always join us when they've finished with their egg duties. Although I think they may be as keen to spend time with Lucas as with anything equine.

When they see us, the ponies come trotting up to the fence. I have the treat of an apple to share between them and split it with my thumbs. I give half to Lucas. 'Hold it flat so they don't nip you. Ringo is allergic to his own hair and he's usually pretty even-tempered, but sometimes it gets him down. He can be a bit out of sorts.' By that I mean he turns into a bitey little bugger. Today, though, he looks quite chilled and both of them usually like having a wash and brush up. I offer my apple and Lucas follows suit. 'That's Buzz Lightyear.'

'I'm not even going to ask,' Lucas says as the pony takes the apple from him.

'We'll take them down to the barn to do this. We've got a horse wash pen there and we can get you suited and booted.' I open the gate and attach halters to the ponies. Lucas looks terrified even though neither of them come higher than his waist.

'I don't know what to do with them,' he admits. 'We've never even had a goldfish at home.'

'Then it will be a steep learning curve.' I'm surprised that Lucas is so chatty, but maybe he's been lonely for so long that he's willing to open up. 'But I'll show you what to do. I'm not going to leave you on your own with them.'

'Thank Christ for that,' he mutters. 'The nearest I've ever got to any animals was when I went to see my father on set.'

'That must have been fun.'

'It was when I was a kid. Now I just find it dull. When he stopped dragging me along, I stopped going. I haven't been for years.'

I feel a bit sorry for Shelby Dacre who, according to Bev, is a much-loved national treasure and respected actor, yet can't seem to do a thing right for his own son.

So we lead the ponies down to our outdoor washing area by the barn and I enjoy feeling the sunshine on my face. I'm not sure that Lucas feels the same. We've already established that he's more of an indoor kind of boy.

I show Lucas how to tie up Ringo and Buzz with a quick release knot, so that they don't hurt themselves if they panic – not that these two usually do. If they get fed up, they'll do a bit of hoof stamping, but nothing more. Both of the boys get hay bags to keep them amused while we wash them. Then I grab all the different equipment we use for grooming and cleaning and talk Lucas through it.

'We'll both work on Ringo first and then if you're happy, you can see how you go with Buzz.'

He nods his acceptance, if not his agreement.

'It's a messy job and you might get wet. Do you want an overall? There's one in the barn.'

'No. I'm good.' Clearly he'd rather be sodden than lose his street-cred.

'Grab some wellies from the barn before we start. You don't want to ruin your boots. Plus they have steel toe-caps in case Ringo accidentally steps on your foot.'

As Lucas lopes off to get his wellies, I fill some buckets for us and make sure that Ringo is securely tied and settled. Lucas is gone for ages and when he comes back he's wearing wellies that look several sizes too big for him.

'I'll bring my own tomorrow,' he says. 'My father has dozens of them in our garage that he never uses. Companies send them to him.'

'They'd be useful here, if they're going begging. We're always short of wellies.'

'OK.'

'If you're comfortable, then we'll begin. One main tip. Don't ever stand behind a horse when you're doing this – even a little one. These two like their baths, but if something spooks them and they decide to kick out, then you'll be out of danger. I don't want to be sending you home bruised or broken or your dad might have something to say.' I hand him a rubber curry comb which he handles as if it's a grenade. 'We use this to loosen the dirt and debris from the coat before we shampoo them.' I show him how and, tentatively, Lucas follows. 'You can be firm, but gentle. Don't rush this. Take your time, then you'll enjoy it and so will the pony.'

After a hesitant start, he quickly gets into a good rhythm and Ringo stands nicely and doesn't fidget or try to nip.

'You're doing well,' I say. 'Now the dandy brush to sweep away what you've loosened. We take that down the legs too, but gently.'

Lucas does as I show him. Instinctively, he steadies Ringo as he moves.

'Good, good. You've got a nice way with him.'

'He's a cute little fella,' Lucas says and as he carries on he talks to him in a soothing way. I smile to myself. A cheeky pony can soften the hardest heart.

'Now we'll soak his coat before we shampoo him. We only use baby products for Ringo as he's allergic to everything else we've tried. Lather him all over and then we'll rinse him off with the hosepipe on a low trickle. Ringo likes water on his face, but he's the only one that does. Just go over him gently with the sponge. Make sure to do his little bit of mane, his tail and his belly.'

Lucas follows my instructions, doing everything thoroughly and gently. I look at him and wonder how it can have all gone so wrong at school for him. I'd take on a dozen boys like Lucas if I could. He's sparky and clearly unhappy, but he doesn't seem to have a destructive nature. Usually, you can tell that straight away.

When he's wet through, Ringo shakes and sprays Lucas with water. The boy laughs out loud as he dodges out of the way. It's a nice sound.

'Don't forget to do under his tail too.'

He looks at me aghast. 'I have to wash a horse's arse?'

''Fraid so.'

'And my father is actually paying good money for me to do this?'

'Yes. Just be careful. Ringo doesn't like cold water round his bottom.'

'Does anyone?' He shakes his head, but picks up his sponge nevertheless. 'To think I could be in a cosy classroom studying Classics.'

'School wasn't working out so well though, was it?'

Lucas's expression hardens. 'I guess not.'

'Want to talk about it?' I ask, casually.

'No,' he says. 'My father employs a ridiculously expensive shrink for that. I'm dragged there once a week too.'

'Is it going OK?'

'No. He's a twat as well.'

'We're all just trying to help you, Lucas.'

'Yeah. I can tell. Washing a horse's arse is going to make me feel great.'

I laugh at that. 'If it's any consolation, it'll certainly make Ringo feel better.'

And though he looks as if he's trying very hard not to, Lucas cracks the glimmer of a smile too. Then, without further complaint, he washes Ringo's bottom.

Chapter Twenty-One

When Lucas has finished his washing duties. I get the kitchen shears and cut his fringe – the pony's fringe, not Lucas's. 'We have to keep his mane and his tail short too, because they give him eczema, otherwise. I'm not the best at this,' I admit, 'but it does the job.'

When I've finished, I can confirm that horse hairdressing is not high in my skill set. Ringo's fringe is lopsided and looks a bit chewed even when I've faffed about with it. Having it this short will at least keep it off his face and while Ringo will stand happily for his bath, he tolerates his hairdo less well and I try to keep it quick as possible.

We give Buzz Lightyear a bath too, following the same routine, and then I show Lucas how to get the excess water from them with a squeegee so that they're nice and dry before we put a scrim on them. Together we lead them back up to their paddock. Sometimes they go and roll straight in the dirt again and you wonder what all your hard work was for, but today we're lucky and they busy themselves with eating grass.

'Let's go and have some lunch,' I say to Lucas. 'Hungry?'

'Yeah.' He sounds surprised that he is.

'You've earned it. Good job.' I hold up a hand and, after only a slight pause, he gives me a high five.

I know that some people might wonder about the benefit of what we do here at Hope Farm, but I only have to see someone like Lucas after a day or two here and I know that it works. There's a lightness in his step as we head back towards the yard, despite his oversize wellingtons tripping him up. The tension he was holding in his shoulders has dissipated. I wonder, once more, what the real story is behind Lucas's disruptive behaviour. Undoubtedly, he's still grieving for his mother, but there's an awful lot of anger directed towards his dad. Which is such a shame.

Everyone else is already in the tea room having lunch. Bev is dishing up cheesy pasta bake that she's just lifted out of the oven. Most days she cooks on site but, occasionally, she'll make a dish at home and bring it in. She spoons some onto plates for us. Lucas and I sit at the end of the communal table.

'Everyone, this is Lucas. Some of you met him this morning but, if you didn't, he's new to us and we'll hope he'll be here regularly.'

There's a variety of responses, from an enthusiastic cheer from Bev to a muted nod from Alan. The girls look at him with even more interest than they did this morning, it has to be said. Lucas holds up a hand, doing his too-cool-to-speak routine.

'There's two hours of lessons this afternoon,' I tell him. 'Everyone else will be attending, but while you're settling in you can choose. Either you can go to lessons or do something else.'

'Something else,' is the swift response.

'Not missing school?'

'Seriously?'

'I went to Glebe Road school,' Tamara says boldly. 'Which did you go to?'

Lucas doesn't lift his head from his cheesy bake. 'St Almsell's.'

87

Tamara is clearly none the wiser, but doesn't pursue it. 'You didn't like it?'

'No.'

'My school was crap too.'

And that's it really. Lucas closes down any hope of conversation by avoiding eye contact and concentrating on his food. Tamara flushes and gives up, her girlish resources exhausted. I wink across at her encouragingly. She's seen enough new students here to know that they pretty much all start out like that – as she herself did. There are some nice kids here and Lucas could do a lot worse than make some friends. I've learned from experience that you can't force it and he'll do it in his own time.

So we chat amongst ourselves and leave Lucas to his own devices. We all help to clear away and Tamara piles the crockery, making a beeline to wrest Lucas's plate from him.

'You'll like it here,' she says. 'You can be yourself.'

He doesn't snarl at her and he doesn't smile either. But, instead of handing over his plate to her, he takes the stack that she's struggling with. 'Let me do that.'

She hands over the plates with a look of awe on her face. I'm just going to stand behind her in case she swoons.

As Bev is washing up, a car pulls in and it's one of the teachers. Today it's the turn of Ms Jessop and they all quite like her. She's young and wears a nose stud. 'Time for lessons,' I say and there's a collective groan – but it's a half-hearted protest. 'Get yourselves round to the classroom. Don't forget to wash your hands.'

There's a giddy five minutes while they get themselves ready and then they all crash out of the door together. Lucas hangs back.

'Sit for a minute.' He does as he's told.

'I think you have some fans there,' I say as I stack the clean dishes back into the cupboard. 'They're good kids and are only trying to be nice.'

Lucas grunts. I wonder if he thinks that people only want him as a friend because of Shelby. 'Do your friends think it's weird that you have a famous dad?'

'I don't have any friends,' he says, flatly. 'Everyone hates me.'

'Not everyone, surely?' Lucas shrugs. 'Because of who you're related to?'

'Yeah. And because I don't fit in. All of this diversity shit is bollocks. If you deviate even slightly from the "norm", you're ostracised.'

'That's sad.'

'It was bad enough before, but it's even worse since he's been going out with *that woman*. There isn't anyone in school who hasn't seen her with her clothes off. Me included.'

'That's tough.'

'It's bloody embarrassing,' Lucas snarls. 'That's what it is. She's fourteen years younger than him. How would he like it if I rocked up with a woman that age? He'd do his pieces. It's grotesque. She hates me too. She just thinks I'm in the way. If it wasn't for me they'd be swanning round Cannes or Venice or somewhere every weekend, doing what "stars" do.'

I can understand that it must be easier for Shelby Dacre to stay away than to come home to an angry, judgemental child, but he's the grown-up here. Can't he see that Lucas needs him?

'Perhaps he's hurting too,' I suggest softly. 'He's lost his wife. It can't be easy.'

'It's as if Mum never existed,' Lucas snaps back. 'He's airbrushed her out of our lives.'

'Maybe the two of you need to sit down together and get this out in the open.'

'If he was ever at home that might be a possibility. You can't talk to someone who isn't there.'

I know that I'm happy with my own company, but it mustn't be easy for someone Lucas's age to go home to an empty house.

No wonder he's feeling miserable. 'So what do you do when you're at home by yourself?'

There's a long pause and an even longer sigh before he says, 'I write poetry.'

That makes me want to smile, but I keep it to myself. 'Poetry, eh?' I confess that I'd expected the answer to be a little more rebellious – smoking weed, watching inappropriate stuff on the internet. Again, I just want to hug him because I think that's what Lucas needs more than anything. 'Sounds interesting.'

'It's no big deal. It's probably shit.'

Then Alan pops his head round the door. 'I'm going up to big field.' He nods towards Lucas. 'Is he coming?'

Lucas folds his arms across his chest defensively, and realising that he's let his guard slip and said too much to me, shuts down again.

The moment is lost, but there'll be more. 'Do you want to spend the afternoon with Alan?' I ask. 'It won't involve any horses' bottoms.'

'Yeah.' He pushes his chair away and stands up.

'We'll talk again, Lucas.'

'Yeah.'

And, I'm pleased to say that it sounds like 'yeah, we might' rather than 'yeah, not on your nelly'.

Chapter Twenty-Two

In the event, it works out that I don't see Lucas again all afternoon. I'm kept busy with Asha who has one of his rare meltdowns and it takes me and Bev half an hour to calm him down. They happened much more often when he first came here, almost daily, but we don't see them so much now. We can't get to the bottom of what kicks it off but afterwards, he's left red-faced, sweating and exhausted. To restore his equilibrium, I sit with him in the rabbit run and we cuddle bunnies. There's nothing like bunny-cuddles to soothe a troubled child.

It's home time when I next see Lucas. He's climbing into his swanky car, so I wave at him and he ignores me.

I close the gate behind the car as it leaves. For some reason, it paints a bleak picture and I block the vision of him going home to an empty house. Sometimes I fail, but I do try hard not to get too emotionally attached to our students. Some of them have significantly more difficult home lives than Lucas does and I have to let them all go at the end of the day. I can't rescue them like I can the animals. I just have to do my best to help them thrive in their environment and give them the best help I possibly can when they're here. I sigh. Sometimes life is shit.

When Bev comes back down to the yard, I have a cup of tea with her, eat some of the cake that's left and listen as she downloads her day.

'How's Shelby Dacre's kid doing?'

'Lucas? I like him. He's just short on love and attention, I think.' I shrug. 'Same old story.'

'Is he signed up as a regular yet?'

'I've told Mr Dacre to come in and complete the paperwork. He told me to call his PA to organise it.' I raise my eyebrows.

'Plonker,' is Bev's verdict. 'I bet the kid has abandonment issues.'

'Yeah,' I agree.

'He's bloody hot in his show though,' she sighs. 'He was in a field with his shirt off last night wielding a scythe.'

'A scythe? Was this in your dreams?'

'No.' She gives me a dark look. 'In the show. He looks like he works out.'

'You've gone all pink.'

'So would you if you saw him in the nip.'

'It's a long, long time since I've seen any gentleman in the nip. I don't feel as if I'm missing out.'

'You are,' Bev says. 'Believe me.' She picks up her bag. 'I'm off. I want to see what Farmer Gordon gets up to tonight.'

'Are we having a bet on Alan's T-shirt?'

Bev strokes her chin and muses before slapping down, 'Radiohead.'

'Nice,' I say, sucking in a breath. 'Very nice.' I give it some thought before coming back with, 'I see your Radiohead and offer The White Stripes.'

'I like it,' Bev says. 'But you won't win.'

'I bet you a bottle of the cheapest red we can find that I do.'

'Done.'

And while Bev goes home to drool once more over Shelby Dacre, shirt or no shirt, I go to my caravan to stress over the finances of the farm.

Chapter Twenty-Three

Account books give me a headache. No matter how long or how hard I puzzle over them, I can never make them balance. I know that I should do outreach or fundraising stuff in the community – Bev tells me often enough – but the very thought of it brings me out in hives. The potential for things to go wrong are many and varied.

I do my late-night round of the animals with a heavy heart. When I get back, I make myself a tomato Cup a Soup for dinner, but that fails to cheer me too. I'm just about to fall into bed at ten o'clock when Big Dog starts to bark.

'Quiet, Big Dog,' I say, but Little Dog simply joins in too. Something's obviously amiss. I should put on my jacket and have a look outside just in case.

Then my phone rings. I don't recognise the number and the overwhelming temptation is not to answer it, but something makes me pick up and say, 'Hello.'

'It's Shelby,' the voice says. 'I'm at your gate.'

'Oh.' That's why the dogs are barking.

'I know it's late, but I'm on my way back from the studio. Can I do the paperwork for Lucas now?'

It's as good a time as any, I suppose. 'I'm in my pyjamas.'

It's Shelby's turn to say, 'Oh.'

'But I don't mind if you don't,' I add hurriedly. I've already learned how busy Shelby Dacre is. I'm not judging him but, most of the time, he doesn't even seem able to spare a few precious hours for his son. My finances are precarious and I need to get this paperwork completed. If I send him away now it could be days, longer even, before we get another chance and that will send me deeper into the red.

'Right. OK. If it's not a problem. Shall I wait here then? The gate's locked.'

'I'll be there in a minute. I'll just make myself decent.' I hang up.

I'm not used to entertaining gentlemen in my caravan, let alone in my pyjamas, and the rashness of my actions hits me. What a fool. Why didn't I ask him to come back in the morning? I feel self-conscious enough in his presence without adding my nightwear into the mix. While I'm still rationalising my decision, I tug a jumper over my jim-jams, pull on my wellies and head out of the van. Little Dog and Big Dog drop into step with me, eager to see if our new arrival is worthy of a lick or a chew.

Anthony has come to the front of the sheep pen and is growling with menace. 'You should be fast asleep by now in the barn,' I tell him. 'And you're a sheep, not a guard dog.' He growls again.

Shelby is sitting patiently at the gate in his car and I hurry to swing it open for him. He drives into the yard and I close the gate behind him. He parks up and is out of his car by the time I reach him. Unlike me, Shelby isn't in his pyjamas. Looking every inch the soap opera star, he's wearing dark jeans and a crisp white shirt. He looks as if he's recently showered as his blond hair sits in damp curls at the nape of his neck and he smells of freshly squeezed lemons.

'Sorry,' he says. 'I'm on my way back from the studio and thought I'd pop in on the off-chance that you were free. I felt I rushed off this morning and that was churlish of me. I should have come by myself with Lucas and stayed longer.' Shelby gives me puppy dog eyes and I wonder if that's an actor-type look. 'Now I realise that this is very thoughtless of me too.' He does look rather shamefaced as he takes in my wellies and pyjamas. 'Sometimes, it's hard to do right for doing wrong.'

We both laugh at that.

'It's fine,' I assure him. 'Your life is infinitely busier than mine. I understand that.'

'Ah. If only Lucas felt the same.'

'I'm not your son, though,' I add and he glances at me as if I've said something really cryptic. I lead him towards the van, regretting that I didn't have time for a quick tidy-up or even think about it until now. 'Sorry about the state of my caravan.'

He looks vaguely horrified. Actually, scratch the 'vaguely'. He looks *totally* horrified and he hasn't seen inside yet. 'This is where you live?'

'Sure is.' In fairness, my caravan has seen better days but I like to think of it as well-loved. I don't know when Hettie bought it, but it's been here as long as I can remember. 'Come on in. Make yourself at home.'

He climbs into the van and his tall frame seems to fill the cramped space. 'Cosy,' he says, then immediately lets rip an enormous sneeze.

'Sorry,' I say. 'It's probably the dog hair. I remember that Lucas said you're allergic to animals.'

'To most things,' he agrees.

'Let me shoo the dogs out.' I hurry Little Dog and Big Dog out and close the door on them. They whine pathetically at such terrible ill-treatment when they have a new friend to play with. 'Though I'm not sure it will make much difference. I hoover regularly but I inherited my vacuum cleaner from my aunt along with everything else. It's probably circa nineteen-fifties.'

'An antique.' Shelby Dacre blows his nose. 'I have antihistamine.' He brandishes a packet at me. 'I have to take it every day, anyway.'

'I'll push the windows open so there's a through draught. It's a warm night.' The ancient window resists my best effort.

'Here. Let me.' Shelby Dacre kneels on the cushion next to me and, as he pushes the window, his forearm brushes against mine and I jump back as if I've been electrocuted. That was a hell of a surge that went between us, but it only seems to be me who noticed. 'That's better.'

A breeze lifts my fringe and I realise that my face is hot. I'd like to take my jumper off, but am aware of my jim-jams beneath and so am destined to boil. 'Do you have to rush away? Let me get you a cup of tea.'

He looks as if he might refuse, but then his shoulders drop slightly and he says, 'Why not? Milk, no sugar, please, Molly.'

'Make yourself at home.'

Shelby scouts around, moves a few cushions, then perches on the edge of the sofa. I try not to smile at his obvious discomfiture as I make tea for us. He sniffles as I hand him his tea and sit down opposite him.

'It must be difficult to be in a role like yours, if you're allergic to all creatures great and small.'

'It has its challenges,' he agrees with a smile.

'As you can see, I really don't have a television.' There's not much in the way of light entertainment in the caravan at all – a few well-thumbed books, mostly Hettie's choices, a jigsaw with several pieces missing that I keep meaning to throw out but can't quite bring myself to and my radio for the times when I do want to fill the silence.

'That's rare in this day and age.'

I shrug. 'The animals keep me busy. By the time I've seen to them all, I don't have a lot of spare hours left for leisure pursuits. But my friend Bev told me all about *Flinton's Farm*. She's a big fan.'

'Good to hear it.' He takes in my cosy surroundings with my frayed carpet, my minimalist kitchen and my jolly gingham curtains. His expression is inscrutable. 'How did you come to be running this place?'

'I lived on the farm with my aunt. When she died I inherited it all. Such as it is.'

Shelby studies me. 'My friends were full of praise for you. They were the ones who urged me to bring Lucas here. They said you could help.'

'I'd like to think that we can.'

He leans on the table and puts his head in his hands and puffs out a wavering breath. When he looks up at me again, his eyes are bright with tears. 'Do you think you can fix Lucas?'

I smile softly at that. 'We're not in the business of "fixing" broken kids, Mr Dacre. We help them to find out who they are, to build their confidence, to teach them how to exist with their various conditions and to get along with others. Sometimes those who can't talk to other humans do very well with animals. We have students here with Asperger's Syndrome, autism, Chaotic Attachment, depression, all manner of mental health issues. Some self-harm, some try to harm others.'

'And what do you think is wrong with Lucas?' he asks me earnestly.

'I think what's "wrong" with him is that he's very angry and unhappy. He's a lost and lonely boy.'

'Is that my fault?'

'It's not really my position to blame anyone, Mr Dacre.'

'Shelby, please.' He looks away from me, staring blankly out of the caravan window. 'I've struggled to relate to him since

Susie, my wife, died. It's a terrible thing to lose a parent at any age, let alone in your difficult teen years.'

'It's not easy to lose your wife either,' I add, sympathetically.

'No.' He takes a moment before he can speak again. 'Susie was the one who kept the home together. I didn't realise it when she was alive, more's the pity. She and Lucas were like two peas in a pod. He's got her looks, her artistic side. I know that he feels cut adrift without her, but I have no idea how to reach him. Susie would have sorted this out in five minutes.' He shakes his head, sadly. 'I've tried to do my best, even though he's made it abundantly clear that he can't stand me near him. We barely exchange a word and when we do it usually results in Lucas shouting at me. Whatever I say is wrong.'

I listen while he speaks, but make no comment.

'I confess that I've taken to staying late on set or going out drinking with colleagues rather than go home to face his anger. It's cowardly of me, I know.'

'But you're grieving too.'

'I don't think that I've let myself do that. I've pushed on because you have to, don't you? If I really thought about what had happened, I'd fall apart.' He puts his head in his hands again.

'It will get better. Give it time.' There's little more that I can offer in the way of solace right now. I'll do all that I can to help them work their way back to each other, but I suspect it's not going to be an easy road. 'How about another cuppa?'

'The British answer to everything.'

'It never hurts.'

Shelby wipes his eyes. 'I don't want to burden you. I'm paying for Lucas to come here. You don't need to counsel me as well.'

I smile at that. 'I'm doing nothing else.'

'Then more tea would be great.' Shelby drains his cup and I take it back to the kitchen. Then he gives another corker of a sneeze and I hand him a bit of kitchen roll to have a good blow.

'We could actually sit outside if you want to. I think it's warm enough and it might be better for your poor nose.'

'I've got a jacket in the car.'

'OK. There are a couple of deckchairs. You can put them out, if you like.'

So, while I brew up again, I show Shelby where my fold-up deckchairs are stored away under the van and he arranges them outside in the lee of the van, out of the breeze. He has to run the gauntlet of Little Dog and Big Dog who try to lick him to death, but they'll settle in a minute. Like me, they're not used to visitors.

Chapter Twenty-Four

The sun has set and now it's the moon's turn to shine brightly. It's high in the sky and the night is so crystal clear that stars are out in force. It's pitch black up here away from the ambient light of any city and it's excellent for stargazing.

Little Dog curls up at Shelby's feet while Big Dog retreats to his favourite spot under the van. I've put Fifty in the pen with Teacup tonight, but I can hear him bleating as he can sense there's something going on and, like any lamb who thinks he's human, wants to be involved. Shelby and I sit side by side in the deckchairs, both silent, and stare heavenwards. He looks lost in thought; I wonder if he's thinking of his wife as he looks up. Perhaps talking about her has sparked some memories.

'So often we think of lost loved ones being up there somewhere, when they're probably nowhere near it at all. Despite that, I still always say hello to my aunt Hettie on nights like this.'

'It's beautiful, isn't it?' he breathes.

'Indeed.' I cradle my cup on my lap.

'All this and yet I rarely stop to look at it. I don't know any

101

of the constellations,' Shelby admits. 'Apart from Orion and everyone knows that.'

'The mighty hunter is all but gone from the sky now, but you can see the Big Dipper.' I lean closer towards him and point it out. 'See? If you follow the handle down, there's a bright orange star called Arcturus. One of the few stars that was mentioned in the Bible.'

He looks impressed. 'You sound as if you know your stuff.'

'I know the stars in the sky better than I do television stars.'

He laughs at that. 'Tell me another one.'

'That's Virgo, the young maiden.' I feel myself flush as I say it, though I could hardly class as young or a maiden. My romantic interludes have been few and far between for sure, but there have been a couple who have got past the holding-hands stage. Not for a long while, though. 'Her brightest star is Spica which is two hundred and fifty light years away.'

He relaxes back in his deckchair and I can see some of the tension ease out of his face. 'This would be a good night for a bottle of wine.'

'I don't think I have any.'

'I should have brought one, but I didn't anticipate staying.'

'We mustn't forget to do the paperwork,' I remind him.

'No.' He lets out a weary sigh as if thinking of that has pulled him back down to earth again while he was content to be among the stars. 'Has Lucas said much to you?'

'Not really. We've had a few chats, but I wouldn't share what we talked about with you. That's part of the deal.'

'Even though I'm the one paying the bill?'

'I'm afraid so.'

He harrumphs at that. 'He doesn't like Scarlett. I suppose he's told you that much.'

Again, it's probably wiser to keep my counsel. When I don't voice an opinion, he continues, 'She's too bloody young for me.

I know that. The tabloid rags never cease to revel in pointing out our age difference.' He blows out an unhappy breath. 'She was good to me when Susie died. I met her at a canapés and cocktails thing. Can't even remember what. I was at a really low ebb and she made me forget I was empty inside. Scarlett's great fun and we have a laugh together. She makes me forget my troubles.'

Scarlett Vincent looks like high-maintenance to me, but then I'm judging a book by its cover and what do I know?

'I don't love her,' he says, sounding defensive. 'But I do like her.'

'Perhaps you and Lucas just need to sit down together and discuss these things.'

'Would that it were so easy. Scarlett likes to be out on the town. She's at the start of her career and wants to be seen in all the right places in all the right clothes.'

Sounds like hell to me.

'I know that it leaves Lucas on his own too much to get up to no good.'

'If you know that, maybe it's the first thing to address.' Seems a bit obvious to me, but even in the darkness, I can see the black expression cross his face. It's quite possible that Shelby Dacre is a man who's used to getting his own way and doesn't like to be told what to do. Someone in his rarefied position must be surrounded by sycophants.

'What did he do here today?'

'We washed two Shetland ponies together,' I tell him. 'Lucas was very good with them. A natural.'

'In that sense, he's not his father's son then.'

'No.' I can only agree. 'You're not an animal lover?'

'Oh, I like them well enough,' he says. 'They just don't like me. I know Susie and Lucas would have loved a house filled with pets, but with these damn allergies, I could never agree to it. I can hardly turn up on set sneezing my head off. If I so much as stroke them, I have to wash my hands straightaway because if I forget and touch my face I come out in great red weals or my eyes itch so much I could claw them out. I manage it as best I can at work, but it's not easy. Playing a farmer while being allergic to animals is, at best, a bit of an embarrassment.'

'I can imagine.'

I'm treated to one of Shelby's dazzling smiles. 'You wouldn't believe how many county shows I'm asked to attend. Every bloody role I get offered now is something to do with the beggars – everyone wants me to play a vet. All I want is a meaty, city detective part. I can't get away from animals. If only they knew. And now I'm here!'

I can only laugh. Shelby laughs too and it's a good sound.

'One of the ponies here is allergic to his own hair. It makes Ringo very miserable. We wash and condition him regularly to help with the itching. I have to cut his fringe and his tail as best I can to keep them away from his skin, but I'm no hairdresser. I suspect Sweeney Todd was a better barber.'

'I sympathise. Poor little bugger.'

'We all have our trials and tribulations,' I quip.

He looks at me, suddenly serious. 'And what are yours, Molly Baker?'

'Money,' I say, honestly. 'That's my only bugbear. I'm always short of money. It not only makes the world go round but it's pretty essential for farms to function too. Especially when we're a unique kind of farm. We don't produce anything, so it's like pouring money into a black hole.'

'That's the best nudge there is to fill in the paperwork.'

'Ah, yes.' The entire point of his visit. Somehow I think we'd both forgotten that. 'Shall we do that inside?'

'Yes.' He hands me his cup and turns his attention to folding up the deckchairs.

Back inside, I spread the paperwork on the table, such as it is. After giving it a cursory glance, Shelby Dacre signs it with a flourish. Clearly, a man more used to dishing out autographs.

'Thank you,' I say. 'I really appreciate it. I hope that Lucas enjoys it here.'

'I hope it stops him from setting fire to things,' is Shelby's more succinct assessment.

'Me too.'

'I'll be going then.' We both stand, awkward in the small space. He leans towards me and kisses me gently on both cheeks.

'Two,' I say a bit giddily. 'Very showbiz.'

'Sorry. I've been a luvvie for far too long.' Then he gives me a long look, confusion on his face. 'I can't remember when I last talked to anyone like this, Molly. I've been Farmer Gordon Flinton for ten years now. I'm too good at pretending. The façade is so easy to maintain that sometimes I actually forget who I am as a person. Thank you for listening.'

'My pleasure.' Then I don't know what possesses me but I touch his arm and give him a reassuring squeeze to comfort him. 'It will work out with you and Lucas. I'm sure of it. Just don't expect too much too soon.'

'I won't. I promise.' His hand covers mine and his fingers are soft and warm against my skin. I get that tingly feeling that I got earlier and it's more than disconcerting. 'Thank you again.'

Embarrassed now, I pull away and hand him his copy of the paperwork. He ducks to go out of the caravan door. I walk him to his car and he takes his jacket off and throws it into the back seat before he eases his long limbs into the passenger seat. Instead of closing the door, he looks at me and I can't read the expression on his face. I feel as if he doesn't really want to leave, but doesn't know how to stay. He seems as if he's about to say something else, but stops himself.

We both pause awkwardly for a moment, before I break it by saying, 'I'll get the gate.'

'Thank you. I hear what you're saying, Molly. I'll try to bring Lucas every morning,' he says. 'I think that will help.'

'It would be a good thing to do,' I agree.

'Goodnight, then.'

'Goodnight, Shelby.' And I walk to the gate and let him out. Then I head back to the caravan feeling strangely light and buzzy, yet knowing full well that it's way past my bedtime and I'm going to be completely bloody knackered in the morning.

Chapter Twenty-Five

Shelby doesn't bring Lucas to the farm the next morning, nor any morning for the next week, which is kind of disappointing. I had hoped for Lucas's sake that he would. I feel let down by him, so I can only imagine how Lucas feels if this is what he does on a regular basis. Why did he say he'd do it, if he had no intention? Actors. All flaky.

Still, with or without his father's help, Lucas quickly falls into the routine of the farm. He and I work well together and he also enjoys spending time with Alan, tinkering with the tractor, rebuilding fences – thanks, big horses – and generally helping around the place. I think he likes the fact that Alan doesn't tax him with too much in the way of conversation, as do many of our kids. There's a healthy glow coming to Lucas's skin too, which I don't dare mention. That won't suit his Goth look at all.

Now that he's gradually coming out of his shell a bit, he's surprisingly good with the other students too – especially the younger ones, who he seems to have a real affinity with. He's proving to be a big hit with Jody and Tamara too who appear to think he's the best thing since sliced bread. Tamara tries to take as many photos as she can of him without him noticing. Lucas can be very funny and charming when he wants to be. He just doesn't want to be that often. They all tend to hang on his every word as he's probably the coolest kid we've had here and it's clear that he's lapping up a bit of hero-worship. If he's always been labelled as the outsider at school, it must be a welcome change for him. I'd like him to be more involved with the group rather than separate, but I'll let him bask in this glory for a bit longer. A little more reluctantly, he's started to join in with the lessons that are taken by a supply teacher too. When I've sat at the back of the class to observe, it's obvious that when he forgets to be sullen and cross, he's precociously bright.

This morning, he and I have cleaned out the stable for the alpacas. They're a nosey trio and kept trying to barge in to have a better look. I should probably have tied them up or put them in another field, but I kind of like having them around being bolshy. It's another animal for Lucas to get used to as well. They might look cute, but they're a skittish bunch, a bit diva-ish and will bite you given half the chance. We've picked up their poo to sell for fertilizer and now it's waiting in the wheelbarrow ready for bagging.

Lucas wipes sweat from his brow with the bottom of his T-shirt and then leans on his shovel. 'I've realised that a lot of the work here involves animal crap.'

'Where there's muck, there's money,' I tell him, quoting my dear aunt.

'There must be easier ways to raise funds.'

'I expect there are,' I say. 'But they generally involve dealing with the public and I'm anti-social.'

'I'd noticed that about you,' he says. 'I'm anti-social too.'

'Then let's wash our hands and be anti-social together.' I pull a chocolate bar from my pocket. 'Half a Twix?'

'Now you're talking.'

So we wash our hands under the hosepipe and disinfect them with gel. We climb out of the alpacas' paddock and sit on the nearest bench. We sometimes have students with disabilities, so we have the luxury of many conveniently placed sitting areas. This rather glamorous bench is hand-carved from a tree trunk and was donated by grateful parents, but sometimes we make do with hay bales. The bench is in the shade of a mature ash tree that I used to climb as a girl and we enjoy the respite from the sun.

I open the wrapper, pass half of the chocolate to Lucas. 'It's a bit melty,' I warn him. 'I should have put it in the shade rather than keeping it in my pocket.'

'It will taste the same.'

He's not wrong. Melted or not, it's wonderful. So we sit in companionable silence for a few minutes enjoying our treat, licking chocolate from our fingers. Little Dog sits at my feet, ever hopeful, even though he knows he's not allowed chocolate.

When we've finished, Lucas and I sit back and take a few moments to relax before I find him something else to do involving animal poo. 'You're enjoying it here?'

He shrugs. 'It's OK. Better than real school. Though there's more shit.'

'What was it you didn't like about school?'

He snorts. 'It's a long list.'

'Top three.'

'Boring lessons. Bullying. Teachers who were total twats.'

I let that hang for a moment before saying, casually, 'You were bullied?'

'Who isn't these days? Most kids are total arses.' I wait while Lucas licks all of his fingers again in the hope of finding residual chocolate. 'They should have sent me to some high-end, private school with kids of rock stars. I wouldn't have stuck out like a sore thumb then.'

'Why didn't they?'

'Daddy wanted me to have a "normal" education. Thanks for that, Father. It worked out really well.'

'And now you've ended up here.'

'Yeah. What kind of normal is this?'

'But why the setting fire to stuff? Where does that come from?'

Lucas sighs. 'Can we change the subject?'

'If you want to.'

'My father's not even called Shelby Dacre, you know. That's made up. His real name is Paul Smith but that's far too ordinary for him. He's such a bloody fake.'

'In fairness, I can see his reasoning. It would probably be hard to stand out as an actor if you were called Paul Smith.'

'Yeah. If you haven't got talent give yourself a funny name.'

I think that's a bit harsh, but before I can answer, our conversation is curtailed as Bev calls out from the yard, 'Someone to see you!'

I look down to the yard, where a man with sharply cut white-blond hair is getting out of what might be a bright red Porsche. Or it could be a Ferrari. Ask me about tractors and I'm your woman. Cars – complete mystery. 'Wonder who it is?'

Lucas gives a belly-laugh. 'You really don't know who that is?'

'Not a clue.'

'Oh, you are in for a treat. Come on!' Lucas runs towards our visitor with me trailing in his wake.

When we reach the yard, Lucas throws himself at the man and, in turn, the man hugs him tightly. They stay locked in a bear hug until, slightly out of puff, I join them.

Lucas is beaming widely and there's a spark in his eyes that I haven't seen before. This man obviously means a lot to him. 'Molly, this is *Christian Lee*.'

I hold out a hand and we shake. 'Nice to meet you.'

Mr Lee is wearing enormous black bug-eye shades, a baggy white jacket, jeans that don't quite reach his ankles, a white T-shirt, red neckerchief – like the geese – and red deck shoes. He looks terribly trendy, if a little overdone for a visit to a farmyard.

Lucas tuts at me, dismayed. 'You still haven't a bloody clue, have you?'

I have to confess that I have not. 'Er . . . sorry. No.' But Bev is all of a flap again, so he must be someone famous.

'Molly lives in a cave,' Lucas declares and I see some of the theatricality of his father seep out.

'A caravan,' I correct. 'But it amounts to the same thing.'

'This is the world's *best* hair stylist,' Lucas declares proudly. 'He does all the celebs – Madonna, the Kardashians, Rihanna. The stars flock to him.'

In my defence, I have heard of Madonna.

'He's the coolest dude on the planet and my godfather,' Lucas tells me. 'It's the one thing my parents did get right. But, dude, what the hell are you doing here?'

'Don't kick off,' Christian Lee says, 'But your old man asked me to drop by.'

At that I see Lucas's shoulders sag a little. 'I might have known he'd be behind it.'

'Cut him some slack,' Mr Lee says. 'He told me that you were here and I wanted to see for myself what you were up to. Sounds like a cool place.'

Lucas kicks at the ground. 'It's OK.'

Mr Lee is having none of Lucas's sulking and pulls him into his shoulder again. 'Don't give me that mardy lip stuff. I'm here on a mission too. I understand that you have a My Little Pony in need of a good haircut.'

I laugh out loud at that. 'You've come to cut Ringo's hair?'

'Looks like it.' Christian Lee holds up a little floral pouch which I'm assuming contains his gold-plated, diamond-encrusted, star-trimming scissors.

Lucas frowns. 'How do you even know about it?'

My turn to fess up. 'I told your dad when he dropped by the other night.'

'He was here?'

'Briefly.' Lucas doesn't need to know the details of our conversation. 'He came to sign some paperwork.'

Lucas looks appeased and Mr Lee says flamboyantly, 'The upshot is that I have my first horsey hairstyle to create.'

'Well, we're very honoured,' I tell him.

He claps his hands and looks more eager than one might imagine. 'So. Let's get started. Do I go to Ringo or does he come to me?'

'I'll bring him down from the paddock.' I cast a glance at his fancy footwear. 'I'm worried that you'll get your shoes dirty.' They look like they're designer shoes, ones with a price carrying many noughts on the end and not something he picked up in Shoe Zone. I don't want him stepping in horse poo or he might sue me. 'Lucas, why don't you make our guest a cup of tea?'

'Will do.' He steers Christian towards the tea room – which is obviously the most attractive of our outbuildings but none of them are exactly Fortnum and Mason.

'Let me get a mug from my caravan,' I shout. 'I have some nicer ones there.'

'We'll be fine,' Christian Lee says.

So I rush up to the paddock, trying not to think about our choice of mugs that range from chipped to very chipped and usually have the logo of an animal feed company on them. I bet he doesn't get that when he goes to do Madonna's hair.

Chapter Twenty-Six

So Christian has his cup of tea in what I believe must have been the most chipped mug that Lucas could possibly find. I'm sure he must have done it on purpose. Even I'm ashamed and you'll have gathered by now that my standards are fairly low. I'm going to throw it in the bin when he's finished. Or perhaps I should auction it on eBay now that it's been held to celebrity lips. I'm going to take a few precious pounds out of petty cash and ask Bev to go to IKEA to get some new ones.

Speaking of my friend, she's rounded up the other kids and, tasks abandoned, has brought them down to the yard to see what's going on. The two girls have selfies with Christian and so does my regularly starstruck assistant. Christian bears it all with the air of a man who is used to being celebrity-spotted. Then, necessary social media opportunities completed, we go out to where Ringo is waiting patiently, tethered in the horse wash by the barn.

Christian looks so incongruous here in his posh clothes that it makes me anxious. 'Can I get you some wellies? I'm really worried about you damaging your nice shoes.'

He seems very doubtful.

'I'll show you.' So I trot into the barn and come back with the least battered ones I can find that look like his size. Believe me, I'm an expert in pairing wellies with feet.

He takes one look at them and recoils. 'I'm not putting my feet in those.'

'Sorry, they're all I've got to offer.'

Looking down at his nice pristine shoes, he says, 'I'll risk it.'

I ditch the wellies. Next hurdle. 'Are you OK with ponies?' I ask.

Christian shrugs. 'I guess we'll find out. Come on, little fella. Let's see what Uncle Christian can do for you.'

Lucas and I lean on the fence along with the other students and Bev to watch the maestro at work. Alan stays in the big field, clearly finding that watching a horse get a haircut is beyond his understanding. If Christian needs any assistance to handle the pony I'll step in, but Ringo is looking quite chilled today, so I can relax and enjoy the show.

Before Christian starts, he gives Ringo a long, hard look and lifts his hair, moving it this way and that. I have to say he doesn't get this much attention when I wield the kitchen scissors.

Soon Christian is snipping away, his scissors flying over Ringo's jagged fringe. He lifts it and feathers it and thins it out, then he kind of chips into it at the ends. I've no idea what the technical hairdressing terms are as I haven't been near a hairdresser since time began. I think they were still doing curly perms when I last ventured through their doors.

'Looking good,' I say to Lucas with a nod towards Ringo.

'He'll be *the* trendiest Shetland pony in Shetland pony land.'

'I hope he appreciates that he has a celebrity stylist.' I just pray that Christian Lee hasn't cast his eye over my own self-mutilated hairdo.

It seems to take for ever until Christian is satisfied, but the little pony stands quite happily for him and when he is finally finished Ringo has the most amazing bobbed fringe. It sits neatly in tidy little layers and when he tosses his head back – as he does proudly – it all settles into exactly the right place again. Much better than my desperate effort. Christian has cut Ringo's mane short too, in the same kind of layers, and he's thinned out his tail and trimmed it neatly. I feel like getting a mirror to show Ringo the back as I'm sure he'd be well impressed.

Everyone gives a round of applause and Christian takes a bow. Tamara takes some photos for Snapchat.

'That looks great,' I say. 'I can't thank you enough. We've all enjoyed watching you at work, haven't we?'

Everyone agrees that we have.

Christian Lee admires his handiwork. 'My pleasure. I never thought I'd say this, but I've found it strangely therapeutic. Anyone else in need of a new look?'

'I'd like my hair done,' Tamara says, quite boldly.

'Do we have a chair?'

'I'll get one,' I say and I bring one out of the barn and set it in the sunshine.

Tamara sits down and Christian Lee fusses with her hair until it's all up in a messy bun with tendrils teased out in all the right places. She takes another selfie of them both and looks very pleased with the finished result.

'I'd like to be a hairdresser,' Tamara admits. It's the first time she's ever expressed any interest in what the future might hold for her. Sometimes tiny glimmers of progress come in the most unusual of places.

'It's a great job,' Christian Lee agrees. 'If you still want to do it when you're old enough, let me know and I'll see if I can help.'

She grins at me, chuffed to bits, and it's nice to see her glowing. Then Christian gives Jody the same treatment so that she's not left out. They'll both be preening all day.

'How can I pay you?' I ask, hoping that he wasn't planning on giving me a bill at his usual rate. 'Will you work for eggs?'

'I'm vegan, darling,' he says. 'But thank you for the thought. How often do you cut Ringo's hair?'

'About every four weeks. Any longer and it starts to bother him.'

'I'll try to drop by regularly then.'

'Seriously?' I've obviously been spending too long with Lucas as I'm starting to talk like him.

'It will be last minute and I'll probably turn up on spec, but I'll be here. My country home is only a short drive away.'

'Well, that would be wonderful. I really appreciate it.'

'I could look at your cut too,' he says, glancing at me in a critical manner. 'It's kind of unique.'

'I usually do it myself,' I admit.

'I'm glad to hear it,' he chuckles. 'If it was a salon they'd be committing crimes against hairdressing.'

I can't help but laugh too. 'I do it with my kitchen scissors.'

He throws his hands in the air, outraged. 'Oh, lordy! You have great hair and good bone structure, what a waste. Go and wash it right away,' he says. 'I'll see what I can do.'

'I don't have a hairdryer,' I confess.

'You really are living off the grid,' he teases. 'We'll manage. As you're *ultra* low-maintenance, there's no point me giving you something that will require GHDs.'

'No,' I agree. Though, in truth, I don't know what he's talking about. I'll try to remember to ask Bev.

So, as instructed, I wash my hair and sit down in the chair. Everyone stands around giggling as they make a sideshow of me getting my hair cut.

'Luckily, I *always* have a hairdryer in my car,' Christian says. 'And spare scissors.'

116

Who doesn't? So I pack Bev off to find an extension cable and then we run it across the yard to my chair.

So I sit as still as I can manage while Christian prowls round me snipping this way and that, occasionally making little tutting noises. If Ringo can bear this stoically, so can I. Closing my eyes, I let the sun warm my face. In a strange way, this could be considered relaxing. I've not been to a salon in years as I'm intimidated just walking past the window. Everyone looks so groomed and polished. Plus the cash that I'd have to stump up would go a long way towards feed.

As Christian is putting the final touches to my new hairdo, fluffing it this way and that, Shelby Dacre turns up in the bling-mobile. Bev, all of a froth at yet another celebrity rocking up, rushes to the gate to let him in while Little Dog and Big Dog bark a greeting. When he gets out of the car, Shelby gives Bev a hug which will, no doubt, turn her into a quivering wreck. Then he strides over to our makeshift salon.

Chapter Twenty-Seven

'I am *never* washing again,' Bev whispers to me with a longing sigh. 'My boobs were against his chest.' She strokes her breasts lovingly.

'*Bev*,' I hiss at her and, thankfully, she stops fondling herself.

Shelby claps Christian on the back. 'Chris,' he booms and they do a man-hug. 'Glad you could make it.'

'Me too. It's been great,' Christian says. 'Couldn't miss out a new challenge or an opportunity to see my gorgeous godson.' He throws an arm round Lucas's slender shoulders so casually that I can see Shelby Dacre wince. I wonder if Shelby wishes he could be as close to his own son.

Shelby takes in the towel round my shoulders, the chair in the middle of the yard. 'I sent you to cut the horse's hair though, not Molly's.'

'I think I made him despair,' I pipe up.

'It looks fantastic,' Shelby says. 'A new woman.' He stops and properly stares at me for a moment before he adds softly, 'You look beautiful.'

'Thanks.' I flush and run a hand over my neck where hair used to be. It's short. Very short. I'm sure that Shelby is only being flattering as it's Christian who's cut it for me.

'You look gorge,' Bev agrees. 'Like Carey Mulligan.'

'Who?'

'Oh, for God's sake!' Bev shakes her head at me, but leaves me none the wiser.

'A small present by way of thanks.' Shelby hands over a bottle to Christian and I'm sure it says Bollinger on the label.

'We should share it together,' his friend says. 'I see so little of you both these days, man.'

'What can I say?' Shelby shakes his head. 'We're both men who are in demand.'

'I see plenty of you running around town with that girl on your arm,' Christian admonishes but in a cheery tone. It still makes Shelby look uncomfortable, though. 'Don't forget your grizzled old mates.'

Shelby shifts awkwardly. 'You know what it's like.'

'We should put a date in the diary or another year will slide by and we'll be even older.'

'We're having a charity fundraiser at the house in the next month,' Shelby says. 'Come. You must have had an invitation.'

'It's probably sitting in the pile of unread post my PA gave me last week.'

'Check your diary. See if you're free?'

'If I'm not, then I will be.'

Shelby claps him on the back again, grinning. 'Good man. That's great news, isn't it, Lucas?'

'Yeah. It will make an interminably dull day infinitely more bearable.'

Christian gives a belly laugh. 'We'll make a party animal of you one day, Lucas.'

Lucas only scowls more. 'I doubt it. There's nothing worse than seeing a load of Z-list stars turn out for *charidee*. I hate people like that. They'd come to the opening of an envelope.'

Shelby snaps back. 'It will raise a lot of money and it was

your mum who set this up. I'm just trying to keep it going in her memory.'

'That's good,' Lucas snarls. 'Because sometimes it feels as if you've forgotten about her altogether.' Then he stomps off towards the fields, even though it's clear to me he has no idea where he's marching off to.

Shelby shouts after him, 'Lucas, get back here! Get back here now.'

But the boy keeps on going.

'Leave him be,' Christian advises. 'He'll come round.' He looks to me and I give a slight nod to confirm my agreement. The last thing Lucas needs now is a confrontation.

'That was a veiled reference to Scarlett, I'm sure.' Shelby's obviously seething. 'I'm not supposed to rebuild my life.'

'It's tough on Lucas. Give him time,' Christian says in a placating tone. 'Let me take you to lunch. We'll have a drink or three, talk about old times, complain about the old farts we've turned into. We can go to that gastro place in the village. I seem to remember they've got some half-decent craft beers.'

Shelby's face softens slightly. 'Sounds like a plan.'

'Good. Shall we both drive down there?' Christian is clearly adept at diffusing tricky situations, maybe that's why he's such a sought-after hairdresser among the celebrities.

'Yeah. I'll follow you. I just need a minute to talk to Molly. Get the beers in.'

'Will do.' Christian holds up a hand. 'See you next month, Molly.'

'Thank you again, Christian. I really appreciate it. Ringo has never looked so good. Nor me.'

'My pleasure.'

We all walk to the cars and Christian lowers himself in.

'Five minutes,' Shelby says as he hangs back. I open the gate and Christian drives away, giving me a friendly wave.

Chapter Twenty-Eight

'He's nice,' I say when Shelby and I are left alone. 'That was very kind of you to send him along.'

'You might be seeing even more of him. The alpacas could soon need a hairdo too,' he says enigmatically.

'How come?'

'I've got a gig for you. If you're interested.' Shelby looks very pleased with himself.

'I'm all ears.'

'The producers of *Flinton's Farm* have decided that they want to vamp things up on the farm, give it a bit of a modern look. Apparently, alpacas are the future.'

'God help us all.'

'They're considering alpaca walks, maybe even a tea room on the farm, but they wanted to give it a bit of a trial run, see them introduced to the farm before they decided on whether they'll become a permanent feature. They wouldn't be on every episode but if their first outing goes well, then they'd become regulars.'

'On the telly?'

'Yes. Showing that Gordon Flinton is a modern and progressive farmer. Lots of farms are diversifying now and this seems like a great opportunity to do something a bit different.'

'I see.' My alpacas, television stars? Wow. They'd be even bigger divas than they are now.

'It's very lucrative.' Shelby tells me how much I'd be paid for letting my babies stand and look pretty.

'Just for a day?' It's a quite staggering sum and I don't really see how I can refuse.

'Yes.' If he needed to twist my arm then he's just done it quite successfully.

'And they won't have to do anything? They're not really performers or, frankly, even house-trained,' I tell him. 'If Johnny Rotten wakes up in a bad mood there's very little we can do with him.'

'I'm sure it'll be fine,' Shelby says as a man who is patently unaware of the old adage 'Never work with children or animals'. 'We always have professional animal handlers on set to look after the animals we use. They can help you.'

If something sounds too good to be true, then it usually is. But I can't look a gift horse – or alpaca – in the mouth, can I? Besides, Bev would kill me stone dead if I turned this down. I'd rather go through the anxiety of agreeing to do this than face telling Bev that I'd refused. I know that she'll love it.

'OK.' It will be an adventure. It will make us some much needed money. My mouth goes dry with fear when I say, 'Let's give it a go.'

'Great.' Shelby looks genuinely pleased. 'It'll be fun. They'll want them soon, though. Next week, probably. Once they have an idea they need it to happen yesterday. I'll give the production secretary your number so that she can set it up, if that's OK?'

'It's fine. I'll await her call.' Yet, despite trying to convince myself that it will be an experience, I'm already wracked with anxiety.

'I'd better go,' Shelby says. 'Don't want my beer to get warm.'

'No.'

'I'll send the driver for Lucas tonight. It will only wind him up if I come.'

'I'll go and find him,' I say, glancing up toward the fields, though he's nowhere in sight. I bet he's gone up to see the ponies. They're always very good at calming down stressed teenagers. 'He *will* be OK.'

'I hope you're right, Molly.' He shakes his head as if bewildered by the ways of the world and climbs into his car. Then, as soon as I've watched him leave, I go in search of Lucas.

Chapter Twenty-Nine

Lucas is leaning on the fence up by the Shire horses, staring into space. The furthest he can get from the yard. He tries to look busy as I approach. The dogs run ahead to see him and he wipes his arm across his eyes. I think he may have been crying.

'The coast is clear,' I tell him. 'Your dad's just gone. It's safe to come back down to the yard now.' I smile encouragingly at him and but all I get is a scowl in return. His face is blotchy, red.

'He gets on my *bloody* nerves,' he spits.

I take up position next to him and, for a few moments, we gaze out over the fields together.

'I get it,' I say, eventually. 'Grief hits us all differently and it can be hard to understand when people don't handle it in the same way as us or in the way that we want them to.'

'Time the great healer,' Lucas scoffs. 'How many times have I been told that?'

'It's kind of true. Though we never get over the loss of a loved one, we simply learn how to live without them.'

Lucas lets out the most careworn sigh I've heard in a long time and I put my arm round him.

'My own mum died when I was quite young – about your age. Even though it was a difficult relationship, I still missed her every day. When Hettie died, I was older and supposedly wiser, yet I thought my world had ended. So I do know how you're feeling.'

'My mum was great,' he says, unhappily. 'Why couldn't someone else have died? Someone horrible? She was so nice to everyone.'

A tear splashes onto his cheek.

I pull him tightly to me. 'Oh, Lucas.' I can feel myself filling up too. 'It will get better. I promise you. Just hang on in there.'

'I don't know how to deal with it,' he sobs. 'It's all knotted up inside me.'

'We can help,' I tell him. 'If you'll let us.'

He cries again and a bubble of snot comes from his nose when he says tearfully, 'I don't think I have any choice.'

'No,' I agree. 'You don't.' I root in my pocket and find a tissue that isn't too manky. I offer it to Lucas and he grimaces at it, but takes it nevertheless. He blows his nose. Little Dog comes and nuzzles against him. 'Talking about it will start to ease the pain.'

'Will it?' I'm not sure he's convinced.

'That plus copious amounts of tea and biscuits.'

He tuts at me. 'I'm not some bloody geriatric who's been told they need a hip replacement.'

I laugh at that. 'Don't underestimate the healing powers of tea and biscuits.'

'Maybe some biscuits would help,' he concedes.

'One of the parents brought KitKats.'

'Luxury,' he deadpans. 'Just when I was growing to love own-brand custard creams.'

I give him one last squeeze as we stand. There's something about his slender frame, his vulnerability, that always touches

125

my heart. My mothering instinct has, up to now, been channelled towards four-legged creatures, but Lucas has definitely sparked deeper nurturing genes. I would have liked a boy and, if I could have chosen, I would have liked a boy just like Lucas. If I could hold him like this for ever and take away his hurt then I would. Instead, I let him go and we head off to the yard together.

'I have got some good news.' I say as we walk. 'And I don't want you to tut at me.' He gives a pre-emptive tut, but I carry on regardless. 'They're going to have some alpacas featured in *Flinton's Farm* and your dad has put our motley crew forward. I'm waiting to hear from the production team.'

Lucas shakes his head. 'I've heard it all now.'

'It will be good for us, Lucas. If nothing else, it will bring in some much-needed money.'

His doubt is unshaken, but I also hope that it will be an opportunity for Lucas to spend some time with his dad. Maybe if he sees him on set then he'll realise that his dad has a lot on his plate. I know that there are worse jobs than being an actor, but it can't be easy either.

However, before I can explain any more, Bev bowls up and says, 'What are you two deep in conversation about? Have you fed the alpacas? If not, I'll go and do it.'

'No,' I admit. 'It was the next job on my list. I was just going to have a cuppa with Lucas.'

'Let me feed Triple Trouble and then we can all have a brew together afterwards. Jody and Tamara will be thrilled to see you, Lucas. I've had a nightmare with them.' Bev shudders. 'I think they're pining for you.'

His pale face flushes slightly.

'Let's get the girls to put the kettle on then and we can walk up to the alpacas together. I've got something exciting to tell you.'

Chapter Thirty

When I recount our news as we reach the alpaca paddock, Bev stops stock-still and her mouth drops open.

'Say something,' I prompt.

'We're going to be on the telly!' She shrieks with joy and does a little dance. 'We're going to be on the telly!' Then she suddenly stops. 'I'll have to get my hair done. And my nails.'

'It's not *us* who'll be on camera,' I remind her. 'Just the alpacas.'

'Yes, but they might need a couple of extras or something. What do they call them now? Additional artists? We could do that.'

'You might be able to, but I'm terrified,' I admit. 'I want to lurk as far in the background as possible. I'm even nervous for this lot.' We lean on the fence and watch Tina Turner, Rod Stewart and Johnny Rotten milling about in their field. They look like harmless innocents, but I know differently. We all do.

'They've just got to stand there,' Bev says. 'You said so your-self. Even our daft lot can't mess that up.'

'No,' I agree, sounding more confident than I feel. Johnny

Rotten is the first to see us and he comes to the fence. I scratch his neck and he doesn't try to bite me so it must be a good day.

'They'll ace it,' Lucas says, fussing him too. He picks up a handful of food pellets from the bucket and holds them out. Johnny takes them gently, but you have to watch because he'll nip your finger given half the chance.

Instantly, sensing food, the others come over to join him and Lucas feeds them too.

'We could be talent-spotted,' Bev says, dreamily. 'They might end up in adverts or West End shows or on the covers of rock albums.'

I grimace. 'Don't you think that you might be getting a bit ahead of yourself?'

'What will I wear?' Bev says, still fantasising. 'I'll have to go through my wardrobe. I don't know what colours look good on screen.'

'We won't be on screen,' I reiterate. 'We'll be the ones panicking in the wings.'

'If I went in proper farm gear, not this tatty stuff, I might get a walk-on part. Maybe even a few lines.'

Lucas and I roll our eyes at each other. That's it, there'll be no stopping her now. I should have kept quiet. Better still, I should have said no.

'Good luck with that,' Lucas says. 'I can't wait to hear about it.'

'But you are coming with us, aren't you?' I automatically thought that Lucas would want to be part of it too. That was part of my cunning plan. 'We could definitely do with an extra pair of hands.'

'No.' Lucas shakes his head vehemently. 'I spent half of my childhood on a TV set. It's interminably boring. It makes watching paint dry seem thrilling.'

'But you know what it's like, you know the ropes. We need you. One person to each alpaca and we have a fighting chance of retaining the upper hand.'

'Not me.' He holds up a palm.

'Please, Lucas.' I'm not adverse to a bit of begging should the situation warrant it.

'I'd rather prise my own eyeballs out with a spoon,' is Lucas's considered conclusion.

That fills me with trepidation. 'Do you think we've done the wrong thing?'

'Nah,' Lucas says. 'Not really. It's money for old rope. These telly types love to splash the cash. We might as well have some of it coming our way.'

'I kind of thought that,' I agree and I also think it's nice that he refers to the farm as 'our.' I hope that means he's starting to feel as if he belongs here and isn't simply coming under duress. 'It was kind of your dad to think of us.'

'There'll be some ulterior motive,' Lucas warns me. 'There always is.'

'He might just be trying to get in your good books,' I suggest.

'Yeah? Well, if he is it's not working. Seriously, count me out.'

Give it time, Molly, I think. *Rome wasn't built in a day*. For all that swagger, there's a scared and lonely kid in there and I'd really like Lucas to come with us to the set, despite what he says.

'You're good with the alpacas and I don't want to be outnumbered when it's important that they behave themselves.' I'll swear alpacas can sense weakness and go for the jugular. If they can cause a riot, they will. 'If you came with us then Alan could stay here and be in charge for the day.'

I can see Lucas weakening and I pounce on his moment of indecision.

'Please, Lucas.' Real tears start to form in my eyes. 'Think about it at least. It's probably not until next week.'

'I won't change my mind.' He's intent on digging his heels in.

I smile to myself. We'll see about that.

Chapter Thirty-One

The production secretary phones me and books us in for our inaugural appearance on *Flinton's Farm* two days later. Which guarantees that I don't sleep a wink until then.

On the morning we're due at the studio, I get up at four o'clock, feed everyone including myself and then turn my attention to the alpacas. Unaware that it's a big day for them, they're as obstreperous as usual. When I call them, Tina Turner and Rod Stewart start to hurtle round the field, intent on ignoring me. Johnny Rotten skulks in the corner of the paddock, refusing to move. I hope he's not having one of his bad days. As usual, it's the lure of food that finally gets their attention.

As they come over to me, I see that Johnny Rotten has a cold. So that's why he was hanging back. An alpaca with a cold is the most disgusting thing you can imagine. Their globules of snot are the size of tennis balls and stink to high heaven. I know that the television company have booked three alpacas but it might be better if I leave him at home. Alpacas are temperamental and tetchy at the best of times, but one with man-flu will be more than a handful.

'That's terrible timing, Johnny. I wanted you all to be at your loveliest.' But he just looks at me dolefully and snorts out some more vile green mucous.

When they've had breakfast, I groom each one in turn, which they *love* – although they hide it very well. Trying to avoid the ensuing kicks, I take a tangle comb and clear them of any debris that they've collected in their coats. I smooth out their fleeces as I go so that they look like the kind of cute alpacas you'd want to see on telly and not like our normally scruffy, badly behaved lot.

Even though I'm still in two minds about taking Johnny with us, I give them all a pep talk. 'Please be nice today,' I coo. 'It'll be a pain in the bum, but it means a lot to the farm. Don't bite or kick anyone. Only poo in designated places. Shall we see if we can manage that?'

They all look doubtful.

'Does that apply to us too?' Bev asks as she comes up behind me.

'We're only to *kiss* designated people,' I tell her. 'We're not allowed to kidnap handsome young soap opera stars or offer them sexual favours.'

'Oh,' Bev says, disappointed. 'That was the bit I was looking forward to the most. Ready for it then?'

'Not really. His Nibs has got a cold.'

She scratches Johnny Rotten's neck. 'Hmm. He doesn't look a hundred per cent.'

'I was just contemplating leaving him behind and hoping that the television company don't notice they're an alpaca short.'

'You'll be all right, mate, won't you?' Bev says. Johnny Rotten flutters his big eyelashes at her. 'They've only got to stand at the back and look cute. He can manage that.'

'If you're sure.'

'No worries. They'll ace it.'

Bev is clearly feeling a lot more bullish than me.

'How do you like the outfit?' Bev gives me a twirl.

My dear friend has turned up in some kind of posh farmer's wife outfit of tweed Barbour jacket, Hunter wellies and beige trousers. 'Where did you get that lot?'

'Borrowed it off a mate,' she says, admiring herself. 'Looking hot, eh?'

'Smoking,' I agree. Whereas I look a complete wreck, not helped by the lack of sleep. 'Your friend knows that it will be covered in alpaca poo by the end of the day?'

'Didn't really spell that out,' Bev admits. 'It will dry clean.'

'We should get this lot in the truck. It's going to take us an hour or more to get there.'

'I've never been on a television set before. I'm beyond excited.'

'Lucas says it's very dull.'

'He's a teenager. He's no idea just how dull life can be.'

True enough.

Bev nudges me in the ribs. 'Besides, Shelby Dacre will be there and in *action*. That always brightens your day.'

Also true enough.

'God, I can't wait! Come on, babies,' Bev says to our alpaca troupe. 'It's time for your big break. This week a soap opera in England, next week Hollywood. All you've got to do is behave yourselves.'

And with that ringing in my ears, we lock and load.

Chapter Thirty-Two

'We're here,' Bev says. 'Just round this corner.'

'Here?' I pull up outside an enormous house with double gates and a plaque that states HOMEWOOD MANOR. I look at the map on Bev's lap. 'This can't be right.'

'Yep. This is the one.'

'Seriously?' We are picking up a still-reluctant Lucas en route. 'Double check the address.'

'Believe me, I have.' Bev is most insistent. 'I was a girl guide. I can read a naffing map. This is Shelby's gaff.' She gives a low whistle. 'Look at the state of it. They must pay him a shitload of dosh on that show.'

Indeed, they must.

With more than a little trepidation, we wind our way down the meandering drive lined with tall poplar trees and acres of grassy parkland on either side. She gapes around as I drive. 'I guess Shelby Dacre was never going to live in a two-up, two-down, but this is like a *proper* country manor house.'

It certainly is.

When we finally reach the house I swing the truck into a huge gravelled area with a fountain splashing away in the middle of it – and not the kind of fountain you might buy on a whim on a Sunday afternoon at the garden centre. This is a *proper* fountain to match the *proper* manor house. Homewood itself is an imposing building – low, wide and constructed in a creamy-coloured stone. There are tall pillars flanking the front door and dozens of windows on either side. Goodness knows how many rooms there must be. On the far side, there's a bank of four pristine garages and I can catch a glimpse of fancy stables behind them, though I know that Lucas can't ride or has ever been close to horses before coming to the farm.

As instructed, Lucas is waiting outside for us outside. He's leaning on the low wall of a raised bed filled with tulips and spring flowers, engrossed in his phone. The truck judders to a halt in front of him and Bev opens the passenger door. He glances up as if surprised to see us there.

'Come on, sunshine!' Bev budges up and Lucas climbs into the truck, squeezing in next to her.

'This is where you live?' I blurt out. 'It's amazing.'

'Oh, yeah,' Lucas says and his cheeks glow red. Suddenly, he's self-conscious again.

I dial it back when I add, 'What a place.' I realise that it's rather different to where I live in my little caravan and wonder if I've made him feel embarrassed by commenting on its opulence. Yet how could I not? It's not your average family home. 'Do just you and your dad live here?'

'We have a housekeeper too,' he divulges rather grudgingly.

Bev raises an eyebrow at me. *A housekeeper*, it says.

'Right. Well. Let's be off.' I coax the gear lever into first as if I'm stirring a pudding. 'Our stars in the back will be getting angsty. Seat belt,' I remind Lucas.

'I'm not five,' he retorts, but buckles himself in anyway.

'Everything OK?'

'Yeah.' He shrugs and then buries himself in his phone again.

We joggle along the country lanes, Bev concentrating on her map-reading.

'You've been here before?' I ask him.

'A million times.' Nothing else is forthcoming.

I try again. 'Johnny Rotten has a cold.'

'Oh, joy.' And that's it. He doesn't say anything else for the rest of the drive.

About an hour later and we're in countryside that I haven't explored before even though it's not actually that far from our farm. The map proves too complicated for our Girl Guide, so we end up following the satnav app on Bev's phone and, eventually, we turn into the lane that leads up to the set. I thought that Hope Farm was secluded, but the set of *Flinton's Farm* is even more so. I guess they don't want fans massing at the gate and the like. It would certainly take the most dedicated to come and hang out here for a glimpse of their favourites. There's nothing but open fields on either side of the lane and a vast open sky above us. We trundle along quite a bit more until we're stopped by a barrier and a burly security guard.

Bev rolls the window down and tells him, 'We're bringing alpacas for the filming.'

He checks his clipboard and, thankfully, decides we're allowed access to the inner sanctum. He points into the distance. 'Park up there and wait. Someone will come to meet you.'

So we head in the general direction he indicated and follow the car park signs. As we climb up a small rise, I can see the set for *Flinton's Farm* spreading out ahead of us.

'It's exactly like a proper village,' I say, slightly awestruck.

And it is. For all the world it looks like a real place. There's a street of a dozen or more houses all with tidy hedges, white picket fences and roses round the doors, a pub called the Farmers' Arms, a church complete with graveyard, a neatly manicured green with a pond and the obligatory ducks. There's an old-fashioned red phone box and a signpost that surely must be left over from the nineteen fifties. It's weird because it all looks so real and yet it isn't. The buildings are stone-fronted – I'm pretty sure that's real and not just painted stone – and yet there are only timber frames behind the façade. All this and yet it's temporary and could all be torn down in a heartbeat.

'They do all the outside shots here.' Lucas deigns to look up from his phone. 'The indoor shots are done at a studio somewhere near Slough. They've got this land on a rolling ten-year lease from the lord of the manor or something. Sometimes they shoot stuff up at the main house too.'

'I'm nearly weeing myself with excitement,' Bev says as we park up.

And I thought it was only the alpacas disgracing themselves that I had to worry about.

Just as we're wondering what to do next, a young woman with long blonde hair and a clipboard comes towards us and Lucas shifts marginally so that Bev can clamber over him. She jumps down from the cab.

I nudge Lucas. 'Coming?'

'Nah. I'm good. I'll wait here until you need me.' He returns to his phone.

I join Bev, standing behind her for protection. As she reaches us, the young woman flicks her hair and asks, 'You're the alpacas?'

'Indeed.'

'You're not due on set just yet. Are you happy to keep them here?'

'Can we walk them round the car park?' I ask. They get all wound up if they're in the truck for too long and this is probably at their outer limits as they're not seasoned travellers. Like me, they very rarely leave the farm.

'Sure. I'll call you when we're ready for you. We're just setting up the scene now. We shouldn't be too long.' She waves an arm towards a huddle of farm buildings. 'There's a catering truck just round the corner. Help yourself to tea and whatever.'

When Clipboard Woman strides away from us, Bev and I look again at the pretty village spread ahead of us. I turn to her. 'Wow.'

'Pinch me,' Bev squeals, doing a little dance in her posh Stepford Wives outfit. 'Pinch me.'

I need pinching myself.

'It's just like on the telly,' Bev says. 'I can't believe that I'm here. They do tours in the summer and I've always wanted to do one. Now look at me!'

In the main street there's obviously a scene being shot. I've no idea what's going on but two actors, surrounded by cameras and crew, are remonstrating with each other quite hotly.

'That's Owen Bart, he's the landlord of the pub,' Bev informs me. 'He's been in the show since time began. That's his wife, Shaz, and she's having an affair with Shelby Dacre.' I must look alarmed as Bev hastily adds, 'Not in real life. Only in the series.'

I lower my voice so that Lucas can't hear. 'I thought he was having an affair with Scarlett Vincent? In real life and in the programme.'

'Yeah.' Bev scratches her head. 'It's complicated.'

'You're telling me.' I'm beginning to think that I might have missed out in life by never having seen a soap.

'This is sooooo totally cool though. Shall we unload Triple Trouble before they decide to kick their way out of the truck and then go and get a cup of tea?'

'Sounds like a plan.' We let the alpacas out of the truck.

They're already getting a little bit skittish from being cooped up. They bounce round in giddy circles trying to tangle us up in their halters and I can only hope that they calm down in time for their big moment.

Lucas finally joins us and he takes Rod Stewart's reins. Rod is looking decidedly nervous.

'Whoa, boy,' Lucas soothes. 'It's just some telly types. Nothing to worry about.'

I hang onto Johnny Rotten who's still a snot bucket. I've brought a kitchen roll with me and I grab it and wipe his runny nose and he backs away, turning his face from me as a toddler would. I look at the pretty village where we're about to make our screen debut and rue that we're not at the glamorous end of farming – if there is one.

Bev takes Tina Turner, who is tossing her head to fluff her pom-pom hair. If anyone is determined to be the star today, it's Tina. A true diva just like her namesake. I hope with all that is good and true that everything goes well. Shelby has put his faith in us and I have everything crossed that we can deliver.

'Once more into the breach,' Bev says. 'Come on, boys and girls. Let's go and have a cup of tea before we throw ourselves into the heady world of stardom and celebrity.'

Lucas sighs heavily and Johnny Rotten blows a bubble of green gloop from his nostrils. And as we walk the frisky alpacas to the tea van, I try to ignore all of my misgivings.

Chapter Thirty-Three

The farm buildings connected to the set are, of course, the kind that Disney would design. They're clean for a start, beautifully maintained and filled with crisp, clean straw that looks as if each strand has been individually arranged. There is not a poo in sight and it doesn't smell of animal wee. Below us, there's a bank of bright lights shining on the open barn and I can see Shelby standing inside talking to someone who looks as if they're in charge.

Bev nudges me again. I'm going to have big blue bruises all along my ribs at this rate. 'There he is.'

'I'd noticed.' He looks so suave in his checked shirt with the sleeves rolled up, jeans and a leather hat with a wide brim. But I have to admit that whatever he wears he looks wonderful to me.

Bev straightens her smart borrowed farm-chic jacket and smooths her hair. I try not to do the same. 'Hold this.' Bev passes me Tina's reins. 'I'll get some tea.'

So Lucas and I stand there on the periphery of it all, hanging onto three twitchy alpacas.

'They're bored,' I say.

'Like me,' Lucas agrees.

'We won't be long. I'm sure.'

He rolls his eyes at me. 'You have *no* idea.'

I glance over at the tea van and see Bev in the queue. In front of her is Scarlett Vincent. She's dressed in tight white jeans and a white shirt. I wonder if she has the 'white' thing in her contract. Her hair is long and glossy and she swishes it more than the alpacas do.

Johnny Rotten's nose runs again and I wipe it with kitchen roll. It's not often that I wonder what I'm doing with my life, but today is one of those times

As Bev arrives with a tray of tea, so does Shelby.

'Hi.' He ruffles Lucas's hair, which I know his son hates. Lucas ducks away from his dad. 'Good to see you here, son. It's been a long time.'

'Not long enough,' Lucas mutters, but Shelby pretends not to hear.

Bev hands him a cuppa. 'I got an extra one. Just in case.'

'Thank you.' He accepts it from her, gratefully, and takes a drink. 'You got here OK?'

'Yes, no problems.' Not yet, anyway. 'This is all very impressive.'

'I guess we're used to it and don't appreciate it as we should. But, yes, it's a very special place.'

'I dressed up especially.' Bev indicates her outfit.

'And you look lovely,' Shelby says.

Bev positively glows and not in a hot flush kind of way. Or maybe it is.

'Any chance of a walk-on part?' Bev asks, boldly.

'I'll certainly ask. I'm sure you could lurk in the background. We shouldn't be long now.' Shelby looks over his shoulder, checking. 'The guys are setting up for the scene. All the alpacas have to do is stand nicely in the background. My body double will settle them.'

I laugh. 'Your what?'

Shelby looks, dare I say, 'sheepish'.

'I don't handle the animals myself,' he admits. 'They can't risk me losing any time due to my allergies. So someone else steps in and does anything that involves touching the animals, usually in close-up. He's over there.'

Sure enough, there's a man dressed in identical clothing to Shelby, though I must say that he doesn't wear it with the same flair and, though handsome, there's not that certain something shining through.

'Who knew?' I say.

'I told you. It's all fake,' Lucas throws in.

But before Shelby has chance to respond someone who looks as if he's important holds up an arm and shouts from the barn, 'Ready when you are, Shelby.'

He nods in acknowledgement. 'That's the director. He's the one who'll tell you what to do.'

'Ah.' So he's in charge. God help him.

'They'll probably want you too in a minute,' he informs us.

'Right.' I'll swear my heart falters.

'It will all be fine.' He sounds so very reassuring that I nearly believe him.

As I watch him walk away Bev slurps hurriedly at her cup and says, 'Drink your tea.'

'You've only just given it to me. It's boiling.'

'Hurry up. We don't want to be late. We need to give them a good impression.'

'You haven't finished yours yet either,' I point out. Though she is glugging it at a rate of knots. In fact, she's too busy drinking to answer, but not too busy to give me a dark look.

While we're still rushing down our tea, Clipboard Woman returns. 'If you could bring the alpacas down to the barn now, that would be great.'

'Ready, gang?' I get nods from Bev and Lucas.

We manage to stop the alpacas from turning in circles and we all troop after her and then wait at the side of the barn behind Clipboard Woman. She's wearing a fluffy cardigan and Rod Stewart decides that he fancies it and rubs against her. Lucas hangs onto him a bit tighter. Clipboard Woman shoots me daggers and moves away.

'Sorry,' I say. 'Very sorry. He must have thought you were a lady alpaca.'

She moves a bit further away.

Lucas supresses a snigger and now he gets daggers too. The last thing we need now is Rod's hormones surging. While Rod Stewart now has a lustful look in his eye, Johnny Rotten is just looking a bit miserable.

I wipe his nose again and he twitches. 'I should have left you at home, poor boy,' I give his neck a scratch. 'Not long now, though.'

Important Man comes bustling over. 'Who's the handler?' he asks.

Despite Bev preening like a peacock, I guess that would be me, so I put my hand up.

'A quick rundown of the script for you. We'll put your alpacas into the barn where Shelby will be discussing getting his new alpacas and his plans for them including the new shop and tea room. When his love interest, Marla – Scarlett Vincent – arrives. Gordon and Marla will have a row.' He frowns at me. 'There will be some shouting. They're not easily startled, are they?'

'Er . . . ' I consider lying, but decide honesty is the best policy. 'Yes, they are.'

'Oh,' he says. 'We'll try to keep the shouting to a minimum.'

'I think that would be a very good idea.' Even the sight of a bumblebee can scatter this lot.

'We'll move the alpacas into place now, have a couple of run-throughs, and hope we won't keep them for too long.'

'Right.' There's not much else I can add. I try to look relaxed and professional, as if we've done this a thousand times while inside, my stomach is churning like a washing machine set to spin. 'We're in your hands.'

'Good, good.' He bustles away again.

'He must be the boss,' Bev whispers. 'I wonder if Shelby remembered to ask him about my part?'

I watch the immaculately dressed Scarlett Vincent move into position. A vision in white. 'He's probably got other things on his mind.'

Clipboard Woman waves us forward and we head to the barn.

Shelby's double comes and shakes me by the hand. 'I'm Graham,' he says. 'I'll be looking after the llamas for you.'

'Great.' Close up, he's beefier than Shelby and looks like a man who could control marauding animals. 'They're actually alpacas.'

He casts his eyes over them. They all have their compliant faces on. 'Nice-looking beasts.'

'Specially groomed this morning. Have you worked with them before?'

'No, but I'll be fine. When I'm not working on *Flinton's Farm*, I deal with lions, stallions, all kinds of wild animals.' He laughs. 'I'm sure I can handle a llama.'

'Alpaca.' One more time.

'Yeah, yeah.'

'They're skittish,' I warn. 'A bit unpredictable. You need to keep your eye on them.'

'I'll take good care of them. I promise,' he says. 'We'll be all right won't we, boys?'

Surely a man used to animals would realise that Tina Turner is a lady alpaca? Perhaps he just didn't look closely enough.

So, with only one sharp stab of reluctance, I hand them over to his tender loving care.

Chapter Thirty-Four

Graham leads the alpacas into their allocated place in the barn and I'm pleased to see that he keeps a good firm grip on them. After a bit of skittering about from Tina Turner and them all trying to wrap Graham in their halters, as is their way, our babies settle. Then we stand like lemons watching on while the crew take some close-ups of him doing animal-type things – scratching their necks, offering some food pellets. No one takes a bite out of him – which is excellent. Perhaps my misgivings are unfounded after all. Only when the crew have finished their fussing does Shelby take up his position.

There's more filming and then Scarlett Vincent sashays on, moving as if she's on a catwalk. She still has on the tight white jeans but now she's sporting a low-cut white top that leaves little to the imagination. Never has a person looked more out of place on a farm. But goodness me, she's pretty.

'Is everyone ready and happy?' Important Man says. Shelby and Scarlett nod. 'Turn over on camera A and B please. OK, stand by, Scarlett. And action!'

'Gordon,' she says breathlessly, breasts heaving. 'We need to talk. We can't go on like this. I think your wife has her suspicions.'

I whisper to Bev. 'He has a wife too?'

'Busy bloke,' Bev whispers back.

Shelby moves towards his love interest. Worryingly, the alpacas skitter a bit behind him and they haven't even got to the shouting bit yet. Tina Turner is looking particularly animated. I'll swear that she has mischief on her mind and I reckon she might like to risk a sneaky bite of Shelby if she can get near enough. Where's Graham gone? The supposed animal handler is nowhere in sight. Who will grab her if she makes a beeline for the star?

My heart goes to my mouth as I murmur to myself, 'Don't get too close, Shelby. Don't get too close.' But he is concentrating on Scarlett and is unaware of the jostling going on behind him.

'No.' Scarlett dramatically holds up a hand. 'Don't touch me. I can't bear it.'

'You're so beautiful,' Shelby says. 'I can't resist you.'

Who writes this, I wonder?

Then, when there's a meaningful pause for them to exchange longing looks, Johnny Rotten comes to the edge of the pen next to them and sneezes loudly. That startles Tina Turner and Rod Stewart who bolt for the fence and, with very little effort, push it over. Clearly, television fencing is not as robust as real farm fencing. Unfettered, they trample the fallen fence and pick up their pace as they exit the barn. Johnny, not to be outdone, runs after them.

'Oh, shit,' I say.

All three of them make a dash for the village green, scattering cameras and crew as they go. It looks as if they make a particular beeline for anyone holding cups of tea and drinks are thrown up in the air, lights are knocked over, camera crew scatter. Clipboard Woman looks as if she's about to expire.

Bev and Lucas dive into action and give chase to them.

Graham, who is supposed to be in control, appears from behind the barn with his phone in his hand, guiltily caught not attending to his charges. A little too late, he follows in hot pursuit. The alpacas crash their way over the green and within seconds the pristine set of *Flinton's Farm* looks . . . well . . . exactly like an actual farm.

'Cut!' Important Man cries.

See, I told you, never work with children or animals. Especially alpacas.

'Sorry, sorry,' I say from the sidelines. 'So sorry.' I can't run after them as humiliation has rooted me to the spot.

There's much laughter from the crew and they try to regroup. Clipboard Woman rushes round picking up dropped cups and papers.

The alpacas, happy to be the centre of attention, run this way and that with Lucas and Bev in hot pursuit.

Eventually, when most of my life has been replayed before me, Bev shouts, 'Got them!'

I could cry with relief as I watch her, Lucas and the rather ineffective Graham grab hold of the Houdini Three and wrestle them back to the barn. If Graham is this useless with alpacas, I wouldn't like to see him with lions. Professional animal handler, my arse. I should have been the one to look after them. I knew it.

As the laughter dies down, I slip into the barn too. I grab Johnny from Graham's slightly ineffectual care and wipe his nose again. 'Bad boy,' I tell him. 'No running away. And we could do without another sneeze, thank you very much.' Then to the crew who all seem to be staring at me, 'So sorry. Very sorry.'

'Ready to go again when you are,' says Important Man with a heavy sigh.

When it seems as if everyone is settled once more and the

bolting alpacas are restored to their pen, Shelby and Scarlett take up their places. Someone else with a clipboard pops in to remind them where they're up to and they talk through the lines.

'Shelby? Scarlett? Good to go?' the Important Man asks.

They both nod and, he says, 'Turn over on A and B. And action!'

Just as they're about to start their scene again, Scarlett glances down. Her scream is ear-splitting. What no one had noticed, especially me, is that she has a big globule of green alpaca snot right in the middle of her chest. It's sliding slowly but inexorably towards her ample cleavage.

'Get it off me,' she shouts. 'Get it off me!'

While she hyperventilates, everyone stands and looks at her, horrified. But not a single person dashes to her assistance. Is no one going to do anything? When it's clear they're not, I sweep in with my kitchen roll, ripping sheets off as I go.

'Do excuse me,' I say to Scarlett, but she is frozen with horror.

I scrape off the worst of the snot, then dab furiously at Scarlett's chest with the kitchen roll while saying, 'I'm sorry. So terribly sorry.'

It's spattered all over her white top too, but I daren't touch that as rage is boiling in her eyes.

Shelby steps forward. 'What a mess,' he says kindly. 'No harm done, though. Off you go to Wardrobe, darling. They'll find you something else to wear.'

A couple of young women now risk rushing in and usher the rather stunned Scarlett away.

I'm mortified. Totally mortified. Yet when I glance at Shelby I can see that behind his hand, he's hiding a smile.

Chapter Thirty-Five

We are summarily dismissed from the set. *Flinton's Farm*, it seems, will fare better without alpacas in its future.

We take our charges back to the truck and load them in. Clipboard Woman stands glowering at us. Clearly checking to see that we leave the premises without causing any more havoc.

'You let me down. You let yourself down,' I tell Johnny Rotten before I close the tail gate. He doesn't look the slightest bit chastened.

'It was bloody funny though,' Bev says, stifling a giggle.

Lucas, Bev and I all jump into the cab. I put my head into my hands. 'Did that really just happen?'

We look at each other and burst out laughing.

'Don't,' I say through my chuckles. 'I'm so ashamed. They hadn't even done anything! They could have sneezed over anyone else and it would have been fine.'

'I'm glad it was her,' Lucas snorts. 'Hil-ar-ious!'

'Did you see her face!' Bev lets out a full-on cackle.

'Stop it,' I say. 'Don't. I'm so embarrassed.'

Eventually, we all manage to stop laughing and calm down enough for the drive home.

'We won't get paid now,' I remind them. 'We came all this way for nothing.'

'I didn't even get my starring role,' Bev complains as she wipes tears from her eyes. 'And my mascara's ruined.'

'At least you're not covered in alpaca snot,' Lucas points out and that starts us off all over again.

'We'll find a tea room and I'll treat us to cake on the way home. It won't hurt the alpacas to wait as they've disgraced us.'

So we compose ourselves again and set off. I'm on driving duty so I trundle along until we spot a nice garden centre that serves tea and cake. We leave the truck and the alpacas out of harm's way in the very far corner of the car park, but we don't linger over our cake just in case.

We drop Lucas at his fabulous home as it's on our way. He looks worn out and I think he's had enough excitement for one day.

'Apologise to your dad for us,' I say. 'It was a nice thought. I wish it had worked out better.'

'He won't come home tonight,' Lucas says. 'He'll go up to London with *her*.'

It shouldn't make any difference for me to hear that, but it does. Lucas stands and watches us as we drive away. He looks so small, so lonely – especially against the backdrop of that big manor house – and it's all I can do not to turn round and scoop him up again.

Even though there's no traffic coming, I pause at the end of the drive and lean on the steering wheel. I ought not to get too involved with Lucas or his father. I should keep my professional head on at all times.

'What?' Bev says.

I turn to her, chewing my lip. 'I could go back for him.'

'Drive, woman,' she says firmly. 'Lucas isn't your responsibility.'

'No.' But that doesn't stop my heart turning inside out.

'We do our best for him.'

'Yes. I can't help think of him there by himself.'

'He's got a housekeeper. Some might say that makes him very privileged.'

'You know what I mean. It's not exactly the same as having family around, is it?'

'You can't save them all.' Bev puts her hand on my knee and pats.

But I don't want to save them all. I just want to save Lucas. Still, I do as I'm told and put the truck into gear. Though as we drive away, I'm still hurting.

Chapter Thirty-Six

Alan, of course, is surprised to see us back at the farm so soon. 'What's up?'

'Our brief flirtation with stardom didn't go quite as smoothly as planned,' I tell him as I unlock the back of the truck.

Alan looks at me blankly.

'Johnny Rotten sneezed all over the star.'

'Oh,' Alan says and I think he might smile, but can't quite tell behind all that beard. 'Alpaca snot is lucky.'

'Isn't that bird poo?' I question.

'Works with alpaca snot too.' Alan, if no one else, looks convinced.

'I'd better go and buy a lottery ticket this week then. I could do with a Ferrari and a house in the South of France,' Bev says. 'I'm off home to get out of this gear before it gets dirty. I can't wait to get my civvies on again.'

'I'll put the alpacas away by myself, shall I?'

'Great,' Bev says, oblivious to my tone. 'See you in the morning!'

We haven't even bet on Alan's T-shirt yet. Off she goes.

'Business as usual then,' I sigh. 'How has today gone here,

Alan? I hope it was better than our day. Has everyone else behaved themselves?'

'Yeah,' Alan says. 'All well.'

'That's good, at least. Want to help me get Triple Trouble back into their field?'

Alan nods, clearly having exhausted his conversational skills.

So we unload the alpacas and put them back in their field. I give them some pellets as a treat even though I'm not sure they deserve it and wipe Johnny's nose again.

'You're a bad lad,' I chide, though I can't help but smile as I say it. I can only hope Shelby will forgive us, if not Scarlett Vincent.

Chapter Thirty-Seven

I text Shelby after what is now known as The Embarrassing Event and apologise profusely, but he just sends two kisses in return. He's a busy man, I guess. I also ask Lucas if he's upset with us, but Lucas just shrugs and says he hasn't really seen him to talk to. All I can do is try to put it to the back of my mind, but the sight of Johnny Rotten's snot all over Scarlett Vincent is not an easy image to erase. I'm sure Scarlett Vincent must feel the same.

I'm still thinking about it when Little Dog and I do my early morning rounds. It was hoofing it down last night, so all the sheep are huddled together in the barn. I can hear the sounds of hungry bleats getting louder and more insistent as I move from one pen to the other in the yard, dishing out brekkie and saying good morning to everyone. When the pigs, bunnies and goats are all catered for, I grab two more buckets of feed for the sheep and head to their corner of the barn.

But when I get there, the pen is open and the sheep are making a beeline for the yard, Anthony at the head of them looking in a very anti-social mood.

'WTF?' I stare at them, dismayed. How on earth have they

got out? I wonder if I didn't secure the gate properly last night? Even in my usual exhausted state at the end of the day, I try to be very careful about things like that.

'Come on, guys,' I say, trying to sound as if I'll stand no messing about. 'Back into the barn. I can't cope if you're all out like this.'

I try to herd them back towards their pen, but they're wandering all over the place. Only Anthony is looking stubborn. He has his shoulders up, his head down, which is never a good thing. Little Dog gives a cursory bark and then decides to hide behind me, which may be a very sensible thing. I'm currently being circled by sheep, all pressing in around me. Anthony is eyeballing me. He looks as if he's up for a fight.

I hold up a hand. 'Stand down, Anthony. I'm the boss here.' Though it doesn't actually feel that way.

But he's having none of it. He's clearly woken up in a vile mood, and he barges towards me and knocks me clean off my feet. The feed buckets hit the deck at the same time as I do and the food scatters everywhere. Wasting no time at all, the sheep dive in. They devour their breakfast, oblivious to the fact I'm lying on the floor beneath them and, to see them in action, you'd think they hadn't been fed for days. I struggle to sit up, but am squashed in by pushing, shoving, munching sheep who are trampling all over me. I'm flat on my back and helpless. Above their bowed heads, I can see Anthony peering over, giving me the evil eye. Obviously, he considers his work here is done.

Then I hear a car at the gate and Little Dog rushes off, barking. I do hope that it's Alan and that in his doggy way Little Dog is trying to alert him to my plight. A minute or so later, above the noise of bleating lambs in a pack, I hear someone shouting my name. 'Molly! Molly!'

'Over here,' I yell back.

Then, thankfully, I see Shelby and Lucas appear.

They clap their hands and dash towards the sheep who take off and scatter to all four corners of the yard. Shelby and Lucas run after them – here and there, mostly in circles, trying to round the sheep back into the pen. It's times like this when I could do with a well-trained sheepdog who could assist, not someone like Little Dog who barks and wags his tail at the excitement of it all and only makes matters worse.

Eventually, Shelby and Lucas manage to secure them all back in their pen. All except for Anthony, of course, who dodges them both and gallops off into the far reaches of the yard to see what other mischief he can find. That terror of a sheep will surely be the death of me.

While Lucas is securing the rest of the recalcitrant escapees into their pen, Shelby comes back to me. I'm sitting, still dazed, on the ground. Shelby holds out his hands and helps me to my feet.

'Thank you,' I say. 'That was a very timely intervention.'

'Glad to be of service,' Shelby says as I stand in front of him a bit frazzled.

'You were almost like a real-life farmer then.'

He laughs. 'Don't tell anyone, it would ruin my image. You're OK?'

'Fine.' Frankly, I've had enough of marauding animals. I'm battered, probably bruised, breathless and have been trampled by the hooves of a dozen sheep. Even though I'm reluctant to let go of his fingers, I have to in order to brush myself down. I'm covered in mud, straw and feed. Even more so than usual. 'Anthony's a nightmare.' I nod towards my most difficult sheep. 'He's more bother than the rest of them put together.'

'Shall I go and see if I can bring him back?'

'No, let him run off steam for a while. He's not going to get into too much trouble.'

'Famous last words,' Shelby notes.

'True enough. Alan should be here soon and we'll rein him in again then. Alan's more used to handling him and when Anthony's being moody he's best left to his own devices.'

Then there's an awkward pause which I try to fill by picking bits of straw from my person.

'It's good to see you again,' Shelby says, eventually.

'You too,' I agree.

'It all ended a bit badly last time.' Though he's all smiles, so it doesn't seem like he's a man who's holding a grudge.

'I can only apologise about the alpacas when they came to *Flinton's Farm*.'

'You seem to have a lot of badly behaved animals,' he observes.

'I do. Was Scarlett very furious?'

He hesitates for a moment before saying, 'Yes.'

Then both of us laugh.

'I did feel terrible, if that's any consolation.'

'I'm not sure it is,' he says. 'But it was quite amusing. I'm sure she'll survive. It will make a great anecdote for the next *Graham Norton Show* that she does.'

'I suppose so.'

'I'm sorry that I've not been around,' he says. 'My life is not my own.'

'It's good to be busy,' I answer somewhat lamely. I've got so used to Lucas being dropped off and collected by a driver that I assumed Shelby wouldn't be doing it again.

Before he can say anything else, Lucas comes back to join us. 'They're all safely in the pen now, little sods. It looks as if part of the fence had fallen over or had been pushed.'

Pushed, if I know Anthony. The devil. Perhaps the alpacas have been giving him lessons.

'Are you OK?' Lucas frowns at me. 'You look a bit shaky.'

'Just a bit winded, I think.'

'Do you want me to feed them properly now?'

'Yes, please,' I say, stretching my back. 'I think I need to sit down for a breather for five minutes.'

'Can I make you a cup of tea?' Shelby says.

I would normally insist that I'm fine and can manage by myself, but this time I feel a shift inside me and actually feel that I want to be looked after for once in my life. 'That would be very nice. Thank you.'

So Lucas heads off to the feed shed, purpose in his stride. I smile to myself. Such a change from the sullen, loping boy who first came here. Shelby takes my arm and I lean on him, letting him help me limp towards the tea room. Perhaps it's not just Lucas who's changing.

Chapter Thirty-Eight

I flop into the sofa, happy to be sitting down and without a sheep on my head, even though this well-loved couch is on the saggy side of soft.

'I brought Lucas this morning because I wanted to have a chat to you,' Shelby says as he busies himself making tea. He brings me over a mug with two chocolate biscuits which I take gratefully. 'I may have mentioned that we have a charity event every year at Homewood.'

I seem to remember him inviting Christian Lee to go along to it. 'Yes.'

'It's a great day. We have musicians, fabulous food, all kinds of entertainment. The great and good of Showbiz attend. How do you fancy it? You could all come too, students and animals, everyone. It would be a great showcase.'

I nearly splutter out my tea. 'You've already been subjected to my disorderly animals. And more than once. Why would you want to do that again? What if they decide to run amok amid your fancy friends?' I tell you, I'll be scarred by the alpaca snot moment for the rest of my days. 'And we know what happens when you add alpacas into the mix.'

He wavers slightly. 'Maybe bring a few animals rather than enough to fill the ark. Leave the boisterous ones at home. Especially Anthony.'

Poor Anthony.

'And Johnny Rotten.'

Poor Johnny.

'They'll go down a storm,' he continues, 'and you can raise some money for the farm. It will be an excellent opportunity.'

It will be a recipe for disaster is my assessment. After the alpaca fiasco, I can't believe that he still wants me to go to his big charity event. 'I don't think I could.'

Shelby spreads his arms. 'What have you got to lose?'

I'm filled with terror just thinking about it.

'I do it every year,' he presses on. 'People give very generously. If they don't, we ply them with lots of alcohol to loosen their wallets. I'll give you a cut of the money we raise.'

Gosh, that sounds so tempting. Our monthly deficit seems only to be growing ever larger. Yet still I hesitate. As well as the animals to contend with, there would be people there – posh ones. I might even have to talk to some of them.

I'm sure Shelby can read my mind as he says, 'I know that it's out of your comfort zone, but it would be good exposure.'

That's exactly what I'm worried about. Do I want to be 'exposed'? I don't think Shelby realises quite how small my comfort zone is. Even stepping beyond the farm gate is traumatic.

'I thought it would help me to get closer to Lucas again. He'd see that I want to be involved in this place, that I care. And I do.'

There's no doubt that would be an excellent idea, but still my terror doesn't subside. That flashing image of alpaca snot again. 'Will Scarlett Vincent be there?'

'Yes. But I'll keep her far away from the alpacas. I don't think she'll need any persuading.' We risk a smile at each other.

'I'm not going to pressure you,' he says. 'But promise me that you'll think about it.'

'I'll think about it,' I agree.

Bev opens the door to the tea room and shouts, 'Anthony's running riot in the yard.'

'I know,' I say wearily. 'We need to go and grab him.'

Then Bev does a little double-take when she sees Shelby and her face softens and she goes all girly. 'Hello. Didn't expect to see you here.'

Shelby rewards her with the full force of his smile. 'I was just asking Molly if she'd consider bringing some of the students and animals to my annual charity fundraiser. And your good self, of course.'

She stares at me. 'And?'

'I said I'd think about it.'

'We'll do it,' Bev says.

'I'm not so sure,' I venture. 'I—'

She fixes me with a threatening stare. 'We'll *do it,* Mols!'

'We'll do it,' I echo, too scared to argue with her.

Shelby Dacre gives me the grin of a man who knows that he's won. 'It's a date.'

Chapter Thirty-Nine

'What were you thinking?' I ask Bev, in despair. 'Why did you agree to this?'

Two short weeks later and it's the day of the charity fundraiser at Shelby Dacre's house and I'm out of my mind with worry. It's not nearly enough time to recover from the last ordeal. I didn't sleep a wink last night. Not helped by the fact that Little Dog, Big Dog and Fifty were hogging the bed. In fact, I've been in a state of heightened anxiety all week. If it had been any longer, then I might well have pulled out. The potential for this to go horribly wrong is enormous. Before I operated in ignorant bliss. Now I know.

I'm standing in the yard, stressing.

'We need more money in,' Bev says, flatly. 'You've not shown me the account books for ages, so I know it must be bad.'

It is.

'This is a fabulous opportunity,' she wheedles. 'It's a no-brainer. Man up, Mols. Just stand there and look cute with your fancy new hairdo. I'll do the talking. All they'll want to do is pet the animals and have some selfies with them. What can possibly go wrong?'

We look at each other, acknowledging The Embarrassing Event, but knowing that it must never be referred to.

'The alpacas will hate it.'

'They hate everything. Tough tittie. They'll have to take one for the team,' is Bev's opinion. 'Their future depends on it. Let's just give Tina Turner an outing. She's less likely to nip anyone. Johnny and Rod can stay at home.'

I chew my fingernails. 'The others will get very anxious without her.'

'It's a day,' Bev points out in an exasperated voice. 'They'll cope. You'll cope.'

Oh, God.

'Just have some tea and get over yourself,' she snaps.

'You still owe me cake,' I throw back, realising that I've lost the previous argument.

The only highlight of my morning is that Alan is wearing a Smiths T-shirt and I so very nearly called it right. I'd said Morrissey which, to me, is kind of the same thing.

'I do not. Morrissey is not the same as the Smiths. The Smiths are not just Morrissey.'

Bev might be pushing against it, but in my mind, I think it means she owes me cake. She's just smarting because she was wildly off-course with Kings of Leon.

'Obviously, we'll take Ringo and Buzz.' She continues in the same vein as before, as if we hadn't interrupted our conversation for Alan's band T-shirt issue. 'They look as cute as feck.'

The girls spent hours yesterday afternoon turning our little ponies into unicorns. There are rainbow-coloured chalks combed through their manes and tails. Their hooves have been painted with purple glittery paint. Bless them both, the ponies stood patiently and bore their makeover with relative good humour. I have silver unicorn horns in a plastic bag to attach to them later. I must point out that this wasn't my idea. Bev assured me that unicorns are all the rage. I bow to her greater knowledge. They do look very cute though.

'Everyone loves them. I've sent Alan up to the field to get them. What about some of the bunnies, plus Dumb and Dumber? Everyone adores a pygmy goat.' She surveys the yard, scratching her head. 'Should we take some of the prettier chickens too? Or have people generally seen a chicken?'

'I think the majority of people only see chickens wrapped in plastic in Waitrose.'

'What do you know of Waitrose?' she snorts.

Got me on that one.

'Let's see how much room we have,' I suggest, placatingly.

It's the first time we've all been on tour, so all this is a new and somewhat frightening experience. We're taking a couple of the sturdier metal barriers to make an ad-hoc enclosure – no one is going to push these bad boys over – and we've got a pull-up banner advertising our work. Bev has printed some leaflets that we can give out too.

'We should be able to squeeze Fifty in too,' Bev adds. 'He'd melt the coldest of hearts.'

'Good plan.'

Alan appears with the ponies and we load them into the truck first. I'm getting more reluctant to take the truck out much because, frankly, it isn't becoming any more reliable. I'll have to cross my fingers all the way to Shelby Dacre's house just in case it crunches its very last gear before going to the big truck stop in the sky. A handful of our regular students and some of the parents are meeting us there. Jack and Seb are coming, Jody and Tamara too – the girls would never miss anything that involved seeing Lucas. He's still quite the heart-throb for them although he insists that he hates every minute of it.

'We ought to get going,' Bev says. 'This thing starts at two and we've got a lot to do when we get there.'

So we scurry about and Tina Turner goes in with the ponies with only a modicum of diva behaviour. The goats will be fine in there for the short journey too. Fifty is squeezed in as well. Little Dog can sit in the cab with me.

When we run out of space, we load up the back of Alan's knackered old estate car with a run full of bunnies and another one with chickens. Some feed and hay go on his front seat. Shelby says they'll have plenty of hay bales if we need to pinch a few. Everything else is stuffed in the truck with me and Bev.

'Is that it?'

'I think so,' Bev says.

'I hope we haven't forgotten anything.' We probably have, but I can't bring it to mind now.

The plan is that Alan will help us to set up, but will come back and look after the rest of the animals for the day, then come and collect his payload again in the evening. The students will be briefly pressed into talking about the animals and giving out some leaflets as part of their learning curve, but I really just want them to have a nice day out.

Finally, we jump in the truck. I'm driving and Little Dog sits on Bev's lap looking out of the window. Big Dog will pine for him all day, but I can't keep my eye on both of them. We leave the farm and I feel jittery just doing that. I've exceeded my annual outing quota in the last few weeks and I'm not feeling relaxed about it. Bev is map-reading and issuing a litany of instructions even though I'm pretty sure I can remember my way to Shelby's swanky place.

We trundle down the country lanes, gears grinding. I'd like to say happily, but I'm still strung like a bow and my palms are sweating on the steering wheel. The last time we did this kind of thing I was operating on the policy of witless optimism, now I know what might lie ahead of us and, quite frankly, I'm crapping myself. Perhaps I'll feel better when we're finally there.

Shelby Dacre's gaff is only about fifteen minutes from where the farm is and the drive takes us through some of the finest English countryside that nature has to offer – the trees are budding with fresh green leaves, the hedgerows are white with blossom where once there was snow and the sun has blessed us with its presence. At least this is a beautiful day for it. We've had some glorious late spring weather and today is no exception.

We keep having to check that Alan is still behind us as he is the world's slowest driver and with chickens and bunnies loaded in the back, he's clearly taking no risks.

'Flipping Nora, we could have walked quicker,' Bev complains as she looks in the wing mirror once more. 'I don't think we've done over twenty miles an hour.'

Quite possibly less. 'We can't be far now, though?'

'We're here,' Bev says and, sure enough, Homewood Manor comes into view and we turn into Shelby's drive once again.

I look down at my worn check shirt and slightly grubby jeans. 'I wish I'd spruced myself up a bit now.'

'You have nothing to spruce yourself up into.'

This is also true. And I was clean when I started the day. Honestly.

Bev grimaces at me. 'I wish I'd borrowed my mate's posh gear again. I didn't think of it.'

If I'm honest, I might have been tempted to raid her wardrobe too. I turn to Bev. 'Now I'm even more terrified.'

'It'll be fine,' Bev says, breezily, but I can see fear in her eyes too. 'We'll get drunk.'

'I'm driving.'

'*I'll* get drunk,' Bev corrects.

'I need you sober and doing schmoozing. I'm going to hide at the back behind Tina Turner.'

'Coward,' she says.

Can't argue with that, so I crunch the truck into gear and

head towards the gates. We're stopped by a security guard and I wind down the window.

'Hope Farm,' I say. 'We're here for the charity day.'

He checks his list and waves us in. 'Have a nice time, ladies.'

'We're in!' Bev says with an air punch. 'I can't wait to get a proper look at this place.'

With my anxiety levels at an all-time high, I can't begin to tell you how relieved I feel when I see Lucas at the front of the house waving to us.

Chapter Forty

I manoeuvre the truck into the huge gravel turning area outside the house, taking care not to knock down the fountain. That wouldn't be a good start. I'm ultra-aware that many dangers are set to trip me up today.

Lucas rushes up to greet us. He looks quite animated and has a flush to his cheeks. If I didn't know him better, I'd say he was quite excited.

'I've made a great area for us,' he babbles as soon as we jump down from the truck. 'Under the shade of the trees, so the animals don't get too hot.'

'Sounds ideal,' I say. 'We can get the boys and girls down there before everyone else arrives.'

'It'll be mad,' Lucas tells me. 'It always is.'

'I appreciate having a veteran of these things to hand. It all seems a bit overwhelming. Can you help us to unload?'

'Yeah, sure.' Together we go round to the back of the truck, lower the tailgate and let our charges out – who, thankfully, seem no worse for wear for their slightly cramped trip.

'Whoa!' Lucas's eyes widen when he sees Ringo and Buzz. 'What happened to these two?'

'They've been unicorned. Apparently it's A Thing. I have accessories in my bag for them.'

'Weird,' is Lucas's verdict. 'They'll be a hit with the kids, though.'

He's probably right.

So Lucas takes the two ponies and I grab Tina Turner and the goats. Bev follows on with Fifty and Little Dog. Alan leaves the bunnies and chickens for now and brings the fencing for our enclosure. Lucas leads us down the side of the house on a path that winds through flowering cherry trees and, if possible, that's even more stunning than the front.

The first thing that takes my breath is the unbroken view across the vale and I'm pretty used to a good view. In the far distance, I can spy another farm, but that's about all. There's a terrace on the back of the house with classy-looking rattan furniture that would seat a dozen or more. Below, there's a swimming pool and the lawn stretches out into a copse of trees in leafy bloom. To one side I can see a tennis court and the back of the stable block. Beyond that is a lake and I can make out a floating pontoon made of wood with two loungers side by side on it. A small rowing boat is tied up by the side. The end of the lake trickles over into an ornamental fountain in the garden. The whole thing is spectacular.

'This is very pleasing on the eye,' I whisper to Bev.

'Not half,' she murmurs back. 'Much like the owner.'

I couldn't even guess at the cost of something like this. In fact, I didn't even know that homes this grand existed.

'This is like a little bit of Hollywood in Buckinghamshire,' Bev coos. 'I could *so* live here.'

'I think you'll find there's already an incumbent.'

'Scarlett Vincent? Pah. He needs a more mature woman. Someone who's down-to-earth and will keep him grounded.'

'You reckon?'

'Of course. You know what these luvvie types are like.'

Actually, I don't. My only meetings with 'luvvie types' have all involved Shelby Dacre. That's the sum and total of my experience.

We make our way across the immaculate lawn, leading our animals. I hold on especially tightly so that they don't go scampering across the picture-perfect flower beds. Already, a few of the stalls are setting out their wares and there's a scattering of deckchairs and hay bales with blankets on them arranged around a small raised platform that forms a makeshift stage. There's a black and white tent marked CHAMPAGNE and a white ornamental cart ready to serve Pimm's.

Bev clocks them both and, rubbing her hands together, declares, 'Now I'm in heaven.'

The whole thing has the air of a mini-festival – a rather upmarket one. Lucas leads us down to the far corner of the huge garden and a shaded area by the copse. It would be nice for lots of people to see the animals, but I don't want it to be too busy for them and this is set slightly apart rather than being in the main thoroughfare. The goats will see a crowd as just more to eat for them, but Tina Turner might get freaked out and we all know how badly that can end.

'Is this OK?' Lucas asks anxiously.

'Perfect choice,' I tell him and he glows with pride.

Alan and Lucas get busy setting up the fences together, while Bev and I sort out the animals – except for Fifty who takes himself off for a wander round. We put up our fancy new banner and secure it to some low branches, so that it doesn't blow over in the breeze. Lucas brings a small table so I pile up the leaflets and stop them from blowing away with a rock.

A woman comes over with a tray of tea in paper cups. 'Mr Dacre asked me to bring these for you,' she says. 'He'll be out to see you shortly.'

'Thank you.' I take one, gratefully, and Bev does too. Though she hisses, 'I wish it was bloody champagne.'

In the opposite corner a string quartet is setting up on the stage area. Some of the students arrive and I give them the unicorn horns to attach to Ringo and Buzz. Tamara and Jody also give them a last minute fluff and take photos for our tea room gallery.

'There's a programme of music too,' Lucas tells me as he follows my gaze. 'And some readings, I think. Dad's sorted that out. It's all his luvvie mates. Nothing to do with me.'

'You're not going to perform some of your poetry?'

'My father doesn't even know that I write it,' he says.

'Really? That's a shame.'

'He'd hate it,' Lucas assures me. 'Not his *thang* at all.'

'You never know.'

'I do,' he says, crisply.

Putting my arm round his skinny shoulders, I pull him to me. 'Thanks for helping us today. I'm scared witless.'

'It's cool,' he says. 'My parents have been holding these since I was a kid. They're nice. If you like that kind of thing. Everyone gets a bit pissed and walks round with smiles on their faces, then they fall asleep in the deckchairs.'

'Sounds wonderful.'

Lucas shrugs. 'I suppose.'

Alan goes off to get the chickens and bunnies and we set them up in their runs. We're going to offer supervised cuddles and selfies in return for donations and Bev has labelled up two buckets with our name in bold letters.

When we're ready, we stand and wait until Bev says, 'I really can't do this without alcohol,' and bolts off towards the champagne tent.

A few minutes later she reappears, grinning. She's carrying two brimming flutes and hands one to me. 'Compliments of the management.'

'I can't possibly drink this,' I say. 'I'm driving.'

'Not for hours. Get it down your neck. The bubbles will take the edge off your nerves. It's a well-known fact.'

'Right.' So I swallow down the cold fizz and, in fairness, Bev's not wrong. It does hit the spot perfectly.

Then I see a few people drift down through the trees and head our way.

'Here they come,' Lucas says.

'Oh, God.' I'm all of a-jitter and go to grab my champagne glass. Bev has beaten me to it. She throws the rest of my fizz down her throat and smacks her lips.

'Brace yourself,' Bev says. 'Incoming!'

Chapter Forty-One

Within half an hour, the place is crowded and our little enclosure is one of the busiest areas. All of the animals are a big hit. Our pony-unicorns are proving particularly popular and I'm glad that I was persuaded to do it. The chickens and bunnies get many cuddles and even more selfies. Money flows into our buckets. Half a dozen of our students join us and, without me having to ask, Lucas supervises them in giving out leaflets. Jody and Tamara disappear into the crowd immediately, but Jack and Seb like to stay near our enclosure, which is fine.

The people all look very smart and talk in loud, confident voices. The women are a bit shrill, giggly and wear lots of make-up, immaculate summer dresses and big sunglasses. The men all look cool in linen shirts and Panama hats. Everyone seems to know each other.

'I'm sure you won't recognise any of these people,' Bev says. 'But they're all off the telly. That's Ricky Wallman, he's in *Doctor Drake's Dilemma*.'

'Nope.'

'Hopeless.' Bev shakes her head and then points at a tall redhead in the distance. 'Caron Dougal? *Legal Team*?'

'Nope.'

'Tell me a television programme you have heard of and I'll tell you if there's someone here from it.'

'Er . . . the six o'clock news?'

'Oh, for heaven's sake.' She rolls her eyes at me. 'Actually, there is a newsreader here, but he's on Sky so there's no point in me even showing him to you.' Bev chews her lip. 'I wonder how I can get sneaky selfies with them?'

'Could you not just ask?'

'Think so?' Her face is wracked with indecision. 'I'll go and try,' she says and bolts off.

The music is playing in the background and there's a friendly hum in the air. The string quartet are playing modern songs that I usually hear when I tune in to Radio Two. There's a considerable queue for the champagne and Pimm's.

I am actually starting to relax, despite Bev deserting me. Lucas is back from leaflet distribution duties and he and Jack are organising selfies with Tina Turner who hasn't done anything to disgrace herself yet. I can't see the girls, so maybe they've gone celebrity-spotting too. I'm sure Tamara will be busy with her phone's camera. Seb seems to be knee-deep in small children, but doesn't appear to be too traumatised so I leave him to it while I supervise some stroking of Ringo and Buzz with Jack.

I'm taking a moment to breathe when Shelby Dacre suddenly appears at my side and my heart starts to race once more. He's wearing cream jeans, a grey tee and has a navy shirt over the top. His eyes are shaded by what I assume are designer sunglasses and his hair looks even more blond than usual in the sunshine. I can't say that I've ever taken note of what any man was wearing before beyond Alan's daily band T-shirts and there's a cake reward on offer for that. Shelby Dacre always looks so smart and even more so today, but then I suppose he's very much on show.

'Can you manage for a minute, Jack?'

'Yes, Molly. Just one minute?'

'Let's say a few minutes. I'll only be over here if you need me.' So I step out of the way and Shelby follows.

When we have our own little space, he kisses me softly on both cheeks and my mouth goes dry. 'How's it going?'

'It's amazing. I've never been to anything so fancy before. Thank you so much for having us.'

'You're going down a storm,' he says. 'I knew you would.'

'I'm very grateful.'

'No need to be. I hope we make a lot of cash. That's the whole point.' He takes in our stand. 'Someone's looking after you with food, drink?'

'We've had tea and Bev blagged us some champagne,' I admit.

He laughs at that. 'I'll get them to put some food aside for you for later. It looks as if you have your hands full at the moment.'

'Thank you.'

'I'd love to pet the animals, but I daren't go near them. I haven't mainlined antihistamine today.'

'I understand.'

Yet he moves closer to me and I'm probably covered in animal detritus and I feel like Bev must, as his proximity suddenly does very weird things to me. Perhaps men like Shelby have more than their fair share of pheromones or something. When he talks to you, it's very hard to tear yourself away from his intense gaze.

'I can't thank you enough for how you're helping Lucas,' he says quietly. 'I know he hasn't been with you for long, but I can tell that he's a different boy already.'

'We haven't done anything but give him some time and attention.' If that sounds barbed then I don't mean it to. 'He's a good kid.'

'I'll take your word for it,' Shelby says, wryly.

'Look at him.' I nod towards where Lucas is helping people with their phones, reminding them to put a pound in the bucket for selfie services rendered, encouraging Jack to do the same.

Then, out of nowhere, Scarlett Vincent appears and links her arm through Shelby's which ends our conversation. She's dressed all in white again today – this time in a clingy jumpsuit that's backless, sleeveless and plunges to her navel. Eye-catching, I think would be the term. Certainly, Shelby's eyes go straight to her cleavage. All I can imagine is alpaca snot sliding down it.

'Hello, darling.' Her voice is husky, sultry and she pronounces darling like daaaaahling. She gives him a lingering kiss. 'I wondered where you'd got to.'

'Just saying hello to Molly.' He smiles at me and gives a little wink. 'Maybe you should steer well clear of the alpacas, but why don't you come and pet one of the goats? They're cute and I'm sure pretty harmless.' He looks at me for confirmation but, frankly, I can't guarantee anything. All of these things pee and poo at will. 'You could have your photograph taken with one.'

Scarlett wrinkles her nose. 'I don't think so. Animals aren't really my thing.' Which means she's not planning to get within ten metres of one. She pulls on Shelby's arm like a bored toddler. 'Don't forget our guests, darling. We should get back to them.'

'I suppose you're right,' he sighs. 'We want those charity buckets to be filled up and I need to press some flesh. Enjoy your day, Molly.'

'Darling . . . ' Scarlett tugs at him again and Shelby rolls his eyes as one would at an indulged child.

'Coming,' he says. Then Scarlett Vincent draws him away and I watch them disappear into the crowd.

Bev comes back as they're leaving and says with disdain, 'Tit tape.'

'What?' Another thing I know nothing of.

'Lots of it,' she continues. 'In fact, that's the only bloody thing holding her together. She could have someone's eye out with those things.'

I assume she's referring to her voluptuous bosom. 'She certainly looks very striking.'

'I'd like to see her step in sheep shit,' Bev says. 'Or fall face-first in it.'

'That's cruel,' I admonish, but I laugh too. 'Haven't we tortured that poor woman enough?'

'Poor woman?' Bev tuts.

As Shelby walks away, I notice that he hasn't really acknowledged Lucas at all. I hope that he hadn't, but I think that Lucas notices it too. I hand Ringo and Buzz over to Bev and I make my way over to him. 'You're doing a grand job.'

'At least I've got something to do,' he says. 'I'm usually hanging round like a spare cock at a wedding.'

'Lucas,' I say sternly, but we both giggle together.

'You're certainly looking better,' a voice says and, when Lucas and I stop sniggering, I look up and see Christian Lee. Today, he's in a bright pink bondage jacket covered in chains and rolled-up white trousers. Is this fashion or Christian's unique style?

'Me or Lucas?' I ask.

'Both of you,' he says. 'Lucas looks as if he's been out in the sunshine instead of cooped up in his room playing those ghastly games and I see that you're managing to keep that hairstyle more or less in check.'

I hadn't even noticed, if I'm honest. Perhaps that shows the quality of the cut. Don't know. I still do the same thing to it that I've always done – wash and run. Sometimes with shampoo, sometimes with washing-up liquid. Depends what's to hand. I'd better not tell Christian that or he might expire in a poof of glitter.

Christian hugs Lucas to him. 'If I'm not mistaken, you look as if you're in very grave danger of enjoying one of your dad's little get-togethers.'

'Yeah?' he says. 'Well, looks can be deceiving.'

I think Christian's right, though, Lucas is definitely looking borderline cheerful. I wonder how long it will last?

'Do you want a selfie with an alpaca?' Lucas asks of his godfather. 'This beauty is Tina Turner.'

'Really?' Christian looks worried by the prospect of getting too close. 'I managed to stroke one of the little horse-unicorn creatures, but this thing looks like trouble. Will it bite me?'

Lucas considers for a moment. 'She hasn't bitten anyone yet.'

'I'll risk it then,' Christian says and he moves in closer. Lucas holds up his phone and they both beam at it as he clicks a photo of them.

'That'll be a tenner,' Lucas says. 'Mates' rates for you.'

Without complaint Christian puts a couple of notes into the bucket. 'Make sure you send me a copy.'

'I'll text it now,' Lucas says.

'I don't know what you've done to him, Molly,' Christian quips. 'But I think I rather like it.'

I smile over at Lucas and he grins back. I like it too.

Chapter Forty-Two

The afternoon goes by quickly and more pleasantly than I could have expected. We're so busy that I don't have time to consider my nerves.

Everyone has oohed and aahed over the animals and they, in turn, have behaved quite nicely. Tina Turner hasn't nipped, hissed at or kicked out at anyone. There have been no unfortunate pee or poo-based incidents – which is never a given. Our bucket has clinked regularly with the sound of small change being deposited in return for selfies.

Our youngsters and their parents have had a lovely time too and I think that I should try to overcome my reticence and get out and about more with them. They've coped better than I could have possibly anticipated and I shouldn't foist my reluctance to meet other people on them. This has been a very good learning experience for all of us and I'm sure as well as raising money for the farm, it's benefited everyone hugely.

Lucas has just brought them all cupcakes from somewhere and is dishing them out. I feel that he's been a perfect host today and has coped admirably. He's been very solicitous of both the animals and his fellow students and I feel quite proud of him. The usual petulance has been little in evidence.

My dear Bev has flitted about like a social butterfly, loving every minute, and I have a feeling her champagne levels are quite high. She's going to be a right handful in the truck on the way home or she'll fall fast asleep. It could go either way.

As the evening beckons, the event starts to draw to a close. The musicians pack up their instruments, the food stalls are selling their last few goods and there's the clinking of glasses as the champagne tent tidies up. Before people start to drift away, Shelby Dacre takes to the stage and I leave the enclosure to stand near the front of the crowd that's gathered around him.

In his deep, rich voice he booms out, 'Thanks to everyone for coming along to support us. It's been a great day and the weather's been kind. Last year we were all in wellies and huddled under umbrellas!'

Everyone laughs.

'The charities who we support really benefit from this. Every penny of profit goes directly to them. This year we've added a new charity to our list – a place that's close to my own heart. I'd like to thank Hope Farm for bringing their students, animals and unicorns along for us to meet. I'm sure everyone has enjoyed that.'

Everyone claps and, if I'm not mistaken, above the gathered audience, Shelby's eyes lock with mine.

'So I'm pleased to announce that we've raised an enormous sum this year.'

He reels off a mind-boggling figure and the crowd of assembled actors and artistes all applaud. There are whistles and cheers too. Collectively, they have raised an awful lot of money. Some of these people must have dug very deep into their pockets.

Shelby holds up a hand. 'Thank you all for coming. Shall we do it again next year?'

More cheering.

'I'll take that as a yes!' Shelby waves to his guests. 'Enjoy the rest of your evening, folks. Drive home safely!'

He steps down and soon everyone starts to drift away. A team of helpers come to pick up litter, fold the blankets, move the hay bales, and put deckchairs away. I stand there feeling quite emotional and more than a little exhausted. It's been a great day and I'm quite overwhelmed by the generosity on display. We might only get a tiny slice of it, but it will make a huge amount of difference. I'm so pleased about how my team managed, too, and feel quite teary about it. I must find Shelby and thank him properly.

I'm desperate for a cup of tea and a sit down, but I need to think about loading up the animals and getting them home. Lucas appears at my side with another plate of cupcakes and two cups of tea.

'I've left Bev and Alan organising the animals with a few of the parents who are still here. You can take a few minutes out.'

'Can I?'

'Yes. They are able to manage without you every now and again, you know. Plus there's a nice view at the back that you should see.' He indicates the copse behind us. 'Want to sit down for a bit? You've been on your feet all afternoon.'

'So have you.'

'Yes, but I'm young and you are very old.'

'Cheeky,' I say to his grinning face. 'Come on then, show me this view.'

Chapter Forty-Three

So I follow Lucas through the narrow band of trees. It's cool beneath them – a welcome respite from the warmth of the day. On the other side, the sweep of the vale dips down before rising to a gentle hill in the near distance. In the field two jet-black horses chew at the grass. Other than that, the view is largely unbroken by any signs of human habitation.

'Beautiful.'

Lucas nods and I see a kind of sofa sculpted out of small hay bales. 'We have someone come in and do it every year,' he says. 'An artist that my father knows.'

'It suits the spot perfectly.' I sit down and he joins me. 'Perhaps we could do our own version at the farm.' He raises an eyebrow at me. 'It would be a good project.'

'If you say so.' Lucas looks around before he sighs and puts the plate of cakes and the tea between us. 'It was Mum's favourite place.'

'I can see why.' After choosing a cake that has a strawberry on the top, I take a swig of my tea which produces a satisfied 'Ooooh.'

'Good?' he asks.

'Great,' I say. 'Much needed. It's very thoughtful of you.'

'My pleasure.' He pulls his battered packet of cigarettes from his pocket.

I frown at him. 'What did I tell you about hay and cigarettes?'

'You told me that they don't mix,' he parrots. 'But this is my turf, my rules. If I want to, I can smoke sixty a day.'

'That would be a very bad idea.'

He shrugs and lights up. 'Doing things that no one approves of is the only pleasure I get at my age.'

'It won't always be like this.'

'Yeah?'

'I promise you.' We both relax back on the hay sofa. I link my arm through his and he doesn't pull away. 'Life is good, Lucas. Truly. Look for the small things every day. That's the way to find happiness.'

He snorts his derision, but doesn't otherwise argue. We sit in silence, taking in the view and, even if Lucas doesn't, I appreciate the few moments of quiet breathing space. Not only have the students and animals done well, but I think I've managed all right too given my aversion to being in public and people in general. I close my eyes and let the sun warm my face. It would be easy to sit here and rest my bones for a very long time. All I can hear is the song of a skylark and I feel my eyes grow heavy.

A few moments later, a voice beside me says, 'I wondered where you two had got to.'

I jolt awake, not even realising that I'd drifted off. I check my mouth for drool. Thankfully, there is none. Putting my hand up to shade the sun, I see Shelby standing in front of us. 'Have I been asleep?'

'Only for ten minutes or so,' Lucas says. 'I didn't want to wake you.' Though he sounds pleasant enough, I feel that his demeanour has changed instantly with the appearance of his father. His expression is back to sullen teenager setting.

183

'I didn't mean to disturb you,' Shelby says. 'I just came to say that you did a great job, Molly. That's a record sum we raised and having the animals here certainly helped.'

'Thank you.'

'I said I'd give you a contribution from the donations. How would two thousand pounds suit you?'

'That would be fantastic. I could get a new clutch for the truck with that.' Shelby laughs even though I don't think I've said anything funny. 'I didn't expect so much. That's very generous. We seem to have quite a lot in our buckets too, if you haven't counted that.'

'Keep whatever you've taken there. Just let me know how much and I can add it to the overall total. I'm pleased it was a success.'

'It was a lovely day,' I have to agree. 'My misgivings were completely unfounded.'

'Glad to hear it. You'll join us for supper? A few of my friends are staying behind.'

'Thank you, but I don't think so. I need to get the animals back and settle them for the night.'

'Ah.' He smiles at his son. 'Lucas, will you eat with us?'

'Have a wild guess,' Lucas snaps back.

Shelby's expression darkens. 'It's been a fantastic day for everyone and yet you have to spoil it. You just love to rain on my parade, don't you?'

Lucas smirks. 'It's my mission in life.'

His father holds up his hands. 'I give up. I'll get some food plated up and left in the kitchen for you.'

'Don't bother.'

Shelby shakes his head sadly, then turns back to me. He takes my hand in his and squeezes it. 'Thanks again, Molly. I'll see you again sometime.'

Then he walks away, hands in his pockets, shoulders slumped.

'Smug bastard,' Lucas mutters as he goes.

I fix him with a sideways glance. 'You're better than that.'

'I can't help it,' he says, defiantly. 'He's such a twat.'

'You were one too,' I tell him straight.

'So what?'

'Two wrong twats don't make a right twat,' I say, solemnly.

'What's that?' He stares blankly at me. 'Some kind of old wives' saying?'

'Yes,' I lie and, despite Lucas being determined to sulk, we both burst into fits of laughter.

Chapter Forty-Four

We load up and trundle home, happy but tired. When I get back to the farm, I feel as if we've done a good day's work and am content. Alan is still waiting patiently for us even though we're later than I had envisaged. I don't think he has much to rush home to, but that isn't the point. He's stayed and I'm grateful that he has.

Alan has already settled and fed the chickens and bunnies. Bev lets the tribe out of the truck and I take Tina's halter. The geese honk their displeasure at being disturbed. My friends must see me yawning behind my hand as they both stay to help me to put the rest of the animals to bed. Little Dog trots at my heel, supervising all of us.

When they're all safely tucked up, Bev hugs me. 'Nice one, Mols. You did really well today.'

'Thanks. I couldn't have managed without you both.'

Alan simply nods and heads towards his car. 'Thank you, Alan,' I call after him. 'You've been great!' He holds up a hand.

'He loved *every* minute,' Bev says and we both giggle as it's always hard to tell with Alan.

'What do we reckon for tomorrow?' Bev asks as we lean on the fence and watch him as he drives out of the gate.

'Hmm. I'm going with The Libertines.' The upside of not having a telly is that I do listen to a lot of music.

'Nice,' Bev says. 'I think I'll take The Kooks.'

'You might be in with a shout there,' I admit. 'We are overdue a sublime victory.'

We high-five each other. 'See you tomorrow, Mols. Love you to the moon and back.'

'Love you too.' I walk her to her car and lean on the door as she climbs in. 'Thanks for making me do it. You were right.'

'I'm always right,' she quips.

'Yeah. Except when it comes to Alan's band T-shirts.'

'Harsh,' she says and we both chuckle.

Closing the door, I then follow her car down to the gate so that I can lock up for the night. Big Dog lies under the van, too hot to be bothered to come on a walk. I do one last round of the animals, taking more time to say goodnight to the ones who haven't been with us today – Teacup, Sweeney and Carter, Johnny Rotten and Rod Stewart. All of my family.

Then I take a slow walk back to the caravan. Now that I'm at home again, the tension I've been holding is starting to go out of my shoulders. It may have been a great achievement today, but I'm glad that I'm back where I belong. It's been a long and busy day and I'm completely exhausted. All of my bones ache. Occasionally, I fantasise about a long, hot bath, but it's so long since I've had one that the image is beginning to fade. I used to be able to close my eyes and feel the warm water lapping over my skin, the scent of bubbles. But not any more. Washing now is a purely functional activity. I could certainly do with a shower – hot or cold – but can't face the rigmarole that involves and so resolve to get up earlier in the morning to do it. I'm just going to have to go to bed smelling of animal.

A teeny-tiny part of me kind of regrets not being able to stay to supper with Shelby. It's not as if I get offers like that every day and I would have loved a peek inside his stupendous palace of a house, but I hate social gatherings like that. They all seemed nice enough today, but what would I have had in common with his arty-farty friends? What would I have said to them? Would they have noticed that I carry with me at all times the faint whiff of sheep?

In the caravan, I force myself to make a cup of tea and a sandwich, both of which I gulp down. Then I sit on the sofa with a heartfelt sigh and, as usual, Little Dog joins me. Sometimes it would be nice to have another person here to talk to. This was a great day, the best, and yet I have no one to share it with. All my happy thoughts are just running round in my own head. I ruffle Little Dog's ears. 'You're not interested, are you, chummie?'

He pricks up his ears, but just nestles further into my lap. There's a pile of post on the table that's been mounting up all week and I really should deal with it. I live in hope that there might be a huge cheque in one of the envelopes. From what, I don't know. Maybe some mystery donor has left us a legacy in their will. Maybe I've won the lottery even though I've never actually bought a ticket.

Pulling the pile towards me, I slit open the envelopes with my thumb. None of it looks terribly interesting. Bills, bills, bills, spam. Bills, bills, spam. Pizza delivery leaflets. Bills. I'm tempted to push the bills down the back of the cushions. Although with our welcome windfall from the charity event today, I do have a chance of paying at least some of them, for once.

Then one catches my eye that makes me frown. This looks way too official for my liking. Letters like this bring me out in a cold sweat. With mounting trepidation, I open it and unfold the letter inside. As my eyes scan the contents, a knot of dread starts to form in my stomach.

Chapter Forty-Five

The heading on the letter is NOTICE TO END TENANCY which is never going to be a good start. It's from our landlord's solicitor and he is actually issuing a notice to say that we have ninety days to leave our farm. I scan it again just to make sure. Ninety days. To leave.

I feel like someone has punched the breath out of me. I sit back on the sofa, panting. I don't think I've ever hyperventilated before, but this feels pretty close to it.

I read on. This can't be right. I've been a good tenant. I've always paid the rent on time – quite frequently by the skin of my teeth – but it's never, ever been even a day late. I always make sure of that. I've lived here for years. And not just me, but Hettie before. It's my home. I've made my life here. I've never caused him a moment's trouble. How can he ask me to leave?

Pressing on, my hands shake as I hold the piece of paper. The land, it seems, has been compulsory purchased as part of the new trainline project, HS2. The track is to go right through here, slicing the farm in two. I have to stop and make myself breathe as I can't quite believe what I'm reading. I'd heard Bev muttering about the plans for this to be built near here, but it never for a moment occurred to me that it would directly affect us. Perhaps if I paid more attention to the news or read the local paper, then I'd have been in the loop. But we don't get the local paper delivered here as no one wants to make the trek up our lane.

I drop the letter onto the table, stunned, shocked. What would Hettie think of all this? What can I do? It looks as if there's no way of fighting this. It's very much presented as a done deal. It's seems as if our landlord has no choice in the matter either. George Brown has, literally, had to sell the land from under us. He must be just as gutted as I am as this farm, this land, has been in his family for generations. Our impending eviction isn't his fault and I wonder if that's why he hasn't come down here to tell me himself.

Staring out of the caravan window and into the darkness beyond, I can't get my mind to focus on what we might do. I'm devastated. That much I know. What will happen to the students? The people who depend on me? I can't fold the charity as I couldn't manage without it either. What will happen to my beloved animals? Where will we go?

Crumpling the letter up, I head to my bed. I don't even get undressed. I just lie on top of the covers and stare at the ceiling. Sensing my despair, Little Dog whimpers as he lies down next to me and I cry myself to sleep for the first time since my dear aunt Hettie died.

Chapter Forty-Six

I barely sleep at all. At four o'clock I give in to wakefulness and get up. Little Dog isn't impressed. He drags himself from under the duvet and mopes around the caravan. I can't face breakfast as my stomach is churning and I feel nauseous, so I don't even make a pretence of opening the cupboards. I feed the dogs and Fifty. Even the smell of the food makes me want to heave.

On auto-pilot, I fill the bucket with warm water and take it out to the shower at the back of the barn. I stand under it, but one bucket fails to hit the spot and instead of feeling refreshed, I simply feel bedraggled. It would be nice to have someone here to fill me another bucket.

I quickly dry myself before the chill sets in. It's a fresh morning, not ideal for outdoor showering. I feel numb today and, when I go back into the caravan, I sit and have another good cry. My brain is spinning with so many questions that I can't even think straight.

When I can't cry any more and my eyeballs are raw, I go through the early morning chores like a robot. Usually, dealing with the animals soothes my soul. Today, I look at them and just feel guilty. Every time I tend to one or other of them, a big ball of emotion lodges in my throat. Teacup grunts at me in greeting as he struggles from sleep and I could lie on the floor next to him and weep. Who will love him as much as I do? Fifty and Little Dog mooch around after me, sensing my sombre mood. What if I end up in some housing association where I can't even have a pet? Lots of them don't allow dogs or even cats. I bet there are precious few that would permit a pet lamb.

I have three months to raise more money and find a new home for them. Is that even doable? At this moment, it seems like an unsurmountable task. But who will take my babies? I'd have to fall on the mercy of various animal charities and they'd be split up. What if they all ended up in different parts of the country or worse? It may sound stupid, but we're like a family. We belong together. Except for Anthony the Anti-Social Sheep, who hates everyone. Yet I couldn't even bear to be parted from him, no matter how many times he tries to headbutt me in the backside.

I walk up to the top fields and feed the ponies and Sweeney and Carter. How do you rehome two Shire horses? These two boys love being in their field together. How can I separate them? My head throbs with the pain of thinking and I rest my face against Sweeney's soft muzzle, whispering to him, 'What am I going to do?'

But it seems that he has no answers.

My mobile rings and it's Bev's number.

'Hey,' she says and her voice is croaky. 'I'm not well. Must be something I ate.'

She certainly sounds like death warmed up. Neither of us mention the word hangover. 'OK.'

'I'll be in later. Can you manage without me for a bit?'

'Yes, of course.' Now isn't the moment to tell her about the letter as I know she'll be as gutted as I am. Plenty of time for that later. Besides, I'm not sure that I could actually get the words out. I hope her hangover clears quickly as I need her calm and clear-headed so that she might come up with the miraculous solution that's staring at us right in the face. 'I'll see you when you get here.'

'You sound like bum too,' she notes.

'I feel like bum.'

'I'll see you as soon as I can get my eyes to focus and we can be bum together.'

'Yeah.'

'Laters.' She hangs up and I sniff back some tears. Bev has no idea what I'm about to hit her with.

Alan arrives wearing Snow Patrol and I could kick myself for not thinking of them. Still, another day, another band T-shirt.

'All right,' he says, but heads straight into the barn without waiting for my reply, so I can't tell him that I'm not all right at all.

Busying myself, I collect the hen's eggs, wash them and, generally, kick round the yard getting sadder by the minute. I wish I could marshal my thoughts into some kind of order and then I might be able to formulate a plan. But joined-up thinking is eluding me. I go and cuddle a chicken instead. Sitting in the corner of the coop with Peg-with-one-leg on my lap, the refrain that's becoming familiar goes on a loop in my head. Who will want a one-legged hen who falls over a lot? Who will take on our blind ladies? For the life of me, I can't think of anyone who will.

When Peg grows bored with me and hops off my lap, I go to see the alpacas. They, at least, will be snapped up, I'm sure. Alpacas are fashionable. They might sometimes behave like evil personified but they look undeniably cute. People like cute.

I get the feed bucket and fill it. Tina Turner, Johnny Rotten and Rod Stewart crowd around me, all jostling for the best place.

'You might be getting a new home soon,' I tell them.

But they don't give a fig. They flounce their pom-pom hair, guzzle their breakfast and generally behave as if they haven't a care in the world. I'm the one who's weighed down with sorrow.

Chapter Forty-Seven

I hear the wheels of a car coming up the lane. Unusually, the first car to arrive this morning is Shelby Dacre's, so I leave the alpacas and head to unlock the gate and let him in. His sleek car sweeps into the yard.

Lucas jumps out first and the boot lid lifts silently. 'Wellies,' he says, brightly, holding a pair aloft. 'I brought loads. I said I would.'

'Thank you.'

He looks up at me and is obviously disappointed by my less than enthusiastic response. 'Don't go too over the top.'

'Sorry,' I say. 'Just a bit distracted. The wellies are fantastic. I'll help you to put them in the barn.'

'I can manage,' Lucas snaps, so easily wounded.

'I'm *really* sorry,' I insist. 'I'm not thinking straight. I've had some bad news.'

That does make Lucas pause and, by then, Shelby is out of the car too.

'What's that? Bad news?' Shelby says and frankly, that's enough to make me burst into tears.

'I'm sorry. So sorry.' I wipe away my tears with my sleeve. 'I shouldn't be troubling you with this.'

'Nonsense.' He turns to Lucas. 'Put the kettle on, son. This is clearly something that requires tea.'

So Lucas abandons the wellies and heads off into the tea room. Shelby touches my arm. 'Yesterday was a triumph,' he says.

'Yes. Thank you for that.'

'No, thank *you*. I wanted to drop Lucas off this morning myself so that I could tell you again. The animals were a big hit. So were the students. You all did very well.'

I think Shelby understands what a trial it had been for me.

'You should have stayed for supper,' he adds. 'You'd have enjoyed it.'

I wouldn't. Perhaps he doesn't understand at all.

'Shall we go and see how Lucas is getting on with that tea and you can tell me what's happened?'

I nod and, to my surprise, he takes my hand and squeezes it gently. He leads me to the tea room and we both sit on the sofa. I'd very much like to curl up under one of the crocheted blankets and pull it over my head.

When we're settled, he says, 'Now then?'

Shelby frowns at me as I start to fill up and have to wait until my throat clears before I can begin to speak. All the time he holds my hand which is both disconcerting and comforting at the same time.

'I've had a letter from my landlord's solicitor,' I eventually manage to tell him in a wavering voice. 'The farm has been purchased under compulsory order to make way for the new HS2 trainline. I've got three months to find somewhere else.' Which, of course, prompts a fresh deluge of tears. 'I have no idea what to do.'

Shelby Dacre sucks in a breath. 'Not good.'

'No.' I can hardly disagree.

'That's shit,' Lucas says over his shoulder. 'Total shit.'

196

I can't disagree with that either.

Shelby lowers his voice so that Lucas can't hear him over the noisy boiling kettle. 'I can tell this is a great place. Though he won't admit it to me, I know that Lucas loves it here. I'm sure that the other kids who come to you feel the same. You only have to look at them. It's brilliant. They can't simply shut it down.'

'Unfortunately, they can.'

Lucas comes over, plonks down three cups of weak, milky tea and sits in the armchair opposite us, scowling.

'There must be something we can do?' Shelby says.

That 'something' is not, currently, apparent. We all sit in silence.

Shelby is the first to speak. 'Look, I'm having some people round for supper on Friday night,' he pipes up. 'Some of the cast from *Flinton's Farm*, some movers and shakers in the industry. Why don't you come along too, Molly, and see if we can come up with any bright ideas? I have contacts who can make things happen.'

'I don't know . . . '

Shelby tuts at me. 'I've already gathered that you hate this kind of thing, but this is how the world works. This is how you raise funds. If you want to survive, it has to be done. Lucas, you'll come along too, won't you?'

Lucas looks horrified at being put on the spot. I know that he'd rather prise out his own eyeballs, yet he turns to me and says, 'I'll go if you'll go.'

'I have nothing to wear.'

Lucas laughs darkly. 'Trust me, that is the *least* of your problems.'

True. And I don't know why I even said that as my personal appearance is, as Lucas noted, a long way down my list of problems. I confess that I had a fleeting vision of Scarlett Vincent sitting across the table from me dressed head-to-toe in a white designer number with her ample charms on show. Not even my very best jumper and jeans can compete with that.

'I'll try to help you all that I can,' Shelby promises. 'People are suckers for animals in peril.'

He can tell that I'm crumbling.

'Say you'll come,' he urges.

Despite my aversion to socialising, I'm desperate and Shelby is being very kind. So, with heaviness weighing down my heart, I say, 'Yes.'

Chapter Forty-Eight

'Fuck,' Bev says when I tell her. She has her head in her hands.

'I know.'

'What are we going to do?'

'I don't know.'

Bev eventually rocked up at eleven o'clock. She looks very fragile. I'm thinking the drinking must have carried on after she went home last night. Though she was quite voluble in the truck on the way back from the Shelby estate.

Despite the hour, I still haven't moved from the tea room. I simply can't mobilise myself today. It's not just my brain that's frozen, it's my body too. Lucas has stepped up to the plate and has taken it upon himself to organise the team. He's supervised loading all the wellies he brought into the barn with the help of Jack and Seb. Then he popped his head round the door to say that he was taking the lads and the rest of the students who are here today up into the fields. I don't know what he's doing with them. I should go and check. He could be teaching them something unspeakable.

However, instead of doing that, I put the kettle on again and make more tea – even though I'm not expecting to find my solution at the bottom of a cup. My limbs are as heavy as lead and I can no more face trekking up the hill than I can flying to the moon. Besides, Bev and I have things to discuss. If the farm has to close, it will affect her as much as it affects me.

'Shelby Dacre's asked me to go to his house for supper on Friday to talk to his influential friends about fundraising.'

'He was here?'

'Early. He dropped Lucas off today.'

'Dammit,' Bev mutters. 'The one day I can't get my back off the bed.'

'I've agreed to go,' I tell her. 'But I'm terrified.'

'I'll go in your place! I had a snoop through the windows when we were at the charity day, but I'd give anything for a good old nosey round his mansion.' She looks a bit dreamy. 'I could play footsie with him under the dining-room table.'

I know she'd stand in for me in a heartbeat and, in many ways, it would be much more sensible. Bev isn't socially inept like me, she could charm the birds out of the trees given a gin and tonic or two. She wouldn't melt like a snowflake in the face of Scarlett Vincent's searing beauty. But, in a weird way, I want to go too. 'I should show willing,' I say, lamely.

'Wow. Hold those horses! Your enthusiasm is making me giddy.'

'This *is* me being enthusiastic about it!'

Bev shakes her head. 'Gawd help us.' She pours us both more tea. 'It's a good opportunity, Mols. You can rub shoulders with some celebs who are keen to flash some cash in a good cause. They're all the same.'

She could be right in her assessment. Bev certainly knows more about the world of celebrity than I do, even if it's vicariously through glossy mags.

'I don't suppose you've got anything to wear?'

'I'm thinking jeans and wellies won't cut it.' When I took over the farm, I sold all my clothes at a car boot sale, just keeping what I needed for working. Space is at a premium in the caravan and I've no room for unwanted clutter. Not that I had much in the way of ballgowns to start with. 'I could go to the charity shop. See what they've got that's suitable for hob-nobbing with celebrities?'

'No. I'll bring something in for you.'

'Nothing too . . . well . . . er . . . ' She gives me a black look as I search for a word that won't offend her. 'Glamorous. Nothing low-cut. Nothing with diamante.'

Bev always looks great when she goes out, but she dresses much more flashily than I ever would. She can carry it off, whereas I'd probably be mistaken for a drag queen.

'Shall I bring a few bin liners and a belt?'

I grin. 'Maybe a little more than that.'

'I'll come and do your make-up too.'

'No make-up.' I hold up a hand. 'It's just not me.'

Her stare says that she despairs of me. 'You've got to look like you've made a bit of an effort, Mols.'

'I will,' I promise. 'I'll pick all of the straw out of my hair. I might even wash it.'

'You kill me,' she says and then sighs heavily. 'We should go and see what these students are up to. Lucas is probably teaching them all swear words.'

'I thought much the same.' Though I do appreciate that he's had the wherewithal to take over the organisation of the younger kids. He obviously appreciated that I'm in no fit state for rational thinking yet and needed some space. That's great progress for him too. It should make him feel good that the other kids are happy to follow him without question.

'He's a nice kid,' Bev says. 'You can't help but like him. He just needs someone to look after him.'

'I've tried to tell Mr Dacre as much, but it's all falling on deaf ears at the moment.'

201

'He seems like a decent enough bloke,' she says. 'Bit self-obsessed, but what actor isn't?'

Again we are straying into the territory of Things-I-Know-Nothing-Of.

'Had enough medicinal tea?'

'Yeah.' Bev forces herself to stand. 'I'm not getting any younger. The menopause is a miserable bitch. Can't tolerate alcohol these days. I just have to remind myself every now and again.'

'Walk up to the field with me?'

Bev nods. We head out of the tea room and across the yard. Bev links her arm in mine and pulls me into her. 'We'll sort something out,' she says. 'You wait and see. I don't want you to worry.'

But, of course I'm going to worry. What else can I do?

'What was Alan wearing this morning?' she asks.

'Snow Patrol.'

She sucks in a breath. 'Didn't see that one coming.'

'Me neither.'

'Have you told him yet?'

'No,' I admit. 'I should go and find him. Perhaps he's got millions stashed under his bed that he'd happily throw our way.'

'You never can tell with Alan,' Bev says sagely and with that, we stride up towards the fields.

But as we round the corner and reach the big barn we can hear Lucas speaking loudly and we both turn to look at each other.

'What's he doing?' I whisper.

Bev shrugs that she's none the wiser than me. 'It sounds like he's taking a class or something?'

We tiptoe towards the sound and stand hidden by the back of the tractor. I'm surprised to see that Lucas has all the students sitting in a line on hay bales and they're rapt with attention –

which in itself is a rare thing. He's spitting out poetry to them – the stuff he writes, I assume. Bev and I exchange another glance, eyebrows raised. He's angry, passionate, chanting his rhymes with great panache. If you ask me, the boy is a born performer. The gangly awkwardness of his body is gone and he moves to the beat of his words, his voice is clear, strong.

'His dad doesn't even know he writes poetry,' I whisper.

'He's good,' Bev whispers back. 'Didn't see that one coming either.'

Me neither.

Chapter Forty-Nine

Friday comes. Too soon, of course.

'You'll be fine,' Bev says.

I won't.

We're in my caravan, the sun is shining and I have a ton of things to do. Every fibre of my being wants to be outside. One of the chickens, Pimms, looked a bit off-colour on my last egg collection and I want to have another look at her. Actually, I need to pop back to check on them all before I go out tonight otherwise I'd worry myself sick.

Bev and I have left Alan in charge while we sloped off for five minutes. The supply teacher is here this afternoon for two hours so all of the students are occupied with lessons. It's the bit they like the least and I have to sympathise. The teachers we have here are, generally, good quality but they are trying to teach pupils who have, so far, proved unteachable in the traditional manner. I'd rather have my job than theirs. Lucas is sulking more than most. He's back in difficult child mode today, so different from the confident young man we secretly saw performing with such aplomb the other day. He's a complex one, that's for sure.

While my mind is still on Lucas, Bev pulls a crumpled dress out of an Aldi carrier bag and holds it up. 'Ta-dah!'

It's leopard-skin print, short and looks pretty low-cut by my standards.

'It doesn't even need ironing,' Bev says. 'Your body heat stretches it out. It kind of clings everywhere.' Then she glances up at me and sees my horrified face. 'What? Don't give me that look. You can *so* carry this off. You're not a flipping pensioner, Mols. You're not even forty. Show some of your figure off. You've got a good body under those shapeless jumpers.'

It's so long since I've seen myself in a full-length mirror that I couldn't tell you whether I have or not.

'I did have something a little more conservative in mind,' I confess. I should have taken myself off to the local charity shop as I suggested and had a good rummage on the rails. A pastime I deplore. I don't know how people get off on shopping. I'd rather clean out a pigsty any day of the week.

Bev tosses the dress to me. 'Get it on, woman. Stop moaning.'

I strip off my jeans and pull it on, wriggling it over my hips. I know how a sausage feels inside its skin.

'Gorgeous,' she pronounces. 'Fits you like a glove.'

A very tight glove. I try to see myself in the caravan windows, but it's hopeless.

'I'd have a shower, if I were you. The smell of horse tends to linger.'

I wonder if I've got any perfume tucked in the back of a drawer somewhere. Sometimes Aunt Hettie liked a spray of *Je Reviens*. 'I'm going to have a shower *and* wash my hair.'

'All of the joys.' She magics another carrier bag from nowhere. 'And, despite your protests, I brought make-up.'

'No.'

'Just a bit,' she insists. 'A flick of mascara. Some lippy.'

'I can't do it now. I've still got jobs to do.'

205

'I'll finish them. Or Alan can. You need time to chill, get in the mood.'

'If I think about it too much, then I won't go at all.'

'Go and have your shower. I'm going to bring Teacup in for the night. He's still out in the paddock with the goats. I'll catch you later.'

'OK.' Bev leaves – her carrier of make-up discarded on the sofa. I'm tempted to hide it, but haven't the nerve. It is easier to submit to make-up than to defy Bev.

I put the kettle on to boil for my shower. Usually, I wait until everyone has left for the day or get up early in the morning as showering outdoors doesn't offer the height of privacy. While the kettle boils, I nip out and manoeuvre the tractor next to the shower to provide a screen. I just hope that Alan doesn't decide he needs it for something in the next ten minutes. In the end I bottle it and find an old swimsuit in the bottom of one of my drawers which I keep on.

As it's a special occasion, I fill two buckets with warm water. I hook one up to the shower attachment and then stand underneath as I tip it over me. Quickly, I wash my hair and then deploy the second bucket to rinse it. This is the equivalent of me enjoying a spa day.

I'm drying my hair, pleased not to have flashed any of my students or distant neighbours, when Bev returns.

'How's Teacup?'

'Adorable,' she says. 'We really should get another pig. He could do with some company.'

'I thought about getting a few more pigs. We could have made a nice, piggy hollow for them near the trees in the bottom field.' I sigh miserably. 'It's not going to happen now though, is it?' I remind her. 'We're going to have to find new homes for everyone soon.'

'Not if you knock 'em dead tonight.' She pulls her carrier

bag of make-up towards her. Damn. 'I'll make you look *so* beautiful that they'll be throwing cash at you.'

'I'm not actually sure that's the impression I want to give.'

'Ah. See what you mean,' Bev says.

'Shall I put the dress on now?'

'Yes. Otherwise you'll have to drag it over your head and it will mess up your hair and make-up.'

As I have no choice but to submit myself to Bev's ministrations, I wrestle myself into her dress once more.

'Very fetching.' She gives me an admiring glance. 'Sit down. Time for your slap.'

'Don't make me look like a pantomime dame.'

'As if.'

So, while I sit wincing, Bev flicks at me with brushes, rubs potions and lotions onto my face. Then she fluffs my hair and sprays things on it until she's deemed that I'm done.

'There,' she says. 'That's better.'

I'm not sure what her definition of 'better' is, but I don't think that I want to look in the mirror.

'You'll be the belle of the ball.'

What I actually want to do is blend quietly into a corner where no one will notice me. But I brave it and have a look in the mirror over the sink that serves as both kitchen and bathroom sink. I'm quite shocked at the person looking back at me. Though in a good way. Despite seeming to apply pounds of foundation and goodness knows what else, the look is surprisingly natural. It enhances my features and highlights some I'd forgotten were there. 'Blimey.'

'You like?'

'Yes,' I admit, grudgingly. 'I do.'

'Under all that cow shit and general farm detritus there lurks a very beautiful woman.'

I look at myself this way and that. 'Who knew?' I still wish that I didn't have so much chest and leg on show. Perhaps I can find one of Hettie's scarves or something. I have sleeves though. I should be thankful for that.

'I'll be off,' Bev says, gathering her make-up into her bag. 'Have a good evening. Relax. Have a couple of glasses of something to loosen you up.'

'Do I want to be loose?'

'Loose but not slack,' is Bev's advice. 'Come back with a plan to rescue the farm.'

'I'll do my best,' I promise.

She kisses my cheek. 'That's all anyone can ever ask of you.'

Chapter Fifty

What Bev doesn't know is that I'm going to pop and see the chickens before I leave – frock or no frock. I pull on my wellies and hurry across the yard. Bev has lent me stilettos to wear too, but as they are potential ankle-breakers, I'm going to put them on at the last possible moment.

Lucas is waiting for me in the tea room. His car is coming a bit later so that it can take us both back to his house. Shelby has kindly organised for me to be brought home later too, so I don't have to worry about driving and can have a drink or three as Bev advised. It's a lovely evening and I wonder if we'll have cocktails served out on the fabulous terrace overlooking the garden and, despite my fears, I get a tickle of excitement in my tummy.

I stick my head round the door. 'Nearly ready, Lucas. I'm just going to have quick look at Pimms, make sure she's all right.'

He glances up from his phone and does a double-take. 'I didn't recognise you all done up like that.' He looks at me a bit goggle-eyed. 'Maybe lose the wellies, though.'

We both regard my muddy boots.

Then Lucas's expression darkens. 'There's no point in going to any effort for *him*, you know. He won't even notice.'

'Bev's idea, not mine,' I say, apologetically. 'I didn't have any choice.'

He makes a mollified, harrumphing noise. 'You look nice though. Hot even.' He grins cheekily at me. 'For a woman of your age.'

'Thanks, Lucas.' We have a giggle together. I smooth down the leopard-print number. 'I'm not a dress kind of person.'

He shrugs. 'Maybe you should wear them more often. It might get Alan hot under the collar.'

'Not sure I could cope with that. Or how I'd even tell.'

'He's a good bloke,' Lucas says. 'I like being with him. He might not say much, but he's kind of cool. In his own way.'

'That's good to know. What did you do today?'

'Oh, this and that. We did some stuff out in the fields. The lesson was as boring as fuck.'

I think they're probably far below Lucas's level. He's a very intelligent boy, quick to learn and he needs a lot of stimulation to keep him interested. I'll have to see what else we can do if he's going to stay on. Perhaps I'll have an opportunity to talk to Shelby about it. I'm sure if I suggested a private tutor for him then money wouldn't be an object. That's definitely not the problem here.

I hoped he'd tell me about performing his poetry for the students, but clearly it's not going to happen without prompting. I'll find my moment though. Now I check my watch. 'Our ride will be here in a minute, I'll nip out to see the hens.'

Lucas pushes himself out of the sofa. 'I'll come with you.'

We never lock up here because a) there's never anyone around and b) there's nothing worth pinching. I do a quick scan as we leave though and am pleased to note that Lucas has done all the washing-up without even being asked. I nod towards the draining board where all the mugs and plates are neatly stacked. 'Thanks for that. I appreciate it.'

He shrugs, never finding it easy to accept praise.

We fall into step together and Lucas opens the gate to the chicken run, letting me pass through first. We dodge under the escape-proof netting.

Pimms is sitting in the corner, looking just as lethargic as she did earlier. 'Hmm,' I say. 'Not good.'

We go over and have a closer look at her. 'Her crop's enlarged,' I tell Lucas. 'Look here.' I show him the lump in her throat. 'It could be lodged food or something more serious. I think I need to get her to the vet.'

'Can we take her on the way to supper?' he asks.

'Sounds like a plan,' I say. 'I'll only worry.'

Lucas's car comes to the gate and toots his horn. 'Looks like our ride is here. I'll get the driver to take us down there.'

'The vet is only in the village. You nip and tell him while I go and find a carry box for Pimms.'

Lucas looks worried. 'She'll be all right, though?'

'I hope so. He's a good vet and well used to us by now.' It doesn't mean that he gives us mates' rates though.

Chapter Fifty-One

The driver drops us right outside the veterinary surgery in the village. It's quite the smoothest ride I've ever had to the vets, even though I had a hen in a box on my lap. Luckily, the vet stays open late each evening and Friday night is often quiet. I know this from long and expensive experience.

We jump out of the car, me thanking the driver profusely. He didn't look too impressed about having either me or the chicken in the back of his shiny Mercedes. Though Pimms seemed happy enough on the ride. In fact she seems to perk up a bit and I wonder if we are on a wild goose chase – or hen chase. You know what I mean. Perhaps this could have waited until morning. Too late to think about that now.

'We shouldn't be long,' I say to the driver as he settles down with a newspaper.

Famous last words.

Lucas and I go into the surgery and my heart sinks as we go inside. Of course – the one and only time I'm in a rush, there's a queue. The waiting room is rammed with people armed with coughing cats, puking puppies, elderly and most likely flatulent dogs. Then there's me bringing up the rear with an ailing chicken.

'Shit,' Lucas mutters as he takes it all in. He wrinkles his nose. 'It smells like cat piss in here.'

'That's probably because, at one time or another, a lot of cats *have* pissed in here,' I hiss. 'It's never going to smell of Chanel No 5, is it?'

Lucas smothers a smile.

I book us in at reception and if the receptionist thinks my leopard-skin-print outfit is a bit OTT for a trip to the vet, she makes no comment. We take our place in the waiting room. I put Pimms on my lap and open her box so that she can have a look round, but she's limp again after her ride in the limo and is not really interested. I stroke her feathers to soothe her.

'We could be here for frigging *hours*,' Lucas notes and he's right as it's much busier than usual.

'You should go on ahead,' I tell him.

'Can't we jump the queue?'

'No.'

He rolls his eyes. He might not like his father's celebrity status but, clearly, there are times when it would come in handy.

'There's no point in us both sitting here. You can still make it in time for supper. Explain to your dad that I'll be along as soon as I can.'

'He'll be *seriously* pissed off.'

'These things happen,' I counter. 'Especially when your life revolves around animals. Unfortunately, they don't care what time the canapés are being served. If you prefer, I'll talk to him and explain.'

'Yeah? Good luck with that. I've been trying to have a conversation for the last year since Mum died. Ain't gonna happen. He's always too busy.'

'Tonight, he does have an excuse.' I think of his guests, chatting, laughing, waiting for us and feel guilty. I do wonder again whether Pimms could have waited for treatment until tomorrow, but you never know, do you? It could be a case of well-aimed antibiotics or it could be something much more serious. And I don't want the guilt of an innocent hen's death on my hands for the sake of a dinner party.

'There's always an excuse,' Lucas bats back. 'Filming, award ceremony, young actress to shag.'

'Perhaps he's lonely.'

Lucas makes a disdainful noise. 'He hides it well.'

'People do strange things when they're grieving.'

'You're telling me.'

I fish in my bag and find a packet of Polo mints in lieu of dinner. I hand them to Lucas. 'We could be here a while.'

He takes one and then, with a sigh, says, 'I'll text him.' So he punches in a message to his father explaining our predicament. We wait for a bit, but there's no reply. Lucas sighs again.

'Want to play I Spy with my Little Eye?'

'No.'

We both sigh. I offer Lucas another Polo. The dog next to us farts and we both waft it away. The puppy next-door-but-one is sick on the floor.

'This is *totally* gross,' Lucas complains.

'You should go to your dad's party.'

'So should you.' We both look at the forlorn chicken on my lap. Lucas doesn't move. We sit there quietly until he eventually says, 'Everybody loves him. But he's a knob, you know?'

'He loves you. Even though he can't show it. I know he does.'

'Tonight would have been hideous,' he continues. 'It proves just how awful, as I'm choosing to sit here in Stinky Central rather than be there. I was only going because of you. When he's with his showbusiness friends he behaves like a wankery actor. Even more than usual.'

'Him being a wankery actor pays all the bills,' I feel the need to point out. 'By all accounts he's very good at what he does.'

'He doesn't want me to go into performing arts. He bangs on about it all the time. He wants me to get a "proper" job.'

This is my moment. 'Is that why you haven't told him about the poetry?'

There's a long pause before he says, 'Yeah. Suppose so.'

'I heard you performing some of your work to the students the other day. In the barn.'

'I didn't know that.' He frowns. 'You sneaked up on me?'

'Yes.' I smile at him to disarm his displeasure. 'I hid behind the tractor to listen. You were good. A natural performer.'

'All you know about is chickens and shit.'

'You're right,' I agree. 'My opinion is entirely pointless.'

He looks up, slightly abashed. 'Sorry.'

The vet's assistant calls out, 'Pickles!' and an ancient couple pick up a carrier with an equally ancient cat inside. I'm guessing they might not have had the offer to attend a celebrity party instead.

'Can you do that as a job?' I ask. 'Be a poet?'

'I don't know.'

'Even if you can, I expect it wouldn't pay much.'

'You sound like my father. It's not all about money.'

'I'm the expert in doing things for love.' We both look at Pimms again. 'It can be a tough way to live, especially if you're—'

'A spoilt brat.'

'I was going to say, especially if you're used to more.' And Lucas is definitely used to having more of everything than most of us.

'You can earn money as a vlogger these days.'

I shake my head. 'You speak a language I don't understand.'

'Christ, Molly, you really do live in a time warp. I record my stuff and put it on my YouTube channel.'

'Really? That sounds terribly enterprising. Can anyone watch?'

215

Lucas rolls his eyes, but he pulls out his phone from his pocket and a set of tiny earphones. 'Stick these in.'

So I do as I'm told and put the earphones in. Lucas fiddles with the phone, then hands it to me. On the screen I can see him performing one of his poems. It just looks like he's in his bedroom filming himself. The poem's called *Without You* and, again, it's angry and poignant.

> *It still goes on without you;*
> *life still goes on for me,*
> *it'll never be the same, though;*
> *not how it's meant to be.*
> *They tell me it gets easier*
> *with every passing day,*
> *but how could I accept that cancer stole my mum away?*
> *It still goes on without you;*
> *life still goes on for us,*
> *but it's a lacklustre alternative,*
> *and ever will be thus,*
> *without you here to guide me;*
> *I won't know what to do,*
> *without you here beside me:*
> *on hand to help me through.*
> *Life still goes on without you;*
> *it still goes on for those,*
> *who kill and maim and terrorise,*
> *because that's just how it goes!*
> *Life goes on without you,*
> *and I'll do the best I can;*
> *I just wish you could have stayed around 'til I was an old man.*

As I listen to the words, I find tears filling my eyes. I hate to think of Lucas with so much pain stored up inside and I'm glad

216

that he's at least found this avenue of release for it. Would that he could channel all his energy this way. He could do great things, I'm sure.

'It's good,' I say with a sniff. 'Very good.'

Lucas looks surprisingly vulnerable when he asks, 'You really think so?'

I do. I want to give him a great big hug and I think that he might let me, but then the vet's assistant calls out 'Pimms!'

So we pick up the chicken and take her to see the vet.

Chapter Fifty-Two

It turns out that Pimms has Sour Crop. Just as I thought. If you're not into chickens then you really don't want to know the ins and outs. Suffice to say that she required a little operation and is being kept in at the vets' over the weekend. Thankfully, she seems to be doing well and I'm not even trying to think about the cost. A sleepover at a vets is never going to be cheap. I could probably check her into The Ritz for less.

It was way too late to go to Shelby's party by the time we'd finished at the surgery. Lucas got the driver to drop me off at the farm before he went home. I texted Shelby to apologise profusely for my absence, even though it seemed a bit lame to blame it on a sick chicken. I wanted to call, but I was too nervous to speak to him. I think I must be a little bit starstruck, like Bev. Needless to say, she was very disappointed that I didn't go on Friday, but could understand why. Kind of. She said that I should have called her and she would have taken over chicken duties as she was only sitting in watching Graham Norton. To be honest, I didn't even think of it.

It was nearly midnight when Lucas and I left the vets. We waited while Pimms had emergency surgery. Then we waited some more until she was out of danger and settled. My eyes were rolling with tiredness when the car dropped me off at the gate before whisking him away.

Despite being emotionally drained, as soon as I was home I did a quick late-night tour of the animals, who were all perfectly fine. When one of your charges is poorly, it kind of makes you paranoid about the others and I gave the rest of them an extra fuss. Back in the caravan, I scrubbed off all my lovely make-up, folded Bev's dress nicely and wondered when the next time would be that I'd get another opportunity to wear something like that.

Saturday went by in a blur of chores, so now it's Sunday and my one day off in the week from students. I still don't get a lie-in as the animals would be bringing the place down for their breakfast, but I can relax a bit for the rest of the time. I should look at the accounts, think about how we're going to shape our future and that kind of thing – but my brain is still largely in denial about it all. The problems seem too vast to surmount.

Getting a deckchair out from under the van, I set it up facing the sun. I should have some novels here as I used to like to read, but I simply never find the time now. I'm sure Bev could lend some to me. Instead, I make a cuppa, settle down and let the weight of the sunshine close my lids.

I think I must be dozing, as I'm roused by the sound of the dogs barking, the geese honking and a car pulling up at the gate. I put a hand to my eyes to see who it is and am surprised that it's Shelby Dacre's car waiting patiently to be admitted.

'Oh, Christ,' I mutter to myself and brush down my jeans. He always manages to catch me off-guard. I scurry off to the gate and unlock it. The dogs are hot on my heels.

I hold up a hand in greeting as he swings into the yard. He pulls up and gets out of the car. The dogs wag their tails, but he doesn't bend to pet them as most people do and Little Dog looks more than a bit miffed that his enthusiastic greeting isn't rewarded. Fifty, roused from snoozing in his favourite sunny spot by Teacup's pen, comes over to have a look too.

Today, Shelby's clad in jeans and a black T-shirt. I'm only telling you what he's wearing as I think you might be interested. Obviously, I'm not. He does look very handsome though, as always. I can see why Bev insists he's the darling of the soap operas.

'Sorry, to drop in on you unannounced,' he says. 'I was passing. Thought I'd see if you were here. On the off-chance.'

'I'm never anywhere else,' I tell him.

'Except at the vets'.'

'Ah, yes. I can only apologise again. I was going to ring but I'm really, really bad at making phone calls.'

He fixes me with a gaze that's quite perturbing. 'It wasn't just an excuse?'

'No. Of course not. I was all dolled up and everything.'

'That I would have liked to see.'

'Well, I think you missed your one chance,' I confess.

'You would have enjoyed it,' he says.

Would I though? I would more likely have found the whole thing a terrible ordeal. 'I'm afraid my life is governed by my animals. It was awful timing. But then these things usually are.'

'Lucas said it was a sick chicken that took you away from me.'

'Yes.'

'The offending chicken is OK now?'

I shrug. 'Maybe. She's still at the vets'. I'm trying not to think of the cost.'

'Will you let me pay the bill?'

'Yes,' I say instantly. 'I have no shame when it comes to accepting handouts for the animals.'

'Consider it done.'

'Thank you. That's very generous.' I let out a breath that I didn't realise I was holding. 'I'm sorry Lucas missed it too.'

'He hates my supper parties – as well as everything else. He only comes under extreme duress.'

'If it's any consolation, I think most kids of his age would feel the same. There aren't many who think that hanging out with their parents is cool.'

'No. I suppose not. Yet he enjoys being with you.'

'He seems to. That's one of life's mysteries as well.' Shelby laughs at that and it emboldens me to say, 'Can I offer you some tea?'

'That would be nice.' We walk back towards the van, animals padding behind us. 'Lucas has gone up to London today. There's some gaming convention he likes to go to. I did think about insisting he stay home so that we try to spend some "quality" time together.' He shakes his head. 'He was so ill-tempered that I realised it was pointless.'

'You couldn't have gone with him?'

'I'd have been stopped every five minutes and he hates that. It was better he went off and enjoyed himself. He said he wanted to be with his friends and he doesn't say that very often. My driver, Ken, took him up to town first thing this morning and I was kicking around the house by myself.' He looks up and, for a fleeting moment, all I see in his eyes is loneliness. 'I thought I'd come up and find out how he's doing. You don't mind?'

'Not at all. I was planning on a quiet day too.'

'And now I'm intruding.'

'A welcome distraction,' I say and then realise that sounds like I'm flirting when I don't mean to.

Chapter Fifty-Three

So we have a cup of tea and sit on the deckchairs together in the sunshine enjoying the view over the fields. At least, I'm enjoying it. Shelby Dacre seems lost in thought.

I'm rubbish at making small talk and Shelby doesn't seem in the mood for idle chatter, so we sit in silence, just sipping our drinks, the dogs and Fifty curled up at our feet. I don't even like to break the mood to ask if he's taken his antihistamine.

After some time, he says, 'We got on well before his mother died, you know. All of us did.' He doesn't look at me but, instead, keeps staring straight ahead. 'We were a tight family unit. We did everything together.'

'The loss of a loved one is a terrible thing. It must have hit you both hard.'

'You think you can prepare for it. But you can't. Susie was wonderful. We'd met when I was a struggling actor and she was a dancer. I wish you'd seen her, Molly. She was such a beauty.' He flicks at his phone and then holds up a photograph of a delicate, dark-haired woman beaming at the camera. She's wearing a floral shirt and jeans and has a warm, open expression. I can see where Lucas gets his looks from.

'Gorgeous,' I agree.

'I think you'd have liked her,' he says softly. 'And she would have loved you and what you're doing with this place. Have you talked to Lucas about her?'

'Not really,' I admit.

'He adored her. As I did. You never know in this business whether someone wants to be with you for who you are or what you can do for them, rather than the person underneath that.'

I say nothing, just letting him talk as he seems in the mood to share with me. Sometimes the hardest thing is to find someone to listen when you need them to. Shelby has such a busy life that it must be difficult to make the space for simply being.

'When Susie and I got together we had nothing. We saved hard out of what we did earn and bought a little terraced house in Leighton Buzzard.' He allows himself a fond laugh. 'We were so proud of ourselves. In reality, the place was falling down round our ears. We had just two deckchairs in the living room for the first year we were there – just like these.' He pats the wooden frame. 'We had one of those Crockpot things in lieu of a cooker. But it served us well. It was our first proper home and we worked on it together. We turned an outhouse into a utility room, painted the cellars, covered all the ancient wood chip with magnolia. All the things that don't seem like chores when you do them with love.' He pauses, gathering his thoughts before continuing. 'When Lucas came along we couldn't have been more thrilled. I was doing OK by then and so we moved to a bigger place. One with a garden for the baby.'

'I bet he was a lovely boy.'

'Oh, he was. We adored him and he could twist us both round his little finger. Neither of us minded. He had great big eyes that would break your heart. Our only sadness was that we didn't have more children. Susie would have liked a huge family. She always wanted a house filled with love and laughter. Loads of animals too. We tried everything to have another baby – went to the best clinics, all of that – but it wasn't to be. Perhaps we doted on Lucas too much as he's our only one. We certainly indulged him.' Shelby sighs and, when I risk a look across at him, his eyes have filled with tears. 'Who'd have thought it would turn out like this?'

'I guess none of us know what the future has in store for us.'

'I don't want to burden you. Or bore you. You don't mind me talking like this?'

'Of course not.' It's nice that he feels able to confide in me.

'We were more privileged than most families. I know that. But all the money in the world can't buy you health or time. It was such a blow when Susie was diagnosed with cancer. We'd had a pretty gilded existence in the years prior to that. Everything was going well with work, we'd moved into the manor and Susie loved it there. Her particular joy was the garden. She was the one who thought it would be a good idea to open the house for charity events.' He halts again, clearly finding it difficult to continue. 'She had so little time when we found out. We thought we'd grow old together and we had such plans. What we weren't going to do! We thought Lucas would be heading off to university, doing his own thing. I was intending to step away from the limelight and we were looking forward to travelling the world together – maybe get a little place in Italy or France, wherever took our fancy.'

'They sound like very good plans.'

'Yes, but look at us now. I have a son who can't stand the sight of me. And I'm floundering around not knowing who I am any more. I stay away from home doing things I don't want to be doing with people I don't want to be with just so I don't have to face him. Lucas doesn't even live in the house now. I came home one night shortly after Susie had died and he'd moved into a tiny cottage in the grounds that was standing empty. Lock, stock and barrel. I think the gardener used to live in it before we moved there. Did he tell you that?'

'No. He didn't mention it at all.'

'It doesn't matter how much I try to reason with him, he won't come back into the house. He refuses point blank. What can I do? I can't force him back into his old room. It's his choice. He comes into the house to get some food and disappears again straight away. And then all this business with school. Setting fire to stuff? Why does he do that? He used to be the model student.' He shakes his head. 'I feel as if I don't know my own son any more. He's become a stranger to me. I want to breach the gap, but I've no idea how to reach out to him.'

'Perhaps you need to work on spending some time together.'

'How? When I walk into a room, he walks out. I go to the cottage, he keeps me at the door. What am I supposed to do? Barge my way in? In the show I deal every day with human relationships and dilemmas – some of them pretty unbelievable – but I can't do it in real life without a script in my hand. You have no idea how frustrating that is.'

How can I tell him that you don't need to be a genius to work out that he needs to be at home and available for Lucas? He could start by ditching the unsuitable girlfriend who his son obviously resents with every fibre of his being, but I'm not really in the position to say that, am I? Instead, I venture, 'I know it's difficult, but are there things that you could let go of that would allow you to concentrate on Lucas? All of his behaviour might indicate the exact opposite, but I'm sure that he needs you now more than ever.'

Shelby lets out a wavering breath and wipes a finger beneath his eyes. 'I'm getting maudlin now. I should go.'

'Take a walk round the farm with me,' I say. 'You can see a little bit of what Lucas gets up to here and why I'm so keen to save it.'

'You know I'm allergic to *all* animals?'

I laugh. 'Yes. Difficult for someone who plays a farmer as his job.'

'My best friend is antihistamine,' he admits. 'I have some in the car.'

'Wellies too?'

'No. Farmer Gordon is such a fake.'

'I'll find you some while you get your tablets. Lucas brought some from your stash and they're in the barn.'

'Ah, yes.' He stands up and stretches. Before he goes, he turns to me. 'Thanks, Molly.'

'No problem. That's what friends are for.'

Then he looks at me and I don't know what passes between us as I've never experienced anything like this before. I suddenly notice the searing intensity of his blue eyes the colour of an English summer sky, the smoothness of his skin, the texture of his straw-coloured hair. I drink in his size, his strength, his maleness that's so alien to me. I feel him doing the same to me and for once in my life, I don't think that I'm found wanting. Is this what they write about in romance novels, this frisson, this electricity that seems to be tingling in my veins? I don't know.

But before I can dwell on it any further, Shelby breaks the moment and says, 'I'll get that antihistamine.'

I watch him go, the unfamiliar trembly feeling inside still not leaving me and wonder what it was that *I* was supposed to go and do.

Chapter Fifty-Four

When he comes back, I'm still standing there like a lemon.

'Wellies,' he says. 'You were supposed to be finding me wellies.'

'Ah, yes. In the barn. I'll just slip mine on.' So I rouse myself and go to put my boots on. Then we walk up to the barn and Shelby kicks off his fancy designer shoes and puts on some of the brand new wellies that he unwittingly donated to us which may or may not be his size.

'Do they fit?' I ask.

'Maybe.' He stamps his feet as if to test them out.

'We won't go too far. I'd like to do my evening round now, if you don't mind.'

'Lead on,' he says. 'I'm in no rush. Lucas will be late back and I have nothing but an empty house waiting for me.'

So with Little Dog and Big Dog at our heels, we wander away from the yard and head up the hill. We stop first at the alpacas who come up to the fence in search of dinner and trouble. I scoop some food pellets from the bins and give them each a handful. Shelby stands back. I can't blame him for not wanting to get too close after what happened.

'Tina Turner is the brown one.'

'That's the one you brought to the house?'

I nod. 'And to the show. She's our most sociable one. Johnny Rotten, with the orange hair, isn't to be trusted. He doesn't really like people or other alpacas. He's the one who caused so much trouble with Scarlett Vincent.'

'Ah,' he says and I feel a bit weird for mentioning her name.

'I was so traumatised by that, it gives me nightmares even now.'

'It's still much talked about on the show,' Shelby tells me.

'Oh, God. We'd have to keep him on a very tight leash if we ever took him out again. Rod Stewart is the one with skinny legs. He's not as spiteful as Johnny, but he'll still give you a nip if you're not paying attention.'

'I always thought alpacas were cute, cuddly things.'

I laugh. 'I guess you won't be getting them now at *Flinton's Farm*?'

'No. You've seen the set. It looks real enough, but our animals are often trained performers.'

'I didn't even know there was such a thing.'

'It's all done with smoke and mirrors,' he confesses. 'I think everyone expected the alpacas to stand in the corner and behave nicely. Me included.'

'Hmm. I'm not sure that was ever going to happen. Alpacas are, shall we say, independent-spirited.'

'Uncontrollable?'

I laugh. 'More unpredictable. They have their uses, though. We sell their fleeces for yarn – for pence, usually. But their poo is more valuable. It makes very good manure, so the gardeners tell me. We have a handful of regulars who pop up for it. Though it's very hard to get the students to do the job of collecting and bagging it. I usually end up doing it myself.'

'I can't imagine Lucas doing this kind of thing. He likes it, though?'

'He does. He's fitted in really well and has a great affinity for the animals. We often find that with even the most troubled of our children.'

'He has friends? That's something I know he's struggling with.'

'There's no particular friend as the other students here at the moment tend to be younger than him. It's just how it's worked out. But they adore him and seem to look up to him. They think he's very cool.' We walk on a little way before I risk adding, 'I heard him performing some of his poetry for them the other day.'

'His poetry? My son? I didn't even know he wrote poetry.'

'He's very good. There's some of it up on YouTube. You should take a look. It might surprise you.'

'I will.' He looks deep in thought as we wander up to the ponies who come trotting across the field to see us. 'This is Ringo and Buzz, our little Shetland boys. You've seen them before too.' I give them both a pat and then check Ringo's skin. Seems to be doing all right. We both must be due a haircut from Christian Lee soon. 'Lucas has been very adept at giving them both a bath.'

'He must really like you,' Shelby says. 'I can't get him to do a bloody thing.'

'It's a very different relationship,' I say, stating the obvious. 'But I admit to having a soft spot for him. We've spent a lot of time together since he's been here.'

'He sounds like a different boy, yet I've seen no change in him at all at home.'

'It'll take time,' I say. 'Though, sadly, that's one thing we may no longer have.'

'What will happen to the people who come here if you have to close?'

'I honestly don't know. They've mostly ended up at the farm because they've tried everywhere else and haven't been happy. We're the last chance saloon.'

We walk on up to the Shire horses. 'These are our big boys, Sweeney and Carter. Ex-police horses. They're our gentle giants. Speak too loudly and Sweeney jumps out of his skin.'

'I'm terrified of horses,' Shelby admits, staying well behind me. 'They have to get in a stunt double when there's any riding to be done.'

'I can't believe that you've been surrounded by animals for all these years and haven't got used to them. You should come and spend some time up here, I'll break you in. Gently, of course.'

He laughs. 'I might take you up on that.'

Chapter Fifty-Five

The evening is still warm, but a gentle breeze stirs the air as we move on, heading towards the goats and sheep, in step together. The dogs wander ahead, finding interesting things to sniff at.

'Between you and me, I'm pretty sick of playing Farmer Gordon Flinton. I've been there too long. We've exhausted pretty much every storyline you can think of. Sometimes the plots are beyond ridiculous. I feel foolish even saying the words. The whole thing seems stale now.' He turns to me and smiles. 'But then you've never watched it.'

'No.' He seems to find that very amusing. 'But I know that a lot of people do. Bev loves it. I never watch anything. It's not that I've singled out your show to avoid.'

'Glad to hear it,' he teases.

'So, if you're fed up with Gordon Flinton, what would be your ideal role?'

'I don't know.' His heart sounds heavy when he says it. 'I came out of drama school wanting to be the next Ian McKellen. It didn't quite pan out like that. I've had very few periods where I haven't worked, which I know most actors would give their eyeteeth for. It's given me a great living and I'm grateful for that.

But it's all been television, adverts. Selling my soul for some trinkets.' He shows me his big, fancy watch which is very big and very fancy. 'I'm the face of Abel Range designer watches.'

'That seems like a nice thing.'

'Double-edged sword. It means that the people who matter don't take you seriously. Plus ten years in the same role means that I don't get approached to try anything more meaty. I'm never likely to be on stage at the Old Vic.'

'Would you want to be?'

'I don't know,' he admits. 'But I'd like to be asked. Between you and me, I'm looking for a new challenge. My agent is putting feelers out.'

'Sounds like a good idea to try something else if you're cheesed off.'

'You won't go running to the tabloids or *Hello!* magazine?'

I laugh. 'Hardly. As well as not having a television, I don't read a newspaper either. Or the glossy mags. I generally find the outside world very much over-rated and try to avoid it as much as possible.'

'I'm beginning to envy your lifestyle very much.'

I'm worried that it's making me sound a bit unhinged. 'I choose to be like this. You'll see why in a minute.'

We walk on until we come to the top of the hill and I stop. We both catch our breath and look out over the vale. The view that greets us is no less stunning than usual. All we can see are green, rolling fields, my sheep, ancient hedgerows and trees. The sun is slowly sinking in the sky and, as evening moves in, the landscape softens in the dwindling light.

'I love this spot. From up here there are very few signs of our modern life. You can't see any houses or roads or unsightly wind turbines. Or people.' I point into the distance and Shelby's gaze follows my finger. 'There's a green lane that runs along the edge of the property and, with a little imagination, I like to think that you can almost see the first farmers here going along it with a horse and cart loaded with hay. It probably hasn't changed very much for hundreds of years.'

'I can see why you don't want to lose this place,' Shelby says. 'It's idyllic.'

'Every time I pause here it lightens my heart. I like to think that we've been good custodians of the land.' Then a knot of emotion tightens my throat and my eyes fill with tears. 'Now there'll be a speeding train going through the middle of it in the name of progress. All to shave twenty minutes off a journey that very few people will actually be able to afford.'

'That is surely a spectacular act of vandalism.'

'I think so. If you ask me it's nothing more than a politicians' vanity project but, sadly, no one did ask me.' The lightness in my heart dissipates as I think of what lies ahead. 'I've no idea how we'll find anywhere to replace it. Especially not at the price we pay. Until now, our landlord has been quite kind to us. I expect our rent is considerably lower than its commercial value. Even if we could find a new location, we may not be able to afford anything else like this.' I feel sick just thinking about it.

'Don't despair. We've got time yet,' Shelby says softly. 'The more I see of this place, the more I want to help you. I promise I'll do all that I can.'

'Thank you, that's very kind.' It's rare that I miss a human touch as I have my dogs, the animals, but I feel as if I'd like to hug Shelby. Of course, I don't. 'I appreciate it.'

'Tell me what I can do.'

'That's the big problem, I don't really know. We'd need to find a new place to house all of us. Somewhere near to here so that it's still convenient for our students. That's a big ask. Land here is so expensive. Even farming land.'

He seems to take it all in, but doesn't offer an immediate solution. Perhaps there isn't one to be had.

'Come on,' I say. 'We'll walk down the hill and I'll introduce you to the sheep.'

I click the dogs to heel and we meander down to the bottom field which is filled with sheep. We started with half a dozen and every year we take in more and more orphans. I have a flock of thirty-eight to manage now which I'd never quite imagined and it grows each year.

As we reach the fence, guess who comes charging right over to see if he's in with a chance of terrorising an unsuspecting person?

'This is Anthony the Anti-Social Sheep.' On cue, Anthony sticks his big head through the fence. 'His pleasure in life is trying to knock over unwary ramblers and me.'

Anthony growls.

'That's terrifying,' Shelby says, backing away. 'Do sheep normally do that?'

'His bark is worse than his bite,' I assure him. 'He's misunderstood.'

Shelby laughs. 'The animals sound as troubled as the kids.'

'They are,' I admit, 'but it makes for an interesting life.'

'My work sounds very vacuous in comparison. Poncing around being a pretend farmer can hardly be classed as life-changing.'

'You provide entertainment and escapism – I think that's a very important job.'

Suddenly he turns to me. 'How can I reach out to Lucas? What can I do to make it better between us?'

'Spend time with him,' I offer. 'Do the things that Lucas likes to do.'

'He wants to sit in his room with his computer.'

'Isn't there a way that you could have gone with him to-day? It might not be your thing, but it might have been a good opportunity.'

'I wish I could have. He made it abundantly clear that he wanted to go alone, as only Lucas can. And he's right, I would have just been a hindrance. Whatever we do, Lucas hates it when we're out together and I get recognised. So it restricts what we can do. I can't even take him to the cinema or to the local pizza place. He gets so angry about it all.'

'That's something else you need to work on then.' I give him a sympathetic smile. 'It's not going to improve overnight, but I'm sure if you try hard enough you'll both find a way.'

Chapter Fifty-Six

It's pushing on into the evening when we get back to the caravan. Shelby slides off his borrowed wellies and puts his designer shoes back on. I expect him to make his excuses and leave, but he doesn't. He hangs about outside the van chatting about nothing until a loud rumbling from my stomach interrupts our conversation.

'Sorry,' he says. 'I'm keeping you talking and you must be hungry.'

Yet still he hesitates. When it's clear he's not in a hurry to leave, I say, 'I'm only planning to throw some pasta in a pot, but I can make enough for two. You're more than welcome to stay.' I'm sure that I see his eyes brighten.

'That's a big house to rattle round in by myself. Pasta sounds very appealing.'

'You don't know what kind of cook I am yet. My repertoire is quite basic and I can't offer you any wine as I don't have any.'

'We could probably both do with a drink. What say I nip to the local shop to grab a bottle? There's one near here?'

'In the village,' I confirm.

'That can be my contribution,' he says. 'Is there anything else you need?'

Probably, but I'm so stunned that I can't even think. I've just asked Shelby Dacre to dinner and he's said yes. 'I'll just rustle something up from whatever's in my cupboard, if that's OK?'

'Perfect. I'll be back as soon as I can.' While I stand there slightly aghast that I'm going to be having a guest for dinner in the caravan – and a celebrity guest at that – he dashes to the gate, opens it up and then shoots off in his car. I wander to close the gate behind him. Then, as I watch his car disappear down the lane, it hits me that I probably have twenty minutes max to make my modest home presentable. So I hurry back and run round the caravan, shoving things into cupboards that haven't been in cupboards for years. I plump the cushions and give a cursory scoot round with the hoover to get up the worst of the dog hair. I don't want Shelby going home with bright red eyes and a streaming nose.

I put on some music. Bev gave me her old CD player and a stack of CDs which I rarely use. This is Lady Antebellum and I think I like their music. I have a rummage for some wine glasses. And I kind of hate myself for this but, if I had more time, I might consider a shower and slipping into Bev's scary dress. I'm not even sure how that makes me feel. I've never been one to have the urge to doll myself up for a man, but this seems different. Instead, I give my hair a cursory comb, scrub my hands and have a look in my veg box. I've got mushrooms, spinach and onions. None of them are too wilty. Looks like a good start.

I'm chopping away when the dogs bark to signal that Shelby has returned. I hear the gate open and my heart starts up a weird pitter-patter beat. I take a couple of deep breaths and, despite my aversion to relying on drink for comfort, think that wine is a very good idea.

A moment later, Shelby knocks at the caravan door and I shout, 'Come on in!'

The minute he's over the threshold Little Dog and Big Dog fall on him and try to lick him to death.

'Away, boys,' I say. 'We can't make our guest sneeze.'

'I'll be fine,' he assures me, but I know that he's only being polite. 'I just have to make sure that I don't stroke them and then touch my eyes or I will be in trouble.'

I can't imagine a life without a relaxed relationship with animals.

He holds up a bottle of wine. 'A good red,' he says. 'Plus they had some fresh basil and a little piece of Parmesan. Is that useful?'

'That's great,' I say. 'What a treat.'

'Can I do anything to help?'

'You could pour the wine.' I push the glasses towards him. 'Also the table comes out from under the sofa and fixes into that bracket in the floor. I don't use it very often, but I feel that we should.' It's warm enough to eat outside, but on a farm you have to consider the amount of flies that are around, so it's probably best if we stay indoors for now.

He pours the wine and we clink the glasses together.

'Cheers,' he says, but we both seem a little self-conscious. Maybe he's now wondering if this really was a good idea.

While Shelby works out the complications of putting up the table, I chop the veg and open a tin of tomatoes. Having found the cutlery drawer, Shelby sets out the knives and forks as I stir the sauce, put the pasta on to cook and grate the Parmesan that he kindly bought.

'Make yourself comfortable,' I say over my shoulder. 'This won't be long.'

I'm glad to see that Shelby kicks off his shoes and shimmies onto the sofa. Little Dog jumps up and sits next to him.

'Down, boy,' I say and my dog pretends that he's deaf.

'I can cope,' Shelby says, bravely. 'I've had my daily dose of antihistamine.'

'Hope it works. Little Dog likes nothing more than to cuddle up to a new friend.'

Ten slightly awkward minutes later, I dish up the pasta – aware that this is a very flung-together affair. As are most of my meals. 'I hope it's OK. You're probably used to eating in Michelin-starred restaurants.'

'I do my fair share of that, but it's a long time since I've had a meal cooked for me. I miss my wife for very many reasons, but one of them is definitely her cooking.'

'Well, I hope this lives up to her standards.'

'I didn't mean it like that,' he says. 'Sorry, that sounded terrible.'

'It's OK. I'm not offended. I know what you mean.'

I sit down opposite him and we tuck in.

'This is very good,' he says. 'Really very good.'

I don't think it is, but he's trying to be nice and that works for me. Shelby tops up my glass. I'm nervous and I'm drinking too quickly.

'In the eyes of most people I must seem to have a glamorous celebrity life, but what I really want is to curl up at home with the person I love.'

Does he think that Scarlett Vincent is a curl-up-at-home kind of person? Obviously, I don't ask that. As Bev pointed out, he may be getting a different kind of solace from someone like her.

'You must wonder what I'm doing with the lovely Scarlett?'

I swear to you I said nothing.

He gulps down his wine. 'She was very good to me when Susie died. Scarlett had just come into *Flinton's Farm* at the time – a brief role, initially. But they liked her and she stayed. Eventually, she became my love interest. In the show and then . . . ' His voice tails away.

I guess these things happen if you're acting passionately with someone. Maybe it is easier for it to tip over into your personal life.

239

He clears his throat. 'We get on well.'

'Good, good.' I can feel myself flush. For some reason, I don't want to think about Shelby getting on well with Scarlett Vincent.

To cover our embarrassment, he tops up my glass again and I don't refuse. Two glasses in and I'm starting to relax. Despite the odd awkward moment, I'm beginning to find it nice to be holed up here with Shelby with a carby dinner and a decent red.

'Despite our age difference, we clicked,' he continues. 'I hadn't laughed since Susie had died and she helped me to take my mind off my grief. We've had a lot of fun.' There's a sparkle in his eye when he talks about her and I feel sad that no one has ever had that look for me. 'She's bloody high maintenance, I'll give you that. But she can be very amusing when she wants to be. However, I'm ashamed to say that I really haven't considered how Lucas is grieving. I can't even deal with my own feelings let alone sort out his.'

'He really misses his mum.' I know that much. 'Losing a parent is difficult at any age, but as a teenager when the world is a scary and confusing place, I'm sure they need more reassurance than ever.'

'And I'm not giving it to him.'

'Only you can tell that.'

'I want to, but we have no common ground. What can I do?'

'Do you want to listen to some of his poetry? That might give you a clue.' I reach for my phone.

When Shelby sees the state of it – the battered case held together with a plaster, the cracked screen – he says, 'Let me,' and reaches for his instead. 'What do I look for?'

'Just type in his name,' I advise as if I'm an expert on these things and am not simply capable of finding Lucas's poetry and little else. 'I confess that I've listened to them all several times since he showed me how. I really love them and find his style very compelling.'

240

'There are tons of them,' Shelby says as he flicks at his screen. 'He's quite prolific.'

'The titles are terrifying. Are they all about him being angry with his father?'

'Some of them are.'

'Christ. Let's not look at those first. You pick one.'

'This is my favourite.' I tap on the screen and Lucas pops up in front of us.

'Weird,' Shelby says with a wavering breath. 'Very weird.'

Yet Shelby turns up the sound and we push our plates away. I scoot over to his side so that we can nestle together on my small sofa, heads together, watching his son spit out his poetry.

Chapter Fifty-Seven

After a few of the least threatening titles, the next one up is called 'Secrets 'n' Lies' which I know is all about his dad – I've watched it enough times. I think about skipping it, but perhaps it's something that Shelby *should* listen to. I hold my breath as Lucas's voice starts up once more. His pale face on the screen of Shelby's phone looks anguished.

> *Who are you?*
> *C'mon an' show me who ya are!*
> *Is anything f'real,*
> *Mr TV star?*
> *Action!*
> *Reaction!*
> *Time t'pour out*
> *y'heart,*
> *but how'm I t'know*
> *what's y'life and what's ya art?*
> *Cards on the table:*
> *time t'bare your soul,*
> *but when you lie for a living,*

ain't life just another role?
How will I know
if what y'telling me is true?
An' if nothing is f'real,
then, does it matter what I do?
Who are you?
I shouldn't really have t'arx,
but I really need to know
if there's a man behind the mask.
Action!
No action;
words are all you got,
scripted 'n' lifted from a cheap soap plot.
Well-versed, rehearsed;
in the character immersed,
two faces; two families,
but which a'them comes first?
They all think they know ya;
they see you as their friends,
but none a'them will be there when the story ends,
so —
Who are you?
That's what I need t'know;
when they turn off the camras
and they wrap up the show.
Action!
Interaction:
that's what I'm looking for,
I shouldn't have to queue at the stage door.
We all got a secret that we're burnin' t'yell,
we're defined by the lies that we're willin' t'tell.
Secrets 'n' lies;
I's no big deal;

all I'm arxin's that y'keep it
a little bit real.
All I'm arxin's that y'keep it
a little bit real.
All I'm arxin's that y'arx y'self:
how I might feel . . .

'That's enough,' Shelby says and he clicks the pause button. He wipes his eyes as he puts down his phone and I wait, anxiously, for his reaction. When he's composed himself, he says, 'Well, that was emotional.' His voice is shaky. 'I didn't know my son had it in him.'

'He definitely has a talent.'

'It was bloody tough to hear. Is that what he really thinks of me?'

I have to put this as tactfully as I can. 'I think in his own way, he's reaching out to you.'

'You think?' He looks willing to believe it.

'I'm sure.'

'Why did I not see this?' Shelby looks drained. 'He's bloody good, isn't he? You think so too? It's not just a father's pride?'

'He's great.'

Shelby blows out a breath. 'I've always tried to put him off being a performer. For the majority, it's such a precarious existence. But he's really got something to offer, something unique. How can we bury our differences so that I can tell him how much I love this?'

'You'll find a way. Take it slowly.'

He looks sad when he says, 'When it comes to my son I seem to spend my life walking on eggshells.'

'I suspect there are a great deal of parents out there who feel the same. The teenage years are a treacherous landscape.'

'I hope you're right.'

The dusk is gathering quickly now and I glance at the clock. 'I should wash up,' I say. 'It's getting late and, unfortunately, the animals don't know the meaning of a lie-in.'

Shelby jumps up. 'I'll help. I'm sure I can remember what to do with the working end of a tea towel. It's been a while though.'

'I do my best thinking while I'm washing up.' We move to the sink and I fill the bowl, add a frugal squirt of washing-up liquid and, as Shelby hands me the dirty plates and glasses, I set to. We're cosied up together in the woeful space of my tiny caravan and I'm aware that Shelby is standing close by my shoulder. I get that funny feeling again. It's nice, but I'm not sure I like it at all, if you know what I mean.

He rubs away with the tea towel.

'You handle that like a pro,' I tease.

'I should do this more often,' he says. 'It's been a great evening, Molly. Thank you. I hope I haven't bored you to tears, droning on about my life.'

'Not at all. I've enjoyed it too. I get precious little company here.'

'I haven't felt this relaxed in years. I've got a six-bedroom mansion, but I realise that it's not a home any more.' He puts down his tea towel and looks at me. 'You're a very easy woman to talk to. I feel as if I can be myself with you. No pretence. No acting.'

He steps towards me and gives me a warm, friendly kiss on the cheek. I don't know how it happens, but suddenly his arms are around me and we're holding each other tight. His fingers are in my hair and, when he kisses my cheek again, it feels different. His mouth lingers against my skin and the atmosphere has definitely changed. Even the air is charged with electricity. My knees feel weak and I want more than anything for him to kiss me properly.

Just when I think he might, his phone rings. Shelby curses.

'Fuck's sake.' He snatches his phone from his pocket and then looks at me. 'Scarlett.'

I try a nonchalant shrug and think I might pull it off. 'You should take it.' What else can I say?

He moves away from me as he answers the phone. 'Hello, darling.'

The words stick a sharp little pin in my heart.

'I can be there in half an hour. Less. Is Lucas at home? Get him to let you in if he is. If not there's a separate bell for the housekeeper's flat, ring that. Pour yourself a drink, I'll join you as soon as I can.' He hangs up and looks guilty when he tells me, 'Scarlett has turned up at the house to surprise me.'

'Ah.'

'I should go.'

'You can't drive.'

'Damn,' he mutters. 'It's too late to call my driver out now. He'll have his feet up watching television. I'll phone a cab instead. Ken can come and collect the car in the morning.' So he makes another couple of calls and organises it, while I put away the dishes and try not to crash them about. I don't want him to go. That's the truth of it. And, if I'm being really candid with you, I particularly don't want him to go to Scarlett.

'The cab will be here in ten minutes,' Shelby says. 'Then I'll be out of your hair.'

I want to tell him that I don't want him out of my hair but, instead, I say, 'Fine.'

'Thank you, Molly. Thanks for today. Thank you very much.'

'My pleasure.' I try not to sound crisp, but I feel a little bit put out that he's leaving.

'Thank you for all that you do for Lucas. He's lucky to have you.'

It's clear that he's babbling now as all he wants to do is hightail it out of here and get home to the comforts of Scarlett.

She wouldn't let him stand and dry dishes, would she? I could kick myself for being so stupid.

A few minutes later, there's the crunch of gravel, the toot of a horn and I can see Shelby sigh with relief. The dogs bark their heads off.

'That must be the cab.' He looks out of the window. 'It is.'

'I'll come out to lock the gate after you.'

We pause and, for a moment, there's a fraction of that spark between us once more.

'Thanks again, Molly.' Tentatively, he touches my arm and, I'm not an expert in these things, but it looks for all the world that he'd still like to kiss me. 'I'll be in touch.'

Then he heads out of the door. The cab is parked up by the gate and I let Shelby out. The driver opens the door and Shelby slips into the passenger seat.

He doesn't look at me as the car makes a tricky three-point turn in the lane, but I'm unable to take my eyes off him and I can't begin to tell you how disappointed I am to see him go.

Locking the gate, I trudge back to the caravan, heavy of heart and deflated. I feel as if someone has burst my party balloon. I have a crush on him. Of that there can be no doubt. Like thousands of other women who watch him in his soap opera. I bet none of them have had him washing up in their caravan.

I down the dregs of the wine, straight from the bottle. Then I get into my pyjamas and climb into bed. For the first time, I'm actually sad to be sleeping alone.

'Fuck,' I say to no one.

Then Little Dog comes into the bedroom and lies down next to me on the duvet and that very nearly makes it all right.

Chapter Fifty-Eight

On Monday, I struggle to get my back off the bed. One late night and I'm thrown for the week. Drinking wine and getting up at five o'clock in the morning are not conducive.

I didn't sleep last night. It seems to be a recurring theme these days and you know why before I even tell you. I couldn't stop thinking about Shelby sodding Dacre. The feel of his mouth on my skin, his fingers toying with my hair. Nothing I did could blank it out. I tried saying the alphabet backwards, counting sheep – including Anthony – and all those other things that they tell you to do to induce a deep slumber. It felt as if I'd had about ten minutes' shut-eye before my alarm went off.

I do my morning round on auto-pilot and barely remember my egg collection. Alan and Bev take the rest of the students out to the sheep paddock before their tutor comes. Alan is wearing a Beyoncé Sasha Fierce T-shirt and neither of us think to comment on it. Must be tired. I have three coffees and they still don't manage to wake me up. I'm standing looking blankly out of the window of the tea room when a cab arrives and Lucas jumps out. He's late, and that's unlike him. Shelby's driver gets out of the passenger seat and crosses to where

Shelby's car was abandoned last night, keys in hand. Lucas lets both vehicles out and then closes the gate. He stomps across the yard.

Instantly, I suss that he's in a right mood and can see the dark scowl on his face from here. What now?

'Good weekend?' I ask as he comes into the tea room, feigning cheerfulness.

'No,' he snarls back. Lucas throws himself into the sofa and becomes riveted to his phone.

I make him a cup of coffee and hand it over. He takes it without thanks.

'Your dad said you'd gone to a gaming convention to meet up with friends. Wasn't it what you expected?'

'It was rubbish,' he snaps. 'And I don't have any friends.'

I guess that was just another cover story to prevent Shelby from going with him. Poor Lucas. Poor Shelby.

'Want to walk up to the barn with me after you've finished your coffee? The pig's hooves need a manicure.' It's known as 'trimming' in the wider farming circles, but we like to embrace Bev's terminology here. 'We can talk about it while we work.'

Lucas glares at me. 'I have nothing to say to you.'

I frown at him. I see. I'm sure I know what this is about, but I want to hear him say it. 'Are you cross with me?'

He looks up at me and there are tears shining in his angry eyes. 'You've seen what he's like,' Lucas says. 'Why did you have to spend time with him?'

Ah. I thought as much. 'He came here to see how you were getting on,' I tell him, softly.

'You cooked dinner for him. He told me everything.'

I wonder if he really did. 'I knocked some pasta together as I would for anyone. He sounded lonely, Lucas.'

'Seriously? He was fucking Scarlett Vincent by the time I got home.' I can tell that he's using coarse language to shock me

249

and I have to admit that it works. What did I think they were going to do? Sit chastely on the sofa holding hands? 'Didn't seem all that lonely to me.'

'He loves you very much, Lucas. He just doesn't know how to tell you.'

I'm sure that I see a tear roll onto his cheek, but Lucas flicks his fringe across his face.

'He's a twat.'

'He's a good man,' I insist. 'He's just forgotten how to be a good father.'

'I can't believe you've fallen under his corny charm spell like everyone else.'

'I'm trying to be impartial. As an outsider, I can see both positions, Lucas. Believe me, from where I stand, it looks as if both of you are hurting.'

'I'm not hurting. I'm fine. I don't need you. I don't need *anyone*.' With that he launches himself at the door and stamps out.

I sigh to myself. If only I wasn't so tired I could perhaps handle Lucas better today, but I can't; my brain is sluggish and I feel as if I didn't say the right things. Bugger.

Instead of chasing after him, I decide it's best to leave Lucas to his own devices for a while. I'll talk to him again later when, hopefully, he'll have cooled off a bit. I'm sad that he's fallen out with me just as we were making good progress. I make myself another coffee, but my bones are aching and my head is still full of cotton wool.

At lunchtime, Bev says, 'I've just taken a call about some newborn lambs. Can we take in some outcasts? Only three of them. It's that time of year.'

Ewes can give birth to twins or triplets, but often only nurture one of the lambs. Sometimes they can be introduced to the mother for feeding, sometimes not. We have a reputation of taking in the rejects for hand-rearing. Most of our sheep have come to us that way. Looks like our thirty-eight are about to become forty-odd.

'You said yes?' I ask her.

'When do we ever turn away a hard-luck case? They'll be here later. I'll deal with it.'

'Put them in the stall behind Teacup. We can set up a feeder and the heat lamps in there.' When they're tiny, they need a bit of extra care on the colder evenings. I bought a feeder last year, so it means that I don't have to do a midnight or three o'clock in the morning feed. With the feeder they can go through the night by themselves. That doesn't mean it stops me from putting my dressing gown on in the dead of night to pop in and check on them.

At lunchtime, when we're all sitting down to eat together, Lucas is late back. I've put him a bowl of veggie curry to one side. When he eventually turns up, he sits as far away from me as possible and picks at his food, still sullen. The boy can certainly give good sulk.

When she's collecting the plates, Bev sidles up to me and whispers, 'What's up with golden boy?'

I get up and go with her to the sink and whisper back, 'He's pissed off with me because Shelby spent the evening here with me.'

Bev's eyes widen. 'He didn't.'

'Nothing happened.' I sound more than a touch defensive.

Her eyes widen further. 'You'd tell me if it did?'

'Of course,' I hiss. 'He came here to talk about Lucas.'

She looks very disappointed by that. I don't tell her that if I'd had time, I would have slipped into her slinky dress. 'Still, Gordon Flinton in your old van!'

I don't like to tell her that it was very much the stripped bare Shelby Dacre. 'He's a nice man.'

251

'He's a smoking-hot, hundred per cent heart-throb!' she murmurs.

'If you say so.'

She looks over her shoulder, checking that Lucas is still at the far end of the tea room. 'So what are you going to do about him?'

'I'll spend some time with Lucas this afternoon. See if I can make it right.'

'He was up with the Shire horses earlier. I don't know what he was doing up there.'

'By himself? Wasn't Alan with him?'

'No. Alan was in the barn. Want me to walk up there and make sure that they're all right?'

'He's a good kid. I'm sure they're fine.' But something nags at me, nevertheless.

Chapter Fifty-Nine

Before I can suggest to Lucas that we go out together in the afternoon, he's disappeared from the tea room. I look round the yard, but he's nowhere to be found. When I go to the chicken run and the alpaca paddock, he's not there either.

I'm back at the yard when Alan and Bev come in from the sheep's field. 'Has anyone seen Lucas?'

'No.' They both shake their heads.

'He must be up at the big field again,' Bev suggests. 'Keeping out of the way.'

'I'll walk up and see if he's there.' So I head out past the ponies, but there's no sign of him. At the big field, I can see that the gate is open – the gate that should at all times be locked – and pick up my pace.

When I reach the field, I can see that Sweeney and Carter have gone walkabout. They've wandered down to the next paddock and have knocked the fence over as they've gone exploring.

'Damn.' More unnecessary expense. More work for Alan.

Rounding up the horses, I marshal them back into their own field and make sure that the gate is locked. Then I double-check it.

I march down the hill, muttering crossly under my breath. As I near the yard, Lucas is coming out of the barn by himself. When he sees me, he looks furtive.

'Lucas, Bev said she saw you up by the horses before lunch. Did you leave the gate open?'

'I don't know,' he says. 'I don't think so.'

'Well, they've been out and have knocked the fence over in the next paddock. Who else has been up here?'

'I didn't do it on purpose.' He folds his arms, defensively. 'Even if it was me.'

'Oh, Lucas. What is wrong with you?' I'm irritable today and it comes out more harshly than I intend.

'I'm a complete fuck-up,' he spits back. 'You know that!'

'You're a bright, intelligent boy. I just wish, sometimes, that you'd use that brain of yours.'

'I've had enough of this place.' He storms off, shouting over his shoulder. 'I'm done. You can't make me stay.'

'Lucas, come back.'

'Fuck you.'

That stings. I shouldn't have shouted at him, but I'm cross and tired. I'm also upset that he may well be right about his father. Was he just acting in the caravan on Saturday? I don't know. I'm annoyed with myself for falling for it if he was.

I chase after Lucas, who's marching ahead, hands jammed into the pockets of his hoodie. Little Dog runs along at my heel, barking excitedly as he thinks it's a wonderful game.

'Let's sit and have a cuppa together and talk this through,' I call out.

'I've phoned the car to be picked up,' he says. 'Then I'm out of here and I'm not coming back.'

'Lucas!'

He runs across the yard, clambers over the main gate and races down the lane. I don't have the energy to chase after him.

254

I stop and stand where I am, heart pounding. Shitshitshit. I feel terrible. Truly terrible. With all my years of experience, I can't believe I handled that so badly.

Chapter Sixty

I follow Lucas down the lane, jogging to try to catch up with him, but to no avail. When I get to the end there's no sign of him. Perhaps he headed into the village to wait for his car. I'm out of breath, unaccustomed as I am to running, so I call his mobile but he doesn't answer.

Resigned to the fact that I won't resolve this today, I head back to the farm. Little Dog, having given up the chase, is waiting patiently at the gate. My first port of call is the tea room in the hope that a good, strong brew will calm me down and put all this into perspective. Bev is sitting in there on the sofa when I arrive.

'You look like a woman with the weight of the world on her shoulders.'

I flop down next to her. 'I feel like it.' She waits for me to continue. 'I've fallen out with Lucas. I think he forgot to lock the gate on the big field this morning. When I went up there to find him, Sweeney and Carter were having a lovely outing. They've broken the fence on the next field. Again.'

'Bugger.'

'I know. More expense that we don't need.' I could actually

cry. 'I'm annoyed with myself at how I handled it. I shouted at Lucas when I really shouldn't have. I'm the grown-up here.'

'Yes, but you're not a saint. You've got a lot to think about at the moment.'

'I'm tired and crotchety. I took it out on him, which was wrong.'

'I'll talk to him if you like. Where is he now?'

'He's stormed off. Last seen legging it down the lane, swearing he was never coming back.'

Bev puts her arm around me. 'He will when he cools down. He loves it here.'

'I don't want to lose him.' I know we shouldn't get emotionally attached to our students, but it's hard not to have your favourites and I feel that Lucas has such untapped potential.

'Want a brew? Everything looks better after a cup of tea.'

'Yes, please. My thoughts exactly.' Though I feel as if I've drunk an ocean of tea in the last few weeks and it hasn't really helped. 'Put two tea bags and about eight sugars in it. A double brandy too, if you've got it.'

She laughs. 'That bad.'

'I could kick myself.'

She goes off to make my tea and brings it over. 'Let's distract ourselves by betting on Alan's T-shirt for tomorrow.'

'Pink Floyd,' I opt for. '*Dark Side of the Moon*. He hasn't worn that for a while.' I'm aware that I'm going over old ground.

'Hmm. Good call.' She drums at her chin with her fingers, deep in thought before announcing, 'I'm going left field with the Stone Roses.'

'May the best woman win.' I down my tea. 'I'd better get out there again. I'm going to have a look at the slurry pond. I think it might need dredging.'

'We have ALL of the fun here,' Bev says. 'There's a bag of leftover cabbage and some sunflower seeds for the chickens, if you want to chuck that in to them on your way.' She nods to a carrier bag propped up by the arm of the sofa.

'Will do.' I know our girls will appreciate such treats. They love nothing better than to scratch about in the dirt looking for seeds.

So I grab the carrier bag and swing by the chicken run, tossing in their treats. I save a bit of cabbage for Teacup too as he also loves it – but then he loves every kind of food. When my favourite pig has been thoroughly fussed and petted, I head towards the pond. Passing near the barn my nose prickles with the faint smell of burning and, as I look up, there's a wisp of smoke coming from the far corner by the hay bales. Shit.

I'm in sprint mode immediately and race over to where I can smell the smoke coming from. Sure enough, there are a few flames dancing on one of the lower bales and I can see glowing embers in the next two bales. It's not too much now, but it's alarming enough and there's no way that we can afford for this to catch hold. Flame and farms are a deadly mix and we're so strict about smoking here, that I wonder how it's started. I grab my phone, punch in the number for the emergency services and give them the details as I race for the nearest hosepipe. Thankfully, there's one at this end of the barn.

Yet, by the time I get back, a couple more bales are starting to smoulder. 'Alan! Bev!' I shout. 'We're in trouble here!' But I've no idea if they're close enough to hear me.

I train the hosepipe on the worst of the flames, wishing that we had some kind of pressure system. This is fantastic for washing horses, not so much for fighting fires. We have fire extinguishers here, as required by our insurance policy, but they're hopeless too. What we need is a water cannon. Little Dog is barking and barking.

A moment later, Alan comes into the barn and quickly clocks what's happening. With an unaccustomed curse, he grabs one of the big buckets and scoops some water from the horse trough to throw on the fire. We move as close to it as we dare and though we work as fast as we can to quell the flames, we seem to be making little impression on it. I can feel the heat increasing and the feel of fear in my chest. Sweat is pouring down my face and back. The billowing smoke fills the barn and starts to make my breathing laboured and my eyes sting.

Bev comes into the back of the barn and sees what's happening. 'You've phoned the fire brigade?'

'Yes. I hope to God they find us quickly.' My face is warm, glowing.

'I'll move the kids to the far side of the farm, then I'll come back for the animals.'

'Take Little Dog too.'

'Come with me, baby.' She grabs Little Dog by the collar and then she dives out again.

'Look out for the fire engine,' I yell after her, but I don't know if she hears me.

Alan and I continue our labours. Him throwing on bucket after bucket of water at the worst of it, never stopping, me dowsing everything with the hosepipe.

'Are you OK, Alan?' I shout over to him.

'Yeah,' he says without looking up from his task.

In the yard, I can hear Bev opening pens and moving the animals out, cajoling those who are reluctant to move with the promise of food.

Alan and I seem to be keeping pace with the fire. It might not be dying down, but it's not taking hold as yet or roaring away from us. I pray to a God that I don't believe in that everything holds. At least there are no animals in the immediate vicinity, but I'm still worried about evacuating them. At what point do we abandon this and turn our attention to moving them just in case?

259

It's a blessed relief when a few minutes later there's the sound of the siren from a fire engine in the lane. I've always worried that we're too remote here, but they seem to have found us with ease and alacrity. It feels as if the cavalry have arrived in the nick of time. I'm sure Bev will go to get the gate as neither of us dare desert our posts.

'Thank God,' I say to Alan who nods at me in response and goes to get yet another bucket of water.

Chapter Sixty-One

Any longer and I think we might have lost control of the fire and the whole barn could have gone up in smoke. As it was, the firefighters arrived in the very nickiest nick of time, took over and saved the day. It would have been a terrible way to end our days at Hope Farm with a disastrous blaze. Yet it was only sheer luck that made me spot it in time. The thought is making me feel very shaky inside.

The stack of hay bales has largely gone and one end of the barn is badly charred, the wood blackened and scarred for ever. It's a miracle that none of the wood actually caught light and, for that, I'm truly grateful. Maybe someone up there was answering my prayers after all. Still, though, there's the pressing question of how it started.

Alan is sitting next to me, staring silently at the mess ahead of us. The barn floor is awash with water from the hoses. It's inching towards us. I turn to Alan and say, 'Thank you. I don't know what I'd have done without you. You were brilliant.'

'No worries.'

My throat closes with pain and emotion.

He puts a hand on my knee and I don't think that Alan has ever touched me before. 'It'll be right.'

'I hope so.'

Bev brings tea and biscuits for the firefighters. She gives me and Alan a mug too. I nurse mine, too shell-shocked to drink.

'The kids are all right,' she tells us. 'Just a bit shaken. I've moved them into the tea room and they've all got drinks. I'll phone their parents or taxis and get them collected as soon as possible.'

'The animals?'

'I've put them all in the alpaca paddock. Tina's not too happy about that, but needs must. They're all OK too.'

'Fifty? The dogs?'

'Just fine. The only casualty is Phantom.' Our elusive barn cat. I didn't even think where he might be. 'Smoke inhalation. The fire fighters are just giving him some oxygen. His fur's a bit singed too. Everyone else is fine. No harm done.'

Poor Phantom. I'm horrified that saving him didn't come into my head. I was too concerned about the barn. Luckily, as in the rest of his life, he was capable of fending for himself. I still feel that I've let down one of my charges.

And I can't stop thinking 'What if? What if? What if?' My teeth might be chattering a bit too. What if this had spread? What if the students had been in danger? What if we'd have had to evacuate the animals? What if our buildings had burnt down to the ground? It doesn't bear thinking about.

'Get that down your neck.' Bev nods at my untouched tea and frowns at me, her expression worried. 'You look dreadful.'

I bet I do. I feel grimy from the smoke and my throat is dry, my eyes are scratchy and my lungs are burning with every breath. The firefighters wanted Alan and me to go and get checked over at the local hospital to see the extent of our smoke inhalation and if any serious damage has been done, but I can't face a five-hour wait in A&E and Alan was reluctant to go too. I'm sure we'll be fine.

I take a sip of the tea and it seems to have a heap of sugar in it and I don't take sugar. 'Thanks, Bev.'

'Why don't you go and have a lie down in your caravan?'

'I'm OK. Really I am.'

She doesn't look convinced.

I'm not OK. There's a nagging feeling in my heart that I don't really want to address. Lucas left here in such a temper and I know that he's got form in this area. He was excluded from school for setting fire to stuff, after all. Could he have been the one to start this deliberately? I don't want to believe it of him, but a little voice in my head won't let the question go. Was he angry enough to do this as a punishment for me? Surely he couldn't be so cruel? Was it an accident? Could he have been smoking in here and carelessly discarded the cigarette butt? Lucas is the only student I know who smokes and I've had to tell him off about it before. I haven't seen him smoking recently, but that's not conclusive proof. I don't want to think badly of Lucas – you know how much I like him – but I can't help but wonder.

The firefighters, having finished their tea and biscuits, are clearing up, putting their paraphernalia away. They couldn't have been better or more supportive and, no doubt, they've saved us from certain disaster. I shudder again to think what could have happened and, despite the mountain of sugar that Bev forced down me, I feel drained now. I'm sitting on the floor as my legs didn't want to hold me up. If anything else lands on my plate, I may never get up again. I wipe my face on my sleeve and cover the fabric in black soot. No wonder I feel filthy dirty and in need of a good scrub down. Already, I know that my bucket shower won't really hit the spot tonight. Sometimes it would be nice to have just a little more luxury in my life or someone else to share the decisions and the difficult times. This is all too much for me to handle by myself. Perhaps I should give it all up, rehome the animals and get myself a proper job in an office or a building society or something. Surely my life would be less stressful. I could pick up my pay cheque and go home at five o'clock every night. There'd be regular money, a pension and weekends off, all of the perks.

But it's no good thinking like that. I have animals and students who depend on me keeping going for as long as I'm able to keep this place open. I have to pick myself up, dust myself down and get on with it, because if I don't, no one else will.

Chapter Sixty-Two

As the firefighters are leaving, I manage to mobilise myself to stand up so that I can shake the hands of our saviours, thanking them profusely. I really don't know what we'd have done if they hadn't arrived so swiftly.

The fire engine is just departing when Lucas comes walking into the yard. His hands are stuffed into his pockets, his fringe is almost covering his face, but what little of it I can see looks ashamed. It seems as if he didn't phone for that car after all. Maybe after stomping around for a bit, he's cooled off. I want to feel pleased to see him but, instead, my shoulders just feel even more weighed down.

He nods at the fire engine as it goes. 'What's going on here then? Have I missed something? It stinks of smoke.'

'Oh, Lucas,' I say sadly and I really hope that he's as innocent as he sounds. I lead him into the barn.

When we go inside his eyes widen and he's clearly horrified to see the extent of the damage that the fire has caused. Is the shock real or is he as good an actor as his father?

'What the fuck?' he says.

'Exactly.'

'Is everyone OK?'

'Yes. People and animals are all fine.' I study him closely when I add, 'Disaster was narrowly averted. I hate to think what would have happened if this had caught hold. My whole life could have literally gone up in smoke.'

'Shit. That was a close call.'

'Yes.' He's obviously shaken, but is that because of what he's seen or what he's done? We stand there awkwardly and that little voice nagging inside me just won't go away. 'I have to ask you this, Lucas. Did you start the fire?'

His face darkens. 'What?'

'I really want to believe that it was nothing to do with you, but given your past history, I can't help wonder.'

He stares at me, aghast. 'You think I did this because you were mad at me?'

'Did you?'

'Fuck off, Molly.'

'Don't speak to me like that,' I say, remaining as calm as I can. 'I want to discuss this rationally. If you did this, then we need to talk about it. I want you to understand just how dangerous it was. You could have endangered our lives and those of the animals.'

'You think I'd do that?'

'You were excluded from school for setting fire to things. How do I know for sure that's all behind you?'

His face screws up and he looks as if he's about to cry. Instead, he spits out, 'Because it wasn't bloody well me in the first place!' He holds up his hands and backs away from me. 'You adults are all the same. You can't see what's under your nose. I didn't set fire to *anything* at school. It was another bunch of kids, but no one would believe me. I took the rap because I was being bullied. Does that make you happy?'

'Why didn't you say anything?'

'Because no one ever listens to me.' He's shaking now and I want nothing more than to give him a hug, yet shock is freezing me to the spot. 'I came back here to apologise for acting like a twat this morning and you try to pin this on me?'

'I'm not trying to pin it on you, Lucas. I'm simply asking you straight. Was this down to you?'

'No,' he snaps. 'No, it wasn't.' He shakes his head at me and I've never seen anyone look more disappointed. I shrivel inside. His eyes fill with tears and two pink spots appear on his chalk-white face. 'I thought you really cared. But you're just like all the rest. This time I'm really going and I'm not coming back.'

He storms away from me, looking like a lost, vulnerable child. But I don't have the energy to follow him. My throat is so scorched that I can't even summon my voice to call out. I watch him march away, all angry angles and hatred emanating from him and I can do nothing.

I look at the barn, the smell of smoke searing my nostrils, the charred wood and, in my heart, I still don't know whether I can believe him or not.

Chapter Sixty-Three

For the rest of the day, I just feel numb. Bev and Alan are fantastic, as always, and step in to look after everyone – kids and animals alike – as I seem to have lost the ability to function properly. Tamara goes round the barn taking loads of photos of charred wood and singed hay to put on social media. I think our students have coped admirably with the dramatic disruption as so many of them don't like any deviation from their routine. This kind of thing is a big challenge for them. For me too. In fact, they're handling it better than I am. No one has gone into meltdown even though there are some anxious faces.

'Go and lie down.' Bev steers me towards my caravan. 'You're no use to anyone like this. Have a good rest and you'll be able to face it all with a clearer head tomorrow.'

My natural instinct is to fight it and soldier on, but instead I take her advice and say, 'Thank you.'

'We'll finish up here,' Bev says. 'I'll see to the students and I'll settle the animals and feed them. There's nothing for you to worry about.'

But there is. Every thought I have causes me to worry.

I click my fingers for Little Dog who trots to my heel. Despite his permanent smile, he looks anxious too. Bending down, I fuss his ears. 'It will be all right, boy,' I assure him. Though I think I could be lying.

We walk towards the van, the smell of smoke heavy in the air, the pattern of the flames still imprinted on my eyes. As well as the barn, the yard is also awash with water from the fire-fighters' efforts and I really need to get out here with the broom, but my limbs are like lead, my head aching. There's nothing in the bank and, once again, the precarious nature of my finances threatens to undo me. If the barn, or anything else, had burned to the ground then I really would be left with nothing but a pile of ashes. If it had caught hold, my caravan could have gone too and then I'd even be without a home. Once again it hits me that I need to do some serious fundraising or have a massive, unexpected windfall.

In the caravan, I close the bedroom curtains and Little Dog and I lie down on the bed. Personal grooming isn't usually high on my list of concerns. It's perfectly normal for me to have dirt under my fingers and uncombed hair, but I feel filthy and in need of a shower. As soon as Bev and Alan have gone, I'll strip off and douse myself. Water always makes you feel better.

I doze off but am restless, dreaming of fire licking at my feet and water engulfing me. Little Dog twitches next to me.

When my phone rings next to my head, it's a struggle to wake up but I'm glad to be free of my dark dreams. I thought it might be Bev as it would be just like her to call to see how I am, but the display says it's Shelby.

Sitting bolt upright, I straighten my tangled hair. 'Hi.'

'I've just got back from filming. Lucas is in a dreadful state.' Shelby sounds bleak. 'He says he won't come to the farm any more, but won't say why.'

I let out a long wavering breath, but can't find any words.

'Molly? Molly? Are you there?'

It takes me an age to answer, 'Yes.'

'This is obviously serious. I'm coming straight up. Is that OK?'

I nod at the phone.

'Ten minutes. That's all I'll be. Come to the gate.'

I nod again and hang up. I've no idea what time it is but my phone tells me it's nearly seven o'clock. My legs are still weak when I get up and Little Dog runs round me looking concerned. 'I'm fine,' I let him know. 'Absolutely fine.'

He doesn't look convinced and I'm not sure that I am either. All this drama has knocked me for six. My thoughts are whirling in my head and I can't latch on to any of them properly.

A text pings in. This time it's Bev. *Are you OK? Didn't want to call & wake you. Bxx*

I text back. *Fine. Still a bit shaky. I'll be as right as rain tomoz. Mxx*

The new lambs need another feed. Everything else is done. Bxx

I'll do it now. I'm not going to mention Shelby's impending visit.

Call if you need me for ANYTHING! Bxx

Thanks. You've done so much already. Mxx

Love you. Bxx

I look in the mirror and am disappointed by what I see. It shouldn't matter what I look like to meet Shelby to talk about Lucas, but I find that it does. New territory for me. Too late to do much about it now. But I do have a quick rub round with a flannel and change my clothes, so that I don't smell like a burnt offering.

On tired legs I walk down to the gate and, only a moment later, Shelby's car sweeps up the lane. I let him in. He looks rattled when he gets out of the driver's seat, but no less immaculately groomed than usual. My heart lurches when I see him

270

and I don't like that at all. I wipe my palms on my jeans, which probably makes them grubbier than they were before, and shake his hand.

'That's very formal,' he says. 'It must be bad.'

'I'm just filthy,' I admit. 'All unnecessary contact should be avoided.'

'Want to tell me why Lucas has locked himself into his cottage and is refusing to speak to me?'

I've no idea how to break this easily to him so, instead, I just say, 'You'd better come this way.'

I lead him towards the barn, aware that he's splashing through puddles in his designer shoes. We reach the ruin of hay bales, the charred wood, the tangle of farm equipment Alan managed to move away from the impending flames.

He stares at it stricken. Then he runs a hand through his beautiful hair and mutters, 'Fuck.'

'Precisely.'

'This was Lucas?'

'I don't know yet. A fire officer is coming out to inspect the damage. Probably tomorrow. They'll try to determine the cause of the fire. I'll have a better handle on it then.'

'But you think it might have been?'

'We had an argument during the day. He was very angry with me. I had to question his behaviour. He insists that it wasn't him.'

'But he has form.'

'The funny thing is he told me that he doesn't. He was quite adamant that it wasn't him who set the fires at his school.'

'They were convinced it was and, by all accounts, he admitted it. That's why he was excluded without the police being called in.'

'Did you know he was being bullied?'

He looks shocked for a moment, but answers, 'No. He never talks to me about anything. What did he say?'

'Not much. Just that it was some other lads who'd done what he was accused of. It sounded like it was easier for him to admit to it rather than tell who the real culprits were.'

'I don't like the sound of this. Talk to him, Molly. You're the only one he seems to relate to. You can get to the bottom of this.'

'I might have blown it,' I confess. 'I didn't handle this situation very well.'

'What was your argument about?'

I wonder if I should tell him the truth and then decide that honesty, usually, is the best policy. 'You.'

'Me?'

'He was unhappy that we'd spent time together, that we'd had dinner – such as it was.'

'But initially, I was here talking about *him*.'

'Believe me, I did try to explain that.' But perhaps I didn't try hard enough.

'What am I going to do about him?' Shelby sounds weary.

'We'll think of something. I've never given up on a student yet and I don't intend to now.' I link my arm through his. 'Walk with me round the farm?'

He nods his agreement and I can see that he's trying to choke down his emotion. Maybe what he actually needs to do is let it all out. Maybe that's what we both need to do.

Chapter Sixty-Four

It's a beautiful evening, warm without a breath of wind. A red kite, wings spread wide to catch the heavy air, soars sedately overhead. The sun is sinking and, once again, I think how blessed that I've been to live in such a wonderful slice of countryside. How sad I am that soon I will have to leave and, instead of my sheep, horses and alpacas, trains will thunder through at such hair-raising speeds that the passengers won't even be able to admire what little there's left of it. This part of England will be destroyed for ever in the name of progress. Today's fire only served to reinforce how attached I am to this land and I feel that my heart is broken into a thousand pieces.

'You're quiet,' Shelby says.

'I think I'm still in shock after today,' I admit.

'But it's more than that. I can tell.'

'The whole thing about losing the farm is very unsettling.' We walk for a minute or two longer before I say. 'I've been onto the council about finding some replacement land, but I'm having no luck so far. Time is running out and I've yet to come up with a solution. If I don't, I've no idea what will happen to my students, my animals. I can't bear to let them down.'

'Are there no other avenues you could explore?'

'If there are, then I've not found them.' I push down the ball of emotion in my raw throat. 'I'm actually thinking of throwing in the towel. I'm not sure how much I can struggle on with all of this.' I feel on the verge of tears but won't let myself cry in front of Shelby again.

He slings an arm round my shoulder and pulls me into his chest. I stand there letting him hold me tight. It feels good to be in the comfort of his embrace and, for a brief moment, I can forget my woes and enjoy the strength and the scent of him.

When we break away, I say, 'I have some new lambs that I want to tend to. Are you happy to head down there?'

He looks strangely sad that the moment has gone yet nevertheless says, 'Yes. Though I actually spend most of my working day trying to avoid animals.'

'I'm sorry, but that still makes me laugh.' And it doesn't fail me this time. A bright spot in what has been a very difficult day.

'I'm glad to be the source of your amusement, Ms Baker,' he chides.

We walk back down to the yard and the stable where the new lambs are being nurtured. 'I'm just going to give them a last feed. Bev finished most of my chores for today.'

'This really is a full-on undertaking, isn't it?'

'It's my life,' I tell him honestly. 'I know nothing else.'

'Don't you ever get the hankering to put on a fancy gown and attend a swanky party?'

'No. It would be my idea of hell.'

'It's my idea of hell too – especially the gown part,' he jokes. 'But these days, I seem to find myself at an awful lot of swanky parties that I don't want to be at. Maybe I'm just getting old.'

'Maybe you've just had enough of small talk.' Shelby gives

me a surprised look that says I may have inadvertently hit the spot.

As soon as we arrive at the stable door, the lambs start bleating in the hope that their dinner waiters have arrived.

'Hello, lovelies. Are you hungry?' They bleat back that they are very nearly on the point of starvation, as always. 'Well, I won't be a moment.'

Treasure that she is, Bev has left three bottles already made up in the stable. 'Want to help?' I offer a bottle to Shelby.

'I'll give it a go,' he says.

'It will mean getting up close and personal with the babies.'

'It might help to build up some resistance if I gradually introduce myself to them.' Though he looks the very picture of reluctance.

'It's not compulsory. You could go back to the van and put the kettle on.' Then I realise it was very presumptuous of me. 'Only if you have nowhere else to be.'

'No. I have no other plans.' He takes the bottle from me, determination on his face. 'I can do this.'

'There are some overalls on the hook. These chaps can be messy. You might want to cover your fancy clothes.'

He looks at the state of the overalls and then at the straw in the stables. 'I think the overalls are probably the lesser of two evils.'

'Good choice,' I tease. 'We do clean the straw regularly, but it hasn't been done today. I'm sorry about that.' Shelby shakes his head, yet he climbs into the overalls. They're dark blue, baggy and have paint stains all over them. At least I think it's paint.

He holds out his hands. 'I'm never going to make the front of a glossy in these.'

'You still look good to me.' And then I blush furiously as I realise what just came out of my mouth. We both ignore it and

Shelby follows me into the stable. 'We're outnumbered, so I'll take two. You can deal with this little one. Hold the bottle like so.' I show him how.

We sit on the straw together in the corner of the stable and, instantly, the lambs pounce on us. They tug at the bottles with all their worth, little tails frantically wagging with joy. We try to avoid giving them names at this point as some of them are so tiny that they just don't make it. We *try* not to give them names, but sometimes we do.

'That's Titch you've got,' I tell Shelby above the bleating. 'He was in quite a bad state when we got him, very underweight and pathetic. But he's thriving now with a bit of extra TLC. I come and cuddle him whenever I can. The others are doing quite well, but Titch isn't very good with the feeder that we have here yet, so I usually check on him in the middle of the night in case he needs a bottle.'

'That's very dedicated of you.'

I shrug. 'What else could I do?'

Titch butts at Shelby's arm, telling him to hold the bottle higher. 'He doesn't seem to be suffering now. He's a feisty little thing.'

'A fighter,' I agree.

'Just like you.'

'I take that as a compliment.'

He fixes me with a disconcerting look when he says, 'It was meant as one.'

I look away from him and concentrate on the lamb that's vying for my attention. 'Your bottle's nearly empty. He's a greedy boy.'

'I'm finding this a strangely therapeutic experience.' Shelby has settled against the wall and Titch is feeding contentedly. 'I just hope that I don't start sneezing any time soon.'

'I'm nearly done now and we can get out of here.' While I'm

finishing up feeding the other lambs, Shelby stays sitting in the hay and I notice that Titch snuggles up to him, sleepy with milk, and that Shelby strokes his head. I can't help but smile to myself. There's nothing like a cute lamb to turn you into an animal lover.

When the bottles are drained and the lambs are all fed, I stand up. 'I'll make you a cup of tea now. If you've got time.'

'That would be great.' Shelby moves Titch from his side and stands up. 'I'd better get out of these overalls.'

He starts to unbutton the front, but one of the buttons is tight and I can see that he's struggling with it. 'Here, let me help.' So I move into him and tweak the button until it undoes. 'There.'

As I go to step away again, Shelby stills my hand to his chest. I can feel his heart beating beneath the cloth. His voice is husky when he says, 'I think the next one might be stuck too.'

So I move my fingers down and unbutton the next one. Then the next. He reaches out and undoes the top button of my shirt. And when he moves lower, I don't stop him.

Chapter Sixty-Five

Shelby kisses me and my head spins. His lips are soft but insistent and I can't think when I've ever been kissed like this before. I want him like I've never wanted any other man. Without speaking, I lead him to the next stall where the newly laid straw is clean, dry and still has the fresh scent of the fields. We undress each other, then lie down on our discarded clothes and make love.

When we're sated and lying in each other's arms, he reaches out and tenderly strokes my face. 'I don't think I've ever made love in a stable before. Not even in *Flinton's Farm*. It's a storyline we're definitely missing out on.'

But is that what we really did, I wonder? Did we make love or merely satisfy an overwhelming but momentary desire?

Shelby lets out a sigh and plays with my hair. 'I feel so contented when I'm here with you, Molly. My troubles seem to melt away. Why is that?'

'I don't know.'

'I want to ask you if you feel the same. I can't read you at all.'

In all honesty, I'm scared of how I feel about Shelby. I don't want to need him as it's only going to end badly for me. He could have the pick of any woman so why would he choose to be with me? And yet he's here and, more than I've ever wanted anything, I do want him. I couldn't bear for him to leave right away. I'd be crushed. If I could stay here in his arms for the rest of the night, I'd be more than happy. How can I tell him that, though? It's too soon and what about Scarlett Vincent? Is this being unfaithful to her or do they have a more fluid and altogether modern arrangement? Maybe that's the way with celebrities? Perhaps that's something I should have asked before I instigated this.

'I want to spend the night,' he says. 'Not necessarily in a pile of straw,' he adds which makes us both laugh. 'But I want to be with you.'

'I'd like that.' You have no idea of the rush of happiness that just hit me. Then, barely a moment later, reality kicks in. Damn my practical brain. 'But what about Lucas?'

He was unhappy enough about me having dinner with his father. How he would hate me for this.

'I need to talk to him, don't I?' Shelby sighs. 'Sooner rather than later.'

'Yes.' There's no denying it.

'Then I'll go home and face him.' He toys with my hair again. 'But not yet.'

He kisses me and, once more, we make love and it takes my breath away that our bodies are so in tune when we hardly know each other. His skin is smooth, firm, deliciously warm against mine. I'm not an advocate of the one-night stand, never have been. I don't see the point of being intimate with someone you don't know and might never see again. What is the point of sharing the most secret part of yourself with them? Yet here I am. And I'm relishing every moment.

Afterwards, we lie together quietly, dozing in each other's

arms. The only sound the bleating of the lambs in the neighbouring stall.

'I should go,' Shelby says, eventually. 'It's going to take me ages to pick the straw out of my clothes. I don't want Lucas to know that we've been tumbling in the hay. Not yet, anyway.'

He'll be furious, I know, and I feel terribly guilty that I've betrayed his trust. 'It's probably best if we keep it to ourselves.'

'There's one thing I know for sure, Molly. You're not the type of woman who'll be running to the tabloids tomorrow morning with the story.'

'It never crossed my mind,' I agree.

'I've only known you for a short while, but I feel that I can trust you. Believe me, that's a very rare thing in my business.'

How sad, I think, to live in a world like that. When you don't know who your friends are and who wants to be with you just because you're someone who's on the telly.

'I smell worse than I do when I've come off the set,' Shelby says, sniffing at his shoulder. 'I do all that I can to avoid contact with the animals at work. Now I'm carrying the aroma of milk, lambs and a hint of sheep poo.'

That makes me giggle. 'We could have a shower?'

'That sounds like a very good plan.'

'Don't get overexcited and think power shower,' I warn him. 'I'm talking bucket shower. An outdoor one at that.'

He looks appalled. 'You are kidding me.'

'No. And we'll have to share a bucket.' Which isn't strictly true. I could quite easily heat up two buckets of water, but the thought of being close to Shelby in the shower is suddenly very appealing.

'Another new experience,' he says and we kiss again.

Chapter Sixty-Six

We share the bucket shower behind the barn as the sun is setting and the dusk deepens. The sky is the colour of marmalade smudged with charcoal. I run my soapy hands over his skin and he does the same to mine. This time I shiver with delight as well as the cold. We linger long after the water has gone, holding each other, tasting each other's mouths. The sun is setting, the night time closing in.

'Much as I don't want to leave, I really should be going,' he murmurs in my ear.

I lean into his shoulder, to hide the disappointment on my face and soak up, once more, the feel of his arms around me.

Afterwards, he wraps me in a towel and, hand-in-hand, we walk back to the caravan. I can only assume that Shelby is lost in his thoughts, as I am.

He gets dressed in the cramped space of my van and I want to tear my eyes away from him but can't. I drink in his handsome face, his toned body, the way he moves, how his face is softened in the fading light. This might be the only time I get to do this and I want to make the most of it. I'm storing up memories to keep in my heart. When I'm old and alone, I want to remember the time when I had this beautiful man all to myself – even if it was for a fleeting moment.

When he's buttoned up his shirt and smoothed his hair, he kisses my cheek – more businesslike now.

'Thank you. This has been . . . it's been . . . well . . . ' He waits patiently while I struggle for the words to encompass my emotions. 'It's been very enjoyable.'

He laughs at that, gently teasing. 'Sweet Molly. I found it *very enjoyable* too.'

I wish that he was staying and not leaving like this.

'I'll call you,' he says. 'Let you know how I get on with Lucas.'

'Yes, do that.'

'Are you going to lock the gate behind me?'

'Gate? Oh, Yes.'

So I follow him to his car, hoping that we might have one last, lingering kiss. But we don't. He climbs into the driver's seat, gives me a little wave and then swings towards the lane. I let him out and watch as he drives away.

He hasn't asked if he can he see me again and I suppose that I'm not really surprised. I guess that this will only happen the once. Fair enough. Shelby hasn't declared undying love and owes me nothing. It was a spur of the moment passion, something I've never felt or done before.

I'm OK with that. Really I am.

Chapter Sixty-Seven

The next day there's a little kernel of glowy warmth in my heart that wasn't there pre-Shelby. I don't know whether to share it with Bev or keep it to myself. She might be pleased for me, but there's an equal chance that she might claw my eyes out.

When I fed the lambs again early this morning, I kept getting delicious flashbacks to last night. If I close my eyes I can still feel his skin against my skin, his mouth on my mouth, his body joined with mine. I want to call Shelby and thank him, but would that be weird? I'm unsure of the etiquette of these things.

Now Bev and I are at the stables together, supervising our students who are mucking out today. This is our regular, thorough strip-down where we take everything out of the stalls and give it a good clean – bedding, feed buckets and even favourite toys and licks. We use the brooms to knock down all the accumulated spiders' webs which usually has at least one or more of the students screaming. Then we disinfect it all before putting it all back nice and tidy. It's my favourite thing to do as I find it so satisfying – like cleaning a dirty oven – but I realise that I'm in a minority.

Currently, the students are attacking it with a high level of enthusiasm which I know from past experience won't last. Depending on how many we have here, we try to rotate the duties so that they only have to do it once a week. Twice at the most. Sometimes three times. Animals poo and wee a lot, what can I tell you?

Bev pauses in her work. 'Despite all your trials and tribulations, there seems to be a distinct sparkle in your eyes.' She stares at me, her own eyes narrowed, as she forks the hay. 'Would you like to tell Auntie Bev why?'

I'm wavering about whether I should 'fess up or not when Alan saunters in, a pace which never varies no matter what he's doing. Today he's sporting a Band of Skulls T-shirt and that's way beyond my musical scope. I look at Bev and she pulls a face at me. Clearly she feels the same.

Alan holds up a small generator. 'Culprit.'

'What?'

'Culprit,' he reiterates. 'It was this bugger what started the fire.'

'You're kidding me.' As soon as the words are out of my mouth, I know that Alan would never joke with me.

'Frayed wire.'

'Seriously? You're absolutely sure that's what caused the barn fire?'

'Yeah. Well, ninety-nine-point-nine per cent recurring,' He offers the offending cable to me to examine.

It certainly does look, even to the untrained eye, that it's burnt out. 'Damn.'

'I thought you'd be pleased,' Bev says, leaning on her pitchfork.

'I am, but it means that I questioned Lucas unnecessarily.' Why didn't I wait until at least we had some evidence of what caused it? I should never have voiced my concerns so soon. 'It wasn't him all along and I've done him a great disservice.'

'At least we know now,' Bev points out, ever practical. 'Phone him and explain. Grovel a bit. Maybe a lot. He'll come back. He's a good kid.'

'I hope you're right.' I touch Alan's arm. 'Thanks, Alan. That's great.'

'We need a new one.'

Marvellous. More expense. 'I'll see what I can do.'

Alan wanders off and Bev and I return to our mucking out. I take a strange pleasure in the monotony of barrowing the manure across the yard to the manure heap. It gives me time to think. Though this morning I brood about how to approach Lucas, cross that I handled it so badly. Before you say anything, I know I'm not Superwoman, that I can't be expected to be perfect all the time, but this was important and I dropped the ball on it. Shame I didn't stop to think it through before launching in.

We move all the mulch, then Bev and I show the students how to clean and maintain the tools, how to store them safely – though Tamara and Jody have lost interest and are entertaining themselves with selfies. I give them both brooms and they sulk. When we've thoroughly swept all the hay debris from the area and the stables are clean and tidy once more, we break for lunch.

I eat my baked sweet potato without tasting it. The kids chatter away happily, seemingly unfazed by yesterday's drama, which is a very good thing. I don't want any of them derailed by this. Plus I've yet to tell them that the future of their beloved farm is about to be derailed, literally. I've that joy to come. Ideally, I hope to have a solution in place before I start to worry them.

While we're clearing up after lunch, I say to Bev, 'I might call Lucas now and apologise.'

She nods at me. 'I'll take this lot to help with the egg collection before their tutor comes.'

'OK.' So they all leave me alone in the tea room and, feeling as if I'd rather eat my own face with a fork, I call Lucas.

I don't know if it's relief or disappointment that washes over me when my call goes straight to voicemail. I wonder if he's identified that it's me who's trying to contact him? I take a deep breath before I launch in.

'Hi Lucas,' I say. 'I'm just phoning to apologise for the other day. Alan's found out what did cause the fire and I know that it wasn't you. I'd like to talk about it. Please call me when you get this message. It's Molly.'

I hang up. Then I sit and don't quite know what to do. Eventually, I decide to leave a message for Shelby as well. My hand shakes as I punch in the number and my heart pounds so much that I think it might just jump out of my mouth.

I get Shelby's voicemail too.

'Hi,' I say as lightly as I can manage. 'Molly here. Just wanted you to know that Alan found the cause of the fire and it wasn't anything to do with Lucas. I hope you're as relieved as I am to hear that. I can only apologise that I thought it might be anything to do with him. Please tell Lucas that if you get the chance. I've called him and left a message too. Anyway, call me if you want to chat about it further.' Then I hesitate. Should I mention last night? Would it seem gauche? I think it probably would. So I finish off with a rather forced and cheery 'Bye,' and hang up.

Then I wait. What else can I do?

Chapter Sixty-Eight

A week goes by and neither Lucas nor Shelby respond to my call. I want to leave more messages, but I don't in case they think I'm a deranged nut job. Still, it leaves me completely unsettled and I go about my chores in a more haphazard and distracted manner than usual. Little Dog is very concerned for my well-being and sticks to me like glue – even more so than usual. Big Dog and Fifty pick up on his distress and latch onto him too which means that I go everywhere with a following of two anxious dogs and a concerned sheep.

If I'm honest, I'm not sure which lack of reply hurts me more – Shelby or Lucas. I'm feeling it like a physical pain in my chest. This is why I stick to animals and don't get too involved with people if at all possible.

The rain is lashing horizontally across the hills today, making all tasks take twice as long. Usually, I don't mind bad weather. It's all part of the deal. Today the rain seems spiteful, the wind malevolent, the clouds cruel and I can't face them. Instead, I grab the opportunity to hibernate in the caravan and spend an hour on the phone to a man at the council whose mission in life is clearly to be as unhelpful as possible. When I hang up, almost weeping with frustration, I'm no closer to finding a solution for our impending homelessness. The end date is looming large and, so far, I have no fall-back plan. None.

Bev sticks her head round the door. 'The weather's a total bitch today.'

'Isn't she just.' Fingers of rain drum against the roof and tap at the windows.

'The kids are cranky buggers.' My friend shakes the rain from her shoulders as she comes in, soaking everything in the vicinity. She shrugs out of her wet things, hanging her coat on the back of the door and kicking off her wellies. 'They hate the rain more than me. I've given up and am letting them sit flicking mindlessly through their phones in the tea room until it stops peeing down.'

'I don't blame you.'

She frowns at me. 'Everything all right in here?'

'Not really,' I admit with a weary puff of breath. 'I've been on the phone for ages, yet I still can't find anywhere for us to go. Especially on our meagre budget.'

'Bum,' she says and comes in to sit next to me. 'Too early for vodka?'

'It's not yet eleven o'clock.'

'A tad then.'

'I'll make us a coffee.'

While I bang about with the cups, Bev says, 'Still no word from Lucas or the rather wonderful Mr Dacre?'

'No.' I make the coffee and hand her a mug. When I sit back down opposite her, I blurt out, 'I slept with him.'

She stares at me, aghast. 'Shelby?'

'Who else?'

'I did wonder for a moment if you meant Alan.'

'He's lovely but, no, not Alan.' I can't imagine Alan ever taking off his band T-shirt. Actually, I *really* don't want to imagine Alan taking off his band T-shirt.

Her eyes widen as she digests my startling announcement. 'You *shagged* Shelby Dacre?'

'I did. Don't look at me like that.'

'Oh, God. You lucky, lucky woman. I wanted first dibs on him.'

'We didn't mean for it to happen.'

'Did you do it here?' She gives a sideways glance to my sofa, clearly intent on an interrogation.

'Er . . . no. Actually it was in the stable. In the hay.'

'Seriously? You dirty cow!'

'I'd hoped for something more encouraging than that.'

'Hay though? All I think of is poo and mice.'

'It was the new stuff in the stable. Untouched by animals or humans.'

'Bugger.' She pulls a jealous face at me. 'That sounds positively romantic.'

She's right. It was.

Bev sighs heavily and gives a wistful little stare. 'Hay or not, I bet he was *flipping fabulous*.'

'I have very little to compare it with, but I'd head towards *flipping fabulous*.'

'I knew it!' she shouts out.

I can feel my cheeks burning. I'm not even going to mention the post-coital bucket shower we took together. Bev might spontaneously combust. The images play in my mind once more. *I* might spontaneously combust!

'And what about Ms Scarlett Moddle-turned-Actress?'

'Strangely, we didn't talk about her.'

'I bet you didn't.' Bev rubs her face with her hands. 'Blimey. I can't leave you alone for five minutes.'

'Can I point out that in all the years you've known me, this is the first time that I've acted out of character? It was purely a spur of the moment thing.'

'So? Are you going to give me all the details?'

'No. It was a one-off. That's all. He hasn't called me since. I didn't expect him to.'

'But, nevertheless, you're disappointed that he hasn't.' Her hand covers mine.

I feel stupid tears prickling behind my eyes as I answer, 'Yes.'

'Oh, Mols. You are not wise in the ways of the world. You *definitely* should have left him to me.'

I laugh and wipe my eyes. 'Is that the best you've got to offer?'

'Look, you've got to forget about Shelby Dacre. He's obviously just like the cad he plays. Put it in a little cupboard at the back of your mind, the one labelled "nice memories", mark it down to experience and don't waste any more time thinking about him.'

'Sound advice.' And it would be so much easier to do if, every time I close my eyes, I didn't see Shelby's face or relive his strong body moving above me.

'Lucas is a different matter altogether. He needs you. Get yourself up to that swanky mansion this afternoon and bang on his door. We can manage without you for an hour or so. He's bound to be there. Where else would he be? Shelby will be on set, so he won't be around. You can talk to Lucas face to face.'

'Do you think I should?'

'You know I'm always right,' Bev asserts. 'Do it.'

'I will.' I need to have closure on this and, surely, it can't do any harm? Can it?

Chapter Sixty-Nine

I take the truck up to Shelby's big posh house. The gears are still grating and grinding as I haven't had time to get it fixed yet. In a matter of weeks, I might not even need a truck for transporting farm animals, so I've put it out of my mind. I also try not to think of the conversation to come and, instead, concentrate on negotiating the country lanes.

Today there's no security guard on the gate, but they're firmly closed against random callers. So I pull up next to the Homewood Manor plaque and, with only a momentary hesitation, lean out of the truck window to press the buzzer in the middle of an intercom box on the high wall.

A minute later, Lucas's voice says, 'Hi. Who is it?'

With a deep breath, I answer, 'It's me. Molly.'

'Oh.'

The gates stay shut. 'Can I come and talk to you?'

'I got your message.'

'Good. I'd like to apologise.'

'No need. Now we both know it wasn't me. I told you that.'

'And I reacted very badly, Lucas. I'm very sorry. I didn't mean to let you down.'

There's a long silence, but I'm determined not to slink away. Not yet, anyway.

When the silence continues, I say, 'I'm not going away.'

More silence.

'If I'd known you were going to keep me out here all afternoon,' I add, 'I'd have brought a flask of tea and some chocolate Hobnobs.'

There's a weak laugh followed by a weary sigh and, clutching at straws, I take that as progress.

Sure enough, a moment later, the gate buzzes and swings open. Lucas says, 'I'll meet you at the front of the house.'

'OK.' I graunch the truck into gear and trundle into the drive.

As I make my way down the tree-lined entrance, I can see Lucas come out of the garden behind the house and plonk himself on a low wall by the fountain to wait for me. No matter how many times I see the house, it's still just as impressive. It's more like a hotel than a home, though. I park, and as I climb down from the cab, Lucas lopes over to me, not meeting my eyes.

'Hi.'

'I'm in a cottage out the back.' He flicks a thumb over his shoulder. 'I don't live in the house any more.'

I don't tell him that Shelby had already mentioned that to me as I don't want us to get off on the wrong foot. Lucas sets off and I fall into step next to him. We make our way into the garden behind the house, down a small path by the swimming pool, cut alongside the tennis court and come out into a smaller, more secluded garden that I didn't notice on my last visit.

There's a single storey building here like a barn. It has a fancy porch and hanging baskets by the door.

'Home, sweet home.' Lucas pushes his way in and I follow. Inside there's a small living area with a galley kitchen to one side. The huge television is on with the sound turned down and

292

there's a recently abandoned games console in the middle of the rug. At the far end, an open door shows a glimpse of an untidy bedroom. Under all the teenage detritus, I think it's tastefully furnished.

'This is nice.'

He shrugs his indifference. 'I suppose you want a cup of tea.'

'That would be lovely. Thank you.'

He clangs about, not speaking, while I stand there a bit awkwardly. Clearly, he's not going to attempt to make this easy for me.

When he comes back with two mugs, he says, 'We can sit in the garden, if you like.'

'Shall we walk up to that place where we sat before? It had a lovely view.'

'OK.'

So we take our mugs of tea into the garden, walk to the far side, away from the house and through the small copse of trees. The view is just as delightful as I remember. We sit down side by side on the bench sculpted from hay. Without speaking, we both take in the rolling countryside.

Eventually, I grab my courage in both hands and break the silence. 'I've missed you.' When he doesn't respond, I add, 'We all have.'

Lucas stares ahead, unmoved.

'I was wrong to think that it was you. But, in my defence, I wasn't thinking at all. My brain just blew a fuse. I didn't know what to make of it. I'm sure you can understand how stressful this all is.'

He makes a disparaging noise.

'You said you were wrongly accused at school too.'

'That doesn't matter now, does it?' He growls like an animal in pain. 'I'm the one who's been kicked out.'

'You didn't try to defend yourself?'

'What was the point? I'm the weirdo kid. The one with no friends. Who's going to believe me against the most popular guy in the school?' He gives me a disgusted look. 'No one. That's who. Not even my own father. He just believed their version.'

'I'm sorry, Lucas. That's awful.'

'It's life,' he says as if he's tired of it all. 'It's shit and then you die.'

'I could go with you to talk to the school, if you'd like.'

'What's the point? Wild horses couldn't drag me back there.'

'At least let's sit down and talk to your dad about it. I left him a message, but he hasn't got back to me yet.'

'You're *way* down his list,' he says, somewhat spitefully. 'He flew off to LA with Scarlett for a few days. That's the last I've heard of him.'

'What for?'

Shrugging. 'No fucking idea.' He stares levelly at me. 'So you see, Molly, there's little reason to try to get me and my dear papa round a table. He's just not that interested.'

'I think, despite how it appears, that he is.' Though I'm disappointed to hear that he's gone off to America and has left Lucas alone at a difficult time for him. 'But I didn't come here to argue with you. I came to ask you to come back to the farm.'

'What's the point when you're going to be closing down soon?'

'I'm still hoping for a miracle,' I tell him, earnestly.

He laughs at that, but not too harshly. 'Christ, you're nauseatingly optimistic.'

'Yeah.' I grin at him. 'That's me. Ms Glass Half-full.'

Then he softens for a moment. 'I wrote a poem about the farm. Want to see it?'

'I'd really love to.'

He pulls out his phone and clicks on to YouTube to play it. I lean over his shoulder to watch and he doesn't move away from me.

On screen, he looks direct to the camera and spits out a rap called 'Save the Farm' in which he extols the virtue of our work and pleads for new land for us.

It's nothing short of criminal:
It's a travesty; a scam.
We're another victim of that HS2 to Birmingham.
Because, despite the work we've done here,
For those with special needs,
The rich man's railway still comes first,
Yes, progress supersedes!
And that leaves us with a problem,
As our work here's far from done,
Our appeal needs to go viral
Reach the hearts of everyone.
All we need is twenty acres,
At a rent that's not too steep;
A place to keep our goats and pigs
And Tony, the angry sheep.

Save The Farm! Save The Farm!
With the alpacas we'll stand tall!
Save The Farm! Save The Farm!
Hear us all at Hope Farm call!
Save The Farm! Save The Farm!
Stand up for what you know is right,
So the work we do can con-tin-ue
Come join us in this fight.

'Cos the work we do here's vital,
It's a lifeline we provide;
For those for whom conventional education
Hasn't been an easy ride.

You see alpacas aren't judgemental,
And goats don't take the mick,
And pigs and sheep don't badger you
For being dyslexic.
They help to normalise anxieties,
Build the confidence to achieve;
They encourage us kids to integrate
And in ourselves believe.
They've been called iconoclastic;
Revolutionary; unique,
We've got all we need to make this work,
It's just the ground space that we seek.

Save The Farm! Save The Farm!
With the alpacas we'll stand tall
Save The Farm! Save The Farm!
Hear us all at Hope Farm call!
Save The Farm! Save The Farm!
Stand up for what you know is right,
So the work we do can con-tin-ue
Come join us in this fight.

There are people who depend on us;
We won't go down without a fight,
But we're an independent entity
And our finances are tight.
There's animal feed and vet bills,
Day-to-days, and at some stage,
Molly would like to draw herself at least a living wage.
So if you're rich and fancy helping us,
Or you've got some land to spare,
Or if you know anyone else who has,
Who could be convinced to care,

Then get in touch; we'd love to hear, or share my video,
On all your social media and with everyone you know!

Save The Farm! Save The Farm!
With the alpacas we'll stand tall
Save The Farm! Save The Farm!
Hear us all at Hope Farm call!
Save The Farm! Save The Farm!
Stand up for what you know is right,
So the work we do can con-tin-ue
Come join us in this fight.

I feel my eyes filling with tears.

'Don't cry,' Lucas says. 'You'll start me off.'

'That's great.' I wipe my tears away with my sleeve.

'What bloody use is it?' he asks.

'I don't know. The students will love it though. You'll be an even bigger hero to them. Plus it's got a hundred thousand views since you put it up. That's a lot, right? You must have tons of followers.'

'Yeah, but they're probably all broke like me.'

'I don't know if it will do any good, Lucas, but it's fabulous nevertheless.' I risk giving him a peck on his cheek and he doesn't rub it off. 'Thank you.'

'My pleasure,' he says reluctantly.

I look at him and try to do my biggest, most imploring doe eyes. 'Does this mean that you're coming back to us?'

He pouts at me in return and mutters, 'I suppose so.'

I punch the air and shout, 'Yay!'

Lucas tries not to smile, but he does.

Chapter Seventy

So the next day Lucas comes back to the farm and throws himself into his work. I watch him, leaning against the fence, as he fills the feed buckets for the alpacas, keeping them at bay with his elbows when they crowd round him as if he's been doing it all his life.

I've missed him so much and am so relieved that my visit to him paid off. I feel one tight little knot of tension loosen from round my heart. There are, however, several more still firmly in place. I've heard nothing from Shelby and I don't even like to ask Lucas whether he has or not. I know that his father isn't back at home yet – which I assume means that his trip to America has been successful.

The driver drops Lucas off every morning and picks him up every night. He stays late after the others have left, having back-of-the-fridge supper with me in the caravan as I can't bear for him to go home alone to that massive place. Our comfortable relationship returns and we spend a pleasant few hours with Lucas showing me random stuff on his phone while Little Dog snuggles into his lap. If it's nice we get out the deckchairs and Big Dog and Fifty join us while we sit and stare at the stars.

I can tell from Lucas's demeanour that all he wants is a

normal life, with someone at home to cook him a bit of dinner and listen to his day. Simply someone to be there for him. I also realise that I'm looking forward to sharing my evenings with human company rather than just my usual canine companions. I'm making a vegetable stir-fry and Lucas is chattering away about nothing in particular, when I look over at him and feel my heart swell with affection for this lost and lonely boy. Perhaps I see myself in him at that age. I want to tell him that everything will work out fine, but sometimes it doesn't. I can hardly hold myself up as a story of success springing from adversity. I muddle along at best. Still, I hope that he'll let me stay alongside him to guide him. My aunt was lovely, but as a confirmed recluse all she wanted to do was keep me on the farm with her. I wonder now if I should have risked going out in the world more. The longer you stay in seclusion, the harder it is to come out of it.

During the day, we all busy ourselves with the dozens of farm chores that have to be completed over and over like a Sisyphean task and soon the week has gone. Sometimes I wonder why we're bothering as that only takes us a week nearer to closure. As I'm contemplating our impending doom, our landlord, George Brown, rocks up. Alan is at the gate to let him in and he parks his Range Rover in the yard.

'While I deal with this, can you look after Jack and Seb for a short while, please?' I say to Lucas.

'OK.'

'You can give the goats some linseed tablets.' It makes their coats nice and shiny, in case you were wondering. 'The horses can have their treat balls filled up too. Oh, and the milk powder needs making up for the lamb's bottles.'

He takes all that in and answers with a serious nod.

'Thank you.' Despite recent events, I do know that I can trust Lucas. It's a testament to his development that I can now assign him tasks like this and know that they will be properly completed.

Leaving him to find the boys, I stride down to meet George. As I reach him, he holds out a hand and shakes mine, nearly crushing my fingers in the process.

'Hello, Molly. How's it going?'

I shrug. 'We're being evicted. What can I say?'

'I know. Bloody awful business. I'm sorry that I haven't been down to see you. This has been a shock for all of us.' He's normally quite brusque – but it seems as if this has taken the wind out of his sails too. I mustn't forget that George's place is being compulsory-purchased from under him and that can't be easy to deal with. The difference is that he at least has the compensation to soften the blow and will have the money to be able to buy another property. 'This farm has been in my family for generations. My great-grandparents planted half of these bloody trees.' He sweeps his arm towards the big field. 'All that history gone, so they can put a bulldozer through it. I wouldn't even mind if it was going to be housing or something useful. But a bloody train?'

A train that most of us probably won't even be able to afford to go on. I can't think when I last went into London, but Bev tells me that the fares are already extortionate.

George continues, 'I think the worst thing is being utterly powerless to stop it. There's strong feeling against it round here and probably in other parts of the country affected by it. But what good does that do us? It's going ahead and that's the end of it.' He puffs out an angry breath. 'I've had one hell of a job sorting out somewhere else to move to. It's not easy when your heart's not really in it. How are you faring?'

'Much the same.' We walk over to the fence together and lean on it, looking out over the sheep paddock. The baby lambs that we're bottle-feeding are out enjoying the sunshine this afternoon, gambolling in the perky way that only little lambs can. We watch them jump and kick the air for the sheer joy of it.

'That's really what I came to ask about,' George says. 'Any news on when you'll be moving? I wouldn't ask but I'm being pressed by the contractors. I know we've got an absolute moving date, but it seems they want us both out as soon as possible.'

'Can they force us out early?'

'No,' he says. 'But it won't stop them from trying.'

'There's been no progress at all,' I admit. 'I've been on the council to help, but no go. Stuff that's commercially available is way out of my price range. If I'm honest, George, I've no idea what I'm going to do.'

'That's tough.' He has the grace to look concerned. Yet I can't really blame him, can I? It's a nightmare for him too.

'Where are you going?'

'We're actually moving away,' he tells me. 'I've got a place lined up in Cornwall. Downsizing in a big way. We're going from all this to a two-bedroomed bungalow.' He tuts in disbelief. 'It's by the sea and all that, so the wife's pleased.'

'It sounds lovely.' I had briefly entertained the hope that George might find a little corner for us in his new farm. Another avenue closed to me.

'We haven't even got half an acre at our new house. It'll be strange, but I couldn't face starting over again. Not at my age.' He shakes his head. 'What about your animals?'

'If I can't find any alternative land, I really should be starting to look for new places for them.' I know that there's only so much more time that I can stick my head in the sand. I have to start addressing this issue otherwise the bulldozers will be moving in and we'll still be here.

'I can give you a couple of numbers. People who might be able to take on a few more.' He glances through the contacts on his phone and then pings some numbers to mine. 'It's worth a try.'

Anything is.

'I appreciate that.' But who in their right mind would want our blind chickens, our anti-social sheep, our troublesome alpacas? Farmers want commercial animals, not a load of lame ducks. Although the one thing that we don't actually have *is* a lame duck.

'I'm sorry about all this, Molly.' George looks genuinely penitent. 'You've looked after this land well. It's a shame to see you go. Bastards. If there was anything I could do to halt this, then I would.'

'I know.'

'It will be terrible if all your good work has to end. There's no one more dedicated than you are. Your aunt would have been proud of you.'

'Thanks.' She'll also be turning in her grave now if she can see the state of affairs we've come to.

'I'd better go,' George says. 'The wife has started packing up already. You should see what's in the bloody loft alone. We've never had a clear-out before. Never needed to. There's stuff up there from my mam and dad. Where will all that go? I'm dreading the move.'

'I hope it goes as well as it can do.' I'm reduced to uttering platitudes.

'It'll be fine,' he says. 'Absolutely fine. I'm sure.' But the tone of his voice is distinctly uncertain. 'Keep me posted on any progress, Molly. If I hear anything that might help, I'll let you know.' Then he looks at me, eyes brimming with tears, the brave face he's putting on it has all but gone. He shakes his head, bewildered. 'I still can't believe they're doing this. It's like a waking nightmare. I feel as if my heritage is literally being ripped out from under us. And for what?'

'I know.' I put my arm around George's burly shoulders and we stand looking out over the beautiful fields together while this rough, gruff mountain of a man has a bloody good cry.

302

Chapter Seventy-One

The next morning, Lucas positively bounces out of his car. He dashes over to where I'm trying, without much success, to unblock a drain in the yard and brandishes his phone at me. He's beaming from ear to ear and Lucas doesn't do beaming. 'Have you seen this?'

'Morning, Lucas!' My urge to instil good manners is never far from the surface. 'Seen what?'

'This.' He flicks his screen and holds it up to my face.

I abandon my drain rods and wipe my hands on my jeans so that I can look properly at what Lucas is trying to show me. I squint at it, the sunshine glaring off the screen. I can just about make out that it's an online glossy mag and the bold headline reads, *Shelby Dacre splits with Scarlett Vincent.*

'Oh, gosh.'

'Gosh? Is that all you can say?' He looks at me aghast. 'It's bloody *brilliant* news. Finally, he's binned her.'

'When did this happen?'

'Dunno. Must have been before he went to LA. I thought she'd gone with him, but she hadn't. These are photographs of her in London.'

He shows me said photos. She has on a hat and massive sunglasses. To be honest, it could be anyone, really. It's her customary white attire and plunging neckline that confirm her identity. Only Scarlett Vincent could stand out like a sore thumb while feigning the desire to remain anonymous.

'No wonder he's been like a bear with a sore head since he got back,' Lucas adds.

He's back? Yet still no word from him.

'If it's online, it's probably in the papers too and he hates nothing more than that.' Lucas closes his phone and sticks it in his pocket, still grinning. 'Or at least he pretends that he does.'

'Have you had chance to talk to him about it?'

'Nah.' Lucas shakes his head. 'He's back on set now. Out first thing in the morning, back late at night.'

'Oh, Lucas.'

'It's cool though,' he says. 'I can live with that. At least *she's* gone.'

'Don't you want him to be happy too?'

He reflects for a moment. 'Yeah, I suppose so. But not with someone half his age who has an aversion to clothing.'

I have to laugh at that. 'You are funny.'

'No, I'm weird,' Lucas says. 'You only think I'm funny because you're weird too.'

'Well, it's nice that we can be weirdos together.' He still doesn't know, as far as I'm aware, that I've slept with his father. I feel terrible keeping it from him, but it was an aberration and I don't know how I'd deal with the fallout if he ever did find out. He'd be furious, I'm sure, and I couldn't bear it if he cut me out of his life again. I can live without Shelby Dacre – I'm sure I can – but I've grown very attached to his son.

It still saddens me that they can't rebuild their relationship, but perhaps now that Scarlett is out of his life, he'll have more time for Lucas. I can only hope. I have my fingers and everything else crossed that he doesn't take up with another younger model straight away. Only for Lucas, you understand. Otherwise, it's nothing to do with me.

'What have we got to do today?' Lucas asks.

'Chores this morning, then this afternoon we can sweep out the barn and fill it with fresh hay.'

The students love these days best of all as they get to do straw-surfing, their favourite pastime. Essentially, they spend hours messing about and diving into the fresh hay. It's always so great to hear everyone playing and laughing together. I've been known to join in a time or two myself.

'Cool,' Lucas says. 'I'll get started.'

'You don't want a drink first?'

'Nah. I'm good to go.' And he positively strides across the yard, his usual lazy lope abandoned.

Bev comes to my side as I'm watching him go. 'Lucas looks remarkably chipper this morning.'

'Shelby has dumped Scarlett Vincent,' I report. 'Or so he tells me.'

'Has he now?' She taps into her phone. 'I'm behind the times.' Bev finds the story and scans it. I resist the urge to read it again over her shoulder. 'Hmm. Means he's on the market again.'

'I *hope* it means that he's going to make Lucas his main priority. Surely anyone can see that the boy blossoms with a bit of fuss and attention?'

'Maybe we're all the same,' Bev says knowingly.

'Shut up,' I say. There are times when I regret telling Bev about my one night with Shelby. This is one of them. In an effort to distract her from my love life or lack of it, I ask, 'What's Alan wearing today?'

'Simple Minds,' she says. 'So obvious and yet our hit rate is tragically poor.'

'We need to up our game,' I agree. 'I'll take Blur for tomorrow.'

Bev sucks in a breath and, after much consideration, says, 'Kaiser Chiefs.'

'I like it,' I say. 'Do you think that Alan has any T-shirts that don't have bands on the front?'

'No.'

I pick up the bucket at my feet. 'What do you want to do – chickens or pigs?'

'Pigs.'

'Straw-surfing this afternoon,' I tell her.

'Fab. I can't wait.'

So we go our separate ways. Bev to Teacup. Me to the chickens. Both of us deep in thought. Bev is probably considering her next T-shirt strategy while I, to my eternal shame, am thinking about Shelby Dacre being available.

Chapter Seventy-Two

It's late afternoon by the time Alan and the students have cleared the barn and have dressed it with fresh hay. They've all worked really hard on it and we've had no tears or tantrums. When I walk up there with Little Dog, I can tell by the screams of delight that the straw-surfing is already in full flow.

Sure enough, as I round the corner, I can see Alan, Bev and the kids flinging themselves into the deep layer of bouncy, fresh straw. I take a run and, shouting, 'Make way! Here I come!' I dive in myself.

I land next to Lucas who is pink from exertion and laughing like I've never heard him laugh before. It's a good sound. We lie on our backs, pretending that we're floating in the sea and kick our legs ferociously while roaring at the roof over our heads. When we've finished we lie there in fits of giggles until we're breathless. This is his inaugural straw-surf and it certainly seems as if he's enjoying it.

'Good fun?' I ask.

'The best,' he confirms with a big grin. This is the first time that I've seen him look unfettered from his cares and my heart tightens with affection for him.

Lucas dives in again and goes to wrestle with one of the younger lads and soon he's in the general tumble with everyone else. That's good to see. He's finally starting to loosen up enough to make friends here.

Although it would be very pleasant to lie here all afternoon, I force myself up and set about the task of picking straw out of my hair and clothing. I think I've even got bits of straw in my pants. As I'm sitting there looking like Worzel Gummidge's scruffier cousin, in a gap between screams and laughter I hear someone clearing their throat. When I look up I see Shelby leaning against the side of the barn.

'Hey,' he says.

When I've recovered from the shock, I manage to find my voice and say, 'Come on in, the straw's lovely.'

'I'm already acquainted with the delights of straw,' he replies calmly, which makes me flush and also gives me a rather torrid flashback to our own tumble in the hay. 'I might sit this one out. Even though it looks like a lot of fun.'

He glances down at his pristine clothes and I can see his point. As always, Shelby looks so handsome but, even from here, I can tell that his features are slightly drawn and there are dark shadows under his eyes. Sleepless nights or nothing more than a touch of jetlag?

Still brushing myself down, I stand up and walk over to him. Lucas, now throwing armfuls of straw over the two shrieking girls, hasn't even noticed his father's presence. As I assume he's come to collect his son, I ask, 'Do you want me to get Lucas for you?'

Shelby shakes his head. 'No. Leave him be. I've been watching for a while. He looks like he's enjoying himself. Besides, it's you I've come to talk to.'

'Oh.' I wonder what about. 'Shall we go down to my van for a cuppa?'

'Sounds like an excellent idea.' We fall into step and, out of the corner of my eye, I see Bev watching as we head back towards the yard. I give her a sign to say 'tea' to let her know where we're going. Little Dog, who was happily barking at the kids, stops what he's doing and trots after us.

Chapter Seventy-Three

Big Dog and Fifty are dozing in a sliver of shade at the door. They look up as we approach, instantly lose interest, and return to their nap. Shelby and Little Dog follow me into the caravan and, once again, I feel very aware of his presence in this small space. He sits down while I put the kettle on. Little Dog leans against his leg and Shelby risks patting him.

'This is awkward,' he says as I place a mug of tea in front of him, trying not to let bits of straw fall into the brew. 'I don't quite know where to start.'

As I perch opposite him, I brace myself for his announcement. What if he's going to take Lucas away from us? 'At the very beginning is usually a good place.'

Shelby pulls the tea towards him and nurses it between his fingers. 'OK. I've split with Scarlett,' he says starkly.

'I know,' I admit with a wince. 'Lucas told me.'

'Lucas?'

'He'd seen it in a celebrity magazine online.' What I don't do is tell him how pleased Lucas was to hear about it. Perhaps I should say that I'm sorry to hear his news, but I'm not. Is that horrible of me? I hope that it means Shelby will be concentrating on his child from now on and not chasing around London with his arm candy.

'He shouldn't have had to find out like that. I should have told him myself.' Shelby shakes his head. 'Why do I always manage to mess up when it comes to my own son?'

'Maybe the two of you can spend more time together now,' I venture.

'Yeah,' he says, but not with the amount of enthusiasm that I'd wished for. 'I realised that wasn't the life for me. I'm not into celebrity parties, standing drinking warm champagne with cold people.' He clears his throat. 'I want to get back to something that's . . . real. Does that sound too airy-fairy? I'm not expressing this very well.'

Before I can say anything else, the caravan door opens and Lucas is standing there. He too has straw in his hair. His face darkens. 'I wondered where you'd got to.'

I feel as if I've been caught in the act of doing something I shouldn't be doing and flush guiltily. 'Your dad came to talk to me.'

'Hello, Lucas,' Shelby says. 'I didn't want to disturb you. Looked like you were having fun.'

'It was OK,' he says reluctantly. 'The kids like it.' Some straw falls out of his hair and I try not to smile. 'I'm ready to go if you are.'

'I wanted to have a private word with Molly, if you don't mind,' Shelby says. 'I'll be with you in a few minutes.'

I can't imagine what else Shelby could have to say to me that couldn't be discussed in front of Lucas yet, nevertheless, I say to him, 'You could just do a quick round of the animals for me? Make sure everyone's all right. If you don't mind.'

'Bev and Alan are already doing it,' he says, pointedly, 'but I know when I'm not wanted.'

'Ten minutes,' Shelby says. 'Then I'm all yours. Maybe we could take in a movie tonight?'

Lucas slams the door.

Shelby throws up his hands. 'What have I said now? Can't I even suggest a movie without him seeing some ulterior motive?'

'I think he feels excluded from your life. Don't be too harsh on him. It must be tough to read about stuff that's going on in your parent's life that you're not party to.'

'You're right,' he says with a sigh. Then he frowns at me. 'You seem to make a habit of being right.'

'It certainly doesn't feel like it.' I put my head in my hands and Shelby reaches out to touch my arm.

'Still no solution to your pressing problem?'

'No,' I admit. 'My head hurts every time I think about it.'

'I might be able to help.' His smile is bright and there's an uncontained note of excitement in his voice as he adds, 'That's what I wanted to talk to you about. I know that I've not been around but, believe me, I haven't forgotten. I've been working away in the background and there's a piece of land that might be ideal. I'd like you to come and look at it.'

'Are you serious?'

'Deadly.'

I can't quite believe what I'm hearing. At the eleventh hour, Shelby might have found us some suitable land. I want to run round the caravan and do a happy dance, but I'm too cautious for my own good. Wonderful things just don't happen like this. 'Is there a catch?'

'Not as far as I'm aware. It's quite close to here. A little smaller – not too much – which I don't think is a bad thing as you can cut costs.'

'Is there a benign benefactor who's going to pay for it all?'

'Kind of,' he says, cagily. 'That's where I come in. I thought we could put on another event at the house. I know all kinds of performers. We could organise a benefit concert at short notice, I'm sure. I can always pull in some favours. Hopefully, that would raise enough money to fund the move and give you some reserves for going forward.'

My chest has tightened and I'm scared to breathe in case this all goes away. 'I'm hearing nothing I don't like yet.'

'Good.' Shelby looks pleased with himself.

In fact it all sounds too perfect. Could this really be the answers to my prayers? The miracle I've been hoping for? I don't want to get my hopes up and then find that they're about to be cruelly dashed. I should definitely wait until I see this land and know more about the costs until I let my feelings run away with me.

'Thank you,' I say to Shelby. 'It's kind of you to do this. I'm very grateful.'

'I see what you can do here and I'd like to help. Can you come and see it tomorrow evening?'

'Of course.'

'I'll text you the directions.'

We grin at each other and then the air becomes suddenly charged. I can hear my own heart beating.

'I have an overwhelming urge to kiss you,' Shelby tells me.

Despite feeling exactly the same, I say, 'I don't think that's a good idea. Lucas might come in and I'm sure he wouldn't be happy. He doesn't know about . . . well . . . *that*.'

'You're probably right.' He laughs. 'Again!'

Shelby stands up. 'I'll see you tomorrow night, then.'

'Yes. Tomorrow.'

'Goodbye, Molly.' And despite what we said about not kissing, his lips brush against mine and linger there for a moment too long.

He leaves the caravan and I just stand there.

I look down at Little Dog who is at my feet and wagging his tail. 'What do you make of that?' I ask him. But, frankly, Little Dog looks as bewildered as I am.

Chapter Seventy-Four

I don't even need to tell you that the next day my feet have wings. I'm not sure I've ever done my chores so quickly or with such a lightness of spirit. Last night I hardly slept a wink, such was the excitement and hope burning inside me. Even being woken by Dick the Cock at a dastardly hour didn't dampen my mood. When I'm feeding Anthony the Anti-Social Sheep and he tries to ouff me over the fence, I smile at him benignly and wonder whether he will like his new home. My heart is over-flowing with love for all of the animals today and mankind in general. I might just have a solution to all of our problems and that couldn't make me any happier.

'Who's put a smile on your face?' Bev asks. 'It wasn't anything to do with the visit from a certain Mr Dacre last night?'

'Actually, it was,' I confide.

'Another cheeky tumble in the hay?'

'No, no, no. Absolutely not,' I say, briskly. 'That's supposed to be a secret. The Thing We Never Mention.'

'Ah.'

'He might have found some land for us to move to.' I can't contain my joy. I was trying to keep it all locked down in case the land isn't suitable for some reason or we can't raise the money, but the pressure of expectation keeps building and I feel like there's a dam waiting to burst inside me. 'I'm going to look at it tonight with him.'

She looks at me in disbelief. 'Blimey! Exciting.'

'I'm trying not to get my hopes too high, but Shelby thinks it's an ideal spot. A bit smaller than the land we've currently got, but not too much.' Despite my sensible words, I want to run round the yard singing for joy.

'I don't suppose you want me to come with you?' she asks hopefully.

'I think I can manage,' I tease. 'Let me check it out first and then we can all go and have an inspection en masse.' If it's not right, I don't think I could shoulder the burden of collective disappointment.

'You just want Shelby Dacre to yourself,' she whispers. 'You little minx.'

'This is purely business,' I assure her, even though I can still feel his lips on mine.

'Well, I have everything crossed that he comes up with the goods. That would take a load off your mind.'

'Wouldn't it just.' Then, as we're talking, Alan pulls up at the gate in his clattery old car.

'Quick, quick. Pick a band. Pick a band.' Bev says. 'We've only got minutes to do it.'

'Er . . . ' I wrack my brain. 'The Jam.'

'Deep.' Bev nods. 'Very deep. I'll have Depeche Mode.'

By which time Alan has parked and is walking towards us. When he gets nearer, we turn to each other, too stunned to speak. Eventually, Bev punches the air and shouts, 'Yeeeeees!' which makes Alan jump.

He eyes us both suspiciously. 'What's up?'

'You beaut!' Bev takes his face in her hands and fights her

way through his bushy beard to plant a noisy, wet kiss on his cheek.

Alan looks more than a little alarmed. 'What's that for?'

'Darling Alan,' she says. 'Every day we bet on what band T-shirt you're going to be wearing and every day we get it wrong. This is the first time in ages that I've hit pay-dirt.'

He looks blankly at us.

'It's a big thing,' I assure him.

Alan still looks bemused. 'What's the prize?'

'Nothing,' Bev tells him. 'Well, cake. Mainly we do it for the glory.'

'Oh.' He looks even more confused now. 'So you've won?'

'Oh, yeah,' Bev says circling her hips and arms in a victory dance.

'I could take you out,' Alan says. 'For something to eat. Somewhere posh. To celebrate.'

Bev laughs at that. 'Don't be soft.'

'I'd wear my best band tee.' I'm not sure if he's joking or not. 'Think about it.'

'Yeah.' Now it's Bev's turn to look bemused. 'I will.'

'Right. I'm off to fix tractor.' Alan wanders off in the general direction of the barn.

Bev stands rooted to the spot, staring after him. 'Did that just happen?'

'Flipping heck,' I say, similarly stunned. 'Depeche Mode got you the offer of a dinner date.'

'Do you think I should go?' Bev asks.

'No. It would be too weird. It's Alan. *Our* Alan.'

'Yeah,' she agrees, a little bit more dreamily than I had expected. 'Though it's the best offer I've had in a very long time.'

Chapter Seventy-Five

Lucas looks moody again when he arrives, but that's probably the joy of teenage hormones. I hope so, anyway.

With a cursory 'hello', he stomps up to the barn where no doubt Alan will instruct him in the mysterious ways of mending tractors. I'm praying that he hasn't had yet another row with Shelby or anything like that. I try not to worry too much about him, but you already know that I have a soft spot for Lucas and don't like to see him unhappy. Still, he's here and, despite one or two setbacks, I believe that he continues to make progress. I don't want to be on at him all the time, so I'll give him some space to try and work out his issues by himself.

Bev is taking the rest of the students on a long walk today around the farm and into the surrounding countryside and maybe she can persuade Lucas to join them. They still are unaware of our impending eviction. Call me a coward, but I can't face addressing it until I have a solution. They are, however, going to take photographs on either their phones or some borrowed cameras to make a record of Hope Farm before we are ousted. Later this afternoon they'll help Bev to set up a Facebook page for the farm and upload the photos to them and do some basic editing – another little bit of learning disguised as fun. It pains me to think that this may be one of the last times that anyone will be able to explore this area freely and I'd love to go with them, but I have other matters to tend to. I've got a mountain of paperwork that I should at least try to scale. I need to order feed too. Just because we're moving it doesn't stop the animals from trying to eat me out of house and home. So I head back to the caravan and set to.

Before I know it, the day has slipped away from me. It's late afternoon and the students – all happy with the photos they've snapped – are leaving for the day. Before I can say anything to Lucas, his car has arrived and he's hopped in. I wonder if he'll come along to look at the land tonight or whether Shelby hasn't mentioned it to him at all. As I'm pondering that, a text pings in and, for one minute, I dread that it might be Shelby messaging me to cancel. But I needn't have worried. The text confirms the address with me and ends, *Look forward to seeing you later. xx*

When I've made sure that all the animals are fed, watered and settled, I have a shower and change into the cleanest pair of jeans that I have and a flowery, floaty blouse that I think must have been my aunt's as I don't ever remember buying it. Though it's not really her style either. Maybe she had it for a family wedding or something – one of her rare social outings. I even look in the mirror to see that all the buttons are done up properly and that I haven't got them all cock-eyed. The shirt makes me think of her and I say out loud, 'Wish me luck, Hettie! Fingers crossed this is just what we need to survive.'

I so hope it is as I can hardly bear to think that her legacy will end here.

Then I bolt down some food and jump into the truck. I check the address and head off. It's quite close to Shelby's manor house, so I know most of the route by now. Before I reach his village,

I turn off and the lanes become steadily more narrow and the houses further apart. Wherever this place is, it's clear that we won't have many neighbours to trouble or to trouble us.

As I round the corner, slightly worried about how close the truck is to the hedges on either side of the lane, I see a sign for Edward's Farm and turn towards it. Shelby's car is parked by the first of the farm buildings and I pull in behind him. He gets out of the car as I approach and comes to kiss my cheek.

'Hey,' he says. 'Very punctual.'

'The animals were all well-behaved tonight. No dramas.' It's not often that I can say that in my life.

'Good. Come on. Let's survey your estate, ma'am.' He grabs my hand, tucks it into the crook of his arm and leads me through to the main area of buildings.

Chapter Seventy-Six

The yard here is situated centrally on the land and is surrounded by neat buildings on three sides – all of them in better condition than our existing ones too. This looks like a place that has had a bit of cash thrown at it. I bet leaky roofs and blocked drains are less in evidence as well. The whole area is swept clean and the stables look as if they haven't been used in a long time. It looks more like the *Flinton's Farm* set than a working farm.

'This is it.' Shelby spreads his hands. 'You've got this place that you could use as your tea room and lunch stop as you do now.' He points at a well-maintained wooden cabin and he's right – it looks ideal. We could all squeeze in there nicely. Shelby leads me on. 'Then there's this huge barn, a couple more stables and stuff.' Plenty of room for the horses and everyone.

He walks me slowly down the yard so that we can inspect them all and I try very hard to take it all in. Already, I can see where all the animals would be at home.

'What do you think?'

'To be honest with you, I'm a bit overwhelmed. It looks amazing. I didn't expect anything like this.' I'd envisaged a bit of rough land, a work in progress, some ramshackle barns. This is beyond my wildest dreams.

'It's smaller in overall size,' he says. 'And there's no house. That's further down the road and was sold off years ago with a large part of the farm. Although there are plenty of barns, there's probably nothing that we'd be allowed to convert for residential use. Planning consent is notoriously difficult to get round here.'

'You know that my own comfort isn't really my priority. It's the students and the animals that I'm more concerned about. As long as they're happy, then I am too.'

'Still, it would have been nice to get you an upgrade in living accommodation.'

'Honestly, I'm fine where I am. Thank you.' Though I'm not entirely sure that my dear old caravan will survive a move. I'm sure it's only held together by love and a lot of cobwebs. Dislodge one of the cobwebs and the whole thing could fall apart. 'Would I be allowed to bring it here?'

'I'm just waiting for confirmation on that, but it's looking positive,' Shelby says. 'Come and see the land. You'll love it.'

We walk away from the array of buildings and Shelby helps me to climb over a stile in the thick hawthorn hedge and I drop down into the field beyond. We stand for a moment, my hand in his, and I can hear nothing but the sound of a skylark above us. This is heaven, right here, right now.

Shelby turns me around and acres of finest, unspoilt Buckinghamshire countryside stretch ahead of me. I shade my brow with my hand and gaze out at it. 'This looks just beautiful.'

'I think so too,' Shelby says, obviously pleased with himself. 'It's not too hilly so the land is all useable, yet it dips down towards the river, so good drainage. I'm not a farmer, but I'd say this was a great space.'

'I didn't think that I could love anywhere as much as my

current home. But this would make the most wonderful replacement.'

'Good.' He grins at me and together we walk over the field and I struggle to take it in as it's all so wonderful.

I don't know how to explain it when, at the end of the day it's another slice of countryside, but it has exactly the same feel to it as Hope Farm does. I believe the land would be kind, accommodating, somewhere that we could make into a nice home. My hearts swells as I look at it. Home. That sounds very lovely, indeed.

I can already picture the animals here too. The alpacas would love it over there by the hedge. If we ever managed to make them into the charmers that people think they are this would be a good place to organise alpaca walks. The ponies and goats could go on the other side while the Shire horses would be very happy next door to them.

We wander down the gently curving slope of the vale until we reach the thin ribbon of meandering river which has carved its way through the landscape over hundreds of years. It's shaded by weeping willows and teasels grow along the bank. Two ducks let themselves drift along on the current and a moorhen on the other side picks at the grass. There's a splash from an unseen fish. It couldn't be more idyllic if it tried.

As we walk along the bank together, Shelby turns to me. 'So, Molly? What do you think?'

'I love it.' To be honest, that really doesn't even begin to sum up how I feel. 'It would be perfect.'

'You could have it on a ten-year lease.'

'Can I afford the rent?'

'It's something we need to discuss further, but I very much hope it will be less than you're paying now.'

I frown at him. 'Then there must be a catch. Is the landlord difficult?'

'Yes,' he laughs. 'An absolute stinker.'

Finally, the penny drops. 'It's *you*, isn't it?' Of course, it's Shelby. Who else would it be?

'Would you mind that very much? I won't be your sole landlord, I'm afraid. I hold this land with two other partners, so it's not entirely mine to do as I please with. I've had to bring them on board as well. That took a bit of persuasion. We bought it years ago as an investment thinking that one day we might get permission to develop it – philistines that we were.'

'Now you've had a change of heart?'

'I can't bear the thought of that blasted trainline ruining the countryside. I wouldn't want to add my bit of development to it even if we could get permission now. Thankfully, we were thwarted in our attempts to build on it.' He gives me an apologetic look. 'So much so that I'd almost forgotten that I owned a bit of it. It's been standing empty for a good few years now and could be put to much better use. If you want to move here, then it would be less intrusive and the land can be used for its intended purpose. I'd love to see your animals here.'

'Me too.' I can't lie, this seems like paradise.

'In time, I might be able to buy out my partners but that's a future negotiation. I didn't dare share with you what was going on before I'd secured their agreement. I checked that there are no restrictions that would prohibit you from operating here and that's fine too. All you need to do now is say yes.'

'It's fantastic, but can I fund it? As you well know, we live from hand-to-mouth.' I don't want to think of the practicalities, but I have to. All I really want to do is sign on the dotted line. 'This rather swift eviction has shown me that I need to be in a more stable financial situation.'

'As I mentioned the other day, I thought we could put on a concert at the manor house to get you up and running. I've floated it to a few friends and they've already agreed to take part. You could bring along some of the students and animals from the farm as you did for the charity day. Would you be up for that?'

'It sounds perfect.' That went off without incident, didn't it? Like me, the animals are becoming a bit more accustomed to people. Besides, Bev would kill me in a particularly slow and painful way if I said no.

'In the long term, the extra barns could give you an opportunity to do more open days and the like.' Perhaps he sees the flash of anxiety on my face as he quickly adds, 'If you want to.'

'It would be a great idea.' I've put a toe in these murky waters now and while I might not be ready to dive headlong into commercialism, I know that I can do it and it would add to our income stream. Look at me with my fancy words. Income stream, eh?

'If you look up at the other side of the vale, you can see the back of my house up there.'

He stands close as he points out the area. I see it now. This is the land that Lucas and I looked out over when we sat together on the hay bales.

He looks at me, expression suddenly serious. 'If you want it, Molly. Then it's all yours.'

'I'd love it.'

Shelby looks relieved. 'It's a deal, then?'

'Yes.' And, without wanting to, I start to cry as all the anxiety of the past few months is lifted. A knot of tension in my heart unfurls and, suddenly, I feel as if I can breathe again. Thanks to Shelby's generosity, I have a home for my dear students and my beloved animals who will love it here. I won't have to send my young people away or scatter the animals to the four corners of the country. We can all stay together and I couldn't be happier. Could I, at last, be getting on top of things once more? Have things finally turned a corner for us? Bev will be overjoyed too. With Alan it will be harder to tell.

'Hush, hush.' Shelby wipes the tears from my cheeks with a gentle rub of his thumb. 'It will all be OK.' He steps in to kiss me and our lips meet, friendly at first, then becoming increasingly more passionate.

I'm the first one to break away and we both look sheepish. I shouldn't do this. It's not that I don't want Shelby. For heaven's sake, this is the first time in my life that I've ever really wanted a man in this way. But he's going to be my landlord now and I don't want to jeopardise my relationship with him. What about Lucas too? If he knew that we were carrying on like this, he'd be furious.

'If you're going to be my landlord and benefactor, we should really keep things firmly on a business footing from now on.' I sound more breathy than I'd like.

'We should,' he echoes.

But we kiss again, nevertheless.

Chapter Seventy-Seven

I feel as if I'm floating on cloud nine as we walk back towards our vehicles. As Shelby locks the gate and we cross the road, he says, 'There's a nice pub a few minutes down the road. Have you got time for a celebratory drink?'

'Yes, of course.' I can think of nothing nicer than spending the evening with Shelby and for once, I have nothing to rush back for. Thankfully, Bev and Alan are feeding the lambs tonight so I don't have to worry about that. The rest of the animals can cope for another hour or two without me. I only have to tuck them in and say goodnight when I go home. I'm glad too that I spent a few minutes upgrading my usual wardrobe. At least I won't now walk into the bar smelling of alpaca poo.

Shelby smiles at me. 'I have something else that I want to share with you too.'

'Sounds good.'

'I think it is,' he says enigmatically.

I'm beginning to like surprises from Shelby and I never thought I'd hear myself say that. I positively spring into the truck and follow him feeling light of spirit and young of heart. After all that worrying, we have a fabulous new home and I can't wait to tell Bev about it. I even sing as I crunch the gears and follow him down the lane and I'm not usually a spontaneous singer.

The pub is low, thatched and looks as if it has served beer to the locals for many a good year now. It's clearly in a gentrified stage as a chalkboard sign outside announces GASTRO PUB. Which, by my limited experience, means expensive with small portions. I expect the beer will be hand-crafted, hand-pumped, high-priced microbrewery stuff and the food will be served on slates.

Shelby locks his car and then waits for me as I park the truck on the road. I'm a pretty dab hand at manoeuvring it, but I think the tiny car park is beyond me – especially as I'm still a bit trembly with happiness. I'm still struggling to believe that amazing place is going to be our permanent home. Already my head is buzzing with ideas for things we can do with it. So, I abandon the truck in the lane, crossing my fingers that other cars will be able to pass easily, and join Shelby to head into the pub.

As it's a lovely evening; a few people are sitting outside under picnic umbrellas and I watch them as they surreptitiously monitor Shelby's arrival. When we open the door and walk in, more heads swivel and I don't think that they're turning for me. Some people gape openly at Shelby and there's a bit of nudging and whispering going on. I hear a few girly giggles too. Others, perhaps more used to him in their local pub, glance up and return immediately to their beer. I see one woman angling her camera to take a sneaky selfie which also includes Shelby too. This is weird. On the rare occasions I come to the pub with Bev, I normally slope in unnoticed. Even when I try to get served with a drink I often go unnoticed. This is the first time I've been out with Shelby in public and I'd drastically underestimated the kind of stir he creates. It must be strange to have people note your every move. Though, credit to Shelby, he doesn't seem to be aware of the ripple of interest that he's causing.

We head to the far end of the bar where it's quieter and he asks, 'What would you like, Molly? A glass of fizz as we're celebrating?'

'Well, I'm driving, but I wouldn't say no to one.'

'What can I get you, Shelby?' the barman says.

'Bottle of Bollinger and a couple of glasses please, Adam.'

'Coming up.'

While the barman gets Shelby's order, I whisper, 'I presume this is your local.'

'Yeah. I don't get out for a drink that often, but when I do I usually come here. The natives are quite friendly. They don't bother me too much.'

I look round. I'm sure I've been in here once before when it was all a bit battered and broken with dark varnished wood everywhere. It seems to have been done up very nicely. The wooden floors are all stripped and sanded. The chairs and tables are mismatched but in a good way. A few people are eating in the bar and the food looks lovely.

'You can leave your truck here overnight, if you like. It'll be safe. I can order a taxi to take you home. I sometimes walk back from here if I've had a few and then send one of the lads for the car in the morning.'

Oh, to have 'lads' to do your every bidding.

'I'm fine. Just the one for me. I've got my rounds to do, so I can't be too late back.' My only pang of guilt is that I've left Little Dog by himself and, as he's used to being about an inch from my heel, he'll be fretting. He might even have ripped up one of the cushions to spite me.

When the barman brings the champagne and two glasses, Shelby flashes a shiny black credit card. I'm alarmed to see the cost ping up on the till. Yikes.

'Enjoy,' the barman says.

Shelby picks up the bottle and glasses and nods towards a quiet corner of the pub. 'You don't mind sitting inside?'

It's a nice evening and one of those umbrella tables looks quite appealing, but I can imagine that it gets tiresome with people gawping at you all the time. 'Not at all.'

So we retreat to a far corner of the bar in a little snug with a booth made just for two. It's cosy here, out of the way, but still heads swivel again when Shelby pops the cork. He fills my glass with bubbles.

Shelby raises his glass. 'To your new home.'

'I still can't quite believe it,' I say, but I toast with the champagne nevertheless.

'There's a lot to do before your deadline,' he says. 'I can help to organise that.'

'It will mainly involve a lot of shuttling back and forth with the animals in the truck.' Already my mind is whirring with the logistics of it. That's a good sign, isn't it? They say if you look at a house and you start to picture your furniture in it, then you should buy it. Same thing with animals and farms, I should think.

I can't believe that this kind man opposite me is enabling this. I know that he's got pots of money – probably more than he knows what to do with. If he can pay these prices for a bottle of fizzy wine, it's clear he has some cash to spare. But he didn't have to choose us. I know that we're trying to help his son, but he's paying for that and there are lots of other very worthy and more high-profile causes where he could be seen to be doing good. We are so low-key we're not on anyone's radar, yet he's chosen us to support. I feel very humble.

We settle back in the seats and I can feel Shelby studying me. It's disconcerting.

'What else was it you wanted to tell me?' I ask.

'Ah. That.' He glugs his champagne and tops up his glass again. A man obviously accustomed to fine wines. I hang on to mine and sip it, wanting to make it last as long as I possibly can. I also calculate how much each mouthful is costing and how much animal feed I could buy for that. 'Promise that you won't breathe a word to anyone, Molly.'

'Of course not.'

'This is top secret. As top secret as it gets.' He looks round to check that no one's listening and I brace myself for his announcement. It must be big, I think, very big.

Chapter Seventy-Eight

Shelby is glowing when he says, 'I've been offered a new part. A *fantastic* new part.'

'That's great.' For one horrible moment, I did wonder if he was going to tell me that he and Scarlett Vincent had got back together and were planning to get married. It's the sort of thing that celebrities do, no? I'm more than relieved that it's simply another acting role. He'd told me that he wanted to cast off Gordon Flinton. 'It's what you wanted, isn't it?'

'Oh, absolutely. You should have seen the other people who were lined up for it.' He reels off a list of names, none of which mean anything to me, but Shelby is obviously impressed to be considered among them. I'll try to remember the names and I'll ask Bev who they are tomorrow.

I lower my voice and ask in conspiratorial tones, 'Will it mean leaving *Flinton's Farm*?'

There's a look that flashes over his face – guilt, discomfort, sadness? 'It will mean leaving a lot of things.'

'Oh.' I've no idea about the nuts and bolts of his world. Perhaps you can't work on more than one thing at a time.

'Have you heard of a big American series called *The Dead Don't Sleep*?'

I really wish I had as this is patently a huge thing for him. But I've never heard of that either and instead, can do no more than look blankly at him.

'It's massive.' He gives a dismissive wave of his hand. '*Enormous*. Everyone watches it.'

Another one for me to check with Bev.

'It's about a zombie apocalypse. People fighting the good fight in the face of adversity.'

Still the blank look.

He seems a little irritated by my ignorance, but presses on. 'Trying to save what's left of humanity.'

'It sounds lovely,' I say.

'It's a *major* role for me.' He's very insistent about that.

'I'm so pleased for you.' And I am. 'You must be thrilled. Do you know what you'll be yet?'

'Of course.' A bit snappy. 'It's one of the lead characters. Each season there's new villain that the survivors come up against. I'm going to be the one for Season Nine.' He leans in towards me. 'If the gossip rags or the fan pages get hold of this I'll be hammered.'

'My lips are sealed,' I assure him. 'So you'll be the villain?'

'After years of playing Gordon Flinton, it's like dream come true. I'm going to be the gun-toting, psycho baddie.'

'And that's a good thing?' If I'm honest, it sounds quite alarming to me. Why would anyone want to do that?

Shelby stares at me aghast. 'It's *huge*. This could really make my name in Hollywood. I'm going straight into one of the biggest shows they have. As a lead. Do you know how many people would *kill* for a role like this?'

I don't, but I'm gathering that it would be a lot. In fairness, if I asked Shelby questions about sour crop in chickens or coccidiosis in alpacas – a parasitic disease in younger ones in case you were wondering – he would look similarly baffled. We each have our own area of speciality.

'If I nail it, they've said they could buck the trend and carry the character to another season. Shake things up a bit for the audience. Imagine that!'

'Wow,' I say in the absence of anything more useful to offer. 'I'm delighted for you. *Really* delighted.'

Then he lets out a long, heavy sigh. 'I'll be able to see you into the farm,' he continues. 'Filming starts shortly after Christmas, so I won't be going until the end of the year.'

Going? 'Going where?'

'Out to LA, Los Angeles, the City of Angels.'

'Oh. You're moving to America?' It's fair to say that I'm just a little bit shell-shocked.

'That's the deal, Molly. I can hardly film it here.'

I never considered that. 'So how long will you be gone for?'

'I'm looking at renting a house out there for a year.'

'A year?' I thought he was talking about a matter of weeks. But a *year*?

'This could be my big break.' He's defensive now. 'I need to be in Hollywood. That's where it all happens. What am I supposed to do?'

'How's that going to work? What will Lucas do?'

For the first time, Shelby looks worried. 'He'll have to go to boarding school.'

I feel myself blanch. 'Tell me you didn't just say that.'

His expression darkens and I can tell that he very definitely did. 'I'm already looking into it. I can afford to pay for the best for him. You know that.'

'And *you* know that he'll hate every minute of it.'

'What exactly am I supposed to do?' Shelby lowers his voice but I can tell that he's cross at being questioned. 'This is my opportunity to get rid of Gordon Flinton for ever. I'll never be anyone else while I'm here.' He glances round the pub. A few heads snap away from staring in our direction. 'You've seen how people look at me. Out there, I can re-invent myself, have a fresh start.'

'But this isn't just about what you want or what's good for you. It's about Lucas too. He's doing brilliantly with us.'

'I am fully aware of the bond you have with my son.'

'You can't palm him off on someone else to look after, just as we're making progress.' I can feel my temper rising and it's a rare feeling for me. Surely, he can't be considering doing this to Lucas? Not now. Not ever. The man must be mad. 'After all he's been through, a settled home life is essential for him.'

'I have to think of my career,' Shelby says through gritted teeth.

I manage to keep my voice sounding civilised when I really want to shout. 'You have to think of your son. Your *only* son.'

'This is the chance of a *lifetime*,' he reiterates, jaw set. 'I *need* to do this.'

'When are you going to get on board with the fact that your son *needs* you? This is a critical time for Lucas. To abandon him now would be an utter disaster.'

'That's unfair, Molly. I wouldn't be abandoning him. I'd make sure he was well looked after. He always has the best that money can buy.'

'And that's your answer, is it? Throw some money at it?'

'I've tried everything else, Molly.' Shelby has raised his voice now and heads in the pub turn to us again. 'Nothing seems to work. Lucas hates me. He doesn't want me anywhere near him. If that's the case, then I might as well do what I want.'

I stand up. I can't listen to any more of this. Of all the stupid, pig-headed things to do. Even though I'm shaking, I shout back at Shelby, 'If you're such a bloody good actor, then it's time that you started acting like a father.'

Then, to the amazement of Shelby and the pub regulars, I storm out.

Chapter Seventy-Nine

I hear nothing from Shelby. Of course, I don't. It was completely out of order for me to tell him how to raise his son. Especially, as he has been so very kind to me. I've texted him twice to apologise, but have had no response and I don't want to try again or he'll think I'm a stalker.

The trouble, as you well know, is that I've grown very fond of Lucas and while I appreciate that this is a fantastic opportunity for Shelby – well, sort of – I don't want Lucas to be dumped at a boarding school, no matter how expensive. He'll hate it. I know he will. It will be the final affirmation that his dad doesn't want him around. Why can't his own father see that?

Also, in voicing my opinion so emphatically, I've probably done us out of that fabulous farm. I haven't slept a wink all week worrying about it. I've had no paperwork, not even an email, so I'm assuming that it's off the cards and we are about to be rendered homeless. I could poke myself in my own eyes for being so stupid. But I couldn't have been party to Shelby's confidence without letting him know how I felt, could I? What if I'd said nothing and simply sat back and watched Lucas be shipped out to God-knows-where.

Bev comes into the caravan, bearing a basket of eggs. I'm sitting at the table with my head in my hands in despair. I don't even try to pretend that I'm not.

'Cheer up, love,' she says. 'It might never happen.'

'It will,' I assure her. 'In just a few short weeks.'

'You've still heard nothing from our tame celebrity?'

'Not so tame, it appears,' I remind her. 'But no, nothing.'

'Fuck,' she says.

'Indeed.'

Bev puts half a dozen eggs in my fridge. 'Time for Plan B then?'

'Plan B involves me phoning round all the local and not-so-local animal sanctuaries to see if they'll take on our babies.' I can feel my eyes well with tears just saying it. How am I going to get through an entire phone call?

Bev sits down opposite and squeezes my hand. 'What a bugger.'

'I don't know what else I can do.' Now my throat closes and when I speak my voice comes out as a pathetic croak. 'We'll have to tell all the students that we're closing, too. How will I break that news to them? Where will they go? I can't palm them off on anyone else. We're unique in what we do here.'

'And, while we've been open, we've done everything we could for them. This isn't your doing, Mols. You can't take the weight of it on your shoulders. It's not as if you've let the farm fail or you're shutting it down to travel the world or something. This is entirely due to that bloody trainline. I wish the people in government could see what their "progress" is doing to real lives.'

But they won't. They never do, do they? Sitting up there in Westminster in their ivory tower, the decisions they make rarely touch their own lives. It's the rest of us who have to pick up the pieces. Now I am crying. Bev comes and gives me a cuddle. She wipes my tears with a dirty tissue she finds in her pocket while I weep all over the carefully written list of people that I might call.

'Tea,' Bev says when my tears have subsided to a snotty sniffle and goes to put the kettle on. When she sits down again, she pushes a mug towards me. 'I don't want to add to your burden, but you do realise that you'll also be homeless. Have you thought about what you'll do?'

That hits me like a slap in the face. With all the worry about the students and the animals, it hadn't even occurred to me that I need to look for a place too. 'No,' I admit.

Bev tuts at me. 'Thought not. You always put everyone else first.'

'I'll find something, I'm sure.' Though my brain is refusing to think what that might be. Even renting these days is prohibitively expensive. I have no money for a deposit, no references, no regular income to speak of. Who'd want to take me on?

'You can have my spare room, you know that,' Bev says. 'It's tiny, but it's better than nothing. Actually,' she looks round my caravan, 'it's better than this.'

I can't help but laugh, even though it makes snot come out of my nose.

'Little Dog can live in the house and maybe we could build a run for Big Dog in the garden. I could even take Fifty and a few of the more pathetic hens if push comes to shove.'

'I'd definitely like to keep our one-legged Peg and Mrs Magoo if I can.'

'Who else would want them?'

Who else would want *any* of them, I think? Our nervous ex-police boys with a penchant for pushing over fences? Ringo with his horsehair allergy and celebrity hairdresser? That's just for starters. I can't even consider the difficulties of finding someone to love Anthony the Anti-Social Sheep or our trio of angsty alpacas. Who will care for them as we do?

'I'd better go,' Bev says, sadly.

'What are the kids up to today?'

'Some of them are with Dumb and Dumber in the barn. They've put the ponies' Happy Horse ball out and the roller. The goats are quite happily chasing them up and down.'

'The rest?'

'Up in the fields with Alan. Lucas is there too.'

I've not seen much of Lucas this week. I think he's been giving me a wide berth. I don't know if he knows about my disagreement with his father or even if he's thinking about jetting off to LA to live. I know that I have to have this conversation with him but frankly, the longer I can avoid it the better.

'I'll leave you to your phone calls,' Bev says.

'What's Alan wearing today?' We might as well add a bit of welcome levity to our situation.

'Supertramp.'

I suck in a breath. 'Old skool.' And miles away from our guesses of the Verve and Primal Scream. 'We need to think more laterally.'

'I'm not sure I want to be getting it right any more,' she says with a worried look on her face.

I can't help but giggle at that. 'Has Alan mentioned your date again?'

'Yeah,' she says. 'He's offered to take me to that posh pub in the village. I haven't been, though I've heard it's good.'

'But you're still not going.'

'Nooooooo. It's Alan, for heaven's sake.'

'He might surprise you,' I offer.

'He won't.' She heads for the door. 'Besides, I'm holding out for your leftovers. You might have blotted your copybook with the sublimely gorgeous Shelby Dacre, but he's still at the top of my To Be Shagged list.'

'I doubt we'll see him around here any more. You'll have to follow him to LA.'

'That would *soooo* work for me. I'll leave you in my house with all the no-hope animals and head off to the sun.' Bev stops dead. 'Actually, that sounds like an absolutely brilliant thing to do. I wonder if he needs a personal assistant? Don't forget that in a couple of weeks I'll be gainfully unemployed too.'

I hadn't really thought what to do about that either, but it doesn't stop me from throwing a cushion at her.

'Get out of here, woman.'

'Hit those phones,' she says as she ducks out of the door. 'We're running out of time.'

That I'm well aware of. So I pick up my list, all blotched with my tears, and dial the first number.

Chapter Eighty

So far I've made twenty-six phone calls and have only managed to find places for the pygmy goats and one of the Shetland ponies at a petting farm that's about ten miles from here. But how can I split up Buzz and Ringo? It seems that no one minds a bit of cute, but anything more complicated is out of the question. They all look at the not inconsiderable cost of vet bills for the afflicted, so I can hardly blame them.

No one wants a ramshackle flock of sheep despite the fact that I didn't even mention Anthony could be used as an attack sheep. Some people might not view that as a bonus. No one, it seems, wants two massive horses who will eat them out of house and home, but will jump at a butterfly alighting in the next field. No one wants a pony that comes with his own hairdressing issues. I hang up on my last call and realise that I've hit a brick wall. I'm all out of begging and pleading for now – it's totally exhausting, even though I've spoken to an awful lot of people who've made sympathetic noises. They 'understand my plight', are 'sorry for my situation', wish they 'could do more', all of those things. But no, they can't help me out by actually taking on any of the animals.

I leave the caravan for a much-needed breath of fresh air. The closer to the deadline I get, the more I feel I need to be out on the land too. Soon it will be churned up by diggers and whatever kind of heavy machinery you need to blight countryside for ever and my heart breaks a bit more. What will happen to the animals if I reach the end of the line and they haven't been rehomed? What then? Little Dog and Big Dog come out of the shade under the caravan and fall into step with me.

Behind the barn I see Lucas washing down Buzz. It's become one of his favourite jobs and I stop for a moment and watch how expert he is at it now. He's grown so much in confidence since he arrived, angry, sullen and lonely. Some days he can still be as moody as hell, but he's a teenager with troubles, so what can I say? He talks to Buzz soothingly as he washes his coat with shampoo.

I go over to him and lean on the fence. As he's been cool towards me, I prepare myself for a rebuff. 'Hey.'

'Do you mean hey or hay?' Lucas asks.

I laugh. Clearly, he's not in a mood today. 'Don't get clever with me, young man.'

Lucas looks up and grins. Little Dog goes to say hello to him, while Big Dog lopes off to find another welcome patch of shade.

'How are you doing?' I venture.

A shrug. 'OK.'

The back of the barn here is still bearing the scars of the fire. As we're moving, we haven't done any of the repairs, so the wood is still charred, the hay there reduced to a blackened mess and the tang of smoke still lingers. The fire officer who came to investigate the blaze advised us to pull it down as, though it's not in imminent danger of collapse, the structure is compromised. Instead, Alan has shored it up as best as he can and we avoid using it. In a short while, it will all be flattened to the ground and any trace of the barn, the farm, lost

342

for good. The fire officer also confirmed that it was the faulty cable that had sparked the fire and I'm so glad we definitively discovered that Lucas didn't do this. I couldn't bear it if it had been him.

He reaches in his back pocket and hands his phone to me. 'Did you see this?'

I scan through the photos on the screen.

'Scarlett Vincent has done an exposé on her relationship with Dad,' he explains as I view them. 'He's been stomping round with a miserable face all week. I guess this explains it. He hates this kind of thing.'

'I'm not surprised.' Though I do wonder if his ill-temper is entirely down to this exposé – horrible as it is. Perhaps he's still cross about what I said to him. He must be. I just wish he'd return my texts and we could talk about it.

'It's on the front page of all the rag mags and the tabloids. They were all piled up on the kitchen table this morning. That's where I saw them. His publicist brought them over. His face was like thunder.'

'It must be difficult,' I venture. 'Living your life in the spot-light.'

'His choice,' Lucas counters.

'I suppose so. Are things between you and him all right?'

'Same as usual. I thought it would be different when he didn't have a girlfriend, but he's still never around. He said we should go for a pizza as there was something he wanted to talk to me about. I'm still waiting. Whether it ever happens or not, your guess is as good as mine.'

I wonder if he's told him about his impending move to LA or if this is going to be the moment he breaks the news to Lucas. My chest tightens at the thought of it.

'Don't just stand there watching me,' Lucas says. 'Get a brush and help. I've got stuff to do.'

'Like what?' Though I grab a brush as instructed and work on the other side of the pony to Lucas.

'Bev asked would I do a poetry class for the kids this afternoon.' He sounds shy when he tells me.

'She did?'

'Yeah. You don't mind?'

'I think it's a great idea. Have you got something prepared?'

'Do you think I'm stupid?'

I take that as Lucas being more organised than I give him credit for. I only hope he's right. This lot can be notoriously difficult to keep focused on a task. 'Are you looking forward to it, then?'

He stops brushing and chews at his lip. 'I'm a bit nervous,' he confesses.

'That's only natural. You'll ace it though. They adore you.'

Lucas snorts with disdain.

'Allow yourself to be the hero, for once,' I tell him.

He looks over at me, his face anxious as he asks, 'What will happen if you don't find another place like this?'

Now I'm the one to pause mid-stroke. 'I honestly don't know, Lucas.'

'You'll find something,' he says with the assurance of the young. 'I know you will.'

And I can't bring myself to tell him that his father came up with the ideal solution, but that I totally and utterly blew it.

Chapter Eighty-One

After we've finished our grooming session, Lucas, Little Dog and I walk Buzz back to his field. The bees meander from flower to flower, drunk with pollen from campion and clover, their contented buzzing the only sound around. The clouds are as fluffy as marshmallows in a sky that's a colour more appropriate to the Mediterranean. I could cry with the sheer beauty of it all. I can't even voice how I feel or I'd definitely be blubbing all over again. So I busy myself with settling Buzz, make a fuss of Ringo and secure the gate behind us.

Then we head back to the yard and have lunch. I notice that Lucas is unusually quiet or perhaps the other students are unusually noisy. It's a busy day today with our full complement of ten students on the farm. Some of them are our most challenging. Lucas is going to have his hands full and I get a flutter of nerves for him. Tamara and Jody are here, so I'm sure his usual fan base will be supportive. But we have a couple of our younger lads with ADHD in the mix today and I hope that Alan has tired Josh and Kenny out a bit this morning with some physical tasks.

When we've cleared away after lunch, I help Lucas to assemble the students in the open-sided part of the barn they use for summer lessons – thankfully, this was unaffected by the fire. They've all chosen to come along to the poetry session which is fantastic. We arrange the chairs so that they're shaded from the sun and with the usual degree of squabbling, they eventually take their seats. One thing I've learned from experience is that there's no point in having a rigid timetable here. Fluidity is our watchword.

Perching at the back on a hay bale, I watch as Bev introduces Lucas and he begins to talk. Little Dog jumps up next to me and I fuss his ears. Fifty wanders in and after a few heckling bleats, settles at my feet. Unfortunately, I can't stay here for long as I have to hit the phones again this afternoon – much as it pains me – but I'm intrigued to see how Lucas will manage his first attempt at a workshop. He sounds nervous as he hands out pieces of paper and tries to calm the kids down enough to listen to his instructions. As a lot of our students have attention issues, even if they're undiagnosed, lessons are often more of a study in crowd control rather than quality learning, but Lucas is persistent and I feel myself smiling at his efforts.

At the front, Lucas raises his voice and shouts out, 'Hey, guys! Listen up! Today, we're going to try to write a poem.'

Good luck with that, I think.

'What's your favourite word?' he says above their chatter. 'Say it out loud to me. Mine is balloon. Or maybe it's drizzle or . . .'

'Fart,' Seb in the front row says to much sniggering. Quickly followed by a chorus of 'bum', 'poo' and 'wee'.

I see a theme developing.

'Let's think of bigger words,' Lucas says, patiently. 'Thunder. Blossom. Garden.'

Asha, tentatively, puts his hand up. 'Sunshine.'

'That's a great word. Anyone else?'

346

Nicely, he's steered them away and I feel quite proud of him for not getting thrown.

'Jelly,' Jack adds, not to be outdone.

'Cool.' Lucas nods his approval and Jack, one of Lucas's biggest fans, preens. 'Write down a few of your favourite words and then pick one. Think of that word as a person. If you've written, say, Thunder, what would Thunder look like? Is it a boy or girl? What would his or her eyes be like? They might be dark and stormy. They might be grey and cloudy. What would they sound like? Would Thunder be loud and frightening? Or would it be exciting? If it was Blossom, would they be soft and pink? Would their voice sound as if it's floating on the air?'

The kids have quietened down a bit now and there's much scribbling going on. I'm impressed. Lucas seems to have a natural rapport with kids of this age. For his debut, he's doing a great job. Some of the supply teachers we have here can't get them to sit down for five minutes.

'What do you think?' I whisper into Little Dog's ear. 'He's pretty good, isn't he?' Little Dog wags his tail in reply.

'What would they be doing?' Lucas asks. 'Thunder might be banging at your windows. Blossom might be blowing down your street like a soft wind. Write down what you think.'

Sadly, I have to leave before I get to find out how the kids have managed with their first poetry lesson, but they certainly seem to be rapt. I jump down from the hay bale and give Lucas the thumbs up. I'm sure he flushes slightly. I'm still grinning as I walk across the yard towards my caravan and, believe me, I find precious little to smile about these days.

As I round the corner, I see Shelby's car parked in the yard and he's talking to Alan. My heart starts to pound in my chest and my mouth goes suddenly dry. Today, Alan is sporting Fleetwood Mac on his chest on a T-shirt that's at least two sizes too small. It's stretched across his chest and looks as if it's

347

cutting off the blood supply under his arms. Bev has been too terrified to guess his T-shirt for the last few days in case he asks her out on a date again.

Shelby, it has to be said, is wearing something entirely more fetching. He has on a plain grey T-shirt and washed-out jeans – intentionally so, and not just faded with age as mine are. I'm still filthy dirty from washing down Buzz with Lucas and have never been more aware of how scruffy I am.

'Visitor,' Alan says and seizes the opportunity to march off in the other direction as Shelby saunters towards me.

'You'll have to excuse my butler,' I quip. 'He's a temp.'

'He seems like a good man to me.'

'Yes,' I agree. 'He is. Don't know what I'd do without him.'

Shelby stares at me and his piercing blue eyes do very strange things to my hormones. 'Things ended badly between us last time.'

'They did.' Can't disagree with that either.

'I'm sorry,' he says. 'You were, of course, right. Which is all the more reason I was angry.'

'It's really none of my business. I was out of order.'

'You could have broken it to me more gently,' Shelby suggests and that makes us both laugh a little.

'Am I forgiven?' I ask.

'You are. Am I? I bring a peace offering.' He holds up a large, brown envelope. 'The contract for the land.'

'Are you sure? I thought I'd blown it.'

'It's yours. If you still want it.'

My heart, which had returned to its normal level of beating, picks up the pace again. I want it more than anything. Of course I do. 'You'd better come to the caravan.'

So he follows me into the van and I push some papers off the sofa so that he can sit down. Little Dog tries to fit into the one clear space with him.

'Tea?'

'I can't stay long,' he says. 'I have an event in London tonight.'

'What about Lucas?'

He frowns. 'Are you intent on making me feel guilty again?'

'That's not what I meant. I could make him some dinner here and the driver could pick him up later. If he wants to stay.'

'I'll text him and see what he wants to do.'

'No need to be so modern,' I tease. 'We can walk up to the barn. He's running his first poetry workshop for the rest of the kids today.'

Shelby looks suitably surprised. 'He is?'

'Yes. And he was making a very good job of it when I left him.'

Shelby shakes his head. 'I still feel that I hardly know him these days.'

'He's written a poem about saving the farm. It's on YouTube.' I flick to the relevant video on my phone and hand it to Shelby. 'He's great.'

He sits quietly while he watches his son on the screen. 'That's fantastic,' Shelby says as he clicks off his screen. 'If only he'd share this with me.'

'I'm sure he will. Just give it time.'

He holds up the brown envelope again. 'Well? Shall we do this?'

I let out a wavering breath. 'I'd love to. It's the answer to all of my prayers. But how can I sign it until I know that I have some money in place? My funds are sorely depleted.' Molly-speak for *I don't have any money at all*.

'I'll cover your costs for the first three months, by which time we'll have the money from the concert.'

'That's unbelievably kind of you, but our monthly bills aren't to be sneezed at,' I warn him. 'Keeping this lot eats through a small fortune.'

'I can only imagine. We can go through the figures when

you're ready. I've already spoken to some of the people I know who I can call favours in from and they're all keen to do a concert for the farm. I've pencilled in a tentative date.' He checks his phone and reels it off.

'That's only a couple of weeks ahead.'

'I thought we should strike while the iron's hot. Besides, you've said yourself, you're running out of time and money.'

True fact.

'I hope that the concert will raise enough to keep you going for the following six months, maybe even longer.' He smiles at me. 'My friends can be quite generous when pressed.'

I can only hope that he's right. 'I'm excited and terrified.'

'That's understandable. It's a big step. If you want to rescue the farm you don't really have any choice. But if it helps, I can assure you that my partners and I will try to be accommodating landlords.'

Yet Shelby will be an absentee one if he jets off to LA without a backward glance and I wonder how that will work. Are his other partners going to be as easy-going?

'I want to do this,' Shelby says, earnestly. 'Please let me. Since Susie died I've been all over the papers, known only for dating unsuitable models and actresses half my age. That's not fair to her memory. It's not fair to Lucas. I realise that now. I'd like to be known for something else. Perhaps this is the start of a new age of altruism for me.'

I hope he's being sincere and that I can trust Shelby Dacre to look after us. I'm putting all of my faith in him. 'Hand over the paperwork,' I say, heart in my mouth. 'Let's do it.'

He pulls the papers out of the envelope and lays them out on the table for me. I find a biro in a drawer and take a couple of deep breaths.

'Sign here, here and here.' He points to the relevant pages, already marked with a red cross.

My hand shakes as I put my name to the legal document, but I think this is a good thing. I'm sure it is.

When I've finished, I stand up and blow out a breath. 'Done.'

Despite being scared witless by the commitment I've taken on, a wave of relief washes over me. My search is over. I have my solution and, not only that, it's a great one. I'm trembling with emotion. Shelby Dacre has come in on his white charger and has saved us.

Shelby gathers the papers and stands up too. 'Welcome to Hope Farm, mark two. I feel as if I should have brought champagne.'

'That would be very welcome right now.' For me, at least, it certainly feels like a momentous occasion deserving of sparkly drinks. Hope Farm is going to continue. My beloved animals will have a home. My dear, dear students will still have a safe place in which to continue their studies and to grow in confidence. 'I couldn't be more grateful.'

'My pleasure.' He holds out his hand and we shake on it. His fingers are strong and warm in mine, we hold on for too long. Then he moves towards me, his lips brush mine and his arms enfold me.

We kiss softly, searchingly, but I pull away and say, 'This is no way for a landlord and tenant to behave. We agreed.'

'So we did.' But I guess that we throw caution to the wind and we kiss more insistently this time, leaving us both breathless.

'Oh, Molly,' he says as we part, his fingers stroking my hair. 'What *am* I going to do?'

I have no idea what to say to that. 'Oh, Molly,' what exactly? He pulls me close again and we hold on tightly to each other. I feel so at home in his arms and I know that I've never wanted anyone or anything as much in my life. But I've not a clue what's going on inside Shelby's head and that frightens me more than you can possibly know.

Chapter Eighty-Two

We leave the caravan, so much unspoken, and walk across to the barn. 'Can I announce this to everyone?' I ask.

'Of course.'

'Does Lucas know already?'

'I haven't had time to speak to him yet,' Shelby tells me and I wonder how they can live in the same home, if not in the same part of it, and yet communicate so little.

I hope that we can catch the end of Lucas's lesson so that Shelby can see what his son is doing here and how he's progressing. I want him to know how popular Lucas is with the kids here, even though they are all younger than him. The only thing that I worry about is that he has no one here of his own age to interact with. Well, it's not the *only* thing that I worry about, but you know what I mean. It depends on our intake who is here at any one time and I hope that we'll have some more students of Lucas's age before too long. Then I realise, if he goes off to boarding school, it won't be an issue at all.

With less than perfect timing, we arrive just as Lucas wraps up his session by shouting, 'That's it! Well done, everyone. You've knocked out some great rhymes there.'

He has a big grin on his face and only falters slightly when he sees me arrive with his father. A shadow crosses his face, but I step up to the front and ask, 'Did you enjoy Lucas's poetry session?'

'Yes!' is the unanimous verdict. Which is good to hear. It will have done wonders for his confidence.

'Shall we ask him to do it again?'

'Yes!'

'Let's give Lucas a big clap.' The students oblige by clapping and cheering.

Lucas takes a bow, smiling.

Shelby claps too. 'Well done, son.'

Lucas spins towards him and his demeanour changes as soon as he speaks to his father. 'What are you doing here?'

'Molly has some news,' Shelby says.

Lucas frowns. 'How does it involve you?'

'You'll see.' Despite his son's cool reception, Shelby still looks more than a little smug.

I touch Lucas's arm. 'It's all fine. No need to worry.' I know that he thinks no good can come of anything that his father's involved with. I hope, this time, he's proved wrong. 'Can you run and get Bev and Alan for me, please?'

Lucas shrugs and dashes off.

As he leaves, Shelby reaches out and squeezes my fingers in his. I nod to him to say that I'm ready. Then I walk to the front of the barn, Little Dog following every step as usual, and clap my hands to get the kids' attention. 'Stay seated just for a moment! I've got something nice to tell you.'

Lucas, Bev and Alan come back and stand next to Shelby.

I try to keep the tremor of excitement from my voice when I say, 'Very soon we have to move from Hope Farm because of the new trainline that's coming. Well, I've been struggling to find us all a new home – you, me, all of the animals.' I make a mental note to send out emails to their parents and carers later tonight, if I can, so that everyone is kept informed. I don't want anyone panicking. 'It's been very difficult and I did worry that we'd never find anywhere just as special.' As you're more than aware, this doesn't begin to explain all that I've been through or how close we have come to closing for good. 'So I'm very pleased to tell you that we have a new home. It's a lovely setting and not very far from here, so we won't have to change our routines at all. Everything will be just the same, if not better. We're very lucky that we'll even have nicer classrooms and all the animals can come with us.' I glance shyly at Shelby. 'Mr Dacre here will be our new landlord. He's made it all possible so I think that we should give him a big round of applause to show him how grateful we all are.'

All the children applaud and Lucas looks at his father in amazement. Shelby is beaming back at me.

'I think this, at least, deserves a conga!' So I gather the kids into a line and get at the head of it. Singing at the top of my voice, I lead a conga round the barn. Bev joins in as we pass and ushers Shelby Dacre in front of her. She's probably going to *love* holding onto his waist for the next few minutes. With very little cajoling, Alan grabs hold of Bev, and he sings along at the top of his voice despite me not really having him down as a conga kinda guy. Even Lucas eventually responds to my beckoning and tags on at the back. When we're all breathless and congaed out, we stand there huffing and puffing.

As soon as I can speak again without keeling over, I shout, 'You can all go down to the tea room and have a drink and a biscuit. You've done really well today. Good work everyone! It's soon going to be home time, so I'll see you all tomorrow.' There's a mad dash out to the yard. I think it was the word 'biscuit' that did it.

I'm not sure that they all understand the significance of

this, but that's the way that it should be. I'm the designated worrier.

'Well done, you beauty,' Bev says as I join the group again. She crushes me to her. 'You're a little star.'

'This is our saviour.' I tip my head towards Shelby.

She lets me go and makes a beeline for him. 'Come on, give us a hug, big boy.' Shelby looks quite startled as she wraps herself around him like a boa constrictor and squeezes.

When he's starting to turn blue in the face, I whisper, 'Put him down now, Bev.' And, thankfully, she lets go. The ink is barely dry on the contract and I don't want my friend crushing him to death with her joy.

Alan nods his approval, but his face – now returned to its usual passive mode – gives nothing away. I'm assuming he's joyously happy like the rest of us, but who knows?

'You're pleased, Alan?' I venture.

'Aye.' He flicks a thumb towards the yard. 'I'm going to see if pig's all right.'

He wanders off. As I said, overjoyed.

'So.' I sidle up next to Lucas. 'Surprised?'

'Stunned is more the word I would have chosen.' He looks at me squarely. 'I did wonder why dad was showing more interest than usual about this place.'

I hope that I don't flush too much. I'm hoping that his father's interest isn't purely out of altruism for the students and animals. I'd like to be in the equation too.

'Cut him some slack,' I say, lowering my voice. 'He's been great and he's helping us to fund the first few months until we get on our feet there.'

'He's loaded,' Lucas points out. 'It's nothing to him.'

'That may be. However, he didn't need to come to our assistance,' I remind him. 'But he has. For that, I'm very grateful. The new site is really beautiful. I can't wait for you to see it.'

'It's just a shame they're going to decimate this one.'

'I know.' I put my arm round his slender shoulders. 'Nothing in life stays the same. Sometimes that's for the better. Sometimes it's infinitely worse. But it's life, Lucas, and we all just have to do our best to work round it.'

'I'm glad that you're not closing Hope Farm. I know that I moan a lot, but I've no idea what I'd do if I couldn't come here every day.' He risks a grin at me. 'I quite like it really.'

I hug him. 'Some days you do hide it well,' I tease. 'But I'm glad you feel like that.'

'Don't get slushy,' he says. 'I can't stand it.'

'OK.' I let my arm drop from his shoulder. 'Let's go and prise your Dad away from Bev.'

How can I tell him that despite our last minute rescue, he might not be coming with us? It's the only thing that's blighting my happiness today and I don't want to burst Lucas's bubble either, especially after he's done so well with the younger kids. Besides, it's Shelby's job to tell him what's going on and the future plans he has. Despite being eternally indebted to the fabulous Mr Dacre, I could still kill him when it comes to how he deals with his own son.

Chapter Eighty-Three

Too soon, it's the day of the benefit concert that Shelby is throwing for us and I'm all of a-jitter. He's called it Hope Farm Festival, which sounds very grand. I'm trying very hard to concentrate on the task in hand, but keep starting something, forgetting what I'm doing halfway through and starting something else. Gah.

We're due at Homewood Manor for six o'clock as Shelby is holding a champagne reception before the concert starts. We're taking a small, hand-picked selection of the more amenable animals and they were all washed and groomed earlier today in the hope that they might actually stay clean for five minutes. Some of them have even managed it. I'll swear that they're worse than a bunch of toddlers.

I've drafted in a handful of our students' parents to help look after the animals during the festival as I want Bev, Alan and our young people to be able to relax and enjoy themselves today. I might even give it a go myself.

I've had nothing to do with the actual organising of this evening, that's all been down to Shelby and the folks who he's press-ganged into helping him. We've exchanged a number of rushed telephone calls about the logistics and updates on progress this week but of our kiss, there's been no further mention. I have been trying to organise one little surprise for the evening, but I've no idea how successful I've been. I have my fingers crossed that I can pull it off.

The weather for the day is set to be fabulous, so that's one less thing for me to worry about. We so rarely have warm, balmy evenings even in the height of summer, but it looks as if we have struck gold. Perhaps all my stars are coming to align or something and the universe is looking kindly at me.

Checking my watch, I realise that we need to be loading up the truck soon. Bev and Alan have been to the Manor this morning to set up our little area, taking the banners to advertise the farm and the fencing to keep the animals from running amok. Thankfully, my reliable volunteers have all arrived and, as soon as they've finished their tea and biscuits, we'll get Buzz, Tina Turner plus Dumb and Dumber all loaded up. Some of the bunnies have already gone down there this morning with Alan and Bev along with a few of the prettier chickens – the ones who have feathers and the usual complement of legs and eyes. We know full well that our challenged chickens tend to be more robust than some of the fluffier breeds – they're survivors against the odds – yet, because of how they look, people can shy away from handling them as they don't want to hurt them.

Once we get the animals loaded, Bev returns. 'Alan's set it all up nicely,' she says. 'It's looking great. I think Shelby has bought up the world's supply of bunting.'

'Good. Good.'

She gives me a hug. 'No need to look so terrified. It will all be wonderful. All we have to do is turn up and drink champagne. How hard can that be?'

'I should go and get changed.'

'Me too. Did you have a shower this morning?'

'Yes, Mum.' I give her a look.

'We adore you even when you smell of pig shit, but the celebrities of Homewood Manor may have delicate noses. They may be more used to Jo Malone and Givenchy than eau de manure.'

'I have washed. I will, eventually, comb my hair.'

'What are you wearing?'

'A dress,' I inform my friend. 'A new one.'

'Never.' She looks at me aghast. 'From where?'

'I popped out and did a quick tour of the charity shops in Aylesbury on Thursday evening.' This is akin to me canoeing the entire length of the Amazon or circumnavigating the earth in a hot air balloon.

'Blimey,' Bev says. 'You are pushing the boat out. You didn't tell me.'

'I don't tell you everything.' I give her a cheeky wink. Though, in all honesty, I thought if I mentioned needing a dress, she'd be fixing me up with her leopard-skin number and I don't think that this is an animal-print kind of do.

We wave the truck goodbye and I try not to fret.

'Come on,' Bev says. 'Let's get a wiggle on. We don't want to be late for our own party.'

My stomach lurches with nerves. 'I just want to go and see if Teacup is OK.'

'He's fine. And, if he's not, it's too late to do anything about it now. ' Bev grabs my arm and marches me towards the caravan. 'I've brought my make-up so that I can do you too.'

I knew she'd want to cover me in slap again and I already realise that resistance is futile. Bev armed with a carrier bag of cosmetics is an unstoppable woman.

Chapter Eighty-Four

Throwing fiscal caution to the wind, Bev and I splash out on a taxi to take us to Homewood Manor. We might well go home in the truck with a bunch of troublesome, smelly animals and Alan, but at least we've arrived in style.

We ask the taxi driver to drop us at the gates so that we can enjoy the walk up the drive to the house. Bev pays and we climb out. Then we pause for a moment and look at the grand house.

'Who'd have thought,' Bev says and links her arm through mine.

'Not me,' I admit.

'You've done us proud, Molly,' she says sounding quite emotional.

'You haven't seen the new land yet,' I tell her. 'But I'm sure you'll love it.'

'It doesn't matter what it's like. It just means that the good work of the farm can continue. The animals won't end up on the scrapheap or in a glue pot and you won't have to go out into the real world to get a proper job.'

I laugh at that. 'You neither. I reckon we'd both be unemployable now.'

'Not if they saw us poshed up like this,' she says. 'Gawd, we look like ladies of the manor.'

'Infinitely better than looking like ladies of the night.' After my extensive tour of charity shops, I found a Coast chiffon dress in Oxfam. It's black with pastel-coloured roses and has a floaty, two-tiered skirt which the assistant told me had a high-low hem – who knew? All I can tell you is that the front stops just above my knees while the back drapes down to the ground. I bought some gold, strappy sandals too and only hope that I don't turn my ankle as my usual footwear of choice is welly boots. I've teamed it with a black cashmere wrap that was Hettie's – which only has one tiny moth hole in it – and a little clutch bag that she had squirrelled away. My hair is freshly washed and trimmed courtesy of the kitchen scissors. I can only hope that Christian Lee doesn't look too closely at it.

'That is one show-stopper of a dress,' Bev says. 'You scrub up well, love. That is *seriously* going to turn heads.'

I know that we'll be mixing with the glitterati tonight and I did want to try and blend in as best I could – given the fact that I'm in a charity shop frock and not Gucci. Besides, there's only one head that I'd like to turn. 'I do feel good in it,' I admit, giving a little swish of my skirt. 'Not bad for a tenner.'

'*Total* bargain,' she agrees. 'Someone, somewhere should regret binning that.'

Bev looks lovely tonight, too. She's wearing a mauve maxi dress with shoestring straps, a sparkly silver shrug and silver sandals.

'I'm *so* going to bag myself a television star tonight,' she says. 'Even a minor one would do. As Shelby Dacre already seems to be taken, I'll try for someone out of *Holby City* or Corrie.'

'Do you think it will all be famous people?' I ask anxiously.

'It bloody well better be. Famous people with fat wallets and loose morals, I hope.'

'They'll be starting without us if we don't get a move on,' I warn.

'Let's go and knock them dead,' Bev says.

So we link arms and make our way down the meandering drive, the scent of summer sweet in the air and a knot of anxious anticipation in my stomach.

Chapter Eighty-Five

At the back of the house, the party is already in full flow. The garden is strung with bunting and hundreds of fairy lights and looks beyond magical. On the stage a string quartet plays an Ed Sheeran tune. There are groups of deckchairs for seating in front of them and hay bales scattered around. The smell of barbecuing food drifts towards us. The set-up might be similar, but the atmosphere is so different to the afternoon event we attended before. It's so sophisticated and grown-up. I don't think that I've ever been to anything remotely like this before. The tickets have, apparently, cost a small fortune and I'm glad that Shelby gave all of us at the farm free passes as we'd never have been able to afford to come. I know nothing about Shelby's world, yet even I can recognise some of the well-known faces among the guests.

Bev and I look at each other and, in unison, say, 'Blimey!'

'This is going to be a good night,' she whispers. 'I can feel it in my water.'

I screw up my nose. 'TMI.'

'The animals are down in the corner where we set up before. We'll take a circuit of the lawn, do some star-spotting and then we'll go to see them. I don't want to smell of goat when I get a selfie with Danny Dyer.' She cranes her neck. 'I thought Alan might be down there already, but I can't see him.'

'I hope he's wearing his best band T-shirt.' I'm certainly glad that I made the effort to spruce myself up. If he turns up looking like he normally does we'll have to hide him.

'Are we having a bet?' Bev asks. 'Just don't tell him if I get it right. He seems to have finally forgotten that he offered me a hot date and I don't want him reminding.'

'Hmm. I'll go for Kings of Leon.'

'Cheeky one,' she says. 'I'll go conservative and have a guess at Coldplay.'

'I like it.'

We cross the terrace and pick up two glasses of chilled white wine as we go. Bev and I clink them together and Bev says, 'To us. Here's to a brilliant night and a secure future.'

'I'll drink to that,' I agree and so we do.

Toast finished, we're about to negotiate walking down the steps onto the lawn when I see Shelby at the other side of the party near the stage. He looks so debonair in a dinner suit that my heart goes into overdrive and pitter-patters so much that I have to stop and take a few deep breaths.

'Holy flipping moly,' Bev whispers. 'He is smokin' hot!'

He is. I can't deny it. Then he looks up and our eyes meet across the crowd. I've never really believed in all this romance stuff, probably because it's never happened to me. But, at this moment, everyone else fades away and it's just Shelby and me. The air feels charged as if there are extra atoms and stuff. Amid the hubbub, a bubble of calm links us. There's definitely a chemistry between us, a connection – I'm sure of it. Though this may be the very reason why he's a national heart-throb. Perhaps every woman feels the same when he looks at her. Ah, well.

Then someone touches his arm and pulls his attention away from me. My heart sinks just a little bit as I come back into the here and now with Bev babbling on beside me. It will be impossible for me to grab even a few minutes with him tonight even though I realise that's not the reason we are here.

'. . . he's on *TOWIE* or is it *Made in Chelsea*? I don't know. One of them.'

'What?' I say.

'Back in the room,' Bev tuts. 'If you're not even listening to me how are you ever going to know your reality stars? Come on, let's get closer to him so I can check him out.'

I've still not a clue who she means.

Yet she yanks on my arm and I move with her. But as Bev and I negotiate the stairs, I see Shelby making his way through the crowd, shaking hands, kissing cheeks, patting shoulders as he goes, but I'm absolutely sure that he's making a beeline for us.

Bev nudges me. 'Incoming,' she says, but I'm already more than aware of it.

With perfect timing, as we reach the bottom of the stairs, Shelby arrives in front of us. 'Ladies,' he says, eyes glittering. 'You're both looking absolutely beautiful tonight.'

'Thanks, Shelby,' Bev says and she leans in for a kiss on the cheek.

Then Shelby reaches forward, puts a hand on my arm and kisses me softly. I'm thrilled when his lips linger a moment too long and I can feel the warmth of his fingers on my skin.

'This looks absolutely fantastic,' I tell him. 'I'm blown away.'

'I'm glad you could make it.'

'You're kidding. I wouldn't have missed it for the world.'

'Let's hope that we raise a ton of money for the farm.'

'I hope so too.'

'You ladies both have a drink?' We hold up our glasses. 'Can I get you anything else?'

'We're hot to trot,' Bev says.

'My role is to mingle tonight, so I hope that you'll excuse me. Molly, I'd like to introduce you to some people even though I know it's your idea of hell.' He grins at me. 'Is that OK?'

'It's the least I can do after you've organised all this.'

'Good.' He gives my arm a gentle squeeze. 'I'll catch up with you later.'

Then he's gone, swallowed by the crowd again.

We both watch him go. Bev says, 'If you do have a fling with him, can I have him when you're done?'

'I'm not going to be having a fling with him,' I assure her. 'Our business relationship is purely platonic.'

'You're forgetting that you told me about getting jiggy with him in the hay?' Bev's eyes widen.

'Sssssh!' I look round to make sure that no one else heard, but no one is paying any attention to us. 'I shared that with you in confidence.'

'And I shall take your sordid secret to my grave with me,' she swears. 'Bet you want to do it again, though.'

I sigh. 'Of course, I do. I'd be mad not to.'

'Tell me again how good he was.'

'No.' I hold up a hand. 'He's my landlord now and that would put me in a very compromising position.'

She snarfs at that.

'You know what I mean. Besides, look at my competition.' I wave a hand at the beautiful people on the lawn. '*Look* at them.'

'Actresses, models, soap stars, singers.' She shakes her head at me. 'I bet none of them can trim the toenails of a stroppy alpaca single-handedly.'

'That's probably quite true. Nor indeed would they need to.'

'Don't underestimate the importance of these skills.'

'You are a fool,' I laugh.

'Let's go and grab some of the grub that's on offer. We can

eat enough to keep us going for the rest of the week, if we're lucky.'

So we tour the different food stations and Bev helps herself to nibbles of satay chicken, little cones filled with salmon mascarpone mousse and bite-sized toad-in-the-holes, while I sample the halloumi bites and tomato bruschetta. There are platters laid out with every kind of food you can imagine and Bev samples each and every one – though she nearly baulks at the oysters. Can't say I blame her. With a grimace, she swallows one.

'Slimy snot,' is Bev's verdict. She necks her wine to take the taste away. 'Shall we go and find our lot, then? I suppose we must.'

So we pick our way through the partygoers, grabbing another glass or two as we do, and go in search of our dear students and animals.

Then Bev says, 'OMG! That's only Ross Kemp. I've *so* got to get a photo. Come with me.'

'No, no, no.' I'd die of embarrassment.

'Catch you in five minutes, then.' With that, Bev dashes off to grab her man and leaves me abandoned in the middle of the lawn.

Chapter Eighty-Six

I give up waiting for Bev to come back and head off towards the Hope Farm enclosure. I spot Lucas before I see anyone else. He's lurking on the very edge of the party by himself and looks forlorn. Like me, the art of socialising does not come easy to him. Tonight, he's clad in an all-black ensemble – shirt, jeans, boots. Which is maybe Lucas's idea of smart. I'm not sure. He's wearing black eyeliner and mascara which makes him look even paler than usual and his hair seems not to have been combed for a week or so. I think that's intentional too.

I never thought that I'd want children of my own, but every time I see Lucas my heart tightens and I think this is as close as I've ever come to maternal love. He touches a softness inside me that I've never experienced before. I can look at a baby animal and go all squishy, but I've never done it with a human before. Of course, I adore all of our students – they all have their own quirks, foibles and downright eccentricities – yet I've never quite connected to any of them in the way I have with Lucas. I want only the best for him and I bet his mum would be really proud to see him now. I want her to be able to hear his poetry, to see that he has such potential, that he's compassionate and caring even though he can be a complete pain in the bum. Is that what loving your own child is like? If it is, then it's a very good feeling.

'Hey,' I say. 'All OK?'

He nods. 'Cool.' Then he holds up a bottle of beer. 'Fourth one in and feeling mellow.'

'You shouldn't even be drinking,' I remind him.

'Daddy Dearest said it was all right.'

'Well, go easy,' I tell him. 'I don't mind clearing up after animals, but I don't want to be doing it after you.'

'We have staff for that.'

'That makes you sound like a brat and you're not. Just relax and have fun . . . '

'But not *too* much fun.'

He's in a weird mood, a bit wired, a bit petulant, a bit agitated. I wonder why? Perhaps, like me, he's anxious for it all to go well tonight. After all, the future financial health of Hope Farm depends on it. I wish I hadn't reminded myself of that and take a swig of my own wine.

'Watch how you go, yourself,' Lucas notes. 'You're not used to strong drink.'

'It's nerve-wracking, isn't it?'

'Yeah,' he agrees. 'Are you sure that getting hammered isn't a really great idea?'

'Positive.' I take another swig. 'How are the kids and the animals faring?'

'Hunky-dory,' he says. 'Dumb and Dumber are sending out cute vibes. Tina Turner hasn't bitten anyone yet. All in the garden is rosy.'

'Your dad's doing a very good thing,' I say to him.

He softens. 'I know.'

'You seem to be so used to battling him that you don't know when to stop.'

'He is an arse a lot of the time,' Lucas counters.

'So are all parents. It's part of the job description.' I wonder if Shelby has told him yet about going to LA. Even the thought of him leaving makes my stomach lurch, so I can't begin to think how it will hit Lucas. Shelby risks losing any chance of a good relationship with his son for ever. Just as bad, it will break my heart to let him go. Still, I don't want to think of that now. Not tonight.

'I'm pleased that the farm is going to continue, though,' Lucas adds.

'Me too. I can't bear to think of what might have happened to us all if your dad hadn't stepped in.'

'Want to walk down to see them all?'

'I hope none of them have rolled in mud since they were washed this morning.'

'The animals or the students?'

I laugh. 'As always, it could go either way.'

'They're doing a great job,' Lucas says. 'Jack and Seb are handling it like pros. Both of the girls look amazing.'

'Oh, yes?' I raise an eyebrow.

'Get a grip,' Lucas snaps. 'They're *children* and don't you dare tell them I said something nice about them or they'll be looking at me all googly-eyed again.'

Tamara, in fact, has recently had a birthday and is just over a year younger than Lucas. Yet in terms of maturity they are miles apart, so I get what he means.

'I was just hopeful for a moment, that you might actually like someone.'

He glares at me. 'I don't really like girls.'

'Do you like boys?' I venture. 'If you do, it's OK.'

'What? Of course it's OK. It's not the dark ages or the 1960s or something.'

'I'm just trying to help.'

'Then stop pretending to be hip. I don't like boys either. What I'm saying is I don't like girls or boys that are *kids*.'

'Oh. I see. Can I point out that you don't like adults much either?'

'You're all right,' he offers grudgingly. 'Mostly.'

I smile at him. 'I think that's what you call damning with faint praise.'

'Yeah, well stop trying to tell me about the birds and the bees and we'll be cool,' he grumbles.

'Is there anything else we need to do for tonight?' I venture, trying to steer us back onto a safer course.

'I made sure there were some deckchairs reserved for everyone at the front.' Lucas points them out to me.

'That's kind of you.'

'I know what this crowd are like.' He flicks a thumb towards the main event. 'They always want to be seen to be doing good, preferably in the front row.'

'As long as they fill the buckets up, I don't mind what they do.'

So we walk together down to the front of the little copse and see the animals in their fenced-off area. All looks reassuringly calm. Sometimes Tina Turner gets a diva mood on her and you can't do a thing with her. Tonight she looks pleasingly compliant. A few people are milling around having photographs taken with them. The parents who volunteered with the preparations this morning have been replaced by the second shift and they're doing a great job. I should encourage this more often. As I generally don't like people, I try to do everything myself and keep other people well out of the mix. Working with Shelby has shown me that great things can happen if you let other people in. Though I'm not sure that I need to let them quite as 'in' as I've let 'in' Shelby Dacre. If you know what I mean. Moving swiftly on . . .

371

The bunnies and the goats are getting lots of cuddles, mostly from people in their finery, which makes me slightly nervous. Buzz is having more selfie action than I thought possible, but he seems to be coping admirably. As Lucas said, our youngsters are doing really well too. They're out in force, chatting to people about the work of the farm and helping them to take photos. It's lovely to see them blossoming. When some of them first came to us they wouldn't have known how to hold a conversation and this is a great mark of their progress. They are all dressed so smartly – and Lucas is right, the girls look great even though they have even more make-up on than I do, which makes them look so grown up. My heart swells with pride to see them.

After a few minutes, Bev joins us and declares, 'I have *totally* snogged Ross Kemp.' She holds up her phone and, on her screen there's a picture of her being pecked rather chastely on the cheek by said celebrity. 'My life is complete.'

'Lovely pic.'

She kisses her screen. 'How's it all going here? Everyone behaving?'

'Yes. No problems.'

'I might go and do another round of celeb-spotting if you don't need me.'

'Fill your boots,' I tell her. 'After all, we might never again be in such close proximity to television royalty and I have plenty of help here.'

Then, as she goes to leave, we see a man striding purposefully towards us. He looks vaguely familiar, but it's only when he gets close that I realise just who it is.

'Well,' Bev says, 'Blow me down with a bloody feather.'

Exactly.

'All right,' Alan says when he reaches us.

We both stare at him, temporarily rendered speechless. Even Lucas is gaping. 'Fuck,' he murmurs to no one in particular

Apart from the fact that I've never seen Alan do anything more than a leisurely saunter, the rest of him is unrecognisable too. His beard has been shaved off, making him look about ten years younger and considerably more handsome than anyone could have imagined. The flowing locks of straggly grey hair have gone and are tamed into a neat man bun. His dinner suit is beautifully cut and, beneath it, his shirt is crisp and white. Not a band T-shirt in sight. Plus, he's holding a bouquet of red roses.

Unlike us, he seems entirely unfazed by his new appearance.

'What?' he says when still no one speaks.

'You.' I stammer. 'You. Look at you.'

He glances down, seemingly surprised that we should, in fact, be at all surprised. 'You said smart.'

'I said smart,' I agree. 'I didn't expect complete and utter transformation.'

Alan merely shrugs, while Bev is standing there like a statue, stunned and apparently struck dumb.

'Flowers,' Alan says. 'For you.' He holds out his bouquet to her. Mine and Lucas's heads swivel towards Bev as if we're watching a tennis match. Transfixed by this new man, she slowly takes them. Her mouth's ajar, but no words are coming out.

I nudge her.

'Thank you,' she squeaks. 'They're lovely.'

Alan nods. 'We'll have that hot date sometime, then.'

'Yes,' Bev manages. 'Next week suits me.'

'Right. That's settled.' Alan claps his hands together. 'Where's the beer?'

Chapter Eighty-Seven

The concert's about to start, so I wrest the students away from the animals and settle them in their reserved deckchairs in the front row of the audience. Lucas and I sit down at the far end of the line.

To great applause, whooping and cheers, Shelby bounds onto the stage and takes a bow. He is the consummate professional and looks so at ease up there. His world couldn't be any more different to mine.

'We've got a great programme for you this evening, ladies and gentleman,' he booms out. 'It's all in a fabulous cause. We're here to support Hope Farm, which you may have visited over in the corner. Molly Baker does fantastic work supporting teenagers with autism, learning difficulties and mental health issues. But it all takes huge amounts of money to keep afloat and that's where you come in. Enjoy the show, avail yourselves of the wonderful food and wine, but please dig deep into your pockets to help fund a great cause.'

More clapping.

Shelby holds up a hand, clearly used to working an audience. 'Enough from me. Let me introduce our first act. All the performers tonight have given their time freely and we couldn't be more appreciative. So, ladies and gentlemen, without further ado, let's give a warm welcome to the cast of *Flinton's Farm*!'

A number of people who I assume are Shelby's colleagues join him on stage. They're all dressed as farm hands in checked shirts and jeans. Scarlett Vincent is obvious by her absence and I assume that it's still all over between them. That shouldn't make me happy, but it does.

Someone strums a guitar and they launch into a comedy song about a combine harvester which gets the audience joining in. Then they sing 'Take Me Home, Country Roads' and McFly's 'All About You'. I feel quite emotional that this is all in aid of Hope Farm. Everyone has put so much effort into it.

The cast leave the stage and are replaced by a folk group, who launch into a lively set with fiddles blazing which gets everyone up and dancing. Despite it being a fast song, Bev and Alan are locked together in an embrace. Lucas grabs my arm and we do what might be classed as a do-si-do. We whoop as we swing each other round until we're dizzy. Out of the corner of my eye, I catch Shelby watching us as he claps along to the beat.

Then a beautiful young girl takes over and sings with a voice like an angel.

'She's good,' Lucas says with an approving nod.

'Who is she?'

'Phoenix Jade. An up-and-coming pop star.'

'Oh.' He looks at her in a very dreamy way and I don't think it's for my benefit. He might not like girls in general, but he seems quite taken with this one.

Two more acts follow and we lose ourselves in the music. Too soon, as the applause is dying down, Shelby comes back on stage to draw the evening to a close. It's all rushed by in a blur, but it's gone beautifully and I'm so grateful to everyone taking part. I've even talked to people – strangers nonetheless – about the farm. Go me!

'Thank you so much, ladies and gentlemen,' Shelby says. 'I think you'll agree that it's been a great evening of entertainment. The performers have all been wonderful and if you haven't donated to keep Hope Farm afloat yet then there are buckets circulating. For credit card donations, see me later! Please put your hands together for all our fantastic supporters.' He waits until the applause finishes again. 'Before we wrap it up, I've got a favour to ask of one very special person here.' He glances towards us and I feel myself colour up. 'My son, Lucas, is a poet and I'd love him to come up and perform the poem he's written about saving the farm.'

Lucas turns and scowls at me. 'You knew about this?'

'I swear I didn't.'

'Fuck,' he mutters.

'You should do it, though,' I whisper to him. 'For your dad. For me. For the farm.'

His look darkens. 'No pressure, then.'

'You can do it,' I assure him. 'You know you can.'

'I haven't got anything prepared and this place is full of professional performers, in case you hadn't noticed.'

I take his hand and squeeze it. 'Then they'll understand how difficult this is for you.'

From the stage, Shelby shouts, 'Come on, Lucas. We'd love to hear you. Wouldn't we, ladies and gentlemen?'

Much cheering from the audience.

'Fuck's sake,' Lucas mutters as he stands. 'I'm going to KILL someone! I'm just not sure who.' But he marches to the stage nevertheless and my heart jumps into my mouth.

Oozing reluctance with every ounce of his being, he climbs the steps to the stage.

'My beautiful boy, Lucas!' Shelby grabs Lucas in a bear hug

376

and ruffles his hair. Lucas shies away. Only the alpacas are more sensitive about getting their hair touched. I could shake Shelby as he has no idea how to handle his own child.

He ushers Lucas to the microphone and then steps away, as a hush falls over the audience. It's so quiet that I can hear the blood rushing in my own ears. Lucas stands there looking like a rabbit caught in the headlights. A rabbit who knows he's about to be involved in a terrible car crash.

Chapter Eighty-Eight

After what seems like an eternity, Lucas finally opens his mouth. His voice comes out as a croak and he says the first line of his poem and then grinds to a halt again. I can see that his hands are shaking and his breath is coming in shallow pants.

'You can do it, Lucas,' someone shouts from the audience and Lucas's head snaps up.

From my seat, I'm willing him to do well. I'm sure that Shelby did it in good faith, but this could crush his son's fragile self-esteem. Lucas's poetry is the only thing that he has that he's brilliant at and I don't want him to fail. If he can't do this it will only make him doubt himself.

'Take deep breaths, Lucas,' I whisper. 'Take deep breaths.'

On the stage, he does just that. Then he starts again, but in a faltering voice. Next to him Shelby steps up to the microphone. He looks directly at Lucas and joins in, feeding him the lines to his own poem.

I can only think that Shelby must have learned the words from the YouTube video I showed him. Lucas is so shocked that he's almost stunned into silence again. But he recovers well and, emboldened by his father's presence, starts to grow in confidence.

'You can do it,' I murmur. My palms are sweating as I watch. 'Come on.'

A few more lines and they're both getting into the rhythm together – although Lucas still looks astounded that his dad knows the words to his poem. As it goes on, Lucas starts to take the lead and I can feel myself breathe once more. Finally, he gets into his stride and his performance starts to flow. Shelby goes to takes a step backwards to leave him to it, but Lucas catches his hand and pulls him back to his side. They finish the poem together with Shelby's arm slung round his son's shoulder, encouraging the audience to join in at the rousing end.

When they're done, Shelby holds up Lucas's hand like a champion and the crowd go wild. As one, they leap from their seats and give Lucas a standing ovation.

Lucas laughs and looks at his dad, bemused.

'That's for you, son,' Shelby says. 'Want to do another one?'

Lucas laughs nervously. 'OK.'

So this time Shelby retreats into the background, the audience remain standing, but quieten as Lucas starts to spit out another rhyme. This time it's an angry and sad poem about love and loss that I haven't heard before. I feel tears spring to my eyes and, at the back of the stage, I see Shelby wipe his eyes with his jacket sleeve. All of Lucas's pent-up emotions pour out and soon, there's not a dry eye in the house. This is the conversation that father and son should have been having and it must be difficult for Shelby to hear all Lucas's hurt performed so openly. It must be hard for Lucas to do it – especially unprepared.

Then he changes up and does a witty rant about people who go to the supermarket in their pyjamas which has everyone laughing. As he stands away from the microphone and takes a bow, the crowd erupt and shout and cheer at him. Lucas, looking bashful, laps up the praise. Shelby goes to wrap his arms round his son and gives him a big bear hug. They hold each other tightly on the stage and I hope that this is a healing moment in their relationship.

When they break apart, Shelby nods at me which is my cue for the little secret surprise I've been working on. 'Come on, gang. We're on.'

Shelby takes the front of stage. 'Ladies and gentlemen, the students of Hope Farm would like to say thank you.'

I shepherd the students, Bev and Alan – still looking like an alien being in his swanky dinner suit – to the stage and we troop on looking like a slightly more eccentric version of the Von Trapps. With much to-ing and fro-ing we manage to form some kind of disorderly huddle around Lucas, who is now beyond confused.

'I know you've just done it, but we thought we'd surprise you with our rendition of "Save the Farm", if that's all right with you?' Shelby didn't know we'd got this planned, just as I didn't know that he'd ask Lucas onto the stage. But I think it bears repeating.

'You've all learned it?'

'Of a fashion,' I tell him.

He pulls a sarcastic face at me. 'Oh, good.'

We've been having secret practice sessions when Lucas was out of sight and Tamara made sure that everyone had the YouTube video on their phone so they could rap along with it at home. It's fair to say though, that at our last group practice, we weren't exactly word-perfect. And the rhythm wasn't exactly spot on. I like to think that we make up for our lack of accuracy with enthusiasm.

'Let's go for it,' Shelby says. 'Ladies and gentleman, feel free to join in at the chorus! Save the farm!'

With a bewildered shake of his head, Lucas kicks off again – this time clear-voiced and confident – and soon we're all joining in.

It's nothing short of criminal:
It's a travesty; a scam.
We're another victim of that HS2 to Birmingham.
Because, despite the work we've done here,
For those with special needs,
The rich man's railway still comes first,
Yes, progress supersedes!

Even I find my voice. Next to me, Shelby slips his arm round my waist. Which, if I'm honest with you, I find more distracting than comforting. I take time to look round at all the students as I want to capture this moment for ever. They might never have a career on the stage, but their faces are shining with joy and there are beaming grins on every face and I know this was the right thing to do.

When it comes to the bit where we all chant 'Save the farm!' the audience join in with gusto and I come over all emotional again.

Save The Farm! Save The Farm!
With the alpacas we'll stand tall!
Save The Farm! Save The Farm!
Hear us all at Hope Farm call!
Save The Farm! Save The Farm!
Stand up for what you know is right,
So the work we do can con-tin-ue
Come join us in this fight.

The audience cheer as we come to the end of our poem and the students clap themselves too. They're going to be talking about this for weeks, months, for ever. And why not? They all deserve some adulation. Especially my dear Lucas. I hope that his mother is looking down on him now as she'd be so proud, as am I.

'Thank you,' I whisper to Shelby as he leads us in a bow.

He winks at me. 'My pleasure.'

We have a bright future ahead of us at Hope Farm and that means more to me than anything.

Chapter Eighty-Nine

I go home floating on a cloud. Tonight was more wonderful than I could possibly have expected. I tried to say thank you again to Shelby before I left, but I had the animals to deal with. When I eventually spotted him, he'd been swallowed up by a crowd of well-wishers and I didn't like to disturb him.

Bev and Alan disappeared in a taxi together. I know! I'm not sure what the biggest surprise of the evening was – Alan rocking up in a dinner suit or Lucas agreeing to get up on stage and perform. Either way, both turned out extraordinarily well.

One of the parents, Jody's dad, who has enjoyed considerably less wine than I have, drives the truck back while I sit content-edly in the passenger seat going over and over the evening in my mind. I wave away his offer to unload the animals and put them to bed, so he calls a taxi to take him home.

It's been a long day for all of us and I thank him profusely for his help. As I see him off, I'm so glad to close the gate and head back to my little caravan. When I step inside, Little Dog greets me as if I've been gone for ten years.

'Down, boy.' I fuss him as he jumps all over my posh flowery dress. 'Did you miss me? Come on then, we've still got work to do.'

So I slip off my dainty sandals and put on my wellies. I don't want to keep the animals waiting in the truck while I get changed into my scruffs again. Instead, I hitch up the back of my lovely floaty dress and tuck it into my knicker legs, so that it's out of the way. In the yard, Big Dog joins us as I take Tina Turner out of the truck and return her to the paddock to join her chums. The alpacas are all instantly skitty and I give them a handful of pellets and talk them down off the ledge. After that, I walk Buzz back up to his field and, when he's settled, I sort out the bunnies and the goats who are much easier creatures. No matter how tired or how drinky you might be, the never-ending task of caring for animals still goes on.

Eventually, when everyone is back to where they should be, I can go to bed myself. Thank goodness that I have a whole day to myself tomorrow. This is the most socialising that I've done in years – possibly ever – and, though I'm also on a high, I feel quite exhausted by it now.

As I head back to my caravan, more than ready to hit the sack, I hear a car coming up the lane. It's a bit late for that and my stomach responds by turning all queasy. We don't get many people finding their way up here at night and, when we do, they're usually up to no good. It's the only time that I feel vulnerable. The dogs set off barking again and I click them both to heel.

Just as I'm about to reach for my phone in case I need to make an emergency call, a text pings in. It's from Shelby and simply says, *I'm at the gate*.

I'd like to tell you that my heart rate returns to normal, but no, this makes it go into even more of a flutter.

'It's Shelby,' I tell the dogs. 'Stand down.' Obediently, they stop barking and wag their tails instead. Dogs' emotions are so much easier to read.

I rearrange my dress so that I'm decent again and we all walk down through the yard in time to see Shelby's driver making a tricky eighteen-point turn in the lane and drive away. I feel a gulp travel down my throat. Does that mean what I think it does? Is Shelby planning on staying here for a while? Quite a while.

He's leaning on the gate when I get there. He's still wearing his dinner jacket, but his bow tie is undone and his shirt neck is open. His usually immaculate hair is a bit messy and, like me, he may be a little bit drunk. There's a bottle of champagne in his hand.

'Hey,' I say as I get there.

He looks so beautiful standing there in the moonlight. The night is turning hot and heavy and I'll swear that the air between us crackles with electricity. 'I've sent my driver away. I hope I can I come in or I'll feel foolish.'

I laugh at that. 'Of course you can.' I unlock the gate and let him through. He fusses Little Dog which comes more naturally to him now. Well, a bit more. He still wipes his hand on his DJ afterwards. We walk up towards my van.

'I tried to speak to you before I headed off, but you were proving very popular.'

'I saw you leave.' His eyes are dark, glittering when he adds, 'But I didn't want our evening to be over.'

'It was wonderful. I didn't want it to end either. I don't think I'll be able to sleep a wink. I'm too wired.'

He holds up the bottle. 'Let's put this to good use, then.'

'It's still warm. I could get the deckchairs out.' See, I have all the best chat-up lines.

'Let me do that. Why don't you go and find us some glasses?'

I take the bottle from him and put it on the step of the van.

While Shelby finds the deckchairs and sets them up, I go into the kitchen. I stand and grip the work surface, trying to steady my breath. What is it about this man that turns me into a trembling wreck? When I've calmed down a bit, I search my cupboard for glasses, but can find none. They're probably scattered far and wide across the farm, so I grab two mugs instead and head back outside.

Shelby pops the cork and I proffer the mugs. 'I'm sorry but I can't find my glasses.'

'These are fine,' he says. 'I always think that champagne tastes better out of mugs.'

Yeah, I bet he does.

'I haven't got the final figure yet, but we raised a lot of money tonight, Molly. With your usual prudent management, it will see you through the next year. Maybe longer.'

'That's fantastic. I don't know if you realise just how much this means to me, to the students and to the animals.'

His eyes hold mine when he says, 'I think I do.'

We clonk our mugs together in way of a toast and settle in our deckchairs. The night is as black as pitch and the moon hangs low, peering over the tops of the trees. Apart from the odd grunt from Teacup or a bleat from Fifty from the yard and the shifting of the dogs under my deckchair, all is silent and still.

I kick off my wellies and pull my knees up, tucking my dress around them.

'You looked beautiful tonight,' Shelby says. 'But I like you even better like this.' With a slow smile, he reaches out, picks some straw from my hair and tosses it to the ground. 'Lucas did a great job, didn't he? I was so proud of him.'

'Me too. It was lovely to see you step forward and help him. All he wants is your attention and approval.'

'I know.'

I don't want to mention Shelby's impending move to Los Angeles as I want nothing to spoil this perfect evening. If Shelby goes off into the starry stratosphere and I never see him again, I will always have this to remember him by. He's secured the future of the farm and, for that, I'm truly grateful.

Chapter Ninety

We sip our champagne in silence, embracing the warmth and stillness of the night.

'I've realised,' Shelby says, eventually. 'What a terrible impediment to romance a deckchair is.' He turns to me and reaches out to take my hand. 'If I had a notion to kiss you, that's a very big gap to bridge.'

I laugh and say, 'If you did by any chance have that notion, we could move into the van.'

'It seems a shame not to fully enjoy this wonderful evening. Do you have a blanket? We could walk up into the fields.'

'That sounds like an excellent idea.' He squeezes my hand tightly and I stand up on legs that are quite wobbly – part drink, part anticipation – to go and find a blanket.

In the van, I dash to the sink and squirt a blob of toothpaste into my mouth and swish it all round with my tongue. If I properly brushed my teeth, he might hear me and think I'm weird. Then I grab a blanket off the sofa and both cushions. I quickly try to brush off the residual dog hair.

Shelby stands to greet me and takes the blanket from me. Hand in hand, we walk up through the yard, up past the ponies and the Shire horses and beyond the big field at the outer reaches of our land. There's no one and nothing else around up here and it feels as if Shelby and I are the only people in the world. If you don't count Little Dog who, of course, has come too.

'Let's sit here.' Shelby chooses a sheltered spot by the trees and sets the blanket down.

I throw the cushions onto it and say, 'We should have brought a picnic.'

We make ourselves comfortable and I think that this is an infinitely better proposition for seduction. Shelby clearly agrees too as, without speaking, he pulls me close to him and his lips find mine. Little Dog, clearly not keen to play gooseberry, wanders off into the trees.

The darkness envelopes us, cradles us. Beneath the vast expanse of starry sky, on the land that I love and with the man that I am coming to love, we explore each other's bodies, slowly and tenderly. With something approaching reverence, Shelby takes off my dress and his eyes devour my body. We lie naked in each other's arms, kissing and every breath, every touch sets my skin on fire. When we make love, it truly feels as if we are joined as one. Shelby is a skilled lover who takes me to the exquisite edge of losing myself. If I were to die tonight, I would surely die a happy woman.

Afterwards, we lie still embracing, drifting towards sleep. I shiver and Shelby covers my nakedness with his jacket. I lay my head on his shoulder and feel that I have never been so content. We must sleep, because when my heavy eyes open the sky is lightening and Little Dog has curled into my back. Sensing I'm awake, he jumps up, wondering if it's breakfast time. I ruffle his ears. In the distance, I can hear the sound of Dick the Cock crowing from the yard. It's time to rouse ourselves and go back to the real world.

I glance across at Shelby who's still sleeping. His face is soft, younger, at rest. I'm sure that people look at someone like him and think that his life must be easy, but I know that he has his troubles like everyone else. I don't want to wake him, but I don't want to doze off again and still be here when Alan and Bev arrive. That wouldn't do at all.

Taking one last lingering look at him, drinking in his image as someone in a desert would do to slake their thirst, I stroke his chest, kiss his cheek, savouring these last quiet moments together. Shelby blinks his eyes open.

'Morning,' I say. 'Well, nearly.'

He's more alert now. 'What time is it?'

'Time we were moving. We could go back to the van for some tea and toast.'

'I can think of nothing nicer. Well,' he says, 'maybe one thing nicer.' He rolls towards me and we're in each other's arms again. 'Toast can wait.'

We make love again and, when we can put it off no longer, we dress and carry our makeshift bed back down to the yard. We're shy with each other in the harsh glare of daylight. Shelby holds my hand, coyly.

When we reach the van, he sighs at me. 'Even now, I don't want to call my driver.'

'Stay,' I say. 'I'll feed you. Though it will have to be quick as there are many, many animals waiting for their breakfast too.'

'I can help,' he says. 'I'm not due on set until later. I'll hang around for a bit and see what I'm taking on.'

'I'm sure there must be some clothes around in one of the barns. I can't vouch for the state of them, though.'

'I'm fine like this,' he assures me. 'But I could do with a shower.'

'Let's do the chores first and then shower. I've learned from bitter experience that's the better way.'

Shelby laughs. 'I bow to your superior knowledge. For

390

someone who's spent years playing a farmer, I know precious little about the real workings of a farm.'

'One baptism of fire coming up,' I inform him. 'I must just get out of my one and only nice dress though. You never know when I might need it again.'

Shelby's eyes twinkle.

'Don't start that cute eyes thing. We'll never get anything done. Although you're clearly an expert at helping me out of my clothes, any further delays and I think the animals will be so hangry, they'll barge the door down. You don't want to be on the wrong side of Anthony the Anti-social Sheep when he hasn't had his brekky.'

As I turn to go inside the van, Shelby catches my hand. 'Thanks for last night. It was very special.'

'My pleasure.' And I shiver with desire, once more.

He sighs heavily at me and, in a very serious tone of voice, says, 'Molly . . . '

But before he can finish his sentence, Alan's car trundles into the yard. When it stops, both Bev and Alan climb out.

'Well, would you look at that,' I say, open-mouthed. 'Wonders will never cease.'

'It seems as if a lot of people were in the mood for love last night,' Shelby remarks.

Then he gives me a look that I can't interpret. Is it longing, regret or something more? But before I can ask, Bev is heading straight for me shouting 'Coooo-eeeee!' and the moment is lost.

Chapter Ninety-One

'You're still in last night's dress.'

Bev misses nothing. '*You're* still with last night's boyfriend.'

'*Touché.*'

Then she looks at the cushions in my hand. 'What are you doing with those?'

'What is this? *Twenty Questions*?'

'Yes.'

I'm never going to get away with withholding information. I glance over to where Shelby and Alan are chatting and lower my voice so that they can't hear us. 'We took a blanket up to the big field and slept up there.'

Bev raises her eyebrows. 'Romantic. Exactly how much *sleeping* was done?'

'Some.' Now *I* raise my eyebrows. 'Where did *you* sleep?'

'Mostly underneath Alan.'

'Hmm. Then we're both quite naughty ladies.'

'Seems so.'

We both have a good giggle into our hands. I'm never naughty and I rather like the feel of it.

'I'm glad it went well with Alan.'

'I'd rather be shagging Shelby Dacre, obvs, you lucky cow. But Alan wasn't too shabby at all. Who'd have thought? In fairness, I had knocked back an awful lot of wine.'

'It will probably be better to have a more considered assessment when strong drink isn't clouding your judgement.'

'I think that's probably a good thing,' she agrees. 'That's why we're going out tonight.'

We both snarf again.

'He's nice,' Bev says, with a quick look over her shoulder. 'Who knew he'd scrub up so well? His cottage is amazing too. As neat as a pin. I think neither of us realised that our Alan had hidden depths. Beneath those scruffy band T-shirts beats a heart of gold.'

'He's always been one of the good guys, but I guess we've just rubbed along with him for all this time.'

'Well, I'm certainly planning to rub along with him a little bit more!'

'Poor man, he'll have no chance now you've set your sights on him. I'm glad for you both.'

'Maybe I'll get to choose his band T-shirt every morning from now on.'

'I do hope so.' If anyone deserves happiness, it's Bev. 'But who will I have band T-shirt bets with?'

'All good things must come to an end,' she says sagely.

Never a truer word spoken, I think.

'Last night was bloody ace though, wasn't it? That Shelby knows how to put on a do.'

'He raised loads of money for us. We'll be able to pay our bills now. All of them. You might even get your wages on time. *Every* week.'

She holds her hands to the sky. 'It's a miracle.'

'Yes, but we'll need another one if the animals are going to get to eat today. We should get started on our chores.'

'I'm feeling pretty sluggish this morning. It could take a while.'

'Shelby's going to stay and help us.'

'Is he now?' We both look over to where the men are. 'Farmer Gordon is going to show us how it's done, is he? Wouldn't it be nice if he was a permanent feature?'

'I don't know if that will ever happen,' I admit. 'But it's been good to have him as a friend, even for a short while. He's still heading off to Los Angeles for his big leap to international stardom.' We didn't talk about it last night and, to be honest, I don't even like to raise the subject. Nothing he's said so far has given me the impression he's decided to stay put.

'Really? Oh, boo to that.'

'Yeah.' I shrug. 'But what can I do?'

'You seem to have done a pretty good job of wrapping him round your little finger so far. Don't give up yet. We don't want to be sitting here watching him on telly while he's sunning himself in California.'

'I don't have a telly,' I remind her.

'Oh, bum.' Bev links her arm through mine. 'Let's hope it doesn't come to that. We should get a wiggle on. But not before we have some strong coffee. I'm going to need at least a dozen cups to get my motor running.'

While Bev makes us all a restorative drink, I get changed into my scruffy jeans. I'm quite sad to be hanging up my pretty frock. I enjoyed dressing up for a while. I press the floaty fabric to my face hoping to catch the scent of Shelby on it, but any trace of him has gone with the rising of the sun.

When I go outside again, Shelby's there in his dress shirt, though it is open-necked, and has his suit trousers tucked into wellington boots.

'You're going to ruin your fine clothes,' I warn him.

'Strangely, I don't care this morning.'

'Well, it will be the smartest waiter service that the animals have ever had.'

He catches my hand and we head towards the feed shed where I show him who has what to eat and we fill up the buckets.

When we've finished in the barn, we go back down to the sheep paddock and I notice that one of the sheep is limping.

'Can you keep Anthony distracted while I have a look at Fluffy? There seems to be something wrong with her front leg.'

Shelby looks worried. 'Isn't Anthony the awkward one?'

'He seems quite placid today.' Currently, he's quietly munching grass in the corner of his field. 'It will only be for a minute. I just need to jump in and have a quick check. He probably won't even notice you.'

'OK,' he says, but not in a way that could be considered keen.

'You'll be fine,' I assure him.

I nod encouragingly towards the field and, with only a slight grimace, Shelby tentatively climbs over the fence. Immediately, Anthony looks up. Hmm. Our dearest anti-social sheep has more of a scowl on his face than I'd imagined.

Shelby notices Anthony's sudden interest too. 'Now what do I do?'

'Distract him.'

He looks at me horrified. 'By doing what?'

But before I can answer, Shelby's driver turns up with Lucas in the passenger seat. 'I need to get the gate,' I tell Shelby. 'Hang on a sec!'

'Don't leave me,' Shelby cries.

'If he starts to run towards you, jump out.' At the moment Anthony just looks menacing. Shelby should be OK.

I dash to open the gate and wave the car through. Then I hurry back to the fence to see how Shelby's getting on. Not well, it seems.

When Lucas climbs out of the car he comes to lean next to me at the fence. There are still smudges of eyeliner round his eyes and he looks more than a little hungover. Lucas yawns.

His father is standing in front of Anthony trying to stop the sheep from head-butting him.

'No, Anthony,' Shelby says, sternly. 'Down, boy. That's being a bad lad. I'm your friend.'

I know that I should jump in and rescue Shelby, but it's too funny to watch and he's not in any danger. Well, not much. Anthony has his head down in charge position and looks as if he means business. He takes a run at Shelby.

I'm giggling away. 'Tell him you're a superstar farmer.'

'You're not helping,' Shelby shouts. Anthony advances again. 'Stop it. Bad boy.'

Anthony cares not for Shelby's celebrity status and tries to ram him in the gentleman's nether regions.

Lucas turns to me. 'Is there a reason why my father is still here dressed in last night's clothes trying to reason with an attack sheep?'

'He's giving me a hand.'

'Not by the look of it.'

I guffaw again as Anthony starts to chase Shelby. 'Don't run,' I call. 'It only makes him worse. Face him off. Show him who's boss.'

'*He's* boss,' Shelby yells and runs back the other way.

'Nice to see Farmer Gordon deigning to get his hands dirty instead of riding around in a Land Rover,' Lucas calls out.

'You can shut up too,' Shelby cries. I don't think he's ever had to run in wellies before. 'No, Anthony. No!'

'Oh, my sides are going to split.' I wipe the tears of laughter from my eyes.

Lucas can't help but laugh too as we watch a sheep getting the upper hand and Lucas is not prone to spontaneous laughter.

Finally, Shelby manages to grab Anthony.

'Tickle him behind the ears,' I advise. 'He likes that.'

'You have got to be kidding me!' We laugh again as Shelby

396

tries to keep Anthony still enough to find his ears. If I'm honest, sometimes Anthony likes it, sometimes he hates anyone going near his ears. Shelby will find out soon enough whether it's an ear-tickling kind of day or not.

Lucas flinches. 'He's not a natural with animals, is he?'

'No.'

'I heard that,' Shelby shouts. 'Give me a break! I was brought up in Muswell Hill. I didn't see a sheep until I was twenty-one.'

I wonder how he ever managed to get cast as a farmer.

Lucas doesn't look at me when he asks, 'So are you two getting it together?'

I pause before answering, 'Would you mind?'

'No. I guess not.' He sighs. 'I've seen it coming for ages. He likes you.'

'I like him too.'

'He seems happier. And he's less of a tit when you're around. He could almost pass as a normal human being instead of being wrapped up in all that star shit.'

'You judge him very harshly,' I say. Then I remember that he'll soon be heading off to LA and he doesn't yet seem to have told Lucas. 'It may not be enough for you, but I believe he tries to do his best. He was great last night.'

'Yeah,' he agrees. 'That was cool.'

'You were brilliant, too.' Lucas looks bashful. 'You've really got something there.'

'I'd like to try and make it as a poet,' he admits. 'Do you think he'll let me?' Lucas nods towards his father. 'He's always said that the last thing he wants me to do is be a performer, but I don't know what else I can do. This feels important.'

'He was *so* very proud of you. Anyone could see that.'

'I wish Mum had been there.'

'Me too,' I tell him. 'I bet she was. Our loved ones never go far from us. Part of her will always be right inside you. Nothing

397

can ever change the fact that you're her son. She'll always be there for you.'

'Thanks, Molly.' He sidles up next to me and I put my arm round his shoulders. Lucas leans against me.

'I'll do all that I can to help you,' I say. 'You know that.' And the first thing will be to persuade Shelby not to send him away to boarding school.

Chapter Ninety-Two

When Shelby has finally gained some kind of control over Anthony, he makes a break for it and quickly climbs out of the field, dropping down from the fence in front of me.

He brushes off his hands and gives me a dark look. 'Thanks for all your help there, Molly. Really appreciate it.'

I laugh again. 'It was great fun to watch.'

'I just hope no one was recording it. If that gets onto YouTube, then Farmer Gordon will lose all his street cred.'

'Damn,' Lucas says. 'Why didn't I think of that?'

'Don't you dare!' Shelby ruffles his son's hair and, as usual, Lucas ducks away from it. 'Still high on performance adrenaline? You did a great job last night.'

'Thanks for helping me out.' It looks as if it's an effort for Lucas to say it, but I'm glad that he does.

'You smashed it,' Shelby says. 'That standing ovation? That was down to you.'

'I want to try to give it a go.' Lucas kicks at the ground with his toe. 'A proper go. Maybe see if I can line up some gigs and stuff.'

'Definitely,' Shelby says. 'I'll see what I can do to help.'

'Just like that?' Lucas is clearly shocked. 'You've always been against it.'

'I didn't actually know, Lucas. You never talked to me about your poetry. It was Molly who spilled the beans. Maybe if you'd told me about it yourself, I could have done more before now.' Shelby sighs. 'Performing isn't the best way to earn a living. Half of the artists and actors out there end up working for peanuts. I wanted to protect you from that, but if it's what you want to do, then you should.' He looks directly at me when he adds, 'We should all follow our dreams.'

I don't know what he means by that. Is he referring to the fact that no matter what has happened between us, he's still off to the USA? Disappointing as that may be, I hadn't expected anything else. Or is he implying that in helping Lucas to achieve his dreams, he should be free to pursue his own? I don't know. You can see why I don't do relationships.

'I should go home,' Shelby says. 'Unless I'm required for more animal duties, I'd like to get a shower and change out of these clothes.'

There's mud on his dinner suit, straw in places there shouldn't be straw and, overall, he's certainly not as immaculately groomed as he usually is. It goes without saying that the crumpled look suits him, though.

'You're relieved of all duties,' I tell him. I'll walk you to your car and see to the gate.' His driver is still sitting patiently waiting for him.

'Catch you later, son,' he says to Lucas. 'We'll talk more tonight. We could get a pizza in or something and make a plan.'

'Yeah. OK.' Lucas watches us carefully as we fall into step and walk away from him.

When we're out of earshot, I say quietly, 'Lucas knows that we've . . . become close.'

'I see.'

'He seems to be OK with it.'

'Good. That's a relief. He always hated Scarlett.' I don't comment that I can understand why. I'd like to think that I'm a very different kettle of fish. Especially when it comes to Lucas.

'I wanted to talk to you about him.'

'Lucas?'

'Don't send him away to boarding school. Please. I think it would be the worst possible thing for him. He's just finding his feet and he's doing really well. If you sent him away, it would really set him back.' Shelby goes to speak, but I press on before he can interrupt my flow. 'You're both getting on a little bit better and I don't want you to jeopardise this. If he goes to boarding school and hates it – as I really think he will – you could lose him for ever, Shelby. I can help. I haven't thought through the details, but I'd be more than happy to take him on.'

'Where would he live?'

'That's one of the little details we'd have to iron out.'

'If you don't mind me pointing out, your caravan is hardly adequate.'

Possibly quite a big detail then. 'I'm sure we could work something out. Couldn't he stay at the house?'

'I'm planning to rent that out,' Shelby says. 'It's a ridiculous size for the two of us. Especially when Lucas chooses to live in the gardener's cottage. I might even sell it and downsize at some point.'

So that's not an option either. I'm at a loss to suggest what else might work and my throat closes with emotion when I say, 'I've grown very fond of Lucas, of you both. Please tell me that you'll at least think about it.'

'I've been thinking about nothing else. I'm even considering taking him out there with me,' Shelby says. 'Lucas would like California.'

I think he'd absolutely hate it, but I say nothing. Lucas loathes the sun. He's like a vampire and will do everything possible to stay out of it. Isn't California all about the beach and roller-blading? Though it seems a feeble argument with which to persuade Shelby to leave his son behind. It looks as if I'll have to steel myself to letting them both go.

Shelby touches my arm and plants a soft kiss on my cheek, but I can tell that he's distracted.

'I'll call you,' he says.

He slides into the passenger seat and I wish there was more that I could say to convince him I'm right. Then his car turns in the yard and I let it pass through the gate. I watch as Shelby is driven away down the lane.

Soon, it will be the last time that I see him do this and my chest tightens just a bit. Get used to it, Molly, I think. You've been alone before, you can do it again. But now that I've had a small taste of what being in love is like, will I *want* to be alone again?

Chapter Ninety-Three

Shelby calls several times. Each time it's to do with the logistics of moving Hope Farm to its new location. We talk about timings, places, volunteers, trucks, utilities, trailers, animals, feed, equipment. All of those things and more. There is so much to do and so little time. As the date of our move grows ever closer, we exchange a dozen phone calls a day and even more texts. What we don't do is mention the blissful night we spent together under the stars. Each time, I feel as if the words hang in the air between us, just waiting for one of us to leap in and grab them. It doesn't happen. As the days go on the feel of his lips on mine, his skin against my skin, his body along the length of mine is slowly fading and I don't want that to happen. What we also don't mention is his infinitely less blissful impending move to America.

Essentially, I'm trying to ignore that it's on the horizon at all. Except perhaps I spend a little longer with Lucas each day, trying to soak up hours with him to store away in case Shelby insists on taking him to California with him. I wonder if he's considered my offer to keep Lucas here with me. If he has, how will that work in reality? Perhaps he's considered it and discounted it as impractical. It's true that I can't offer Lucas the type of accommodation that he's been used to. But I can't bear to think about him leaving. Or Shelby, if I'm being honest with you. Would Lucas come back to see me at the farm or will he forget all about us as soon as he moves? Could be the latter. Such is the fickleness of youth. I can't blame him for that. While all this is going through my head, Lucas, on the other hand, is carrying on with his tasks, mood borderline sunny, which makes me think that he is, as yet, happily unaware of what's about to hit him.

Still, I have more pressing issues to address. In two days' time we will have to shift about fifty or more uncooperative animals to their new home. Much as Shelby hasn't mentioned his relocation to the USA, I've not told the animals that we're upping sticks either. Though I'm sure Little Dog can sense something's afoot. He's been twitchy all week and more clingy than usual. The students, on the other hand, are all completely hyperactive and it's difficult to keep them on task. It's nice to see them all excited by the move though instead of stressed by it. We've decided to let them help with the change of premises to the new place so that they feel involved and invested in it. I have everything crossed that this is going to prove to be the best approach.

As I hang up the phone to his father, Lucas swings through the door of the tea room. He's all smiles. Well, as smiley as Lucas ever gets. He's not scowling darkly, let's put it that way. It's pouring it down today, but it seems as if even torrential rain can't dampen his spirits. He's been like a changed boy since the night of the concert. I can feel that his self-esteem has been bolstered and there's an air of delicate confidence about him. It's good to see.

Lucas shakes the rain from his jacket and then stands dripping on my floor. 'It's tanking it down out there.'

'I hope it's not a day like this for the move or we'll all be up to our eyeballs in mud.'

'Yeah. Not long now,' Lucas observes. 'I've been packing up tools in the barn with Alan. We need to ask you some stuff. He thinks some of it needs throwing away.'

For weeks now Alan has been sorting out what we have to take with us and what we can do without. It's been an arduous task. My natural instinct is to keep it all, just in case, but I know that realistically a lot of old tools and machines that are hanging on by the skin of their teeth need to go to farm equipment heaven.

'Do you want to come up there and see what you think?' Lucas asks.

'Yes. I've just finished on the phone to your dad.'

'Cool. I haven't seen him in days,' he says.

'Me neither,' I admit.

Lucas frowns. 'I thought you two were getting it together.'

'I think we both have other things on our mind at the moment.' Which is the best stalling tactic I can think of.

'So where's he been going every night?'

'I don't know.' But I do know that my stomach sinks a little bit when I hear this. Where has he been going? To make arrangements for his new life, to rekindle old flames? I don't know and I'm not sure that I want to either.

'The new farm will be totally cool,' Lucas says. 'I can't wait to see it.'

My heart breaks a little bit more. I took Alan and Bev up there one evening so that they could help me with the planning of what and who is going to go where. I should have taken Lucas too, but there never seemed to be the right moment.

'It's got much better accommodation,' I tell him. 'We'll have farm buildings and barns coming out of our ears.' It's just a shame there's no house there as Lucas and I could be quite comfortable there. I know that Hettie and I managed in the caravan together, but it was a long way from civilised. Besides, we were two women and relatives at that. It wouldn't be suitable for a young man. Lucas needs his own space, his own privacy.

'Maybe we could put on a bit of a festival of our own – poetry and stuff,' he says. 'That would raise some more money. I could sort it out. A kind of project.'

'I like the sound of that.' And I do. Really, I do. I just hope that Lucas will be here to execute it.

I leave the paperwork on my table and stand up. Then I can't help it, I put my arms round Lucas, even though he's completely soggy, and give him a big hug. I love this boy to bits and I've fallen in love with his father too. 'Whatever happens, in the future, it will all work out fine.'

'You're creeping me out.' Lucas frowns at me. 'You're not dying, are you?'

Only a little bit inside, I think. 'No, no. Nothing like that. It's all a bit much. I'm just overcome with emotion. Ignore me.'

'You're bloody *weird*,' Lucas says. 'That's why I like you.' Then, in a rare and very welcome display of affection, he hugs me back.

Chapter Ninety-Four

The day of moving finally arrives and I can't begin to tell you how I'm feeling. My head is all over the place and yet I'm trying to hold it together so that I, our students, the animals and our incumbent paraphernalia end up in the same place with minimal fuss.

I don't even need Dick the Cock's best efforts to rouse me from my sleep as I'm wide awake long before our vociferous cockerel is. It will be hard to leave this place as it's been my home, my refuge for so long. Although Hettie's been gone for a long time now, I feel as if I'm leaving her behind and that's tough. Her ashes are scattered on this land and she's still so much a part of this. When we move to the new farm, it will be just me, alone. I'm gripped by an unbearable sense of loss yet somewhere, floating beneath the surface, I'm almost certain that there are gossamer threads of hope. If only I could catch hold of them.

Little Dog is asleep on my chest, but there's a crushing weight there anyway that's not to do with my doggy companion. It's hours before Shelby and his crew are due, but I get out of bed and put the kettle on. Shelby's assembled a work force to help us today from his actor friends and the cast of *Flinton's Farm* which is fantastic. But still I'm fretting about whether it will go well and our animals will end up there with the same amount of legs they started with – even though many of them don't enjoy a full complement of limbs now.

We've chosen to do this on a Saturday as the cast don't do any filming at the weekend. It also means that we'll have the Sunday to try to get organised in time for the students to come back on Monday. Despite their best intentions, I think this might take twice as long as it would without them as I'll have to focus on keeping the kids in check as well as doing my best animal herding.

I make myself tea and use up the last of the stale bread for toast. In an effort to run down supplies before the move, I've found myself woefully short of food – though I did manage to empty the dregs of the Corn Flakes box for last night's supper. Most of my life is in cardboard cartons around me ready for the off and I realise how little I actually have to show for my almost forty years on earth.

There's one box full of Hettie's stuff that I can't bear to part with. It's not much, a few bits of jewellery – mostly worthless, but priceless to me in sentimental value. That's the kind that you can't ever replace. There's the little clutch bag I used for the charity evening and a few scarves. On top of the pile are a handful of photographs of me as a child with her. I don't know who took them as I don't remember her ever having a camera. Perhaps it was my mum. I pick them up, one by one, and look at them. They're all in colour, but it's that greeny-yellow colour that photos were then in the days before smartphones and digital images. Photographs were expensive to take too, so there aren't a lot of them. I'm leaning against Hettie in most of them and we look more like mother and daughter than aunt and niece. She might have been my mother's older sister, but she was nothing like her. Thank goodness. There's not a day goes by that I don't think of Hettie and I wish she was here with me now – although it would break her heart to move away from Hope Farm. Just as it's breaking mine. I put the photograph back.

When both Little Dog and I have had our breakfast, I pull on my clothes and we head out into the yard. I want to take one last look round the farm as I'm sure once Shelby and his crew arrive then mayhem will ensue and I won't be able to find time to myself to do it.

'Come on, boy.' I click Little Dog to heel and he kind of obliges me. 'Let's go and say goodbye to our home.'

So we walk up to the fields and I give everyone their breakfast as I go. I pause at every paddock, taking time to bid adieu to my home and having one last lingering look at every view so that it's seared into my mind.

'We'll be OK, won't we?' I say to Little Dog. He wags his tail and his odd smile widens. He looks happy enough.

I think if I had a tail, I'm not sure I'd quite manage a wag today. I just have to try and be positive about it. Any other outcome would have been unthinkable. We have somewhere wonderful to go to and I have to focus on that.

The sun is rising nicely and it looks as if we are going to have a good day for our move. To do this in a downpour or on a miserable, grey morning would be too depressing. Little Dog leans against my leg as I stand at the top of the hill and look down into the vale below. The fields, myriad soft shades of green, a hundred or more if I could count them, roll away from me into the distance. It's so beautiful and peaceful in this spot and soon it won't be. It's hard to say goodbye, but I think it would be even worse to come back here and see what they've done to it, how shaving a few minutes off the journey North will wipe away this idyll for ever. So I'll say my farewell and never come back here again, except in my heart.

Chapter Ninety-Five

By the time I get back to the yard Alan and Bev have arrived. All is going well there. I might even go as far as to say they were loved-up. If Bev's not staying at Alan's house, Alan is staying at Bev's. Alan's beard is always neatly trimmed now, his flowing grey locks held in place by a tidy man bun or a neat plait. His band T-shirts are washed and pressed, which means our gambling game has been somewhat thwarted as Bev knows what he's going to be wearing every day – just as she predicted. Still, it's a small price to pay for her happiness.

'God, I bet you're all of a dither,' Bev says when she sees me. 'I know I am.'

'I'm OK,' I say and it's not much of a lie. I'm filled with trepidation and turmoil, but I know it's going to turn out all right in the end. Hopefully.

'I'll get the truck.' Sometimes Alan now speaks in entire sentences, but not often.

'See you later, lover,' Bev shouts after him. When he's gone, she turns to me. 'That man's *insatiable*.'

I screw my nose up. 'TMI!'

'You're only jealous,' she says. 'What time is Hot Stuff getting here?'

'Shelby? He should be here soon.'

She puts her arm round me. 'It will be all right, you know. You saved the farm. That's all that matters.'

'I still can't believe we've done it.'

'*You've* done it,' she insists.

I smile. 'Your belief in me is touching, but I think we should give Shelby Dacre a bit of credit. This is all down to him.'

'Yeah. I suppose. All he needs to do now is make an honest woman of you.'

'I don't think that's ever going to happen, Bev. He'll be off to California soon and he'll forget all about us here at Hope Farm. We'll be a distant memory for him.' It will be the beginning of his dream and the end of mine. He'll find a scantily dressed young starlet, fall in love and will grace the gossip pages once more. I have to learn to live with that. It's Lucas that I worry about. He's done so well and I don't want him falling between the cracks.

'Nonsense. If he gets any notions of escaping from us, we'll hunt him down and bring him back.'

'That's creepy,' I tell her.

She puts her hand on my arm. 'He's done all this for you,' she says. 'He must care. Don't let him go without a fight. Tell him how you feel.'

'I'm not sure how I do feel.'

'You love him,' Bev says. '*That's* how you feel.'

'It isn't that easy.'

'It is. You love him. And I think he loves you. If he doesn't, then he should.'

However, any discussion about the state of my heart or Shelby's is curtailed as there's a toot at the gate and the man himself has arrived.

411

'He's here,' I say pointlessly.

'Go and throw yourself at him,' Bev says with a wink. 'See how he copes with that.'

But I think that Shelby is entirely used to lovelorn women throwing themselves at his feet. Nevertheless, I head to the gate, a smile pinned on my face and get ready to embrace whatever the day brings.

There are two mini-vans filled with people waiting to be let in. I open the gate and they drive through. A moment later Shelby jumps out of the first van and comes over to me.

'Hey,' he says and plants a warm kiss on my cheek.

It's only been a few weeks since I've seen him, but my heart leaps when I set eyes on him again. His fair hair is tousled, his blue eyes shaded by dark glasses, and his square soap-star jaw makes me go all of a quiver. I said for them all to come in working clothes, but Shelby's turned up in a tight black T-shirt and grey jeans. I'd swear to you that they're both designer label clothing. Well, by the end of the day they'll both be covered in animal detritus. He does have welly boots in his hand, so I'll give him that.

'What are you smiling at?' he asks.

'Nothing. Just taking it all in.'

'You're feeling OK?'

'I've just been through this with Bev. I'm fine. Really.'

'I know this must be hard,' he says. 'I'm here for you.'

'Thank you. It would have been a lot harder if you hadn't offered us the fabulous place we're going to.'

He winks at me and says, 'My pleasure.'

'I suppose we'd better get started then.'

'Yeah. It's going to be a long day. I do, however, bring you a lot of press-ganged help.' He slides open the van door and a lot of colourfully dressed people climb out. There are one or two in sensible overalls, more than one or two in sparkly drag queen outfits and a guy who's dressed in a top hat, green feather boa, tutu, striped tights and pink wellies. I don't think that I'd better give him Anthony the Anti-Social Sheep to deal with.

'Right.' This is going to be a fun day.

Shelby spreads his hands. 'My friends, at your disposal. Tell them your bidding and they'll fulfil it.'

You might be surprised to learn that we do have a plan. Shelby and I knocked a spreadsheet together over our many phone calls with the hope that it would go as smoothly as possible. The animals need to go to their new homes in shifts otherwise it would be one mad scramble with chickens and sheep everywhere.

'The students and parents that are coming to help will be here soon too.'

'We'd better get started then.' Shelby sounds very decisive.

I look again at the motley and very colourful crew of celebrities he's brought with him and smile. 'You're right. We should.'

Chapter Ninety-Six

Chaos reigns. Of course it does. Despite being the cast of a farm-based soap and portraying farmers and country folk, it's clear the actors have never dealt with animals before. I think that some of them may never have been in the *actual* countryside before.

When handling animals it's best to keep them firmly in control rather than letting them run amok. Today we're favouring the running-amok style. Anthony knocks three of the actors over before we even start. But, eventually, they work out how to get their hands dirty and we manage to load the animals into the truck in their allotted order. Bev and I go up with the first truckload which contains a grumpy Anthony, two bleating goats, two honking geese, three skittish alpacas and Fifty. We're followed by a minibus full of giggly kids, unsuspecting parents and animated actors. Alan, Lucas and Shelby are to stay behind and get the next lot ready.

Bev drives and Little Dog sits on my knee looking out of the window. I am, as usual, a nervous wreck, but as Bev turns the truck into the entrance of Edward's Farm, I feel my tension leave me. This is to be our new home and what a fine place it is. We'll be happy here, I know we will.

Bev turns to me and smiles. 'Good job, Molly. This is a great place.'

Alan and I have been up here in the week, working hard, so several of the pens and stables are ready for our animals and they simply have to be installed into their new home – though we still have some preparation to do. We've fenced off a couple of areas, but there are still paddocks that need to be secured and I'll get a couple of the burlier-looking guys onto that. In the yard, there's a catering truck already set up – Shelby's idea. They're going to supply us with tea, cake, halloumi chips and chickpea wraps throughout the day. Apparently, actors do their best work on full tummies. Given the way that they head straight for the food I'm sure Shelby must be right. Jack gets tea for everyone. The girls take lots of selfies with the actors. I've tasked Tamara with making a record of today and I only hope that she remembers to take more than just pictures of herself.

Bev and I unload the truck. The actors quickly learn to give Anthony a wide berth as he growls at them – probably quite wisely. So I take our troublesome ram to his new paddock, but he's determined to be bad-tempered and unappreciative of his wonderful view. Little Dog, more easily pleased, runs round sniffing and weeing in every corner excitedly. The goats are a frisky handful when we let them out, but are quickly settled with a bit of fussing.

The alpacas look as if they're trying to do a Zumba workout, prancing this way and that, and it takes more than a modicum of wrangling until we finally get them under control too. The man in the tutu proves to have quite a knack with them. Then, while I allocate jobs, Bev takes the truck back to load up again.

The animals keep coming throughout the day until the last ones arrive at their new home. I even see Phantom, briefly, before he dashes off into one of the barns – though I've no idea who brought him here. But I'm glad that someone did.

'That's it.' Bev wipes her hands on her jeans. 'Nearly all

Chapter Ninety-Seven

When I get back to the farm, Alan, Shelby and Lucas are in the yard. As I climb out the cab, I try to feel upbeat, but I can't quite manage it and sadness descends. I'd like to walk round the farm, one last time by myself – but I've already said my goodbyes and I don't think that I could bear to do it again. I need to leave now without a backward glance. I don't want to return and see what they do to this place. It would be far too heartbreaking. This is all out of my hands and I must move forward without regrets.

Shelby comes over to the truck. 'How's it going?' he asks. 'Feeling OK?'

'Yes,' I lie. 'I've been too busy to worry about anything. Everyone seems to be settling in well at the other end. Your friends are working very hard.' I don't tell him that they're eating for England too. I wouldn't like the bill for all that halloumi.

'Shall we get your caravan hooked up?' Shelby says. 'If you reverse the truck, then Alan and I can connect it to the tow bar.'

So I do as I'm told and manoeuvre the truck into place. Alan, Shelby and Lucas get busy at the back end, removing the blocks from in front of the caravan wheels that have kept it in place since time began and hitch it up. I've tidied up inside and all of my belongings, such as they might be, are boxed up for the short journey.

After a few minutes, Shelby bangs on the side of the truck. 'She's all yours, Molly. Take it slowly.'

So I inch forward as carefully as I can and, behind me, I hear the caravan creak and groan as it moves for the first time in forty-odd years – possibly longer. I look in the wing mirror, but the caravan seems still very much attached to the land – as reluctant to leave as I am. I rev the engine a bit more, the truck strains a little and the sounds of creaking and groaning grow ever louder. Then suddenly there's a moment of release and an almighty crash. I assume that the caravan has finally started to move.

'Ok! Easy, easy!' Shelby shouts. 'She's all yours.'

I leave the engine idling and get out of the cab.

'The last of the chickens are loaded into Alan's car. Dick's in there too looking very tetchy,' Lucas says. 'I'll go with him and we'll see you there. Dad can ride in the truck with you.'

'Good idea. We'll be right behind you.'

So he and Alan jump in the car and head out with the sound of chickens squawking in the back and Dick crowing indiscriminately. When they've gone the farm seems strangely quiet and it's unsettling to see it so deserted.

'This really is it,' I say to Shelby, tears not far from my eyes. 'It's just us that's left.'

He nods.

'This has been a good home,' I tell him, tearfully. 'I have nothing but fond memories of my time here.'

'And they'll always stay with you.' He catches my hand and holds it tight.

'I'd feel infinitely better if we were moving out of choice and it wasn't being torn away from beneath us. At least we've got a

418

new home to go to.' I smile at him, even though my heart feels as heavy as lead. 'Thank you for stepping in to save us.'

'I didn't save you, I *helped* you,' he says. 'You're the one that's done all the hard work and you're the one that will continue to do so. Do you need a minute by yourself?' he asks.

'No, I simply need to leave now. Get it over with.'

'Your call,' he says.

So we climb into the truck together and, gingerly, I tow the caravan down to the gate. Lucas has left it open for us now that there are no animals who might take the chance of bolting to freedom, so I drive straight through and then pause in the lane. 'One last time,' I say to Shelby. 'I'll do it.'

I get out and swing the gate closed before sliding the bolt. I lean on it for a moment and look out over the land that I've loved so much. It's a mellow evening and the sun is starting to sink in a sky that's already warming to pink. I think it will be a beautiful sunset tonight and the stars will be out in force. I'll miss this place. I'll miss it so very much.

'Bye, Hettie,' I whisper. 'Love you. Wish me luck.'

Then with a lump in my throat I climb back into the truck.

'All right?' Shelby asks.

I nod and blink back the tears that are behind my eyes.

Grinding the truck into gear and with Shelby's hand resting gently on top of mine, I drive away.

Chapter Ninety-Eight

I trundle along as carefully as I can taking my caravan to its new site, but every pothole I hit makes me grind my teeth with terror. The caravan is making some alarming noises and I wonder if that's usual.

'It's holding up nicely,' Shelby assures me with a glance in the wing mirror. By that, I think he means it's still attached to us. 'We're nearly there. Just a few more twists and turns.'

I squeeze through the narrow lanes, dreading meeting anything coming the other way – I've no idea what I'd do if we did. I'm quite adept at handling the truck, even when it's full of animal cargo, but towing a caravan with it takes me to a whole new level of anxiety. How people take these away on holiday and enjoy it is beyond me. I don't think I've ever done any driving that's been more stressful.

'Not far now,' Shelby encourages. 'Home straight.'

Thank goodness.

At last, the farm comes into sight and I turn into the lane, breathing a sigh of relief. The yard is still full of colourful people, using colourful language, but all the animals – as far as I can tell – are still safely in their assigned homes. Lucas and

Alan are unloading the chickens who'll go into their new run.

There's a piece of hard-standing conveniently near to the barn and I'll set up the caravan on that. I'll be near to the gate, near to the animals and I can set up my trusty bucket shower once more behind the buildings for some privacy. Perfect. And do you know what? My heart lifts just that little bit.

'I'll back the caravan into place,' I tell Shelby.

'It would be a lot easier if you could reverse straight into the pitch,' he says, rubbing his chin. 'This looks slightly tricky. The angle's not easy. Have you reversed while towing a caravan before?'

'No.' But how hard can it be?

'Just take it very slowly,' he advises, a more worried expression on his face than I'd like. 'Keep looking over your shoulder to see where you want to be and then turn the wheel in the opposite direction to the way you would if you were reversing without anything attached to the back.'

'Right.' I think I got that. Look one way. Reverse the other.

'It will move quite quickly, but make sure you hold it or you'll jack-knife.'

And we definitely don't want that. I feel a gulp travel down my throat.

'Then when you get to where you want to be on the pitch, turn the wheel in the opposition direction again. Got it?'

'Yes,' I say more confidently than I feel. Opposite direction. Opposite to the one it went in before or a different opposite? I'm not sure. I'm certain it will all become clear when I start to move.

Shelby must see the fear on my face as he says, 'We can always push and pull it into place, once you've got it more or less on the pitch. We've got plenty of muscle here.'

Though the muscle are all currently standing and watching me while stuffing their faces. So are the students. In fact, it

421

seems as if everyone has stopped to watch. Bev looks frightened to death. My mouth goes dry. 'Can you get out and guide me in?'

'Will do.' He turns towards me and smiles. 'You did well, Molly. I'm proud of you.'

I feel myself flush. 'Thanks.'

Then he jumps out of the truck and goes to stand at the back of the caravan. I wind down the window so that I can hear his instructions. I manoeuvre forwards and line up with the rectangle of concrete, which seems to look quite a bit smaller now.

He waves me backwards. 'This way. This way.'

I reverse as steadily as I can.

'Left hand down, Molly. Left hand down.'

I've got an audience now and I'm starting to sweat.

'Left! Left! The other left!' Shelby shouts.

I steer back the other way. There's a feeling of resistance and then, suddenly, the caravan seems to let go.

'Whoa! Whoa!' Shelby shouts. There's an alarming crash followed by a collective gasp from the gathered crowd. Have I overshot the concrete to one side? I didn't think so.

Leaning out of the window, I call back, 'Is it stuck?'

Shelby grimaces worriedly at me. 'Maybe a little worse than that.'

Instantly, I'm out of the cab and go to see what the problem is.

'Oh.' I stand and survey the damage.

'This may be terminal,' Shelby says.

He's not joking. Though I'm perfectly parked on the hard-standing, only the floor of the caravan is still very much attached to the tow bar. Unfortunately the rest of it isn't. The top of my home and its contents have parted company with the bottom and is currently sitting forlornly in the patch of dried-up mud beyond the concrete, sides collapsed in, windows popped out.

I'm too shocked to speak or to cry. 'Did I do that?'

'I think it may have just spontaneously died,' Shelby offers. 'The move was clearly too much for it.'

I knew that my dearly beloved, knackered caravan was fragile, but I thought it would live to fight another day. Seems I was wrong. I run my hands through my hair and look at the wreckage that was once my home. We'll have to tear our way in to get my boxes out. My crockery is likely to be smashed to smithereens. I could have done with another five years out of that. Maybe more. It looks as if that may have been optimistic. 'That's the end of it, isn't it?'

Shelby puts his arm round my shoulders. 'I'd say so. It's gone to the big caravan park in the sky.'

'I'm homeless,' I say more calmly than I feel. 'Where am I going to stay?'

'This is probably a good time to point out that I have a perfectly serviceable six-bedroomed manor house not a ten minute drive from here.'

'That might as well be the moon,' I point out. 'I have to be with my animals. I can't leave them. They need me here.'

Shelby raises his eyebrows. 'How did I know you were going to say that?'

But it's true. I can't leave them and go swanning off. What would they do without me?

Chapter Ninety-Nine

It's been a long, tiring day and more than a little emotional but, finally, we get it all done. There's a little lingering warmth in the sun when Shelby brings a case of champagne from one of the mini-buses and pops open half of the bottles.

'Thanks to everyone for coming today. Couldn't have done it without you, guys,' Shelby says to everyone. 'To Hope Farm Mark 2! And to Molly!'

'To Molly!' they echo.

So we toast our new farm with warm fizz in paper cups. The kids get orange juice.

Bev comes to hug me and we hold onto each other without speaking, rocking gently.

'Bloody love you,' she sniffs eventually and we both cry a bit.

When we've drained our cups, I thank all our helpers and shake their hands. They've done a great job and I couldn't have managed without them. Amid much back-slapping and air-kissing and high-fiving, they troop back to their minibus and throw up dust as they leave. The kids and the parents who are still here also head off for the day and I can't wait to see them all again on Monday. The catering truck packs away its wares and departs too.

Bev and Alan come over and my friend says, 'We're going now. Will you be all right?'

'I'll be fine.'

'Have you actually got anywhere to sleep tonight?'

'Not yet,' I admit, 'but I'll sort something out.'

'I suppose there's no point me asking you to come home with us?'

'Not a lot.'

She shakes her head at me. 'We'll be back in the morning. First thing.'

'Have a lie-in,' I tell her. 'I've got it covered. Couldn't have managed without you today.'

She hugs me once more and I can tell that Bev is on the verge of tears again. She strokes my hair like Hettie used to. 'You'll be OK here. I promise you.'

'I will,' I assure her.

'Look after her,' Bev says to Shelby. Then she and Alan climb into his car that's probably full of chicken feathers and worse and off they go.

The only people left are Shelby, Lucas and me.

We walk over to the gate and lean on it while we look out over the fields. The actors have made a great job of putting up some new fencing. Sweeny and Carter are in one field, the alpacas opposite them. Buzz and Ringo are beyond them. All is well. I let out a happy, but weary sigh.

'Tired?' Shelby says.

'Exhausted.'

'Don't tell me. You've still got all the animals to feed.'

I laugh. 'Of course. It's business as usual. They'll probably be cross that dinner's later than usual.' From the plaintive bleating that's coming from the sheep, you'd think they were all starving to death.

'I'll start them, Molly,' Lucas says. 'You and Dad finish this off.' He passes me a half-full bottle of champagne and then heads off into our new feed shed with Little Dog and Big Dog at his heels.

'I'll be fit for nothing after this,' I say nodding at the fizz.

'You'll certainly sleep soundly,' Shelby agrees. 'Speaking of which, where might that be?'

'We've got plenty of barns. Some of them are probably less leaky than the caravan and there's fresh new straw in every one.'

'Hmm,' Shelby says. 'This is sounding more appealing than I first thought.'

'You're staying?'

He sighs at me. 'Of course I am. You don't think I'd let you be here by yourself?'

'I'll be fine. I promise.'

'I'm staying,' he insists and frankly, I'm not going to argue with that.

'We could see if we can break into the caravan and grab some blankets?'

'All of the joys,' Shelby teases.

'Shall we do it now?'

'Not yet.' He takes the bottle from me and fills our cups. Then he looks at me and I can't tell what's written on his face, but he takes a deep breath before he says, 'I have something that I need to tell you.'

Chapter One Hundred

'It's about Hollywood,' Shelby says and he stares ahead, unseeing, deep in thought.

I've been bracing myself for this announcement, but the minute it raises its ugly head, my stomach turns to liquid. I'm dreading this moment. In my mind, I'd hoped that Shelby would stay here not just for the night, but long enough to see us properly settled here before departing for his new life in America. It looks as if I'm about to be disappointed. I can't even bear to hear what arrangements he's made for Lucas. Shelby hasn't discussed them with me, so I can only assume that I'm not to be included in them.

When he doesn't say anything further, I venture to ask, 'When are you planning to leave?'

He turns to me and gives me a half-smile. 'That's the thing, Molly. I'm not.'

It takes me a moment to process that. 'You're not going to America?'

'Correct.'

'What about the job as gun-toting, psycho-baddie?'

'It won't be me after all. I turned it down.'

'Should I be pleased or sad for you?' On a personal level I know that I'm happy for myself that Shelby won't be going away, but I also know just how much this role meant to him. It was his move into the big time, the starry stratosphere.

'A bit of both, I guess,' Shelby says. 'It was a fantastic opportunity and Malibu did look quite nice.' There's a mischievous twinkle in his eye as he says it, but a hint of regret too. 'But you helped me to see that there were too many sacrifices to be made for it. I need to stay here for Lucas, you're quite right. If I've got to play Farmer Gordon Flinton for the rest of my life then I'll do it. I'll do it for my son.'

'There'll be other chances, I'm sure. When Lucas is a little bit older and is back on his feet again. Hollywood won't forget you.'

'I think that they very much will. Besides, I'm not sure that I want it any more,' he confesses. 'There's a big price to be paid for that kind of fame and fortune. It sounds alluring and I have to admit that I was flattered to be offered it. Who wouldn't be? It's been spending time with you and at the farm that has made me realise the important things in life. The kids here are fantastic. They've overcome so many difficulties. You, Bev and Alan have so much patience and show them a level of care I could never have imagined possible. My world has always been so shallow and, if I never work again, I've been amazingly lucky. Most people would kill for half of the success I've enjoyed.'

'I'm sure it hasn't all been a walk in the park. You've had your share of sadness too.'

'I know. But it seems so silly, so vacuous to go chasing that pot of gold at the end of the rainbow, when I already have so much.'

'Did you ever tell Lucas about the job?'

'No,' Shelby says. 'I think it's best that he doesn't know I was even considering it.'

'My lips are sealed.'

'If I'm going to be around more, I'd like to help him to achieve his dream of being a poet. I don't know exactly what I can do, but I'll help him all that I can.'

'He'll be pleased to know that. He's very good.'

'I can see that and I've been blind to Lucas for a long time.'

'But not now,' I remind him.

He grins at me. 'Not now.'

In the background, over by the barn, I can hear Lucas moving from pen to pen, saying hello to the animals, chatting away as he feeds them. He's such a changed boy since he started here and I can't tell you how happy I am that he's going to be staying here too.

'I was so frightened that you'd take Lucas away and I wouldn't see him again.'

'I know. While I was examining my soul and my conscience, I did very much take that into account. I realise that you care for him way beyond your professional duties.'

I laugh. 'I shouldn't have favourites, but I've had a soft spot for Lucas since the minute he arrived.'

'You've done wonders with him,' Shelby tells me and I feel myself glow with pride. 'And that's another reason that I wanted to stay here. I want us to be together too.'

I look at him open-mouthed. 'Us?'

'Is that so strange?'

'No, no. I'd quite like it.'

Shelby rolls his eyes at me. 'Good, because I'd *quite* like it too.'

'What I mean is . . . well, of course . . . that would be wonderful.' Then I run out of words. I can't say fancy things. If I think of them at all, it's about three hours after the relevant moment. Yet I know that Shelby understands how I feel without me having to spell it out. He wouldn't be here if he didn't. Of all the ways that I'd pictured this day would end, this didn't feature in it at all. 'But do you think Lucas would be happy for us? Would he like us to be together permanently? I don't want him to think that I'm trying to replace his mother.'

Shelby twines his arm round my waist and pulls me closer to him. 'I might give up my chance of stellar stardom for him, Molly, but I don't plan on giving up you.'

He draws me in, kisses me deeply and my head spins. What a glorious way to end an amazing day, in the arms of the man that I've come to love.

Chapter One Hundred and One

As Lucas approaches, he bangs on the bucket he's carrying. 'Oi, you two. Get a room.'

I pull away from Shelby, guiltily, but he keeps me close to him, arm protectively around me. 'Sorry, sorry.'

'You're frightening the animals,' Lucas teases.

'Are they all OK?' I ask.

'Fine,' he tells me. 'They don't seem to mind where they are as long as their dinner is served on time. Speaking of which, is anyone planning on feeding me tonight?'

'We're definitely the ones who missed out on the all-day delights of the catering truck,' I note. It looked very nice too. 'I should have thought to grab something from them before they left.'

'I could phone the Chinese takeaway in the village and get them to deliver,' Shelby suggests. 'I thought we'd stay here for the night with Molly as she refuses to move into the house.'

Lucas looks slightly taken aback. 'Our house?'

Shelby nods. 'I know it's moving at quite a pace, but I've made some decisions over the last few days. I want to be more involved in your lives – yours and Molly's. I'm going to cut back on my filming schedule and help out here more.' He looks at me. 'If Molly will have me.'

As if I'm going to say no.

'Do you think we could make a future together, all of us?' Shelby asks his son.

'The animals too,' I put in.

'That goes without saying,' Shelby agrees.

Lucas looks quietly pleased. 'That would be cool.'

'Come and give us a hug,' Shelby says and, with only a moment's hesitation, Lucas joins us too.

'You're not going to make me call you Mum, are you?' he asks me. 'That would be *too* weird.'

'I wouldn't dream of it,' I say. 'But it could be nice if we can make our own odd little family.'

'OK,' he says with a shrug and I guess that's the closest we're going to get to out-and-out approval.

'I'd like to help you to find an outlet for your poems,' Shelby says. 'They deserve a wider audience.'

Lucas looks even more pleased by that suggestion.

'You could do some more workshops here for the students if you want to,' I chip in.

'I'd like that. Does it mean I can stay here and not go back to regular school?'

'I'm sure we can work something out,' Shelby says. 'But we can't do it on an empty stomach.' So he takes our order and phones it in.

'Shall we go and find some blankets from the caravan? Might as well make ourselves comfortable.'

'Your idea of comfort and mine definitely differ,' he points out.

With Little Dog at our heels, we walk over to the carnage of my caravan, nevertheless.

Together we survey the crumpled mess. Blimey. I look at the

remnants of my home sadly. 'It looks a bit sorry for itself.'

'It's a blot on the landscape,' Shelby notes. 'Why don't you let me buy you one of those fancy caravans, with hot and cold running everything and a proper shower?'

'I don't know,' I say, anxiously. 'It's not really my style.'

'You have to live *somewhere*,' he points out. 'And, if I'm going to be staying over more regularly – which I hope I am – it would be nice to do it in a fairly civilised manner.'

As Lucas is here, I don't point out that we have slept under the stars together with nothing but a holey blanket for comfort and have shared an outdoor bucket shower which he seemed to quite enjoy. Probably best that we keep that to ourselves.

'I hope that you notice I've hardly sneezed at all today,' he says.

I hadn't but I'm pleased if that's the case.

'A new antihistamine,' he tells me. 'I'm hoping that it will mean I can be more hands-on with the animals.'

'That would be great.'

'Though I think Little Dog might have to stop sleeping on the bed when we share it.'

I gasp at that and Little Dog's ears prick up. I'll swear that his perma-smile falters a little.

'Compromise, Molly. That's what all relationships involve.'

And he's right, of course. Shelby will have to get used to my ways, but I'll have to make changes to work round his. We can do this, though. I'm feeling confident. I'll make a proper farmer of him yet.

Shelby roots around in the wreckage, risking opening the caravan door. It creaks alarmingly. Yet we manage to make our way inside while it shivers and shakes around us. We carefully rummage about until we find blankets and the deckchairs, hoping that it doesn't heave a final sigh and collapse on us. A few plates and mugs have survived and, though the cutlery drawer has tipped its contents all over what remains of the floor, that's intact too.

'It could be worse,' I note, tentatively kicking at the ruins with my toe. 'If this is the only casualty of the day, that's not too bad. At least none of the animals or actors came to any harm.'

Shelby starts to laugh. 'And that's why I love you,' he says. 'You're a glass half-full kind of woman.'

He *loves* me! I pinch myself to check that I'm not dreaming. I'm absolutely sure that's what he said. Just wait until I tell Bev.

Chapter One Hundred and Two

The Chinese takeaway arrives, eventually. Once it goes dark, you can't see anything up here. The delivery driver had a hell of a job finding us, but Shelby tipped him handsomely for his trouble. I'll have to get better signage sorted out. Add it to the list of jobs. Perhaps we'll rename it Hope Farm while we're at it.

I've cobbled together makeshift beds in the cleanest barn for the three of us on top of nice, fresh straw. It doesn't look too bad and I think we'll all be comfy here – relatively. I just hope Shelby has dosed up. This will test his new medication to the full. But, perhaps he's right, it's time to have a bit more luxury in my life – especially if it makes life easier for him and Lucas too. In the meantime, there's a loo in one of the outbuildings and a sink. I'm sure we could shoehorn a shower in there as well and I could rig up something basic again. I haven't stopped thinking about Shelby's offer to buy me a nice caravan with all mod cons, but should I let him do that when he's already done so much? I don't know. I'll ask Bev. She'll know.

'I have a surprise for you,' Lucas says and while we stand and watch, he flicks a switch in one of the sheds and the yard lights up with the soft glow of fairy lights. 'I nicked them from the festival evening and some of the guys strung them up this afternoon. I've got bunting too, but we didn't get round to that.'

'Oh, it looks lovely,' I say.

'Nice one, Lucas,' his dad agrees.

Lucas gives one of his rare grins. 'Cool.'

So we break bits from the caravan and get a fire going in an old drum, well away from the barns – lesson learned – although all of them here are built of steel and brick and we have yet to stack them with hay bales.

Actually, we manage to get quite a blaze going and I never knew that caravans burned so well. It's a shame to see the old thing go up in smoke, but perhaps it was its time. We sit round the fire on the rescued deckchairs, although I'm sure one is more wonky than it used to be. Lucas is laid out on a blanket toasting his toes and staring at his phone, willing it to have a signal.

'Who are you trying to phone?'

'Phoenix Jade gave me her number.' He aims for a 'no big deal' voice and fails miserably.

The young singer at the festival, I seem to remember. 'Oh yeah?'

'I said I'd let her know how the move went. That's all.'

'So you've been chatting with her?'

'"*Chatting*"?' He shakes his head in despair, but I'm not really sure why.

'Do I need to buy a hat?' Shelby and I exchange a wry glance.

'Get a life, Molly,' he retorts, but he tries his phone one more time with feeling.

Little Dog is as close to the fire as he can possibly get without scorching and, as I go to throw on another piece of caravan to keep us warm, I nudge him away with my toe. He inches right back, so I leave him be. I'm sure we'll smell it if he starts to sinter. Big Dog has settled under Shelby's deckchair for the duration and Shelby lets out a delicate sneeze in acknowledgement. I have my fingers crossed that his new antihistamine is as good as he thinks.

The night is as black as tar with no ambient light at all, save for the mellow glimmer of the fairy lights in the yard and the spark of our fire. The stars are putting on a splendid show for us – a lovely night to welcome us to Hope Farm Mark Two. There's no noise apart from the crackle of the burning wood and the occasional bleat or snuffle from one of the animals as they too settle for the night.

I smile to myself. I think Hettie would definitely like this place. I hope I've done her proud and I don't think I've left her behind at all. I can feel her here in the warmth of the night air, in the scent of the fresh hay in the breeze. She's still very much with me and I'm pleased about that. Her spirit has sustained me through many a difficult time and I know it will do as I move into a new phase. We have a busy day tomorrow to get ready for the return of our young people on Monday but, for now, I can relax.

'Mushroom chop suey for you.' Shelby reads the scribble on the top of the cartons and hands them out accordingly. 'Sweet and sour prawns for Lucas.'

Lucas sits up and takes his carton. 'I like it here,' he says. 'It feels like a good place, even though the phone signal is seriously crap.'

No finer accolade.

I've given the cutlery and plates a wash under the tap and I'm sure they're more chipped than I remember, but I dish out anyway. We sit back and enjoy our al fresco meal. I eat with relish, not realising how hungry I really was. It's the best food I've tasted in a long time. Perhaps it's the company or the atmosphere. So much better than eating alone. And I never thought I'd hear myself say that.

When we're finished, Shelby takes my hand. 'Listen to that.' He cups an ear, theatrically. 'Silence! Lots of it!'

'I'm glad that you're here,' I tell him, sincerely. 'I couldn't have done it without you.'

He sighs contentedly. 'I could get used to this.'

'You could?' I risk asking, 'You don't think you'd get bored? Miss the bright lights?'

'Never,' he says. 'How can they compare with this?' He takes it all in and nods happily. 'I think Farmer Gordon would very much approve.' Then he turns to me and in the glow of the fire, I can see the love for me shining in his eyes. 'We've all had such a journey here that I might even suggest it as my next big storyline.'

I wonder who'd portray me on the television screen? I shudder to think. I try to be supportive, though. 'That sounds like a great idea.'

Shelby turns to his son. 'What do you think, Lucas? Would that perk up a jaded old soap star?'

'Sounds cool,' he agrees. 'Just please make sure there aren't any arsey alpacas in it. I couldn't stand the strain.'

We all laugh and it's such a joyful, uncomplicated sound that it makes tears come to my eyes. Shelby's right, we have all come on such a journey together. One that I hope will continue for a very long time. Who knew when Lucas arrived at the farm, feeling all angry and unloved, that we would end up here? I couldn't love him more if he was my own child and I want nothing but the best for his future. He has so much potential and I know that he'll make it whatever he sets his mind to do. Looking at him, my heart swells with affection and I feel contentment right in the very centre of my soul.

He glances up at me, tearing himself from his phone. 'What?'

'Nothing. I'm just thinking how happy I am.'

'Weirdo,' he says, but he smiles as he focuses back on his screen.

Then there's Shelby. I thought that'd I'd spend my life alone with just my animals for company. I thought no one would love me for who I am. And yet I gaze across at the man by my side and know that I've been lucky enough to find a love that I didn't believe existed. If I could stay here, like this, for the rest of my life then I would know true happiness even though I'm a beginner at it.

As I'm enjoying my reverie, there's a terrible crashing noise and the gate to the sheep's enclosure in the barn flies open and Anthony comes careening out, knocking over a feed bucket as he goes. The rest of the flock are hot on his heels.

'I locked the bloody gate,' Lucas yells. 'I swear.'

We're all on our feet instantly and Little Dog sets off barking, while Big Dog decides to howl. Dick the Cock wakes up and crows, throwing his head back to let out an ear-splitting cock-a-doodle-do even though he's only just gone to bed.

'Not now, Dick,' I call. 'Too soon!'

The silence of the night is filled with the sound of sheep bleating anxiously. Anthony heads one way, the rest of the sheep in the other direction. He stampedes past us, only pausing briefly to check out what's in our abandoned Chinese cartons.

'Anthony,' I shout after him. 'Come back here. Don't you dare run off!'

He runs off.

'You get Anthony,' Shelby yells. 'Lucas and I will round up the rest of the sheep.' They're currently charging round the yard making themselves giddy.

'Right.' So we split up, running in opposite directions, giving chase to our errant animals.

And, as I pound after my anti-social sheep, my heart swells with even more happiness to know that on our first night in our new home, it's very much business as usual. Except, for once, I'm not having to do it alone.

Author Note

My dear friend Donna is a force of nature. Well, just forceful really. So when she asked me to join her one Friday night to feed baby orphaned lambs at a local farm, how could I refuse? Actually, I couldn't refuse, it would be pointless. Donna is a lady who doesn't take no for an answer. In fairness to her, my default setting is also to say yes as you never know what life might bring you, do you? So, despite being allergic to all things fluffy and furry – think anything from guinea pigs to horses – I loaded up with antihistamine and set off.

It was a bitterly cold night and as the farm is in a fairly (very) exposed situation, the wind howled round us. Yet we snuggled down in the corner of a barn and set to feeding a dozen or more very hungry and quite demanding tiny lambs. I like animals, but wouldn't necessarily class myself as an animal lover, as such. Being brought up in a northern, industrial town I don't think I saw a sheep until I was twenty-one and, being allergic to everything, I've tended to keep my distance. I'm out of my comfort zone with animals. Yet these tiny, warm, wriggly bodies would melt anything but the hardest of hearts. They were well worth my sneezes and itchy eyes.

While we sat there amidst the straw, multi-tasking with two bottles of formula at a time, Donna explained that this wasn't any old farm, it was actually a unique place. I learned that Animal Antiks is a life-enriching establishment. As I've said, it's not a traditional farm, but has been set up to provide animal-assisted learning for students – children and young adults – with a variety of challenges including behavioural difficulties, mental health issues and autism. The farm aims to provide an environment that allows individuals to feel safe to flourish and grow so that they can reach their full potential. The students come along and interact with the animals by helping to look after them. They learn about teamwork and responsibility in a caring way.

Being a typical author, I needed to know more and Sarah and Nick who run Animal Antiks very kindly welcomed me to show me how they work. Interestingly, they quickly sussed me out and now give me very pleasant tasks to carry out when I go to the farm – cuddling goats, collecting eggs, turning ponies into unicorns with glitter paint – and don't make me muck out pigs. I found out that many of the animals at the farm have troubled backgrounds or behavioural issues too. Don't get me started on the naughty alpacas! Of course, the more I learned, the more I thought it would make a brilliant basis for a story.

Sarah, Nick, Donna and her husband, Paul, have been fantastic at helping with my research. Paul penned the excellent poems in the book. I've also met some of the brilliant students who go there. To see children who are unable to cope with traditional forms of education become engaged through inter-acting and working with animals is wonderful. The ethos of the farm is 'opening hearts and unlocking minds' which I felt was a perfect fit for the kind of warm-hearted fiction that I like to write and *Happiness for Beginners* was born! Thank goodness for my dear Donna being a ninja at getting people to do things that they don't think they want to!

As with many charities, Animal Antiks are always short of funds. Unlike the book, a work of pure fiction, they have no gorgeous soap-star patron – though I feel they most definitely should! They rely on donations and if you'd like to find out more about them, they're on Facebook and Twitter, as below.

Hope you've enjoyed the book and you might love it a little bit more now that you know what's at the heart of it.

Website: www.animalantiks.co.uk

Twitter: @animal_antiks

Facebook: www.facebook.com/animalantiks

Instagram: AnimalAntiks

Acknowledgements

I want to thank, most sincerely, Sarah Kettlety and Farmer Nick Sear, who run the Animal Antiks farm – the inspiration behind this story. They have been so generous with their help. The students are great and the animals they look after are characters in themselves!

Also I must thank the wonderful Donna Ray and Paul Eccentric without whom none of this would have happened. Paul is one half of the music and poetry duo The Antipoet, and author of the poems created especially for this book. You are both totally bonkers and we love every minute we spend with you. I'm so grateful to be able to call you our friends.

If you haven't heard The Antipoet you should check out their work. They're rude, lewd and will play for food: make sure to book them for weddings, christenings and important tea parties involving the vicar.

Facebook: https://www.facebook.com/AntipoetThe/
Twitter: @theantipoet
  Website: http://www.theantipoet.co.uk/

Carole Matthews

Christie Chapman is a single mum who spends her days commuting to her secretarial job in London and looking after her teenage son, Finn. It's not an easy life but Christie finds comfort in her love of crafting, spending her spare time working on her beautiful creations, and it's not long before opportunity comes knocking.

Christie can see a future full of hope and possibility for her and Finn – and if the handsome Max is to be believed, one full of love too. It's all there for the taking. And then, all of sudden, her world is turned upside down.

Will Christie find her happy ending in *Paper Hearts and Summer Kisses*.

'I laughed and cried and marvelled'
CATHY BRAMLEY

Ruby Brown is ready for a change.

She's single for the first time in years and ready to dive into this brave new world with a smile on her face and a spring in her step. The last thing she's looking for is a serious relationship.

Mason represents everything Ruby wants right now: he's charming, smooth and perfect for some no-strings-attached fun. Joe on the other hand is kind and attractive, but comes with the sort of baggage Ruby wants to avoid.

Ruby thinks she knows what she wants, but is it what she needs to be truly happy? It's about to get emotional in *Million Love Songs*.

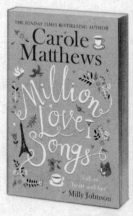

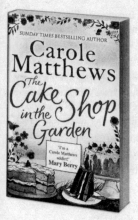

Fay Merryweather runs her cake shop from her beautiful garden. She whips up airy sponges, while her customers enjoy the gorgeous blooms. Looking after the cake shop, the garden and her cantankerous mother means Fay is always busy, but if she doesn't do all this, who will?

Then Danny Wilde walks into her life and makes Fay question every decision she's ever made.

When a sudden tragedy strikes, Fay doesn't know which way to turn. Can she find the strength to make a life-changing choice – even if it means giving up the thing she loves the most?

Life, love and family are about to collide in *The Cake Shop in the Garden*.

'Perfect for lifting spirits'
HEAT

Fay and Danny are madly in love and it's all Fay's ever dreamed of. But she left everything – including the delightful cake shop she used to run – to be with Danny on his cosy canal boat. And she soon finds out, making delicious cakes on the water isn't always smooth sailing!

hen Fay gets a call that sends her back to where it all began: the Cake Shop in the Garden. Even Fay returns happily to dry land and her passion for baking, she knows it will be hard being away from Danny, especially with Christmas round the corner. But their relationship is strong enough to survive… isn't it?

Can Fay really get everything she ever wanted in *Christmas Cakes and Mistletoe Nights*?

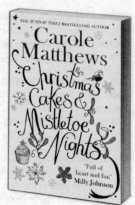

Grace has been best friends with Ella and Flick forever. The late-night chats, shared heartaches and good times have created a bond that has stood the test of time.

When Ella invites them to stay for a week in her cottage in South Wales, Grace jumps at the chance to see her old friends. She also hopes that the change of scenery will help her reconnect with her distant husband.

Then Flick arrives; loveable, bubbly, incorrigible Flick, accompanied by the handsome and charming Noah.

One week will change all their lives for ever in *A Cottage by the Sea*.

'Simply brilliant' *CLOSER*

In the dead of night, Ayesha takes her daughter, Sabina, and slips quietly from her home, leaving behind a life full of pain. Boarding a coach to London, all Ayesha wants is a fresh start.

Hayden, a former popstar, has kept himself hidden away for years. He's only opened up his home to two people – Crystal, a dancer with a heart of gold, and Joy, an ill-tempered retiree with a soft spot for waifs and strays.

When Crystal asks Hayden if Ayesha and Sabina can stay with them, he reluctantly agrees. As different as they may be, they all form an unlikely bond and start to build ***A Place to Call Home*.**

Cassie Smith has been out of work for a while but she has an idea. Drawing on her love of Christmas, she begins charging for small things: wrapping presents; writing cards; tree-decorating. She's soon in huge demand and Cassie's business, Calling Mrs Christmas, is born.

Carter Randall wants to make Christmas special for his children, so he enlists Cassie's help, and his lavish requests start taking up all her time. Thank goodness she can rely on her loving partner Jim to handle the rest of her clients.

When millionaire Carter asks Cassie to join his family on a trip to Lapland, she knows she shouldn't go … **But could love be *Calling Mrs Christmas*?**

'Full of heart and fun'
MILLY JOHNSON

Louise Young is a devoted single mother whose only priority is providing for her daughter, Mia. Louise has a good job and she's grateful for it. The only problem is her boss who can't keep his hands to himself, but Louise can handle him.

What she really doesn't have time for is romance – until she meets the company's rising star, Josh Wallace.

It's the office Christmas party, and Louise has decided to let her hair down. But she's completely unaware that others around her are busy playing dangerous games.

The Christmas Party **will be a night to remember.**

For Lucy Lombard, there's nothing that chocolate can't cure. From heartache to headaches, it's the one thing she knows that she can rely on – and she's not alone.

Fellow chocolate addicts Autumn, Nadia and Chantal share her passion and together they form a select group known as The Chocolate Lovers' Club. Whenever there's a crisis, they meet in their sanctuary: a cafe called Chocolate Heaven.

And with a cheating boyfriend, a flirtatious boss, a gambling husband and a loveless marriage, there's always plenty to discuss in *The Chocolate Lovers' Club*.

THE SUNDAY TIMES BESTSELLING AUTHOR

The Chocolate Lovers' Club

'Simply brilliant'
Closer

Carole Matthews

'Warm, witty and hopeful'
SARAH MORGAN

Survival tips for times of stress:

1. Take deep breaths
2. Count to ten
3. Eat chocolate

Lucy thought she had got her happily ever after with the gorgeous Aidan but things aren't turning out the way she had hoped they would.

And she's not the only one with problems: Autumn's new boyfriend has yet to meet her parents, Nadia's husband has sworn he's given up gambling but she's finding that hard to believe, and Chantal is doing all she can to save her marriage.

It's clear these girls are going to need a lot of support in *The Chocolate Lovers' Diet*.

THE SUNDAY TIMES BESTSELLING AUTHOR

The Chocolate Lovers' Diet

Carole Matthews

Christmas is just around the corner but the women of The Chocolate Lovers' Club have more to worry about than present shopping...

Lucy's love life is in all sorts of trouble, and the last thing Nadia wants it's a man. Chantal is loving being a new mum but so its tough, and Autumn is feeling unsupported when she needs it most.

Can friendship overcome all in *The Chocolate Lovers' Christmas*.

'Delightful and humorous'
WOMAN'S WEEKLY

The ladies of The Chocolate Lovers' Club should be gearing up for the wedding of the year but life keeps getting in the way...

Lucy is worried about her financial situation, Nadia needs a change, Autumn's best laid plans ve gone awry, and Chantal gets some bad news.

And yet, despite all the ups and downs, the Chocolate Lovers' ladies know they can get through it all as long as they have each other.

They're not going to let anything get in the way of their happy-ever-afters in *The Chocolate Lovers' Wedding*.